The Story of Our Hymns

by
ERNEST EDWIN RYDEN

To the Sweet Memory
of Our Bonnie Boy
Richard Edward Ryden
Who at the Age of Ten Years Went
Home to Sing with the
Angels.

He is not dead: he only sleeps,
Safe in the arms of Him who keeps
His lambs secure from earth's alarm,
From grief and sin and foes that harm.
He is not dead: he is at rest,
Content upon his Saviour's breast;
Dear little child, we loved you so,
But Jesus loved you more, we know.
He is not dead: the Shepherd came
To call His little lamb by name;
The gentle Shepherd watch will keep,
While His beloved child doth sleep.
He is not dead: by angel bands
Now welcomed to the heavenly lands,
With theirs a childish voice shall sing
Hosannas to the children's King.
He is not dead: though tears may flow,
Faith whispers: "It is better so."
With joy we'll meet on that fair shore,
Where God's own children weep no more.

FOREWORD

The hymn lore of the Christian Church offers a fascinating field for profitable research and study. To know the hymns of the Church is to know something of the spiritual strivings and achievements of the people of God throughout the centuries. Henry Ward Beecher has well said: "Hymns are the jewels which the Church has worn, the pearls, the diamonds, the precious stones, formed into amulets more potent against sorrow and sadness than the most famous charm of the wizard or the magician. And he who knows the way that hymns flowed, knows where the blood of true piety ran, and can trace its veins and arteries to the very heart."

This volume has been inspired by a desire on the part of the author to create deeper love for the great lyrics of the Christian Church. In pursuing this purpose an effort has been made to present such facts and circumstances surrounding their authorship and composition as will result in a better understanding and appreciation of the hymns themselves.

A hymn is a child of the age in which it was written. For this reason the author has followed a chronological arrangement in an endeavor, not only to set forth the historical background of the hymns, but also to trace the spiritual movements within the Church that gave them birth.

The materials contained in this volume have been gathered from sources too numerous to mention here. The author feels a special sense of gratitude for information drawn from David R. Breed's "The History and Use of Hymns and Hymn-Tunes," Edward S. Ninde's "The Story of the American Hymn," and John Julian's monumental work, "Dictionary of Hymnology." No claim is made to originality, except in the manner of presentation and interpretation. A popular style has been adopted in order to appeal to the lay reader.

Thus we send forth this book with the earnest prayer that it may inspire many hearts to sing with greater devotion the praises of Him who redeemed us with His blood and made us to be kings and priests unto God.

Ernest Edwin Ryden.

St. Paul, Minnesota, November 14, 1930.

TABLE OF CONTENTS

PART I: EARLY CHRISTIAN HYMNODY
The Early Christian Chants 13
Greek and Syriac Hymns 19
The Rise of Latin Hymnody 25
An Ancient Singer Who Glorified the Cross 31
The Golden Age of Latin Hymnody 35
PART II: GERMAN HYMNODY
Martin Luther, Father of Evangelical Hymnody 43
The Hymn-Writers of the Reformation 53
Hymnody of the Controversial Period 59
The King and Queen of Chorales 65
Hymns of the Thirty Years' War 69
A Hymn Made Famous on a Battle Field 77
The Lutheran Te Deum 81
Paul Gerhardt, Prince of Lutheran Hymnists 85
Joachim Neander, the Paul Gerhardt of the Calvinists 93
A Roman Mystic and Hymn-writer 99
Hymn-writers of the Pietist School 103
The Württemberg Hymn-writers 111
How a Great Organist Inspired Two Hymnists 117
Gerhard Tersteegen, Hymn-writer and Mystic 123
Zinzendorf and Moravian Hymnody 127
Two Famous Hymns and some Legends 131
Hymnody in the Age of Rationalism 135
Hymns of the Spiritual Renaissance 141
PART III: SCANDINAVIAN HYMNODY
The Swedish Reformers and Their Hymns 149
A Hymn-Book That Failed 155
David's Harp in the Northland 161
The Golden Age of Swedish Hymnody 169
The Fanny Crosby of Sweden and the Pietists 177

Kingo, the Poet of Easter-Tide 185
Brorson, the Poet of Christmas 191
Grundtvig, the Poet of Whitsuntide 197
Landstad, a Bard of the Frozen Fjords 203
PART IV: ENGLISH HYMNODY
The Dawn of Hymnody in England 209
Isaac Watts, Father of English Hymnody 215
Doddridge: Preacher, Teacher, and Hymnist 221
Wesley, The Sweet Bard of Methodism 225
A Great Hymn that Grew out of a Quarrel 233
The Bird of a Single Song 239
England's First Woman Hymnist 245
A Slave-trader Who Wrote Christian Lyrics 249
An Afflicted Poet Who Glorified God 253
An Irish Poet and His Hymns 259
The Hymn Legacy of an English Editor 263
Heber, Missionary Bishop and Hymnist 269
An Invalid Who Blessed the World 275
How Hymns Helped Build a Church 279
A Famous Hymn by a Proselyte of Rome 285
Henry Francis Lyte and His Swan Song 291
Sarah Adams and the Rise of Women Hymn-writers 297
A Hymn Written in a Stage-coach 301
An Archbishop's Wife Who Wrote Hymns 305
Bonar, the Sweet Singer of Scotland 311
Two Famous Translators of Ancient Hymns 317
Baring-Gould and His Noted Hymn 323
Frances Ridley Havergal, the Consecration Poet 327
A Unitarian Who Gloried in the Cross 333
A Model Hymn by a Model Minister 337
Matheson and His Song in the Night 341
Part V: AMERICAN HYMNODY
The Beginning of Hymnody in America 347
America's First Woman Hymnist 353
Thomas Hastings, Poet and Musician 359
Francis Scott Key, Patriot and Hymnist 363
America's First Poet and His Hymns 367
The Hymn-writer of the Muhlenbergs 371
The Lyrics of Bishop Doane 375
The Quaker Poet as a Hymn-writer 379
America's Greatest Hymn and Its Author 383
Samuel Smith, a Patriotic Hymn-writer 389
Two Famous Christmas Hymns and Their Author 395
Harriet Beecher Stowe and Her Hymns 399
A Hymn Written on Two Shores 407
A Hymn That Grew out of Suffering 411
A Famous Hymn Written for Sailors 415
A Tragedy That Inspired a Great Hymn 419
Anna Warner and Her Beautiful Hymns 423

Phillips Brooks and His Carols 427
Women Who Wrote Hymns for Children 431
Fanny Crosby, America's Blind Poet 435
One of America's Earliest Gospel Singers 441
The Lyrist of Chautauqua 445
Gladden's Hymn of Christian Service 449
A Hymn with a Modern Message 453
A Lutheran Psalmist of Today 457
Survey of American Lutheran Hymnody 463
Index of Notable Hymns 471
Alphabetical Index of Hymns and Sources 477
Authors' and General Index 493
Bibliography 503

PART I
Early Christian Hymnody

The Angelic Hymn

Glory be to God on high, and on earth peace, good will toward men. We praise Thee, we bless Thee, we worship Thee, we glorify Thee, we give thanks to Thee for Thy great glory, O Lord God, Heavenly King, God the Father Almighty.

O Lord, the Only-begotten Son, Jesus Christ; O Lord God, Lamb of God, Son of the Father, that takest away the sin of the world, have mercy upon us. Thou that takest away the sin of the world, receive our prayer. Thou that sittest at the right hand of God the Father, have mercy upon us.

For Thou only art holy; Thou only art the Lord; Thou only, O Christ, with the Holy Ghost, art most high in the glory of God the Father. Amen.

THE EARLY CHRISTIAN CHANTS

The first Christians sang hymns. The Saviour went to His passion with a song on His lips. Matthew and Mark agree that the last act of worship in the Upper Room was the singing of a hymn. "And when they had sung a hymn, they went out unto the Mount of Olives."

How we wish that the words of that hymn might have been preserved! Perhaps they have. Many Biblical scholars believe that they may be found in the so-called Hallel series in the Psaltery, consisting of Psalms 113 to 118 inclusive. It was a practice among the Jews to chant these holy songs at the paschal table. Fraught as they were with Messianic hope, it was fitting that such a hymn should ascend to the skies in the hour when God's Paschal Lamb was about to be offered.

The Christian Church followed the example of Jesus and His disciples by singing from the Psaltery at its worship. Paul admonished his converts not to neglect the gift of song. To the Ephesians he wrote: "Be filled with the Spirit; speaking one to another in psalms and hymns and spiritual songs, singing and making melody with your heart to the Lord." And his exhortation to the Colossians rings like an echo: "Let the word of Christ dwell in you richly; in all wisdom teaching and admonishing one another with psalms and hymns and spiritual songs, singing with grace in your hearts unto God."

The praying and singing of Paul and Silas in the midnight gloom of the Philippian dungeon, their feet being made "fast in the stocks," also is a revelation of the large place occupied by song in the lives of the early Christians.

The double reference of the Apostle to "psalms, hymns and spiritual songs" would indicate that the Christian Church very early began to use chants and hymns other than those taken from the Psaltery. The younger Pliny, in 112 A.D., wrote to Emperor Trajan from Bithynia that the Christians came together before daylight and sang hymns alternately (invicem) "to Christ as God."

These distinctively Christian chants were the Gloria in Excelsis, or the "Angelic Hymn," so called because its opening lines are taken from the song of the angels at Jesus' birth; the Magnificat, Mary's song of praise; the Benedictus, the song of Zacharias, father of John the Baptist; and the Nunc Dimittis, the prayer of the aged Simeon when he held the Christ-child in his arms. Other chants that were used very early in the Christian Church included the Ter Sanctus, based on the "thrice holy" of Isaiah 6:3 and Revelation 4:8; the Gloria Patri, or "Lesser Doxology;" the Benedicite, the "Song of the Three Hebrew Children," from the Apocrypha; and the Te Deum Laudamus, which is sometimes regarded as a later Latin chant, but which undoubtedly was derived from a very ancient hymn of praise.

Eminent Biblical scholars believe that fragments of other primitive Christian hymns have been preserved in the Epistles of Paul and in other portions of the New Testament. Such a fragment is believed to be recorded in 1 Timothy 3:16:

He who was manifested in the flesh,
Justified in the spirit,
Seen of angels,
Preached among the nations,
Believed on in the world,
Received up in glory.

The "faithful saying" to which Paul refers in 2 Timothy 2:11 also is believed to be a quotation from one of these hymns so dear to the Christians:

If we died with Him,
We shall also live with Him:
If we endure,
We shall also reign with Him:
If we shall deny Him,
He will also deny us:
If we are faithless,
He abideth faithful;
For He cannot deny Himself.

It will be noted how well these passages adapt themselves to responsive, or antiphonal, chanting, which was the character of the ancient Christian songs. Other passages that are believed to be fragments of ancient hymns are Ephesians 5:14; 1 Timothy 6:15, 16; James 1:17, and Revelation 1:5-7.

There are strong evidences to support the claim that responsive singing in the churches of Asia Minor was introduced during the latter part of the first century by Ignatius, bishop of Antioch, a pupil of the Apostle John. The Gloria in Excelsis was used in matin services about this time, while the Magnificat was sung at vespers. Ignatius suffered martyrdom about 107 A.D. by being torn to pieces by lions in the circus as a despiser of the gods.

Liturgies also were employed very early in the worship of the Christian Church. An ancient service known as the "Jerusalem" liturgy was ascribed to the Apostle James, while the so-called "Alexandrian" liturgy claimed as its author Mark, fellow laborer of Paul and companion of Peter. There is much uncertainty surrounding these claims, however.

Both Tertullian and Origen record the fact that there was a rich use of song in family life as well as in public worship.

The singing of the early Christians was simple and artless. Augustine describes the singing at Alexandria under Athanasius as "more like speaking than singing." Musical instruments were not used. The pipe, tabret, and harp were associated so intimately with the sensuous heathen cults, as well as with the wild revelries and shameless performances of the degenerate theatre and circus, that it is easy to understand the prejudice against their use in the Christian worship.

"A Christian maiden," says Jerome, "ought not even to know what a lyre or a flute is, or what it is used for." Clement of Alexandria writes: "Only one instrument do we use, viz., the word of peace wherewith we honor God, no longer the old psaltery, trumpet, drum, and flute." Chrysostom expresses himself in like vein: "David formerly sang in psalms, also we sing today with him; he had a lyre with lifeless strings, the Church has a lyre with living strings. Our tongues are the strings of the lyre, with a different tone, indeed, but with a more accordant piety."

The language of the first Christian hymns, like the language of the New Testament, was Greek. The Syriac tongue was also used in some regions, but Greek gradually attained ascendancy.

The hymns of the Eastern Church are rich in adoration and the spirit of worship. Because of their exalted character and Scriptural language they have found an imperishable place in the liturgical forms of the Christian Church. As types of true hymnody, they have never been surpassed.

The Oldest Christian Hymn

Shepherd of tender youth,
Guiding in love and truth

Through devious ways;
Christ, our triumphant King,
We come Thy Name to sing,
And here our children bring
To join Thy praise.
Thou art our holy Lord,
O all-subduing Word,
Healer of strife:
Thou didst Thyself abase,
That from sin's deep disgrace
Thou mightest save our race,
And give us life.
Ever be near our side,
Our Shepherd and our Guide,
Our staff and song:
Jesus, Thou Christ of God,
By Thine enduring Word,
Lead us where Thou hast trod;
Our faith make strong.
So now, and till we die,
Sound we Thy praises high,
And joyful sing:
Let all the holy throng
Who to Thy Church belong
Unite to swell the song
To Christ our King!
Clement of Alexandria, about 200 A.D.

GREEK AND SYRIAC HYMNS

Very soon the early Christians began to use hymns other than the Psalms and Scriptural chants. In other words, they began to sing the praises of the Lord in their own words. Eusebius informs us that in the first half of the third century there existed a large number of sacred songs. Some of these have come down to us, but the authorship of only one is known with any degree of certainty. It is the beautiful children's hymn, "Shepherd of Tender Youth."

Just how old this hymn is cannot be stated with certainty. However, it is found appended to a very ancient Christian work entitled "The Tutor," written in Greek by Clement of Alexandria.

Clement, whose real name was Titus Flavius Clemens, was born about 170 A.D. He was one of the first great scholars in the Christian Church. An eager seeker after truth, he studied the religions and philosophical systems of the Greeks, the Assyrians, Egyptians, and Jews.

In the course of time he entered the Catechetical School conducted by Pantaenus at Alexandria, Egypt, and there he became a convert to Christianity. Some years later

Clement himself became the head of the institution, which was the first Christian school of its kind in the world. Among the students who received instruction from Clement was the famous Origen, who became the greatest scholar in the ancient Christian church. Another of his pupils was Alexander, afterwards Bishop of Jerusalem, and still later Bishop of Cappadocia.

One of Clement's most celebrated works was "The Tutor." It was in three volumes. The first book described the Tutor, who is Christ Himself; the second book contained sundry directions concerning the daily life and conduct; and the third, after dwelling on the nature of true beauty, condemned extravagance in dress, on the part of both men and women.

Two poems are appended to this work, the first of which is entitled, "A Hymn to the Saviour." This is the hymn known as "Shepherd of tender youth."

The "Hymn to the Saviour" in all the manuscripts in which it is found is attributed to Clement himself, but some critics believe that he was merely quoting it, and that it was written by a still earlier poet. Be that as it may, we do know that, aside from the hymns derived from the Bible, it is the oldest Christian hymn in existence, and it has always been referred to as "Clement's hymn."

Clement was driven from Alexandria during the persecution of Severus in 202 A.D. Of his subsequent history practically nothing is known. It is believed he died about 220 A.D.

A number of other beautiful Greek hymns have come down to us from the same period, but their date and authorship remain in doubt. Longfellow has given us an exquisite translation of one of these in "The Golden Legend":

O Gladsome Light
Of the Father immortal,
And of the celestial
Sacred and blessed
Jesus, our Saviour!
Now to the sunset
Again hast Thou brought us;
And seeing the evening
Twilight, we bless Thee,

Praise Thee, adore Thee,
Father omnipotent!
Son, the Life-giver!
Spirit, the Comforter!
Worthy at all times
Of worship and wonder!

An inspiring little doxology, also by an unknown author, reads:

My hope is God,

My refuge is the Lord,
My shelter is the Holy Ghost;
Be Thou, O Holy Three, adored!

Doctrinal controversies gave the first real impetus to hymn writing in the Eastern church. As early as the second century, Bardesanes, a Gnostic teacher, had beguiled many to adopt his heresy by the charm of his hymns and melodies. His son, Harmonius, followed in the father's footsteps. Their hymns were written in the Syriac language, and only a few fragments have been preserved.

The Arians and other heretical teachers also seized upon the same method to spread their doctrines. It was not until the fourth century, apparently, that any effort was made by orthodox Christians to meet them with their own weapons. Ephrem Syrus, who has been called "the cithern of the Holy Spirit," was the greatest teacher of his time in the Syrian Church, as well as her most gifted hymnist. This unusual man was born in northern Mesopotamia about 307 A.D. His zeal for orthodox Christianity was no doubt kindled by his presence at the Council of Nicaea in 325 A.D., and thenceforth he was ever an eager champion of the faith. Not only did he write hymns and chants, but he trained large choirs to sing them. He exerted a profound influence over the entire Syrian Church, and even today his hymns are used by the Maronite Christians.

The greatest name among the Greek hymnists of this period is Gregory Nazianzen. Born in 325 A.D., the son of a bishop, he was compelled by his father to enter the priesthood at the age of thirty-six years. He labored with much zeal, however, and eventually was enthroned by the Emperor's own hand as Patriarch of Constantinople. Through the machinations of the Arians he was later compelled to abdicate his office, whereupon he retired to his birthplace. Here he spent the last years of his life in writing sacred poetry of singular beauty and lofty spirit.

Another of the important writers of the early Greek period was Anatolius. Concerning this man very little is known except that he lived in the seventh or eighth century. He has left about one hundred hymns, among them, at least three that are still in common use, "Fierce was the wild billow," "The day is past and over," and "A great and mighty wonder." This last is a little Christmas hymn of unusual charm. His description of the storm of Galilee is one of the classics of Greek hymnology:

Fierce was the wild billow,
Dark was the night;
Oars labored heavily,
Foam glimmered white;
Trembled the mariners,
Peril was nigh;
Then said the God of God,
"Peace! It is I."

To John of Damascus, who died about 780 A.D., we are indebted for two of the most popular Easter hymns in use today, namely, "The day of resurrection" and "Come, ye faithful, raise the strain." Further reference to these will be found in the chapter on the great translator of Greek and Latin hymns, John Mason Neale.

When John of Damascus forsook the world and left behind him a brilliant career to enter a monastery founded in 520 A.D., by St. Sabas, he took with him his ten-year-old nephew, Stephen. The boy grew up within the walls of this cloister, which is situated in one of the deep gorges of the brook Kedron, near Bethlehem, overlooking the Dead Sea. Stephen, who came to be known as the Sabaite, was likewise a gifted hymnist, and it is he who has given us the hymn made famous by Neale's translation: "Art thou weary, art thou languid?" Stephen died in 794 A.D.

The last name of importance among the great hymn-writers of the Greek Church is that of Joseph the Hymnographer, who lived at Constantinople in the ninth century. It is he who wrote the hymn on angels for St. Michael's Day:

>Stars of the morning, so gloriously bright,
>Filled with celestial resplendence and light,
>These that, where night never followeth day,
>Raise the "Thrice Holy, Lord!" ever and aye.

As early as the fourth century the Council of Laodicea had decreed that "besides the appointed singers, who mount the ambo, and sing from the book, others shall not sing in the church." How far this rule may have discouraged or suppressed congregational singing is a subject of dispute among historians. However, it is a matter of record that hymnody suffered a gradual decline in the Eastern division of the Christian Church and eventually assumed more of a liturgical character.

An Ambrosian Advent Hymn

Come, Thou Saviour of our race,
Choicest Gift of heavenly grace!
O Thou blessed Virgin's Son,
Be Thy race on earth begun.
Not of mortal blood or birth,
He descends from heaven to earth:
By the Holy Ghost conceived,
God and man by us believed.
Wondrous birth! O wondrous child
Of the virgin undefiled!
Though by all the world disowned,
Still to be in heaven enthroned.
From the Father forth He came,
And returneth to the same;
Captive leading death and hell—
High the song of triumph swell!
Equal to the Father now,
Though to dust Thou once didst bow,
Boundless shall Thy kingdom be;
When shall we its glories see?
Brightly doth Thy manger shine!
Glorious in its light divine:
Let not sin o'ercloud this light,

Ever be our faith thus bright.
Aurelius Ambrose (340-397 A.D.)

THE RISE OF LATIN HYMNODY

The first hymns and canticles used in the Western churches came from the East. They were sung in their original Greek form. It was not until the beginning of the fourth century that any record of Latin hymns is found. Isadore of Seville, who died in the year 636 A.D., tells us that "Hilary of Gaul, bishop of Poitiers, was the first who flourished in composing hymns in verse." Hilary, who died in the year 368, himself records the fact that he brought some of them from the East. His most famous Latin hymn is Lucis largitor splendide.

The father of Latin hymnody, however, was the great church father, Aurelius Ambrose, bishop of Milan. It was he who taught the Western Church to glorify God in song. Concerning this remarkable bishop, Mabillon writes:

"St. Ambrose took care that, after the manner of the Eastern Fathers, psalms and hymns should be sung by the people also, when previously they had only been recited by individuals singly, and among the Italians by clerks only."

The father of Ambrose was prefect of the Gauls, and it is believed that the future bishop was born at Treves about 340 A.D. The youthful Ambrose, like his father, was trained for government service, and in 374 A.D. he was appointed Consular of Liguria and Aemilia. During the election of a bishop in Milan, a bitter conflict raged between the orthodox Christians and the Arians, and Ambrose found it necessary to attend the church where the election was taking place in order to calm the excited assembly.

According to tradition, a child's voice was heard to cry out in the church, "Ambrosius!" This was accepted at once by the multitude as an act of divine guidance and the whole assembly began shouting, "Ambrose shall be our bishop!" Ambrose had been attracted to the Christian religion but as yet had not received baptism. He therefore protested his election and immediately fled from the city. He was induced to return, however, was baptized, and accepted the high office for which he had been chosen.

The story of his subsequent life is one of the most remarkable chapters in the annals of the early Christian Church. Selling all his possessions, he entered upon the duties of his bishopric with such fervent zeal and untiring devotion that his fame spread far and wide. He early recognized the value of music in church worship and immediately took steps to introduce congregational singing. He was the author of a new kind of church music, which, because of its rhythmical accent, rich modulation, and musical flow, made a powerful appeal to the emotions. Withal, because it was combined with such artless simplicity, it was easily mastered by the common people and instantly sprang into great popularity. By the introduction of responsive singing he also succeeded in securing the active participation of the congregation in the worship.

Empress Justina favored the Arians and sought to induce Ambrose to open the church of Milan for their use. When Ambrose replied with dignity that it did not behoove the state to interfere in matters of doctrine, soldiers were sent to enforce the imperial will. The people of Milan, however, rallied around their beloved bishop, and, when the soldiers surrounded the church, Ambrose and his congregation were singing and praying. So tremendous was the effect of the song that the soldiers outside the church finally joined in the anthems. The effort to compel Ambrose to yield proved fruitless, and the empress abandoned her plan.

Augustine, who later became the most famous convert of Ambrose, tells of the great impression made on his soul when he heard the singing of Ambrose and his congregation. In his "Confessions" he writes: "How mightily I was moved by the overwhelming tones of Thy Church, my God! Thy voices flooded my ears, Thy truth melted my heart, the sacred fires of worship were kindled in my soul, my tears flowed, and a foretaste of the joy of salvation was given me." Ambrose himself has left us this testimony: "They say that people are transported by the singing of my hymns, and I confess that it is true."

Ambrose was no respecter of persons. Although he was a warm friend of the Emperor Theodosius, he denounced the latter's cruel massacre of the people of Thessalonica, and, when Theodosius came to the church of Ambrose to worship, he was met at the door by the brave bishop and denied admittance.

"Do you," he cried, "who have been guilty of shedding innocent blood, dare to enter the sanctuary?"

The emperor for eight months refrained from communion; then he applied for absolution, which was granted him after he had done public penance. He also promised in the future never to execute a death sentence within thirty days of its pronouncement.

It was at Milan that the pious Monica experienced the joy of seeing her tears and prayers answered in the conversion of her famous son, Augustine. The latter, who had come to Milan in the year 384 as a teacher of oratory, was attracted at first by the eloquence of Ambrose's preaching. It was not long, however, before the Word of God began to grip the heart of the skeptical, sensual youth. At length he was induced to begin anew the study of the Scripture, and his conversion followed. It was on Easter Sunday, 387 A.D., that he received the rite of holy baptism at the hands of Bishop Ambrose. There is a beautiful tradition that the Te Deum Laudamus was composed under inspiration and recited alternately by Ambrose and Augustine immediately after the latter had been baptized. However, there is little to substantiate this legend, and it is more likely that the magnificent hymn of praise was a compilation of a later date, based on a very ancient Greek version.

As Athanasius was the defender of the doctrine of the Trinity in the East, so Ambrose was its champion in the West. It is natural, therefore, that many of the hymns of Ambrose center around the deity of Christ. There are at least twelve Latin hymns that can be ascribed with certainty to him. Perhaps his best hymn is Veni, Redemptor gentium, which Luther prized very highly and which was one of the first he translated into German. The English translation, "Come, Thou Saviour of our race," is by William R.

Reynolds. Another Advent hymn, "Now hail we our Redeemer," is sometimes ascribed to Ambrose.

The beloved bishop, whose life had been so stormy, passed peacefully to rest on Easter evening, 397 A.D. Thus was seemingly granted beautiful fulfilment to the prayer Ambrose utters in one of his hymns:

> Grant to life's day a calm unclouded ending,
> An eve untouched by shadows of decay,
> The brightness of a holy deathbed blending
> With dawning glories of the eternal day.

While Ambrose was defending the faith and inditing sacred songs at Milan, another richly-endowed poet was writing sublime Latin verse far to the West. He was Aurelius Clemens Prudentius, the great Spanish hymnist. Of his personal history we know little except that he was born 348 A.D. in northern Spain, probably at Saragossa.

In early life he occupied important positions of state, but in his latter years he retired to a monastery. Here he exercised his high poetic gifts in writing a series of sacred Latin poems. He was preeminently the poet of the martyrs, never ceasing to extol their Christian faith and fortitude. Bentley called Prudentius the "Horace of the Christians." Rudelbach declared that his poetry "is like gold set with precious stones," and Luther expressed the desire that the works of Prudentius should be studied in the schools.

The finest funeral hymn ever written has come to us from the pen of this early Spanish bard. It consists of forty-four verses, and begins with the line, Deus ignee fons animarum. It is sometimes referred to as the "song of the catacombs." Archbishop Trench of England called this hymn "the crowning glory of the poetry of Prudentius," and another archbishop, Johan Olof Wallin, the great hymnist of Sweden, made four different attempts at translating it before he produced the hymn now regarded as one of the choicest gems in the "Psalm-book" of his native land.

An English version, derived from the longer poem, begins with the stanza:

> Despair not, O heart, in thy sorrow,
> But hope from God's promises borrow;
> Beware, in thy sorrow, of sinning,
> For death is of life the beginning.

A Prophetic Easter Hymn

> Welcome, happy morning! age to age shall say,
> Hell today is vanquished, heaven is won today.
> Lo, the Dead is living, God for evermore!
> Him, their true Creator, all His works adore.
> Welcome, happy morning! age to age shall say.
> Maker and Redeemer, Life and Health of all,
> Thou from heaven beholding human nature's fall,
> Thou of God the Father, true and only Son,

Manhood to deliver, manhood didst put on.
Hell today is vanquished; heaven is won today!
Thou, of life the Author, death didst undergo,
Tread the path of darkness, saving strength to show;
Come then, True and Faithful, now fulfil Thy word;
'Tis Thine own third morning: rise, O buried Lord!
Welcome, happy morning! age to age shall say.
Loose the souls long prisoned, bound with Satan's chain;
All that now is fallen raise to life again;
Show Thy face in brightness, bid the nations see;
Bring again our daylight; day returns with Thee!
Welcome, happy morning! Heaven is won today!
Venantius Fortunatus (530-609 A.D.)

AN ANCIENT SINGER WHO GLORIFIED THE CROSS

The joyous, rhythmical church-song introduced by Bishop Ambrose made triumphant progress throughout the Western Church. For three centuries it seems to have completely dominated the worship. Its rich melodies and native freshness made a strong appeal to the human emotions, and therefore proved very popular with the people.

However, when Gregory the Great in 590 A.D. ascended the papal chair a reaction had set in. Many of the Ambrosian hymns and chants had become corrupted and secularized and therefore had lost their ecclesiastical dignity. Gregory, to whose severe, ascetic nature the bright and lively style of Ambrosian singing must have seemed almost an abomination, immediately took steps to reform the church music.

A school of music was founded in Rome where the new Gregorian liturgical style, known as "Cantus Romanus," was taught. The Gregorian music was sung in unison. It was slow, uniform and measured, without rhythm and beat, and thus it approached the old recitative method of psalm singing. While it is true that it raised the church music to a higher, nobler and more dignified level, its fatal defect lay in the fact that it could be rendered worthily only by trained choirs and singers. Congregational singing soon became a thing of the past. The common people thenceforth became silent and passive worshipers, and the congregational hymn was superseded by a clerical liturgy.

One of the last hymnists of the Ambrosian school and the most important Latin poet of the sixth century was Venantius Fortunatus, bishop of Poitiers. He was born at Ceneda, near Treviso, about 530 A.D., and was converted to Christianity at an early age. While a student at Ravenna he almost became blind. Having regained his sight through what he regarded a miracle, he made a pilgrimage to the shrine of St. Martin at Tours, and as a result of this journey the remainder of his life was spent in Gaul.

Although all of the poetry of Fortunatus is not of the highest order, he has bequeathed some magnificent hymns to the Christian Church. No one has ever sung of the Cross with such deep pathos and sublime tenderness:

Faithful Cross! above all other,
One and only noble tree!
None in foliage, none in blossom,
None in fruit thy peer may be;
Sweetest wood and sweetest iron!
Sweetest weight is hung on thee.
Bend thy boughs, O Tree of Glory!
Thy relaxing sinews bend;
For awhile the ancient rigor
That thy birth bestowed, suspend;
And the King of heavenly beauty
On thy bosom gently tend!
Thou alone wast counted worthy
This world's Ransom to uphold;
For a shipwrecked race preparing
Harbor, like the Ark of old;
With the sacred blood anointed
From the smitten Lamb that rolled.

And again:

O Tree of beauty, Tree of Light!
O Tree with royal purple dight!
Elect on whose triumphal breast
Those holy limbs should find their rest:
On whose dear arms, so widely flung,
The weight of this world's Ransom hung:
The price of humankind to pay,
And spoil the spoiler of his prey.

Fortunatus' famous Passion hymn, Pange lingua glorioso, is also the basis for the beautiful Easter hymn:

Praise the Saviour
Now and ever!
Praise Him all beneath the skies!
Prostrate lying,
Suffering, dying,
On the Cross, a Sacrifice;
Victory gaining,
Life obtaining,
Now in glory He doth rise.

Another Easter hymn, "Welcome, happy morning! age to age shall say," has a triumphant ring in its flowing lines. His odes to Ascension day and Whitsunday are similar in character.

That Fortunatus had a true evangelical conception of Christ and His atonement may be seen in his well-known hymn, Lustra sex qui jam peregit:

Holy Jesus, grant us grace

In Thy sacrifice to place
All our trust for life renewed,
Pardoned sin and promised good.

A Tribute to the Dying Saviour

O sacred Head, now wounded,
With grief and shame weighed down,
Now scornfully surrounded,
With thorns Thine only crown!
Once reigning in the highest
In light and majesty,
Dishonored now Thou diest,
Yet here I worship Thee.
How art Thou pale with anguish,
With sore abuse and scorn!
How does that visage languish,
Which once was bright as morn!
What Thou, my Lord, hast suffered,
Was all for sinners' gain;
Mine, mine was the transgression,
But Thine the deadly pain.
Lo, here I fall, my Saviour,
'Tis I deserve Thy place:
Look on me with Thy favor,
Vouchsafe to me Thy grace.
Receive me, my Redeemer;
My Shepherd, make me Thine,
Of every good the Fountain,
Thou art the Spring of mine!
What language shall I borrow
To thank Thee, dearest Friend,
For this, Thy dying sorrow,
Thy pity without end!
O make me Thine forever,
And should I fainting be,
Lord, let me never, never,
Outlive my love to Thee.
Bernard of Clairvaux (1091-1153 A.D.)

THE GOLDEN AGE OF LATIN HYMNODY

During the Middle Ages, when evil days had fallen upon the Church, there was very little to inspire sacred song. All over Europe the Gregorian chants, sung in Latin, had crowded out congregational singing. The barbarian languages were considered too crude for use in worship, and much less were they regarded as worthy of being moulded into Christian hymns. Religious poetry was almost invariably written in Latin.

However, in the midst of the spiritual decay and worldly depravity that characterized the age there were noble souls whose lives shone like bright stars in the surrounding darkness. Their sacred poetry, a great deal of which was written for private devotion, bears witness of their deep love for the Saviour.

The beautiful Palm Sunday hymn, "All glory, laud, and honor," was composed by Bishop Theodulph of Orleans in a prison cell, probably in the year 821. The immortal Veni, Creator Spiritus also dates from the same period, being usually ascribed to Rhabanus Maurus, archbishop of Mainz, who died in the year 856.

The religious fervor inspired by the Crusades, which began in the year 1098, resulted in the production during the twelfth century of Latin poetry of singular lyrical beauty. This may be regarded as the golden age of Latin hymnody.

It was during this period that the most touching of all Good Friday hymns, "O sacred Head, now wounded," was written. It is ascribed to Bernard of Clairvaux, preacher of the Second Crusade, and one of the most brilliant of Latin hymn-writers.

Although composed in the twelfth century, the hymn did not achieve unusual fame until five centuries later, when it was rendered into German by the greatest of all Lutheran hymnists, Paul Gerhardt. Lauxmann has well said: "Bernard's original is powerful and searching, but Gerhardt's hymn is still more powerful and profound, as re-drawn from the deeper spring of evangelical Lutheran, Scriptural knowledge and fervency of faith."

Gerhardt's version in turn was translated into English by James W. Alexander of Princeton, a Presbyterian. Thus, as Dr. Philip Schaff puts it: "This classic hymn has shown in three tongues—Latin, German and English—and in three confessions—Roman, Lutheran and Reformed—with equal effect the dying love of our Saviour and our boundless indebtedness to Him."

Yet another Lutheran, none other than John Sebastian Bach, "high priest of church music," has contributed to the fame of the hymn by giving the gripping tune to which it is sung its present form. Strangely enough, this remarkable minor melody was originally a rather frivolous German folksong, and was adapted by Hans Leo Hassler in 1601 to the hymn, "Herzlich thut mich verlangen." It was Bach, however, who moulded the tune into the "Passion Chorale," one of the world's masterpieces of sacred music.

Many touching stories have been recorded concerning this famous hymn. In 1798, when Christian Schwartz, the great Lutheran missionary to India, lay dying, his Indian pupils gathered around his bed and sang in their own Malabar tongue the last verses of the hymn, Schwartz himself joining in the singing till his voice was silenced in death.

Of Bernard of Clairvaux, the writer of the hymn, volumes might be written. Luther paid him an eloquent tribute, when he said: "If there has ever been a pious monk who feared God it was St. Bernard, whom alone I hold in much higher esteem than all other monks and priests throughout the globe."

Probably no preacher ever exerted a more profound influence over the age in which he lived than did this Cistercian monk. It was the death of his mother, when he was twenty years old, that seemed to have been the turning point in his life. The son of a Burgundian knight, he had planned to become a priest, but now he determined to enter a monastery. He did not go alone, however, but took with him twelve companions, including an uncle and four of his five brothers!

When he was only twenty-four years old, in the year 1115, he founded a monastery of his own, which was destined to become one of the most famous in history. It was situated in a valley in France called Wormwood, a wild region famous as a robber haunt. Bernard changed the name to "Clara Vallis," or "Beautiful Valley," from which is derived the designation "Clairvaux."

Among his pupils were men who afterwards wielded great influence in the Roman Church. One became a pope, six became cardinals, and thirty were elevated to the office of bishop in the church.

As abbot of Clairvaux, the fame of Bernard spread through all Christendom. He led such an ascetic life that he was reduced almost to a living skeleton. His haggard appearance alone made a deep impression on his audiences. But he also was gifted with extraordinary eloquence and deep spiritual fervor.

Frequently he would leave his monastery to appear before kings and church councils, always swaying them at will. During the year 1146 he traveled through France and Germany, preaching a second crusade. The effect of his preaching was almost miraculous. In some instances the whole population of cities and villages seemed to rise en masse, flocking to the crusade standards.

"In the towns where I have preached," he said, "scarcely one man is left to seven women."

Emperor Conrad and Louis, King of France, were easily won to the cause, and in 1147 the vast horde of crusaders started for the Holy Land. Probably only one-tenth reached Palestine, and the expedition resulted in failure. A miserable remnant returned home, defeated and disgraced. The blame was thrown on Bernard and it was no doubt this sorrow that hastened his death, in the year 1153.

His noble Good Friday hymn, which in Latin begins with the words, Salve caput cruentatum, alone would have gained undying fame for Bernard, but we are indebted to this gifted monk for another remarkable poem, De Nomine Jesu, from which at least three of our most beautiful English hymns have been derived. One of these is a translation by the Englishman, Edward Caswall:

Jesus, the very thought of Thee
With sweetness fills my breast;
But sweeter far Thy face to see
And in Thy presence rest.
A second by the same translator is equally beautiful:

O Jesus! King most wonderful,

Thou Conqueror renowned,
Thou sweetness most ineffable,
In whom all joys are found.

The third derived from Bernard's Latin lyric is by the American hymnist, Ray Palmer:

O Jesus, Joy of loving hearts!
Thou Fount of life! Thou Light of men!
From fullest bliss that earth imparts,
We turn unfilled to Thee again.

Throughout the Middle Ages the verses of Bernard were a source of inspiration to faithful souls, and it is said that even the Crusaders who kept guard over the holy sepulchre at Jerusalem sang his De Nomine Jesu.

A noted contemporary, Bernard of Cluny, shares with Bernard of Clairvaux the distinction of occupying the foremost place among the great Latin hymn-writers. This Bernard was born in Morlaix in Brittany of English parents very early in the twelfth century. After having entered the Abbey of Cluny, which at that time was the most wealthy and luxurious monastery in Europe, he devoted his leisure hours to writing his famous poem, De contemptu mundi. This poem, which is a satire against the vices and follies of his age, contains 3,000 lines. From this poem have been derived three glorious hymns—"Jerusalem the golden," "Brief life is here our portion," and "For thee, O dear, dear country."

Other noted Latin hymn-writers who followed the two Bernards included Thomas of Celano who, in the thirteenth century, wrote the masterpiece among judgment hymns, Dies irae, dies illa, of which Walter Scott has given us the English version, "That day of wrath, that dreadful day"; Adam of St. Victor, who was the composer of more than one hundred sequences of high lyrical order; Jacobus de Benedictis, who is thought to be the writer of Stabat mater dolorosa, the pathetic Good Friday hymn which in its adapted form is known as "Near the cross was Mary weeping"; and Thomas Aquinas, who was the author of Lauda, Sion, salvatorem, a glorious hymn of praise. With these writers the age of Latin hymnody is brought to a close.

PART II
German Hymnody

The Battle Hymn of the Reformation

A mighty Fortress is our God,
A trusty Shield and Weapon,
He helps us in our every need
That hath us now o'ertaken.
The old malignant foe
E'er means us deadly woe:
Deep guile and cruel might
Are his dread arms in fight,

On earth is not his equal.
With might of ours can naught be done,
Soon were our loss effected;
But for us fights the Valiant One
Whom God Himself elected.
Ask ye who this may be?
Christ Jesus, it is He,
As Lord of Hosts adored,
Our only King and Lord,
He holds the field forever.
Though devils all the world should fill,
All watching to devour us,
We tremble not, we fear no ill,
They cannot overpower us.
For this world's prince may still
Scowl fiercely as he will,
We need not be alarmed,
For he is now disarmed;
One little word o'erthrows him.
The Word they still shall let remain,
Nor any thanks have for it;
He's by our side upon the plain,
With His good gifts and Spirit.
Take they, then, what they will,
Life, goods, yea, all; and still,
E'en when their worst is done,
They yet have nothing won,
The kingdom ours remaineth.
Martin Luther, 1527?

MARTIN LUTHER, FATHER OF EVANGELICAL HYMNODY

The father of evangelical hymnody was Martin Luther. It was through the efforts of the great Reformer that the lost art of congregational singing was restored and the Christian hymn again was given a place in public worship.

Luther was an extraordinary man. To defy the most powerful ecclesiastical hierarchy the world has known, to bring about a cataclysmic upheaval in the religious and political world, and to set spiritual forces into motion that have changed the course of human history—this would have been sufficient to have gained for him undying fame. But those who know Luther only as a Reformer know very little about the versatile gifts and remarkable achievements of this great prophet of the Church.

Philip Schaff has characterized Luther as "the Ambrose of German hymnody," and adds: "To Luther belongs the extraordinary merit of having given to the German people in their own tongue the Bible, the Catechism, and the hymn book, so that God might speak directly to them in His word, and that they might directly answer Him in their songs." He also refers to him as "the father of the modern High German language and literature."

Luther was divinely endowed for his great mission. From childhood he was passionately fond of music. As a student at Magdeburg, and later at Eisenach, he sang for alms at the windows of wealthy citizens. It was the sweet voice of the boy that attracted the attention of Ursula Cotta and moved that benevolent woman to give him a home during his school days.

The flute and lute were his favorite instruments, and he used the latter always in accompanying his own singing. John Walther, a contemporary composer who later aided Luther in the writing of church music, has left us this testimony: "It is to my certain knowledge that that holy man of God, Luther, prophet and apostle to the German nation, took great delight in music, both in choral and figural composition. I spent many a delightful hour with him in singing; and ofttimes I have seen the dear man wax so happy and merry in heart over the singing that it is well-nigh impossible to weary or content him therewithal. And his discourse concerning music was most noble."

In his "Discourse in Praise of Music," Luther gives thanks to God for having bestowed the power of song on the "nightingale and the many thousand birds of the air," and again he writes, "I give music the highest and most honorable place; and every one knows how David and all the saints put their divine thoughts into verse, rhyme, and song."

Luther had little patience with the iconoclasts of his day. He wrote in the Preface to Walther's collection of hymns, in 1525: "I am not of the opinion that all sciences should be beaten down and made to cease by the Gospel, as some fanatics pretend, but I would fain see all the arts, and music, in particular, used in the service of Him who hath given and created them." At another time he was even more emphatic: "If any man despises music, as all fanatics do, for him I have no liking; for music is a gift and grace of God, not an invention of men. Thus it drives out the devil and makes people cheerful. Then one forgets all wrath, impurity, sycophancy, and other vices."

Luther loved the Latin hymns that glorified Christ. He recognized, however, that they were so permeated with Mariolatry and other errors of the Roman Church that a refining process was necessary in order to rid them of their dross and permit the fine gold to appear. Moreover, the Latin hymns, even in their most glorious development, had not grown out of the spiritual life of the congregation. The very genius of the Roman Church precluded this, for church music and song was regarded as belonging exclusively to the priestly office. Moreover, since the entire worship was conducted in Latin, the congregation was inevitably doomed to passive silence.

Brave efforts by John Huss and his followers to introduce congregational singing in the Bohemian churches had been sternly opposed by the Roman hierarchy. The Council of Constance, which in 1415 burned the heroic Huss at the stake, also sent a solemn warning to Jacob of Misi, his successor as leader of the Hussites, to cease the practice of singing hymns in the churches. It decreed: "If laymen are forbidden to preach and interpret the Scriptures, much more are they forbidden to sing publicly in the churches."

Luther's ringing declaration that all believers constitute a universal priesthood necessarily implied that the laity should also participate in the worship. Congregational singing therefore became inevitable.

Luther also realized that spiritual song could be enlisted as a powerful ally in spreading the evangelical doctrines. During the birth throes of the Reformation he often expressed the wish that someone more gifted than himself might give to the German people in their own language some of the beautiful pearls of Latin hymnody. He also wanted original hymns in the vernacular, as well as strong, majestic chorales that would reflect the heroic spirit of the age.

"We lack German poets and musicians," he complained, "or they are unknown to us, who are able to make Christian and spiritual songs of such value that they can be used daily in the house of God."

Then something happened that opened the fountains of song in Luther's own bosom. The Reformation had spread from Germany into other parts of Europe, and the Catholic authorities had commenced to adopt stern measures in an effort to stem the revolt. In the Augustinian cloister at Antwerp, the prior of the abbey and two youths, Heinrich Voes and Johannes Esch, had been sentenced to death by the Inquisition for their refusal to surrender their new-born faith.

The prior was choked to death in his prison cell. The two youths were led to the stake at Brussels, on July 1, 1523. Before the faggots were kindled they were told that they might still be freed if they would recant. They replied that they would rather die and be with Christ. Before the fire and smoke smothered their voices, they sang the ancient Latin hymn, "Lord God, we praise thee."

When news of the Brussels tragedy reached Luther the poetic spark in his soul burst into full flame. Immediately he sat down and wrote a festival hymn commemorating the death of the first Lutheran martyrs. It had been reported to Luther that when the fires began to lick the feet of Voes, witnesses had heard him exclaim, "Behold, blooming roses are strewn around me." Luther seized upon the words as prophetic and concluded his hymn with the lines:

> "Summer is even at the door,
> The winter now hath vanished,
> The tender flowerets spring once more,
> And He who winter banished
> Will send a happy summer."

The opening words of the hymn are also significant, "Ein neues Lied wir heben an." Although the poem must be regarded as more of a ballad than a church hymn, Luther's lyre was tuned, the springtime of evangelical hymnody was indeed come, and before another year had passed a little hymn-book called "The Achtliederbuch" appeared as the first-fruits.

It was in 1524 that this first Protestant hymnal was published. It contained only eight hymns, four by Luther, three by Speratus, and one probably by Justus Jonas. The little hymn-books flew all over Europe, to the consternation of the Romanists. Luther's enemies lamented that "the whole people are singing themselves into his doctrines." So great was the demand for hymns that a second volume known as the "Erfurt Enchiridion" was published in the same year. This contained twenty-five hymns, eighteen of which were Luther's. "The nightingale of Wittenberg" had begun to sing.

This was the beginning of evangelical hymnody, which was to play so large a part in the spread of Luther's teachings. The number of hymn-books by other compilers increased rapidly and so many unauthorized changes were made in his hymns by critical editors that Luther was moved to complain of their practice. In a preface to a hymn-book printed by Joseph Klug of Wittenberg, in 1543, Luther writes: "I am fearful that it will fare with this little book as it has ever fared with good books, namely, that through tampering by incompetent hands it may get to be so overlaid and spoiled that the good will be lost out of it, and nothing kept in use but the worthless." Then he adds, naively: "Every man may make a hymn-book for himself and let ours alone and not add thereto, as we here beg, wish and assert. For we desire to keep our own coin up to our own standard, preventing no one from making better hymns for himself. Now let God's name alone be praised and our name not sought. Amen."

Of the thirty-six hymns attributed to Luther none has achieved such fame as "A mighty fortress is our God." It has been translated into practically every language and is regarded as one of the noblest and most classical examples of Christian hymnody. Not only did it become the battle hymn of the Reformation, but it may be regarded as the true national hymn of Germany. Heine called it "the Marseillaise of the Reformation." Frederick the Great referred to it as "God Almighty's grenadier march."

The date of the hymn cannot be fixed with any certainty. Much has been written on the subject, but none of the arguments appear conclusive. D'Aubigné's unqualified statement that Luther composed it and sang it to revive the spirits of his friends at the Diet of Augsburg in 1530 can scarcely be accepted, since it appeared at least a year earlier in a hymn-book published by Joseph Klug.

The magnificent chorale to which the hymn is sung is also Luther's work. Never have words and music been combined to make so tremendous an appeal. Great musical composers have turned to its stirring theme again and again when they have sought to produce a mighty effect. Mendelssohn has used it in the last movement of his Reformation symphony; Meyerbeer uses it to good advantage in his masterpiece, "Les Huguenots"; and Wagner's "Kaisermarsch," written to celebrate the triumphal return of the German troops in 1870, reaches a great climax with the whole orchestra thundering forth the sublime chorale. Bach has woven it into a beautiful cantata, while Raff and Nicolai make use of it in overtures.

After Luther's death, when Melanchthon and his friends were compelled to flee from Wittenberg by the approach of the Spanish army, they came to Weimar. As they were entering the city, they heard a little girl singing Luther's great hymn. "Sing on, my child," exclaimed Melanchthon, "thou little knowest how thy song cheers our hearts."

When Gustavus Adolphus, the hero king of Sweden, faced Tilly's hosts at the battlefield of Leipzig, Sept. 7, 1631, he led his army in singing "Ein feste Burg." Then shouting, "God is with us," he went into battle. It was a bloody fray. Tilly fell and his army was beaten. When the battle was over, Gustavus Adolphus knelt upon the ground among his soldiers and thanked the Lord of Hosts for victory, saying, "He holds the field forever."

At another time during the Thirty Years' War a Swedish trumpeter captured the ensign of the Imperial army. Pursued by the enemy he found himself trapped with a swollen river before him. He paused for a moment and prayed, "Help me, O my God," and then thrust spurs into his horse and plunged into the midst of the current. The Imperialists were afraid to follow him, whereupon he raised his trumpet to his lips and sounded the defiant notes: "A mighty fortress is our God!"

George N. Anderson, a missionary in Tanganyika Province, British East Africa, tells how he once heard an assembly of 2,000 natives sing Luther's great hymn. "I never heard it sung with more spirit; the effect was almost overwhelming," he testifies.

A West African missionary, Christaller, relates how he once sang "Ein feste Burg" to his native interpreter. "That man, Luther," said the African, "must have been a powerful man, one can feel it in his hymns."

Thomas Carlyle's estimate of "Ein feste Burg" seems to accord with that of the African native. "It jars upon our ears," he says, "yet there is something in it like the sound of Alpine avalanches, or the first murmur of earthquakes, in the very vastness of which dissonance a higher unison is revealed to us."

Carlyle, who refers to Luther as "perhaps the most inspired of all teachers since the Apostles," has given us the most rugged of all translations of the Reformer's great hymn. There are said to be no less than eighty English translations, but only a few have met with popular favor. In England the version by Carlyle is in general use, while in America various composite translations are found in hymn-books. Carlyle's first stanza reads

> A sure stronghold our God is He,
> A trusty Shield and Weapon;
> Our help He'll be, and set us free
> From every ill can happen.
> That old malicious foe
> Intends us deadly woe;
> Arméd with might from hell
> And deepest craft as well,
> On earth is not his fellow.

The greater number of Luther's hymns are not original. Many are paraphrases of Scripture, particularly the Psalms, and others are based on Latin, Greek, and German antecedents. In every instance, however, the great Reformer so imbued them with his own fervent faith and militant spirit that they seem to shine with a new luster.

The hymns of Luther most frequently found in hymn-books today are "Come, Thou Saviour of our race," "Good news from heaven the angels bring," "In death's strong grasp the Saviour lay," "Come, Holy Spirit, God and Lord," "Come, Holy Spirit, from above," "Lord, keep us steadfast in Thy word," "Lord, Jesus Christ, to Thee we pray," "Dear Christians, one and all rejoice," "Out of the depths I cry to Thee," and "We all believe in one true God."

A Metrical Gloria in Excelsis

All glory be to Thee, Most High,
To Thee all adoration!
In grace and truth Thou drawest nigh
To offer us salvation.
Thou showest Thy good will toward men,
And peace shall reign on earth again;
We praise Thy Name forever.
We praise, we worship Thee, we trust,
And give Thee thanks forever,
O Father, for Thy rule is just
And wise, and changes never.
Thy hand almighty o'er us reigns,
Thou doest what Thy will ordains;
'Tis well for us Thou rulest.
O Jesus Christ, our God and Lord,
Son of the Heavenly Father,
O Thou, who hast our peace restored,
The straying sheep dost gather,
Thou Lamb of God, to Thee on high
Out of the depths we sinners cry:
Have mercy on us, Jesus!
O Holy Ghost, Thou precious gift,
Thou Comforter, unfailing,
From Satan's snares our souls uplift,
And let Thy power, availing,
Avert our woes and calm our dread;
For us the Saviour's blood was shed,
We trust in Thee to save us!
Nicolaus Decius, 1526, 1539

THE HYMN-WRITERS OF THE REFORMATION

The hymns of the Reformation were like a trumpet call, proclaiming to all the world that the day of spiritual emancipation had come. What they lacked in poetic refinement they more than made up by their tremendous earnestness and spiritual exuberance.

They faithfully reflect the spirit of the age in which they were born, a period of strife and conflict. The strident note that often appears in Luther's hymns can easily be understood when it is remembered that the great Reformer looked upon the pope as

Antichrist himself and all others who opposed the Lutheran teachings as confederates of the devil.

In 1541, when the Turkish invasion from the East threatened to devastate all Europe, special days of humiliation and prayer were held throughout Germany. It was for one of these occasions that Luther wrote the hymn, "Lord, keep us steadfast in Thy word." In its original form, however, it was quite different from the hymn we now sing. The first stanza ran:

> Lord, keep us in Thy word and work,
> Restrain the murderous pope and Turk,
> Who fain would tear from off Thy throne
> Christ Jesus, Thy beloved Son.

When Luther, on the other hand, sang of God's free grace to men in Christ Jesus, or extolled the merits of the Saviour, or gave thanks for the word of God restored to men, there was such a marvelous blending of childlike trust, victorious faith and spontaneous joy that all Germany was thrilled by the message.

The popularity of the Lutheran hymns was astonishing. Other hymn-writers sprang up in large numbers, printing presses were kept busy, and before Luther's death no less than sixty collections of hymns had been published. Wandering evangelists were often surrounded by excited crowds in the market places, hymns printed on leaflets were distributed, and the whole populace would join in singing the songs of the Reformers.

Paul Speratus, Paul Eber, and Justus Jonas were the most gifted co-laborers of Luther. It was Speratus who contributed three hymns to the "Achtliederbuch," the first hymn-book published by Luther. His most famous hymn, "To us salvation now is come," has been called "the poetic counterpart of Luther's preface to the Epistle to the Romans." It was the great confessional hymn of the Reformation. Luther is said to have wept tears of joy when he heard it sung by a street singer outside his window in Wittenberg.

Speratus wrote the hymn in a Moravian prison into which he had been cast because of his bold espousal of the Lutheran teachings. Immediately upon his release he proceeded to Wittenberg, where he joined himself to the Reformers. He later became the leader of the Reformation movement in Prussia and before his death in 1551 was chosen bishop of Pomerania. His poetic genius may be seen reflected in the beautiful paraphrase of the Lord's Prayer which forms the concluding two stanzas of his celebrated hymn:

> All blessing, honor, thanks, and praise
> To Father, Son, and Spirit,
> The God who saved us by His grace,
> All glory to His merit:
>
> O Father in the heavens above,
> Thy glorious works show forth Thy love,
> Thy worthy Name be hallowed.
> Thy kingdom come, Thy will be done
> In earth, as 'tis in heaven:
> Keep us in life, by grace led on,

Forgiving and forgiven;
Save Thou us in temptation's hour,
And from all ills; Thine is the power,
And all the glory, Amen!

Eber was the sweetest singer among the Reformers. As professor of Hebrew at Wittenberg University and assistant to Melanchthon, he had an active part in the stirring events of the Reformation. He possessed more of Melanchthon's gentleness than Luther's ruggedness, and his hymns are tender and appealing in their childlike simplicity. There is wondrous consolation in his hymns for the dying, as witness his pious swan-song:

In Thy dear wounds I fall asleep,
O Jesus, cleanse my soul from sin:
Thy bitter death, Thy precious blood
For me eternal glory win.
By Thee redeemed, I have no fear,
When now I leave this mortal clay,
With joy before Thy throne I come;
God's own must die, yet live alway.
Welcome, O death! thou bringest me
To dwell with God eternally;
Through Christ my soul from sin is free,
O take me now, dear Lord, to Thee!

Another hymn for the dying, "Lord Jesus Christ, true man and God," breathes the same spirit of hope and trust in Christ. During the years of persecution and suffering that followed the Reformation, the Protestants found much comfort in singing Eber's "When in the hour of utmost need."

Justus Jonas, the bosom friend of Luther who spoke the last words of peace and consolation to the dying Reformer and who also preached his funeral sermon, has left us the hymn, "If God were not upon our side," based on Psalm 124.

From this period we also have the beautiful morning hymn, "My inmost heart now raises," by Johannes Mathesius, the pupil and biographer of Luther, and an equally beautiful evening hymn, "Sunk is the sun's last beam of light," by Nicholas Hermann. Mathesius was pastor of the church at Joachimsthal, in Bohemia, and Hermann was his organist and choirmaster. It is said that whenever Mathesius preached a particularly good sermon, Hermann was forthwith inspired to write a hymn on its theme! He was a poet and musician of no mean ability, and his tunes are among the best from the Reformation period.

The example of the Wittenberg hymnists was quickly followed by evangelicals in other parts of Germany, and hymn-books began to appear everywhere. As early as 1526 a little volume of hymns was published at Rostock in the Platt-Deutsch dialect. In this collection we find one of the most glorious hymns of the Reformation, "All glory be to Thee, Most High," or, as it has also been rendered, "All glory be to God on high," a metrical version of the ancient canticle, Gloria in Excelsis. Five years later another edition was published in which appeared a metrical rendering of Agnus Dei:

O Lamb of God, most holy,
On Calvary an offering;
Despiséd, meek, and, lowly,
Thou in Thy death and suffering
Our sins didst bear, our anguish;
The might of death didst vanquish;
Give us Thy peace, O Jesus!

The author of both of these gems of evangelical hymnody was Nicolaus Decius, a Catholic monk in the cloister of Steterburg who embraced the Lutheran teachings. He later became pastor of St. Nicholas church in Stettin, where he died under suspicious circumstances in 1541. In addition to being a popular preacher and gifted poet, he also seems to have been a musician of some note. The two magnificent chorals to which his hymns are sung are generally credited to him, although there is a great deal of uncertainty surrounding their composition. Luther prized both hymns very highly and included them in his German liturgy.

A Beautiful Confirmation Hymn

Let me be Thine forever,
My gracious God and Lord,
May I forsake Thee never,
Nor wander from Thy Word:
Preserve me from the mazes
Of error and distrust,
And I shall sing Thy praises
Forever with the just.
Lord Jesus, bounteous Giver
Of light and life divine,
Thou didst my soul deliver,
To Thee I all resign:
Thou hast in mercy bought me
With blood and bitter pain;
Let me, since Thou hast sought me,
Eternal life obtain.
O Holy Ghost, who pourest
Sweet peace into my heart,
And who my soul restorest,
Let not Thy grace depart.
And while His Name confessing
Whom I by faith have known,
Grant me Thy constant blessing,
Make me for aye Thine own.
Nicolaus Selnecker, 1572, et al.

HYMNODY OF THE CONTROVERSIAL PERIOD

Many of our great Christian hymns were born in troublous times. This is true in a very special sense of the hymns written by Nicolaus Selnecker, German preacher and theologian. The age in which he lived was the period immediately following the Reformation. It was an age marked by doctrinal controversy, not only with the Romanists, but among the Protestants themselves. In these theological struggles, Selnecker will always be remembered as one of the great champions of pure Lutheran doctrine.

"The Formula of Concord," the last of the Lutheran confessions, was largely the work of Selnecker. Published in 1577, it did more than any other single document to clarify the Lutheran position on many disputed doctrinal points, thus bringing to an end much of the confusion and controversy that had existed up to that time.

Selnecker early in life revealed an artistic temperament. Born in 1532 at Hersbruck, Germany, we find him at the age of twelve years organist at the chapel in the Kaiserburg, at Nürnberg, where he attended school. Later he entered Wittenberg University to study law. Here he came under the influence of Philip Melanchthon, and was induced to prepare himself for the ministry. It is said that Selnecker was Melanchthon's favorite pupil.

Following his graduation from Wittenberg, he lectured for a while at the university and then received the appointment as second court preacher at Dresden and private tutor to Prince Alexander of Saxony. Many of the Saxon theologians at this time were leaning strongly toward the Calvinistic teaching regarding the Lord's Supper, and when Selnecker came out boldly for the Lutheran doctrine he incurred the hostility of those in authority. Later, when he supported a Lutheran pastor who had dared to preach against Elector August's passion for hunting, he was compelled to leave Dresden.

For three years he held the office of professor of theology at the University of Jena, but in 1568 he again found favor with the Elector August and was appointed to the chair of theology in the University of Leipzig. It was here that Selnecker again became involved in bitter doctrinal disputes regarding the Lord's Supper, and in 1576 and 1577 he joined a group of theologians, including Jacob Andreae and Martin Chemnitz, in working out the Formula of Concord.

Upon the death of Elector August the Calvinists again secured ecclesiastical control, and Selnecker once more was compelled to leave Leipzig. After many trials and vicissitudes, he finally returned, May 19, 1592, a worn and weary man, only to die in Leipzig five days later.

During the stormy days of his life, Selnecker often sought solace in musical and poetical pursuits. Many of his hymns reflect his own personal troubles and conflicts. "Let me be thine forever" is believed to have been written during one of the more grievous experiences of his life. It was a prayer of one stanza originally, but two additional stanzas were added by an unknown author almost a hundred years after Selnecker's death. In its present form it has become a favorite confirmation hymn in the Lutheran Church.

Selnecker's zeal for his Church is revealed in many of his hymns, among them the famous "Abide with us, O Saviour dear." The second stanza of this hymn clearly reflects the distressing controversies in which he was engaged at the time:

This is a dark and evil day,
Forsake us not, O Lord, we pray;
And let us in our grief and pain
Thy Word and sacraments retain.

In connection with his work as professor in the University of Leipzig, he also served as pastor of the famous St. Thomas church in that city. It was through his efforts that the renowned Motett choir of that church was built up, a choir that was afterward conducted by John Sebastian Bach.

About 150 hymns in all were written by Selnecker. In addition to these he also was author of some 175 theological and controversial works.

One of the contemporaries of Selnecker was Bartholomäus Ringwalt, pastor of Langfeld, near Sonnenburg, Brandenburg. This man also was a staunch Lutheran and a poet of considerable ability. His judgment hymn, "The day is surely drawing near," seems to reflect the feeling held by many in those distressing times that the Last Day was near at hand. It was used to a large extent during the Thirty Years' War, and is still found in many hymn-books.

Another hymnist who lived and wrought during these turbulent times was Martin Behm, to whom we are indebted for three beautiful lyrics, "O Jesus, King of glory," "Lord Jesus Christ, my Life, my Light," and "O holy, blessed Trinity." Behm, who was born in Lauban, Silesia, Sept. 16, 1557, served for thirty-six years as Lutheran pastor in his native city. He was a noted preacher and a gifted poet. His hymn on the Trinity is one of the finest ever written on this theme. It concludes with a splendid paraphrase of the Aaronic benediction. Two of its stanzas are:

O holy, blessed Trinity,
Divine, eternal Unity,
God, Father, Son and Holy Ghost,
Be Thou this day my guide and host.

Lord, bless and keep Thou me as Thine;
Lord, make Thy face upon me shine;
Lord, lift Thy countenance on me,
And give me peace, sweet peace from Thee.

Valerius Herberger was another heroic representative of this period of doctrinal strife, war, famine, and pestilence. While pastor of St. Mary's Lutheran Church at Fraustadt, Posen, he and his flock were expelled from their church in 1604 by King Sigismund III, of Poland, and the property turned over to the Roman Catholics. Nothing daunted, however, Herberger and his people immediately constructed a chapel out of two houses near the gates of the city. They gave the structure the name of "Kripplein Christi," since the first service was held in it on Christmas Eve.

During the great pestilence which raged in 1613, the victims in Fraustadt numbered 2,135. Herberger, however, stuck to his post, comforting the sick and burying the dead. It was during these days that he wrote his famous hymn, "Valet will ich dir geben," one of the finest hymns for the dying in the German language. The hymn was published with the title, "The farewell (Valet) of Valerius Herberger that he gave to the world in the autumn of the year 1613, when he every hour saw death before his eyes, but mercifully and also as wonderfully as the three men in the furnace at Babylon was nevertheless spared."

The famous chorale tune for the hymn was written in 1613 by Melchior Teschner, who was Herberger's precentor.

Other Lutheran hymn-writers of this period were Joachim Magdeburg, Martin Rutilius, Martin Schalling and Philipp Nicolai. The last name in this group is by far the most important and will be given more extensive notice in the following chapter. To Magdeburg, a pastor who saw service in various parts of Germany and Hungary during a stormy career, we owe a single hymn, "Who trusts in God a strong abode." Rutilius has been credited with the authorship of the gripping penitential hymn, "Alas, my God! my sins are great," although the claim is sometimes disputed. He was a pastor at Weimar, where he died in 1618.

Schalling likewise has bequeathed but a single hymn to the Church, but it may be regarded as one of the classic hymns of Germany. Its opening line, "O Lord, devoutly love I Thee," reflects the ardent love of the author himself for the Saviour. It was entitled, "A prayer to Christ, the Consolation of the soul in life and death," and surely its message of confiding trust in God has been a source of comfort and assurance to thousands of pious souls in the many vicissitudes of life as well as in the valley of the shadow.

Although Schalling was a warm friend of Selnecker, he hesitated to subscribe to the Formula of Concord, claiming that it dealt too harshly with the followers of Melanchthon. For this reason he was deposed as General Superintendent of Oberpfalz and court preacher at Heidelberg. Five years later, however, he was appointed pastor of St. Mary's church in Nürnberg, where he remained until blindness compelled him to retire. He died in 1608.

A Masterpiece of Hymnody

Wake, awake, for night is flying:
The watchmen on the heights are crying,
Awake, Jerusalem, arise!
Midnight's solemn hour is tolling,
His chariot wheels are nearer rolling,
He comes; prepare, ye virgins wise.
Rise up with willing feet,
Go forth, the Bridegroom meet:
Alleluia!
Bear through the night your well trimmed light,
Speed forth to join the marriage rite.
Zion hears the watchmen singing,
And all her heart with joy is springing,
She wakes, she rises from her gloom;
Forth her Bridegroom comes, all-glorious,
The strong in grace, in truth victorious;
Her Star is risen, her Light is come!

All hail, Thou precious One!
Lord Jesus, God's dear Son!
Alleluia!
The joyful call we answer all,
And follow to the nuptial hall.
Lamb of God, the heavens adore Thee,
And men and angels sing before Thee,
With harp and cymbal's clearest tone.
By the pearly gates in wonder
We stand, and swell the voice of thunder,
That echoes round Thy dazzling throne.
To mortal eyes and ears
What glory now appears!
Alleluia!
We raise the song, we swell the throng,
To praise Thee ages all along.
Philipp Nicolai, 1599.

THE KING AND QUEEN OF CHORALES

At rare intervals in the history of Christian hymnody, we meet with a genius who not only possesses the gift of writing sublime poetry but also reveals talent as a composer of music. During the stirring days of the Reformation such geniuses were revealed in the persons of Martin Luther and Nicolaus Decius. We now encounter another, Philipp Nicolai, the writer of the glorious hymn, "Wachet auf."

Nicolai's name would have been gratefully remembered by posterity had he merely written the words of this hymn; but, when we learn that he also composed the magnificent chorale to which it is sung, we are led to marvel. It has been called the "King of Chorales," and well does it deserve the title.

But Nicolai was also the composer of the "Queen of Chorales." That is the name often given to the tune of his other famous hymn, "Wie schön leuchtet der Morgenstern." Both of Nicolai's great tunes have been frequently appropriated for other hymns. The "King of Chorales" has lent inspiration to "Holy Majesty, before Thee," while the "Queen of Chorales" has helped to glorify such hymns as "All hail to thee, O blessed morn," "Now Israel's hope in triumph ends," and "O Holy Spirit, enter in."

Some of the world's greatest composers have recognized the beauty and majesty of Nicolai's inspiring themes and have seized upon his chorales to weave them into a number of famous musical masterpieces. The strains of the seventh and eighth lines of "Wachet auf" may be heard in the passage, "The kingdoms of this world," of Handel's "Hallelujah chorus." Mendelssohn introduces the air in his overture to "St. Paul," and the entire chorale occurs in his "Hymn of Praise." The latter composer has also made use of the "Wie schön" theme in the first chorus of his unpublished oratorio, "Christus."

The circumstances that called forth Nicolai's two great hymns and the classic chorales to which he wedded them are tragic in nature. A dreadful pestilence was raging in

Westphalia. At Unna, where Nicolai was pastor, 1,300 villagers died of the plague between July, 1597, and January, 1598. During a single week in the month of August no less than 170 victims were claimed by the messenger of death.

From the parsonage which overlooked the churchyard, Nicolai was a sad witness of the burials. On one day thirty graves were dug. In the midst of these days of distress the gifted Lutheran pastor wrote a series of meditations to which he gave the title, "Freuden Spiegel," or "Mirror of Joy." His purpose, as he explains in his preface, dated August 10, 1598, was "to leave it behind me (if God should call me from this world) as the token of my peaceful, joyful, Christian departure, or (if God should spare me in health) to comfort other sufferers whom He should also visit with the pestilence."

"There seemed to me," he writes in the same preface, "nothing more sweet, delightful and agreeable, than the contemplation of the noble, sublime doctrine of Eternal Life obtained through the Blood of Christ. This I allowed to dwell in my heart day and night, and searched the Scriptures as to what they revealed on this matter, read also the sweet treatise of the ancient doctor Saint Augustine ("The City of God") ... Then day by day I wrote out my meditations, found myself, thank God! wonderfully well, comforted in heart, joyful in spirit, and truly content."

Both of Nicolai's classic hymns appeared for the first time in his "Mirror of Joy." As a title to "Wachet auf" Nicolai wrote, "Of the voice at Midnight, and the Wise Virgins who meet their Heavenly Bridegroom. Mt. 25." The title to "Wie schön" reads, "A spiritual bridal song of the believing soul concerning Jesus Christ, her Heavenly Bridegroom, founded on the 45th Psalm of the prophet David."

It is said that the melody to "Wie schön" became so popular that numerous church chimes were set to it.

Nicolai's life was filled with stirring events. He was born at Mengerinhausen, August 10, 1556. His father was a Lutheran pastor. After completing studies at the Universities of Erfürt and Wittenberg, he too was ordained to the ministry in 1583. His first charge was at Herdecke, but since the town council was composed of Roman Catholic members, he soon was compelled to leave that place. Later he served at Niederwildungen and Altwildungen, and in 1596 he became pastor at Unna. After the dreadful pestilence of 1597 there came an invasion of Spaniards in 1598, and Nicolai was forced to flee.

In 1601 he was chosen chief pastor of St. Katherine's church in Hamburg. Here he gained fame as a preacher, being hailed as a "second Chrysostom." Throughout a long and bitter controversy with the Calvinists regarding the nature of the Lord's Supper, Nicolai was looked upon as the "pillar" of the Lutheran Church, and the guardian of its doctrines. He died October 26, 1608.

A Tribute to the Dying Saviour

Ah, holy Jesus, how hast Thou offended,
That man to judge Thee hast in hate pretended?
By foes derided, by Thine own rejected,

O most afflicted!
Who was the guilty? Who brought this upon Thee?
Alas, my treason, Jesus, hath undone Thee!
'Twas I, Lord Jesus, I it was denied Thee:
I crucified Thee.
Lo, the Good Shepherd for the sheep is offered;
The slave hath sinned, and the Son hath suffered;
For man's atonement, while he nothing heedeth,
God intercedeth.
For me, kind Jesus, was Thine incarnation,
Thy mortal sorrow, and Thy life's oblation;
Thy death of anguish and Thy bitter passion,
For my salvation.
Therefore, kind Jesus, since I cannot pay Thee,
I do adore Thee, and will ever pray Thee:
Think on Thy pity and Thy love unswerving,
Not my deserving.
Johann Heermann, 1630.

HYMNS OF THE THIRTY YEARS' WAR

Times of suffering and affliction have often brought forth great poets. This was especially true of that troublous period in European history known as the "Thirty Years' War." Although it was one of the most distressing eras in the Protestant Church, it gave birth to some of its grandest hymns.

It was during this dreadful period, when Germany was devastated and depopulated by all the miseries of a bloody warfare, that Johann Heermann lived and wrought. He was born at Rauden, Silesia, October 11, 1585, the son of a poverty-stricken furrier. There were five children in the family, but four of them were snatched away by death within a short time. Johann, who was the youngest, was also taken ill, and the despairing mother was torn by fear and anguish. Turning to God in her hour of need, she vowed that if He would spare her babe, she would educate him for the ministry.

She did not forget her promise. The child whose life was spared grew to manhood, received his training at several institutions, and in 1611 entered the holy ministry as pastor of the Lutheran church at Koeben, not far from his birthplace.

A few years later the Thirty Years' War broke out, and all of Germany began to feel its horrors. Four times during the period from 1629 to 1634 the town of Koeben was sacked by the armies of Wallenstein, who had been sent by the king of Austria to restore the German principalities to the Catholic faith. Previous to this, in 1616, the city was almost destroyed by fire. In 1631 it was visited by the dreadful pestilence.

Again and again Heermann was forced to flee from the city, and several times he lost all his earthly possessions. Once, when he was crossing the Oder, he was pursued and nearly captured by enemy soldiers, who shot after him. Twice he was nearly sabred.

It was during this period, in 1630, that his beautiful hymn, "Herzliebster Jesu," was first published. One of the stanzas which is not usually given in translations reflects very clearly the unfaltering faith of the noble pastor during these hard experiences. It reads:

Whate'er of earthly good this life may grant me
I'll risk for Thee; no shame, no cross shall daunt me;
I shall not fear what man can do to harm me,
Nor death alarm me.

The hymn immediately sprang into popularity in Germany, perhaps through the fact that it reflected the feelings of Protestants everywhere, and partly because of the gripping tune written for it in 1640 by the great musician Johann Crüger.

Heermann has been ranked with Luther and Gerhardt as one of the greatest hymn-writers the Lutheran Church has produced. Because his hymns were written during such times of distress and suffering, they seemed to grip the hearts of the German people to an extraordinary degree.

One of his hymns, published in 1630 under the group known as "Songs of Tears," is entitled "Treuer Wächter Israel." It contains a striking line imploring God to "build a wall around us." A very interesting story is told concerning this hymn. On January 5, 1814, the Allied forces were about to enter Schleswig. A poor widow and her daughter and grandson lived in a little house near the entrance of the town. The grandson was reading Heermann's hymns written for times of war, and when he came to this one, he exclaimed, "It would be a good thing, grandmother, if our Lord would build a wall around us."

Next day all through the town cries of terror were heard, but not a soldier molested the widow's home. When on the following morning they summoned enough courage to open their door, lo, a snowdrift had concealed them from the view of the enemy! On this incident Clemens Brentano wrote a beautiful poem, "Draus vor Schleswig."

Another remarkable story is recorded concerning Heermann's great hymn, "O Jesus, Saviour dear." At Leuthen, in Silesia, December 5, 1757, the Prussians under Frederick the Great were facing an army of Austrians three times their number. Just before the battle began some of the Prussians began to sing the second stanza of the hymn. The regimental bands took up the music. One of the commanders asked Frederick if it should be silenced. "No," said the king, "let it be. With such men God will today certainly give me the victory." When the bloody battle ended with victory for the Prussians, Frederick exclaimed "My God, what a power has religion!"

Other famous hymns by Heermann include "O Christ, our true and only Light," "Lord, Thy death and passion give" and "Faithful God, I lay before Thee."

Many other noted hymn-writers belong to the period of the Thirty Years' War, among them Martin Opitz, George Weissel, Heinrich Held, Ernst Homburg, Johannes Olearius, Josua Stegmann, and Wilhelm II, Duke of Saxe-Weimar.

Opitz was somewhat of a diplomat and courtier, as well as a poet. He was a man of vacillating character, and did not hesitate to lend his support to the Romanists whenever it served his personal interests. However, he has left to posterity an imperishable hymn in "Light of Light, O Sun of heaven." He is credited with having reformed the art of verse-writing in Germany. He died of the pestilence in Danzig in 1639.

Homburg and Held were lawyers. Homburg was born near Eisenach in 1605, and later we find him practising law in Naumburg, Saxony. He was a man of great poetic talent, but at first he devoted his gifts to writing love ballads and drinking songs. During the days of the dread pestilence he turned to God, and now he began to write hymns. In 1659 he published a collection of 150 spiritual songs. In a preface he speaks of them as his "Sunday labor," and he tells how he had been led to write them "by the anxious and sore domestic afflictions by which God ... has for some time laid me aside." The Lenten hymn, "Christ, the Life of all the living," is found in this collection.

Held, who practiced law in his native town of Guhrau, Silesia, also was a man chastened in the school of sorrow and affliction. He is the author of two hymns that have found their way into the English language—"Let the earth now praise the Lord" and "Come, O come, Thou quickening Spirit."

Weissel, a Lutheran pastor at Konigsberg, has given us one of the finest Advent hymns in the German language, "Lift up your heads, ye mighty gates."

Olearius, who wrote a commentary on the Bible and compiled one of the most important hymn-books of the 17th century, has also bequeathed to the Church a splendid Advent hymn, "Comfort, comfort ye My people."

Stegmann, a theological professor at Rinteln who suffered much persecution at the hands of Benedictine monks during the Thirty Years' War, was the author of the beautiful evening hymn, "Abide with us, our Saviour."

Wilhelm II, Duke of Saxe-Weimar, who wrote the inspiring hymn, "O Christ, Thy grace unto us lend," was not only a poet and musician, but also a man of war. He was twice wounded in battle with the Imperial forces, and was once left for dead. He was taken prisoner by Tilly, but was released by the emperor. When Gustavus Adolphus came to Germany to save the Protestant cause, Wilhelm after some hesitation joined him. However, when the Duke in 1635 made a separate peace with the emperor, the Swedish army ravaged his territory.

Johann Meyfart also belongs to this period. He was a theological professor at the University of Erfürt, and died at that place in 1642. One of his hymns, "Jerusalem, thou city fair and high," has found its way into English hymn books.

The beautiful hymn, "O how blest are ye," which was translated into English by Henry Wadsworth Longfellow, comes to us from the pen of Simon Dach, another Lutheran theologian who lived during these stirring days. Dach, who was professor of poetry and dean of the philosophical faculty of the University of Königsberg, wrote some 165 hymns. They are marked by fulness of faith and a quiet confidence in God in the midst of a world of turmoil and uncertainty. Dach died in 1659 after a lingering illness. The first stanza of his funeral hymn reads

O how blest are ye, whose toils are ended!
Who through death have unto God ascended!
Ye have arisen
From the cares which keep us still in prison.

Tobias Clausnitzer, who has bequeathed to the Church the hymn, "Blessed Jesus, at Thy Word," was the chaplain of a Swedish regiment during the Thirty Years' War. He preached the thanksgiving sermon at the field service held by command of General Wrangel at Weiden, in the Upper Palatine, on January 1, 1649, after the conclusion of the Peace of Westphalia. He afterwards became pastor at Weiden, where he remained until his death in 1684.

Johann Quirsfeld, archdeacon in Pirna, has given us a very impressive Good Friday hymn, "Sinful world, behold the anguish." Quirsfeld died in 1686.

Christian Knorr von Rosenroth, a noted Orientalist, scientist and statesman of the seventeenth century, in addition to duties of state edited several Rabbinical writings and works on Oriental mysticism. He also wrote hymns, among them "Dayspring of eternity," which has been referred to by one writer as "one of the freshest, most original, and spirited of morning hymns, as if born from the dew of the sunrise." He died at Sulzbach, Bavaria, May 8, 1689, at the very hour, it is said, which he himself had predicted.

The extent to which Lutheran laymen of this period devoted themselves to spiritual exercises is revealed in the life of Johann Franck, a lawyer who became mayor of his native town of Guben, Brandenburg, in 1661. To him we are indebted for the finest communion hymn in the German language, "Deck thyself, my soul, with gladness." He also was the author of such gems as "Light of the Gentile nations," "Lord, to Thee I make confession," "Lord God, we worship Thee," "Jesus, priceless Treasure," and the glorious song of praise:

Praise the Lord, each tribe and nation,
Praise Him with a joyful heart;
Ye who know His full salvation,
Gather now from every part;
Let your voices glorify
In His temple God on high.

It was Franck who began the long series of so-called "Jesus hymns," which reached their fullest development in the later Pietistic school of hymnists. Franck held that poetry should be "the nurse of piety, the herald of immortality, the promoter of cheerfulness, the conqueror of sadness, and a foretaste of heavenly glory." His hymns reflect his beautiful spirit of Christian cheerfulness and hope.

The last name that we would mention is Heinrich Theobald Schenk, a pastor at Giessen. Not much is known of this man except that he was the writer of a single hymn, but it is a hymn that has gained for him the thanks of posterity. There is scarcely a hymn-book of any communion today that does not contain, "Who are these, like stars appearing?" Schenk died in 1727, at the age of 71 years.

The Swan-song of Gustavus Adolphus

Be not dismayed, thou little flock,
Although the foe's fierce battle shock
Loud on all sides assail thee.
Though o'er thy fall they laugh secure,
Their triumph cannot long endure,
Let not thy courage fail thee.
Thy cause is God's—go at His call,
And to His hand commit thine all;
Fear thou no ill impending;
His Gideon shall arise for thee,
God's Word and people manfully
In God's own time defending.
Our hope is sure in Jesus' might;
Against themselves the godless fight,
Themselves, not us, distressing;
Shame and contempt their lot shall be;
God is with us, with Him are we;
To us belongs His blessing.
Johann Michael Altenberg, 1631

A Hymn Made Famous on a Battle Field

"Be not dismayed, thou little flock" will always be known as the "swan-song" of the Swedish hero king, Gustavus Adolphus.

No incident in modern history is more dramatic than the sudden appearance in Germany of Gustavus Adolphus and his little Swedish army during the critical days of the Thirty Years' War. It was this victorious crusade that saved Germany, and probably all of northern Europe, for Protestantism.

The untimely death of the Swedish monarch on the battlefield of Lützen, November 6, 1632, while leading his men against Wallenstein's host, not only gained immortal fame for Gustavus, but will always cause the world to remember the hymn that was sung by his army on that historic day.

When Gustavus Adolphus landed in Germany in 1630 with his small but well-trained army, it seemed that the Protestant cause in Europe was lost. All the Protestant princes of Germany had been defeated by Tilly and Wallenstein, leaders of the Imperial armies, and the victors were preparing to crush every vestige of Lutheranism in Germany.

The Margrave of Brandenburg and the Duke of Saxony, however, furnished a few troops to Gustavus, and in a swift, meteoric campaign the Swedish king had routed the army of the Catholic League and had marched all the way across Germany. In the spring of 1632 Gustavus moved into the heart of Bavaria and captured Munich.

The Imperial forces who had sneered at the "Snow King," as they called him, and who had predicted that he would "melt" as he came southward, were now filled with dismay. The "Snow King" proved to be the "Lion of the North."

Wallenstein rallied the Catholic forces for a last stand at Lützen, the battle that was to prove the decisive conflict.

On the morning of November 6, 1632, the two armies faced each other in battle array. Dr. Fabricius, chaplain of the Swedish army, had been commanded by Gustavus to lead his troops in worship. The king himself raised the strains of "Be not dismayed, thou little flock," and led the army in singing the stirring hymn. Then he knelt in fervent prayer.

A heavy fog prevented the Protestant forces from moving forward to the attack, and, while they were waiting for the fog to lift, Gustavus ordered the musicians to play Luther's hymn, "A mighty Fortress is our God." The whole army joined with a shout. The king then mounted his charger, and, drawing his sword, rode back and forth in front of the lines, speaking words of encouragement to his men.

As the sun began to break through the fog, Gustavus himself offered a prayer, "Jesus, Jesus, Jesus, help me today to do battle for the glory of Thy holy name," and then shouted, "Now forward to the attack in the name of our God!" The army answered, "God with us!" and rushed forward, the king galloping in the lead.

When his aid offered him his coat of mail, Gustavus refused to put it on, declaring, "God is my Protector."

The battle raged fiercely. For a time the outcome seemed ominous for the Lutherans. At 11 o'clock Gustavus was struck by a bullet and mortally wounded. As he fell from his horse, the word spread quickly throughout the Swedish lines, "The king is wounded!"

It proved to be the turning point in the battle. Instead of losing heart and fleeing, the Swedish troops charged the foe with a fierceness born of sorrow and despair, and before the day was ended another glorious victory had been won. The Protestant cause was saved, but the noble Gustavus had made the supreme sacrifice.

The authorship of his famous "battle-hymn" has been the subject of much dispute. The German poet and hymnologist, Albert Knapp, has called it "a little feather from the eagle wing of Gustavus Adolphus." Most Swedish authorities, too, unite in naming their hero king as the author. However, the weight of evidence seems to point to Johann Michael Altenberg, a German pastor of Gross Sommern, Thüringen, as the real writer of the hymn. It is said that Altenberg was inspired to write it upon hearing of the great victory gained by Gustavus Adolphus at the battle of Leipzig, September 7, 1631, about a year before the battle of Lützen.

In any event, it is a matter of record that the Swedish king adopted it immediately, and that he sang it as his own "swan-song" just before he died at Lützen. Someone has aptly said, "Whether German or Swede may claim this hymn is a question. They both rightly own it."

Rinkart's Hymn of Praise

Now thank we all our God,
With hearts and hands and voices,
Who wondrous things hath done,
In whom His earth rejoices;
Who from our mother's arms
Hath blessed us on our way
With countless gifts of love,
And still is ours today.
O may this bounteous God
Through all our life be near us,
With ever joyful hearts
And blessed peace to cheer us;
And keep us in His grace,
And guide us when perplexed,
And free us from all ills,
In this world and the next.
All praise and thanks to God
The Father now be given,
The Son, and Him who reigns
With them in highest heaven;
The One eternal God,
Whom earth and heaven adore;
For thus it was, is now,
And shall be evermore!
Martin Rinkart (1586-1649).

THE LUTHERAN TE DEUM

    The last of the great Lutheran hymn-writers belonging to the period of the Thirty Years' War was Martin Rinkart. Except for the time of the Reformation, this period was probably the greatest creative epoch in the history of Lutheran hymnody. But of all the glorious hymns that were written during those stirring years, there is none that equals Rinkart's famous hymn, "Now thank we all our God."

    The date of this remarkable hymn is obscure. The claim has been made that it was written as a hymn of thanksgiving following the Peace of Westphalia, which in 1648 brought to an end the long and cruel war. This claim has been based on the fact that the first two stanzas are a paraphrase of the words of the high priest Simeon, recorded in the Apocryphal book Ecclesiasticus 50:29-32: "And now let all praise God, who hath done great things, who hath glorified our days, and dealeth with us according to His loving-kindness. He giveth us the joy of our hearts, that we may find peace in Israel as in the days of yore, thus He lets His loving-kindness remain with us, and He will redeem us in our day." Inasmuch as this was the Scripture passage on which all regimental chaplains were ordered to preach in celebration of the conclusion of peace, it has been inferred that Rinkart was inspired to write his hymn at that time.

It is probable, however, that these circumstances were merely a coincidence, and that the hymn was written several years previous to 1648. In Rinkart's own volume, "Jesu Hertz-Buchlein," it appears under the title "Tisch-Gebetlein," or a short prayer before meals, and many believe that it was originally written for Rinkart's children. It will be noticed that, while the first two stanzas are based on the passage from Ecclesiasticus, the last stanza is the ancient doxology, Gloria Patri.

No hymn except Luther's famous "A mighty Fortress is our God" has been used more generally in the Lutheran Church than Rinkart's glorious paean of praise. In Germany, where it has become the national Te Deum, it is sung at all impressive occasions. After the battle of Leuthen, the army of Frederick the Great raised the strains of this noble hymn, and it is said that even the mortally wounded joined in the singing.

In his history of the Franco-Prussian War, Cassel tells of a stirring incident that took place on the day following the battle of Sedan, where the Germans had won a decisive victory over the French. A multitude of Prussian troops who were marching toward Paris were billeted in the parish church of Augecourt. They could not sleep because of the extreme excitement of the day. Suddenly a strain of music came from the organ, first very softly but gradually swelling in volume until the whole sanctuary shook. It was the grand old hymn—"Nun danket alle Gott!" Instantly men and officers were upon their feet, singing the stirring words. Then followed Luther's "Ein feste Burg," after which the terrible strain seemed relieved, and they laid themselves down to peaceful slumber.

It is recorded that the hymn was also sung at the opening of the magnificent Cathedral of Cologne, August 14, 1880, as well as at the laying of the cornerstone of the Parliament building in Berlin, June 9, 1884. It has also achieved great popularity in England, where it was sung as a Te Deum in nearly all churches and chapels at the close of the Boer War in 1902.

Rinkart's life was a tragic one. The greater part of his public service was rendered during the horrors of the Thirty Years' War. He was born at Eilenburg, Saxony, April 23, 1586. After attending a Latin school in his home town, he became a student at the University of Leipzig.

In 1617, by invitation of the town council of Eilenburg, he became pastor of the church in the city of his birth. It was at the beginning of the Thirty Years' War, and, because Eilenburg was a walled city, it became a refuge for thousands who had lost everything in the conflict. Famine and pestilence added to the horror of the situation, and the other two pastors of the city having died, Rinkart was left alone to minister to the spiritual needs of the populace.

Twice Eilenburg was saved from the Swedish army through the intercession of Rinkart, first in 1637 and again in 1639. A levy of 30,000 thaler had been made on the city by the Swedish general to aid the Protestant cause. Knowing the impoverished condition of his townsmen, Rinkart went out to the Swedish camp to plead their cause, but to no avail. Turning to those who were with him, Rinkart exclaimed, "Come, my children, we can find no mercy with men, let us take refuge with God." He then fell on his knees and uttered a fervent prayer, after which they sang the hymn of Paul Eber so much used in those trying days, "When in the hour of utmost need." The scene made such an impression on the Swedish commander that he relented and reduced his demand to 2,000 florins or 1,350 thaler.

Rinkart lived only a year after the close of the bloody war. He died, a worn and broken man, in 1649.

A Joyous Christmas Carol

All my heart this night rejoices,
As I hear,
Far and near,
Sweetest angel voices:
"Christ is born," their choirs are singing,
Till the air
Everywhere
Now with joy is ringing.
Come and banish all your sadness,
One and all,
Great and small,
Come with songs of gladness;
Love Him who with love is yearning;
Hail the star
That from far
Bright with hope is burning.
Hither come, ye heavy-hearted,
Who for sin,
Deep within,
Long and sore have smarted;
For the poisoned wounds you're feeling
Help is near,
One is here
Mighty for their healing.
Faithfully Thee, Lord, I'll cherish,
Live to Thee,
And with Thee
Dying, shall not perish,
But shall dwell with Thee forever,
Far on high,
In the joy
That can alter never.
Paul Gerhardt, 1656.

PAUL GERHARDT, PRINCE OF LUTHERAN HYMNISTS

The greatest Lutheran hymnist of the seventeenth century, and perhaps of all time, was Paul Gerhardt.

Not even the hymns of Martin Luther are used so generally throughout the Christian world as those of Gerhardt. More of the beautiful lyrics of this sweet singer have found their way into the English language than the hymns of any other German writer, and with the passing of years their popularity increases rather than diminishes.

In the Lutheran church at Lübden, in Germany, there hangs a life-size painting of Gerhardt. Beneath it is this inscription: Theologus in cribro Satanae versatus, "A divine sifted in Satan's sieve." That inscription may be said to epitomize the sad life-story of Germany's great psalmist.

Gerhardt was born March 12, 1607, in Gräfenhaynichen, a village near the celebrated Wittenberg. His father, who was mayor of the village, died before Paul reached maturity. When he was twenty-one years of age he began the study of theology at the University of Wittenberg. The Thirty Years' War was raging, and all Germany was desolate and suffering. Because of the difficulty of securing a parish, Gerhardt served for several years as a tutor in the home of Andreas Barthold, whose daughter Anna Maria became his bride in 1655.

It was during this period that Gerhardt's poetic gifts began to flourish. No doubt he was greatly stimulated by contact with the famous musician Johann Crüger, who was cantor and director of music in the Church of St. Nicholas in Berlin. In 1648 many of Gerhardt's hymns were published in Crüger's Praxis Pietatis Melica.

Through the recommendation of the Berlin clergy, he was appointed Lutheran provost at Mittenwalde, and was ordained to this post November 18, 1651. Six years later he accepted the position of third assistant pastor of the Church of St. Nicholas in Berlin. His hymns continued to grow in popularity, and his fame as a preacher drew large audiences to hear him.

The controversy between the Lutherans and Calvinists, which had continued from the days of the Reformation, flared up again at this time as the result of efforts on the part of Elector Friedrich Wilhelm of Prussia to unite the two parties. Friedrich Wilhelm, who was a Calvinist, sought to compel the clergy to sign a document promising that they would abstain from any references in their sermons to doctrinal differences. Gerhardt was sick at the time, and, although he had always been moderate in his utterances, he felt that to sign such a document would be to compromise the faith. Summoning the other Lutheran clergymen of Berlin to his bedside, he urged them to stand firm and to refuse to surrender to the demands of the Elector.

Soon after this the courageous pastor was deposed from office. He was also prohibited from holding private services in his own home. Though he felt the blow very keenly, he met it with true Christian fortitude.

"This," he said, "is only a small Berlin affliction; but I am also willing and ready to seal with my blood the evangelical truth, and, like my namesake, St. Paul, to offer my neck to the sword."

To add to his sorrows, Gerhardt's wife and a son died in the midst of these troubles. Three other children had died previous to this, and now the sorely tried pastor was left with a single child, a boy of six years. In May, 1669, he was called to the church at Lübden, where he labored faithfully and with great success until his death, on June 7, 1676.

The glorious spirit that dwelt in him, and which neither trials nor persecutions could quench, is reflected in the lines of his famous hymn, "If God Himself be for me," based on the latter part of the eighth chapter of Romans:

Though earth be rent asunder,
Thou'rt mine eternally;
Not fire, nor sword, nor thunder,
Shall sever me from Thee;
Not hunger, thirst, nor danger,
Not pain nor poverty,
Nor mighty princes' anger,
Shall ever hinder me.

Catherine Winkworth, who has translated the same hymn in a different meter under the title, "Since Jesus is my Friend," has probably succeeded best in giving expression to the triumphant faith and the note of transcendent hope and joy in the final stanza:

My heart for gladness springs;
It cannot more be sad;
For very joy it smiles and sings—
Sees naught but sunshine glad.
The Sun that lights mine eyes
Is Christ, the Lord I love;
I sing for joy of that which lies
Stored up for me above.

Because of his own warm, confiding, childlike faith in God, Gerhardt's hymns have become a source of special comfort to sorrowing and heavy-laden souls. They not only breathe a spirit of tender consolation but of a "joy unspeakable and full of glory." We have a beautiful example of this in his Advent hymn, "O how shall I receive Thee":

Rejoice then, ye sad-hearted,
Who sit in deepest gloom,
Who mourn o'er joys departed,
And tremble at your doom;
He who alone can cheer you
Is standing at the door;
He brings His pity near you,
And bids you weep no more.

In Gerhardt's hymns we find a transition to the modern subjective note in hymnody. Sixteen of his hymns begin with the pronoun, "I." They are not characterized, however, by the weak sentimentality so often found in the hymns of our own day, for Gerhardt never lost sight of the greatest objective truth revealed to men—justification by faith alone. Nevertheless, because of his constant emphasis on the love of God and because his hymns are truly "songs of the heart," they possess a degree of emotional warmth that is lacking in the earlier Lutheran hymns.

His hymns on the glories of nature have never been surpassed. In contemplating the beauty of created things he is ever praising the Creator. His famous evening hymn, "Nun ruhen alle Wälder," has been likened to the beauty and splendor of the evening star. In a marvelous manner the temporal and the eternal, the terrestrial and the celestial are contrasted in every stanza. It was a favorite hymn of the great German poet, Friedrich von Schiller, who first heard it sung by his mother as a cradle song. Probably no hymn is so generally used by the children of Germany as an evening prayer as this one. The most familiar English translation begins with the line, "Now rest beneath night's shadow." A more recent translation of rare beauty runs:

> The restless day now closeth,
> Each flower and tree reposeth,
> Shade creeps o'er wild and wood:
> Let us, as night is falling,
> On God our Maker calling,
> Give thanks to Him, the Giver good.

The tune to which this hymn is sung is as famous as the hymn itself. It is ascribed to Heinrich Isaak, one of the first of the great German church musicians. It is believed to have been composed by him in 1490, when he was leaving his native town, Innsbruck, to establish himself at the court of Emperor Maximilian I. It was set to the plaintive words, "Innsbruck, ich muss dich lassen." According to tradition, Isaak first heard the beautiful melody sung by a wandering minstrel. Bach and Mozart regarded it as one of the sublimest of all chorales, and each is said to have declared that he would rather have been the composer of this tune than any of his great masterpieces.

Gerhardt wrote 123 hymns in all. In addition to the hymns already mentioned, probably his most famous is "O sacred Head, now wounded," based on the Latin hymn of Bernard of Clairvaux. Other hymns in common use are "Immanuel, we sing Thy praise," "Holy Ghost, dispel our sadness," "O enter, Lord, Thy temple," "Shun, my heart, the thought forever," "Commit thou all thy griefs," "All my heart this night rejoices," "Beside Thy manger here I stand," "Awake, my heart, and marvel," "Go forth, my heart, and seek delight," "O Saviour dear," and "A pilgrim and a stranger."

Only the briefest mention can be made of other German Lutheran hymn-writers of this period. One of these, Johan Rist, pastor in Wedel, was crowned poet laureate of Germany by Emperor Ferdinand III in 1644, and nine years later was raised to the nobility. Rist wrote some 680 hymns, but all are not of uniform excellence. Among those in common use to-day are "Arise, the kingdom is at hand," "Help us, O Lord, behold we enter," "Rise, O Salem, rise and shine," "O Living Bread from heaven," "O Jesus Christ, Thou Bread of Life," "Father, merciful and holy," which has also been translated "Soul of mine, to God awaking," "O darkest woe," and "Arise, arise ye Christians."

Georg Neumark, court poet and secretary of archives under Duke Wilhelm II of Saxe-Weimar, has left us the hymn of trust in God: "Let, O my soul, thy God direct thee," which is also known by the English translation, "If thou but suffer God to guide thee." The hymn was written in 1641, at Kiel, when, after being robbed of practically all he possessed except his prayer-book, Neumark succeeded in obtaining employment as tutor in a wealthy family. He was a destitute student at the time.

Michael Schirmer, an educator and poet who lived in Berlin during the Thirty Years' War and for two decades after its close, is the author of a number of beautiful hymns, among them the Pentecost hymn, "O Holy Spirit, enter in." Because of poverty and afflictions suffered during a period of war and pestilence, he has been called "the German Job."

Ahasuerus Fritsch, chancellor and president of the Consistory of Rudolstadt, is credited with the authorship of "Jesus is my Joy, my All," a hymn that reflects the spirit of true evangelical piety. He died in 1701.

Caspar Neumann, another of Gerhardt's contemporaries, has bequeathed to the Church the sublime hymn, "God of Ages, all transcending," the last stanza of which is unusually striking in language:

Say Amen, O God our Father,
To the praise we offer Thee;
Now, to laud Thy name we gather;
Let this to Thy glory be.
Fill us with Thy love and grace,
Till we see Thee face to face.

Neumann, who was a celebrated preacher and professor of theology at Breslau from 1678 to 1715, was the author of some thirty hymns, all of which became very popular in Silesia. He was also author of a famous devotional book, "Kern aller Gebete."

A Glorious Paean of Praise

Praise to the Lord, the Almighty, the King of creation!
O my soul, praise Him, for He is thy health and salvation!
All ye who hear,
Now to His temple draw near,
Join me in glad adoration.
Praise to the Lord, who doth prosper thy work and defend thee!
Surely His goodness and mercy here daily attend thee;
Ponder anew
What the Almighty can do,
If with His love He befriend thee!
Praise thou the Lord, who with marvelous wisdom hath made thee,
Decked thee with health, and with loving hand guided and stayed thee.
How oft in grief
Hath not He brought thee relief,
Spreading His wings to o'ershade thee!
Praise to the Lord! O let all that is in me adore Him!
All that hath life and breath, come now with praises before Him!
Let the Amen
Sound from His people again;

Gladly for aye we adore Him.
Joachim Neander, 1680.

JOACHIM NEANDER, THE PAUL GERHARDT OF THE CALVINISTS

While all Germany during the latter half of the seventeenth century was singing the sublime lyrics of Paul Gerhardt, prince of Lutheran hymnists, the spirit of hymnody was beginning to stir in the soul of another German poet—Joachim Neander. This man, whose name will always be remembered as the author of one of the most glorious hymns of praise of the Christian Church, was the first hymn-writer produced by the Reformed, or Calvinistic, branch of the Protestant Church.

Hymnody in the Reformed Church had been seriously retarded by the iconoclastic views of Calvin and Zwingli. These Reformers at first frowned on church choirs, organs, and every form of ecclesiastical art. Even hymns, such as those used by the Lutherans, were prohibited because they were the production of men. God could be worshiped in a worthy manner, according to Calvin's principles, only by hymns which were divinely inspired, namely, the Psalms of the Old Testament Psaltery.

This gave rise to the practice of versifying the Psalms. Calvin's insistence that there should be the strictest adherence to the original text often resulted in crude paraphrases. The exclusive use of the Psalms explains the development of so-called "psalmody" in the Reformed Church as over against "hymnody" in the Lutheran Church.

Psalmody had its inception in France, where Clement Marot, court poet to King Francis I, rendered a number of the Psalms into metrical form. Marot was a gifted and versatile genius, but not inclined to piety or serious-mindedness. However, his versified Psalms became immensely popular with the French Huguenots and exerted a great influence in the struggle between the Protestants and the papal party. When Marot was compelled to flee to Geneva because of Roman persecution, he collaborated with Calvin in publishing the famous Genevan Psalter, which appeared in 1543.

Following the death of Marot in 1544, Calvin engaged Theodore de Beza to continue the work, and in 1562 the Genevan Psalter was published in completed form, containing all the Psalms in versified dress. The musical editor during the greater part of this period was Louis Bourgeois, to whom is generally ascribed the undying honor of being the composer of probably the most famous of all Christian hymn tunes, "Old Hundredth."

The Genevan Psalter was translated into many languages, and became the accepted hymn-book of the Reformed Church in Germany, England, Scotland, and Holland, as well as in France. In Germany the most popular version was a translation by Ambrosius Lobwasser, a professor of law at Königsberg, who, oddly enough, was a Lutheran.

For more than 150 years Lutheran hymn-writers had been pouring out a mighty stream of inspired song, but the voice of hymnody was stifled in the Reformed Church. Then came Joachim Neander. His life was short—he died at the age of thirty—and many of his hymns seem to have been written in the last few months before his death; but the influence he exerted on the subsequent hymnody of his Church earned for him the title, "the Gerhardt of the Reformed Church."

Neander's hymns are preeminently hymns of praise. Their jubilant tone and smooth rhythmical flow are at once an invitation to sing them. They speedily found their way into Lutheran hymn-books in Germany, and from thence to the entire Protestant world. Neander's most famous hymn, "Praise to the Lord, the Almighty," with its splendid chorale melody, grows in popularity with the passing of years, and promises to live on as one of the greatest Te Deums of the Christian Church.

Joachim Neander was born in Bremen, Germany, in 1650. He came from a distinguished line of clergymen, his father, grandfather, great grandfather and great great grandfather having been pastors, and all of them bearing the name Joachim Neander.

Young Joachim entered the Academic Gymnasium of Bremen at the age of sixteen years. It seems that he led a careless and profligate life, joining in the sins and follies that characterized student life in his age.

In the year 1670, when Neander was twenty years old, he chanced to attend services in St. Martin's church, Bremen, where Theodore Under-Eyck had recently come as pastor. Two other students accompanied Neander, their main purpose being to criticize and scoff at the sermon. However, they had not reckoned with the Spirit of God. The burning words of Under-Eyck made a powerful impression on the mind and heart of the youthful Neander, and he who went to scoff came away to pray.

It proved the turning point in the spiritual life of the young student. Under the guidance of Under-Eyck he was led to embrace Christ as his Saviour, and from that time he and Under-Eyck were life-long friends.

The following year Neander became tutor to five young students, accompanying them to the University of Heidelberg. Three years later he became rector of the Latin school at Düsseldorf. This institution was under the supervision of a Reformed pastor, Sylvester Lürsen, an able man, but of contentious spirit. At first the two men worked together harmoniously, Neander assisting with pastoral duties, and preaching occasionally, although he was not ordained as a clergyman. Later, however, he fell under the influence of a group of separatists, and began to imitate their practices. He refused to receive the Lord's Supper on the grounds that he could not partake of it with the unconverted. He induced others to follow his example. He also became less regular in his attendance at regular worship, and began to conduct prayer meetings and services of his own.

In 1676 the church council of Düsseldorf investigated his conduct and dismissed him from his office. Fourteen days after this action was taken, however, Neander signed a declaration in which he promised to abide by the rules of the church and school, whereupon he was reinstated.

There is a legend to the effect that, during the period of his suspension from service, he spent most of his time living in a cave in the beautiful Neanderthal, near Mettmann, on the Rhine, and that he wrote some of his hymns at this place. It is a well-established fact that Neander's great love for nature frequently led him to this place, and a cavern in the picturesque glen still bears the name of "Neander's Cave." One of the hymns which tradition declares was written in this cave bears the title "Unbegreiflich Gut, Wahrer Gott alleine." It is a hymn of transcendent beauty. One of the stanzas reads:

> Thee all the mountains praise;
> The rocks and glens are full of songs of Thee!
> They bid me join my lays,
> And laud the mighty Rock, who, safe from every shock,
> Beneath Thy shadow here doth shelter me.

Many of Neander's hymns are odes to nature, but there is always a note of praise to nature's God. Witness, for instance:

> Heaven and earth, and sea and air,
> All their Maker's praise declare;
> Wake, my soul, awake and sing,
> Now thy grateful praises bring!

"Here behold me, as I cast me," a penitential hymn by Neander, has found favor throughout all Christendom.

In 1679 Neander's spiritual friend, Pastor Under-Eyck, invited him to come to Bremen and become his assistant in St. Martin's church. Although his salary was only 40 thalers a year and a free house, Neander joyfully accepted the appointment. The following year, however, he became sick, and after a lingering illness passed away May 31, 1680, at the age of only thirty years.

During his illness he experienced severe spiritual struggles, but he found comfort in the words, "It is better to hope unto death than to die in unbelief." On the day of his death he requested that Hebrews 7:9 be read to him. When asked how he felt, he replied: "The Lord has settled my account. Lord Jesus, make also me ready." A little later he said in a whisper: "It is well with me. The mountains shall be moved, and the hills shall tremble, yet the grace of God shall not depart from me, and His covenant of peace shall not be moved."

A Hymn Classic by Scheffler

> Thee will I love, my Strength, my Tower,
> Thee will I love, my Joy, my Crown;
> Thee will I love with all my power,
> In all Thy works, and Thee alone;
> Thee will I love, till Thy pure fire
> Fill all my soul with chaste desire.
> I thank Thee, uncreated Sun,
> That Thy bright beams on me have shined;
> I thank Thee, who hast overthrown
> My foes, and healed my wounded mind;
> I thank Thee, whose enlivening voice

Bids my freed heart in Thee rejoice.
Uphold me in the doubtful race,
Nor suffer me again to stray;
Strengthen my feet with steady pace
Still to press forward in Thy way;
That all my powers, with all their might,
In Thy sole glory may unite.
Thee will I love, my Joy, my Crown;
Thee will I love, my Lord, my God;
Thee love beneath Thy smile or frown,
Beneath Thy scepter or Thy rod.
What though my flesh and heart decay?
Thee shall I love in endless day.
Johann Scheffler, 1657.

A ROMAN MYSTIC AND HYMN-WRITER

In Johann Scheffler we have the singular example of a man who forsook the Lutheran Church to become a Romanist, but whose hymns have been adopted and sung by the very Church he sought to oppose and confound.

Scheffler was a contemporary of Gerhardt and Neander. He was born in Breslau, Silesia, in 1624. His father, Stanislaus Scheffler, was a Polish nobleman who had been compelled to leave his native land because of his Lutheran convictions. Young Scheffler became a medical student at Strassburg, Leyden, and Padua, returning to Oels, Silesia, in 1649 to become the private physician to Duke Sylvius Nimrod of Württemberg-Oels.

During his sojourn in foreign lands he had come in contact with the writings of various mystics and he began to lean strongly toward their teachings. At Oels he began to flaunt his separatist views by absenting himself from public worship and the Lord's Supper. When the Lutheran authorities refused to permit the publication of some poems he had written, because of their strong mystical tendencies, Scheffler resigned his office and betook himself to Breslau, where he joined himself to a group of Jesuits. Here he pursued the study of the medieval mystics of the Roman Catholic Church, and in 1653 was confirmed as a member of that communion. At this time he took the name of Angelus Silesius, probably after a Spanish mystic named John ab Angelis.

In 1661 he was ordained a priest of the Roman Church. He became a prolific writer and took special delight in directing bitter polemics against the Church of his childhood. Of these writings, it has been well said: "He certainly became more Roman than the Romans; and in his more than fifty controversial tractates, shows little of the sweetness and repose for which some have thought he left the Lutheran Church."

Scheffler, however, was a poet of the first rank. His poems, always tinged by the spirit of mysticism, sometimes attain to sublime heights, and again they descend to a coarse realism, particularly when he describes the terrors of judgment and hell.

His hymns, on the other hand, are almost uniformly of a high order. They are marked by a fervent love for Christ the heavenly Bridegroom, although the imagery, largely based on the Song of Solomon, is sometimes overdrawn, almost approaching the sensual. Few of his hymns reveal his Catholic tendencies, and therefore they were gladly received by the Protestants. Indeed, they came into more general use among the Lutherans than among the Catholics. They were greatly admired by Count von Zinzendorf, who included no less than 79 of them in his Moravian collection.

The mysticism of Scheffler often brought him dangerously near the border-line of pantheism. Vaughn, in his "Hours with the Mystics," compares Scheffler with Emerson, and declares that both resemble the Persian Sufis. Something of Scheffler's pantheistic ideas may be seen in the following lines:

God in my nature is involved,
As I in the divine;
I help to make His being up,
As much as He does mine.
And again in this:

I am as rich as God; no grain of dust
That is not mine, too: share with me He must.

Duffield, commenting on these astonishing lines, observes, "We need not wonder that this high-flown self-assumption carried him to the door of a Jesuit convent. It is in the very key of much that passes with Romanist theology for heavenly rapture and delight in God."

The pantheistic views of Scheffler may be discerned even in his dying prayer: "Jesus and Christ, God and man, bridegroom and brother, peace and joy, sweetness and delight, refuge and redemption, heaven and earth, eternity and time, love and all, receive my soul."

However, we must agree with Albert Knapp in his judgment of Scheffler's beautiful hymns, that "whencesoever they may come, they are an unfading ornament of the Church of Jesus Christ." The gem among them is "Thee will I love, my Strength, my Tower." Others that have come into general use are "Earth has nothing sweet or fair," "Thy soul, O Jesus, hallow me," "Come, follow me, the Saviour spake," "Jesus, Saviour, come to me," "Thou holiest Love, whom most I love," and "Loving Shepherd, kind and true."

A Gem among Pietistic Hymns

O Jesus, Source of calm repose,
Thy like no man nor angel knows,
Fairest among ten thousand fair!
E'en those whom death's sad fetters bound,
Whom thickest darkness compassed round,
Find light and life, if Thou appear.
Renew Thine image, Lord, in me,
Lowly and gentle may I be;

No charms but these to Thee are dear;
No anger may'st Thou ever find,
No pride, in my unruffled mind,
But faith, and heaven-born peace, be there.
A patient, a victorious mind,
That life and all things casts behind,
Springs forth obedient to Thy call,
A heart that no desire can move,
But still to praise, believe, and love,
Give me, my Lord, my Life, my All!
Johann Anastasius Freylinghausen, 1704.

HYMN-WRITERS OF THE PIETIST SCHOOL

Spiritual revivals in the Christian Church have always been accompanied by an outburst of song. This was true of the Reformation, which witnessed the birth of the Lutheran Church, and it was also characteristic of the Pietistic movement, which infused new life and fervor into that communion. The Pietistic revival, which in many respects was similar to the Puritan and Wesleyan movements in England, had its inception in Germany in the latter part of the 17th century and continued during the first half of the 18th century. It quickly spread to other Lutheran countries, particularly Scandinavia, and its influence has been felt even to the present time.

The leader of the movement was Philipp Jacob Spener, pastor of St. Nicolai Church, in Berlin. Spener, although a loyal and zealous son of the Lutheran Church, was not blind to the formalism and dead orthodoxy which had overtaken it following the Thirty Years' War and which threatened to dry up the streams of spiritual life. To stimulate spiritual endeavor and personal piety, Spener and his followers organized Bible study groups. They also encouraged private assemblies for mutual edification. These were known as collegia pietatis, which gave rise to the name, "Pietists."

August Hermann Francke, the foremost disciple of Spener, succeeded the latter as leader of the movement. The University of Halle, where Francke was called as professor in 1691, became the center of Pietism. Here Francke laid the foundations for the remarkable philanthropic and educational institutions that made his name known throughout the Christian world. It began in 1695 when the great-hearted man opened a room in his own house for the instruction of poor children. Within a few years he had established his great orphanage, a high school, and a home for destitute students. The orphans' home was erected on a site where there had been a beer and dancing garden.

When Francke began he had no money, nor did he receive any support from the state, but as the marvelous work progressed funds poured in from all quarters. In the year of his death, 1727, more than 2,000 children were receiving care and instruction from 170 teachers. Altogether, some 6,000 graduates of theology left Halle during Francke's career, "men imbued with his spirit, good exegetes, and devoted pastors, who spread their doctrines all over Germany, and in the early decades of the 18th century occupied a majority of the pulpits."

Halle also became the cradle of the modern missionary movement. From this place, in 1705, Bartholomew Ziegenbalg and Henry Plütschau, were sent forth as the first missionaries to India, nearly a century before William Carey left England for the same field. At Halle the youthful Count von Zinzendorf became a pupil under Francke and received the inspiration that in later years led to the establishment of the far-reaching missions of the Moravians. To Halle the founder of Methodism, John Wesley, came in 1738, shortly after his conversion in London, in order to become more familiar with the teachings of Luther and the Pietists.

The secret of the marvelous success of Francke's efforts may be read in the simple inscription on the monument erected to his memory in front of the famous orphanage at Halle. It reads: "He trusted in God."

Neither Francke nor Spener were hymn-writers of note, although each composed a few songs. The Pietist movement, however, gave birth to a great revival in hymnody in Germany, both in Lutheran and Reformed circles. At Halle it was Johann Anastasius Freylinghausen who not only became the representative hymnist of the Pietists, but also succeeded Francke as head of the great Halle institutions.

Freylinghausen was a student at the University of Jena when he first heard the preaching of Francke. Shortly afterward he followed him to Halle, and in 1695 became Francke's colleague. He preached at vesper services, conducted midweek meetings, taught classes in the orphanage school, and delivered lectures on homiletics. He served without salary for ten years, since Francke was obliged to use all his income for the support of his institutions of mercy. In 1715 Freylinghausen married Francke's only daughter. At her baptism as an infant he had been her sponsor, and she had received his name, Johanna Anastasia. It was after Francke's death in 1727 that the Halle institutions reached their highest development under the direction of Freylinghausen. When the latter died in 1739, he was buried beside his beloved friend.

Freylinghausen's "Geistreiches Gesangbuch" became the standard hymn-book of the Pietistic movement. The first edition appeared in 1704 and contained 683 hymns. A second hymn-book was published in 1714, containing 815 additional hymns. The two collections were combined in 1741 by G. A. Francke and published as one hymn-book, containing 1,582 hymns and 600 tunes. Freylinghausen was the author of forty-four of these hymns, and is also said to have composed some of the melodies.

The hymns of Freylinghausen are the most worthy of all those produced by the Pietistic school. They are marked by genuine piety, depth of feeling, rich Christian experience, and faithfulness in Scriptural expression. The tunes employed, however, were often a distinct departure from the traditional Lutheran chorales, and were not always suited to congregational worship. Freylinghausen's most famous hymn, "O Jesus, Source of calm repose," was greatly admired by John Wesley, who translated it into English in 1737. The so-called "Jesus hymns," which reached their greatest development among the Pietists, find their sweetest expression in Freylinghausen's:

Who is there like Thee,
Jesus, unto me?
None is like Thee, none above Thee,

Thou art altogether lovely;
None on earth have we,
None in heaven like Thee.

It is not strange that from Halle, from whence such mighty missionary influences flowed, should also go forth the first Protestant missionary hymn. It was in 1750 that Karl Heinrich von Bogatzky, while working among the orphans of the Franckean institutions, wrote his famous hymn, "Awake, thou Spirit, who didst fire."

Bogatzky, who came from a noble Hungarian family, was disowned by his father when he chose to enroll as a theological student at Halle rather than to prepare for a career as an army officer. His health failed him, however, and he was unable to enter the ministry. For many years he devoted himself to hymn-writing and devotional literature. He also traveled as a lay preacher. Because of his noble birth he was able to exert a considerable influence in the higher circles of German society. From 1746 to his death in 1774, he lived at the Halle orphanage. He was the author of some 411 hymns, but few of them possess the poetic and spiritual fire of his missionary hymn. Two of its glorious stanzas read:

Awake, Thou Spirit, who didst fire
The watchmen of the Church's youth,
Who faced the foe's envenomed ire,
Who day and night declared Thy truth,
Whose voices loud are ringing still,
And bringing hosts to know Thy will.

O haste to help, ere we are lost!
Send preachers forth, in spirit strong,
Armed with Thy Word, a dauntless host,
Bold to attack the rule of wrong;
Let them the earth for Thee reclaim,
Thy heritage, to know Thy Name.

Johann Jacob Rambach was another important hymn-writer of this period. The son of a cabinet maker of Halle, young Rambach attended the free school established by Francke and came under the direct influence of the great Pietist leader.

Like many a youth, however, he felt that his education was complete at the age of thirteen years, at which time he left school to work in his father's shop. The Lord, on the other hand, seems to have had other plans for the lad, and it was not long before young Rambach suffered a dislocated ankle. Confined to his bed for several weeks, he again turned to his books, and, before he had recovered, the desire to resume his studies took possession of him.

Rambach eventually became one of the outstanding theologians of Halle, as well as preacher at the school church. In 1731 he removed to Giessen to become superintendent and first professor of theology. Here he found conditions vastly different from those at Halle. He was particularly grieved over the fact that his preaching did not seem to bear fruit. Often his efforts to bring about healthier spiritual conditions met with opposition and scoffing on the part of his adversaries. He died in 1735 at the early age of forty-two years—from intense sorrow over the spiritual indifference of his flock, so it has been said.

Rambach wrote many splendid hymns, among them the confirmation hymn, "Baptized into Thy Name most holy." His fame rests principally on his work as a hymnologist, however. During his life-time he published a number of collections from all sources. These hymns were chosen with fine discrimination, and Rambach was the first hymn editor to make a distinction between hymns for congregational worship and those particularly suited for private devotion.

The beautiful Advent hymn, "Rejoice, all ye believers," as well as the Epiphany hymn, "O Saviour of our race," also date from the Pietistic period. Both hymns apparently were written in 1700 by Laurentius Laurentii, cantor and director of music in the Lutheran cathedral at Bremen. Laurentii was not only a splendid musician, but also a hymn-writer of high order, and no less than thirty-four of his hymns were included in the Freylinghausen collections.

Other hymnists of the Pietistic school include Christian Scriver, writer of the famous devotional book, "Seelenschatz;" Gottfried Arnold, a noted church historian; Ernst Gottlieb Woltersdorf, founder of an orphanage at Bunzlau, and Christian Richter, a pious physician and an associate of Francke. Few of their hymns, however, are in common use today.

A Hymn of Longing for Christ

O Son of God, we wait for Thee,
We long for Thine appearing;
We know Thou sittest on the throne,
And we Thy Name are bearing.
Who trusts in Thee may joyful be,
And see Thee, Lord, descending
To bring us bliss unending.
We wait for Thee, 'mid toil and pain,
In weariness and sighing;
But glad that Thou our guilt hast borne,
And cancelled it by dying.
Hence, cheerfully may we with Thee
Take up our cross and bear it,
Till we the crown inherit.
We wait for Thee; here Thou hast won
Our hearts to hope and duty;
But while our spirits feel Thee near,
Our eyes would see Thy beauty;
We fain would be at rest with Thee
In peace and joy supernal,
In glorious life eternal.
We wait for Thee; soon Thou wilt come,
The time is swiftly nearing;
In this we also do rejoice,
And long for Thine appearing.
O bliss 'twill be when Thee we see,

Homeward Thy people bringing,
With ecstasy and singing!
Philipp Friedrich Hiller, 1767.

THE WÜRTTEMBERG HYMN-WRITERS

The Pietistic movement quickly made its influence felt in all parts of Germany. In some quarters, especially in the latter stages of the movement, it assumed more radical forms. Sometimes it developed into emotionalism and mysticism. The hymns were often of a subjective type, which led the worshiper to think more about his own inner processes and feelings than to direct his thoughts to Him alone who can redeem and sanctify.

Some of the Pietistic hymnists, notably Woltersdorf, were given to the use of inordinate language and even sensuous descriptions for the purpose of arousing intense emotion. In one of Woltersdorf's passion hymns, he dwells morbidly on every detail of the physical sufferings of Christ, and in another hymn he borrows Scheffler's figure which likens the soul to a bee deriving sustenance from the crimson wounds of Christ.

On the other hand, the Pietistic hymn is exemplified in its highest and noblest form in the writings of the so-called Württemberg school of hymnists, the chief exponent of which was Philipp Friedrich Hiller. Württemberg was blessed with the famous scholar and theologian, Johann Albrecht Bengel, whose sound doctrinal views and profound understanding of human nature not only led to a healthy development of Pietism in southern Germany, but also left a lasting impression on all the theological students who came under his influence at the training schools at Denkendorf, near Esslingen. Hiller was one of these.

Hiller's hymns and those of the other Württemberg hymnists never indulge in the weak emotional effusions of which the later Halle hymn-writers were often guilty.

Hiller was a man sorely tried in the school of adversity. Shortly after he began his pastorate at Steinheim, in 1748, he lost his voice and was unable to continue his pulpit duties. However, he believed implicitly in the Pauline teaching that "to them that love God all things work together for good," and, when his voice became silent, his spirit began to sing hymns richer and sweeter than ever. Witness, for example, the note of tenderness in the last stanza of his baptismal hymn, "God, in human flesh appearing":

Feeble is the love of mother,
Father's blessings are as naught,
When compared, my King and Brother,
With the wonders Thou hast wrought;
Thus it pleased Thy heavenly meekness;
Pleasing also be my praise,
Till my songs of earthly weakness
Burst into celestial lays.

Hiller was a prolific writer, his hymns numbering no less than 1,075 in all. Most of these were written for his devotional book, "Geistliches Liederkästlein," a work that holds an honored place beside the Bible in many pious homes in southern Germany. Indeed, it has been carried by German emigrants to all parts of the world. It is related that when a Germany colony in the Caucasus was attacked by a fierce Circassian tribe about a hundred years ago, the parents cut up their copies of the "Liederkästlein" and distributed its leaves among their children who were being carried off into slavery. Hiller's hymns, though simple in form and artless in expression, have retained a strong hold on the people of Württemberg and are extensively used to this day. Among the more popular are "O boundless joy, there is salvation," "Jesus Christ as King is reigning," and "O Son of God, we wait for Thee."

Hiller's rule for hymn-writing, as set forth in one of his prefaces, could be followed with profit by many modern writers of sentimental tendencies. He says: "I have always striven for simplicity. Bombastic expressions of a soaring imagination, a commonplace and too familiar manner of speaking of Christ as a brother, of kisses and embraces, of individual souls as the particular Bride of Christ, of naive and pet images for the Christ-child,—all these I have scrupulously avoided, and serious-minded men will not blame me if, in this respect, I have revered the majesty of our Lord."

Another representative of the Württemberg school was Baron Christoph Carl Ludwig von Pfeil, a diplomat of high attainments and noble, Christian character. In September, 1763, he was appointed by Frederick the Great as Prussian ambassador to the Diets of Swabia and Franconia. He was created a baron by Emperor Joseph II shortly afterwards.

Pfeil began writing hymns at the age of eighteen years and continued it as his chief diversion throughout life. He was a prolific writer, his published hymns numbering about 850. He was a warm friend of Bengel, who wrote the introduction to one of Pfeil's hymn collections. Pfeil wrote hymns on various phases of civil life. His hymn on the Christian home is typical:

O blest the house, whate'er befall,
Where Jesus Christ is All in all;
Yea, if He were not dwelling there,
How poor and dark and void it were!

The Silesian pastors, Johann Andreas Rothe and Johann Mentzer, also may be regarded as belonging to the more conservative Pietistic hymn-writers. Rothe was pastor at Berthelsdorf, having been brought there through the influence of Count von Zinzendorf, who had heard him preach in Silesia. The Moravian community of Herrnhut formed a part of Rothe's parish, and he took a keen interest in the activities of Zinzendorf and his followers. However, when Rothe, in 1737, found it necessary to report to the ecclesiastical authorities that the Moravians were deviating from sound Lutheran doctrine, the friendship between him and Zinzendorf ceased, and Rothe found it advisable to remove to Thommendorf, where he died in 1758.

Rothe wrote approximately forty hymns, the most famous of which is "Now I have found the ground wherein." This hymn was greatly admired by John Wesley and was translated by him in 1740. Because it first appeared in the Moravian hymn-book, the Lutherans suspected that Zinzendorf was the author. Upon discovering that it was by Rothe, they quickly adopted it. The first stanza reads:

Now I have found the ground wherein
My soul's sure anchor may remain:
The wounds of Jesus, for my sin
Before the world's foundation slain;
Whose mercy shall unshaken stay
When heaven and earth are fled away.

Mentzer, who has given us the beautiful hymn, "O would, my God, that I could praise Thee," was born at Jahmen, Silesia, in 1658. For thirty-eight years he was pastor at Kemnitz, Saxony, at which place he wrote his hymns, about thirty in number. There is an exalted strain in his hymns of praise:

O all ye powers that He implanted,
Arise, keep silence thus no more,
Put forth the strength that He hath granted,
Your noblest work is to adore;
O soul and body, be ye meet
With heartfelt praise your Lord to greet.

This hymn sometimes begins with the line, "O that I had a thousand voices."

A Noble Hymn of Worship

Light of light, enlighten me,
Now anew the day is dawning;
Sun of grace, the shadows flee,
Brighten Thou my Sabbath morning.
With Thy joyous sunshine blest,
Happy is my day of rest!
Fount of all our joy and peace,
To Thy living waters lead me;
Thou from earth my soul release,
And with grace and mercy feed me.
Bless Thy Word, that it may prove
Rich in fruits that Thou dost love.
Kindle Thou the sacrifice
That upon my lips is lying;
Clear the shadows from mine eyes,
That, from every error flying,
No strange fire may in me glow
That Thine altar doth not know.
Let me with my heart today,
Holy, holy, holy, singing,
Rapt awhile from earth away,
All my soul to Thee upspringing,
Have a foretaste inly given,
How they worship Thee in heaven.
Benjamin Schmolck, 1715.

HOW A GREAT ORGANIST INSPIRED TWO HYMNISTS

While all the hymn-writers of Germany in the early part of the eighteenth century were more or less influenced by the Pietistic movement, there were some who nevertheless refused to be carried away by the emotional extravagances of which some of the Halle song-writers were often guilty. In the hymns of these more conservative psalmists we find a happy blending of objective teaching and a warm, personal faith that reminds us of the earlier hymns of Gerhardt.

The chief representatives of this more typical Lutheran school were Benjamin Schmolck, a beloved pastor and a poet of rare ability, and Erdmann Neumeister, creator of the Church Cantata. It was the age in which John Sebastian Bach lived and wrought, and this prince of Lutheran organists, whose title of "high priest of church music" has never been disputed, gave of his musical genius to help make the hymns of Schmolck and Neumeister immortal.

Next to Gerhardt, there is no German hymnist whose name is so frequently found in hymn-books today as that of Schmolck. Born at Brauchitzdorf, Silesia, where his father was pastor, he was sent to school at Lauban at the age of sixteen. After an absence of five years the young man returned home and was invited to fill his father's pulpit. The sermon he preached so pleased the father that he determined to send him to the University of Leipzig to study for the ministry. In 1697 he returned to Brauchitzdorf to be ordained as his father's assistant.

In 1702 Schmolck became pastor of Friedenskirche at Schweidnitz, in Silesia. According to the terms of the Peace of Westphalia in 1648, all of the churches in this district had been turned over to the Catholics, and only a "meeting-house," built of timber and clay and without tower or bells, was allowed to the Lutherans. Here Schmolck labored patiently for thirty-five years under the most trying circumstances, not even being permitted to administer communion to the dying except by consent of the Catholic authorities.

Schmolck's hymns and spiritual songs, numbering 1,183 in all, brought him fame all over Germany. Many have been translated into English. His fervent love for the Saviour is beautifully reflected in the hymn:

My Jesus, as Thou wilt!
O may Thy will be mine!
Into Thy hand of love
I would my all resign;
Through sorrow or through joy,
Conduct me as Thine own,
And help me still to say,
"My Lord, Thy will be done!"

"Light of light, enlighten me," a noble hymn of praise and adoration, has been happily wedded to a glorious chorale by Bach. Other hymns that have won renown throughout the Christian world include "Open now thy gates of beauty," "Welcome,

Thou Victor in the strife," "Blessed Jesus, here we stand," "What our Father does is well," "My God, I know that I must die," "Hallelujah, Lo, He wakes," "My truest Friend abides in heaven," and "Precious Word from God in heaven." The joyous spirit in many of Schmolck's hymns may be seen reflected in the beautiful temple hymn:

> Open now thy gates of beauty,
> Zion, let me enter there.
> Where my soul in joyful duty
> Waits for Him who answers prayer;
> O how blessèd is this place,
> Filled with solace, light, and grace!

Neumeister followed the example of Schmolck in becoming an ardent champion of the older, conservative Lutheranism. Although he was greatly influenced as a youth by the writings of Francke, he later became convinced that there were dangerous tendencies in the Halle and Herrnhut movements, and he did not hesitate to issue violent polemics against them.

His hymns, on the other hand, offer a curious contrast to his other writings. Often they reveal a warmth and tenderness of feeling that would have merited a place for them in any Pietistic hymn-book. This may be seen in the hymn, "Jesus sinners doth receive," which has also been translated "Sinners may to Christ draw near:"

> "Jesus sinners doth receive!"
> Word of surest consolation;
> Word all sorrow to relieve,
> Word of pardon, peace, salvation!
> Naught like this can comfort give:
> "Jesus sinners doth receive!"

Neumeister became pastor of St. James church in Hamburg in 1715, where he remained for forty-one years until his death in 1756. His fame does not rest merely upon his hymns, although he wrote 650 in all, but Neumeister will also be remembered as the originator of the Church Cantata. In this new field of musical art he was fortunate in having the coöperation of such a genius as Bach.

Bach belonged to the fifth generation of a remarkable family of musicians. As many as thirty-seven of the family are known to have held important musical positions. John Sebastian, who is by far the greatest musician the Protestant Church has produced, was born in Eisenach, on March 21, 1685. The greater part of his life was spent in Leipzig, where he labored from 1723 until his death in 1750 as cantor of the Thomas school and director of music at the Thomas and Nicolai churches.

Bach's devotion to the Lutheran Church has been likened to that of Palestrina to the Catholic Church. There is no loftier example of musical genius dedicated to the service of the Christian religion than we find in the life of Bach. He felt that his life was consecrated to God, to the honor of his Church, and to the blessing of mankind. Although it was the age when the opera was flourishing in Europe, Bach gave no attention to it, but devoted all his remarkable talent to church music.

As master of the organ, Bach has never been equaled. His chorales and passion music also belong in a class by themselves. A famous critic has written: "Mozart and Beethoven failed in oratorio, Schubert in opera; the Italian operas of Gluck and Handel have perished. Even in the successful work of these men there is a strange inequality. But upon all that Bach attempted—and the amount of his work is no less a marvel than its quality—he affixed the stamp of final and inimitable perfection."

With the passing of years, Bach's genius is being recognized more and more throughout the Christian Church. The performance of his cantatas by the Catholic Schola Cantorum of Paris "is one of the many testimonies to the universality of the art of this son of Lutheranism." There is something in his mighty productions that touches the deepest chords of religious emotion, regardless of creed or communion.

A Hymn on the Mystical Union

Thou hidden love of God, whose height,
Whose depth unfathomed no man knows,
I see from far Thy beauteous light,
Inly I sigh for Thy repose:
My heart is pained, nor can it be
At rest; till it find rest in Thee.
Is there a thing beneath the sun
That strives with Thee my heart to share?
Ah! tear it thence, and reign alone,
The Lord of every motion there.
Then shall my heart from earth be free,
When it hath found repose in Thee.
O hide this self from me, that I
No more, but Christ in me, may live!
My base affections crucify,
Nor let one favorite sin survive;
In all things nothing may I see,
Nothing desire, or seek, but Thee.
Each moment draw from earth away
My heart that lowly waits Thy call!
Speak to my inmost soul, and say:
"I am thy Love, thy God, thy All!"
To feel Thy power, to hear Thy voice,
To taste Thy love, be all my choice!
Gerhard Tersteegen, 1729.

GERHARD TERSTEEGEN, HYMN-WRITER AND MYSTIC

While Benjamin Schmolck must be regarded as the greatest of Lutheran hymn-writers in Germany during the eighteenth century, Gerhard Tersteegen holds the same distinction among German Reformed hymnists. Except for the Wesleys in England, no man during his age exerted so great a spiritual influence in evangelical circles of all lands as did Tersteegen. In some respects his religious views bordered on fanaticism, but no one could question his deep sincerity and his earnest desire to live the life hidden with Christ in God.

Born at Mörs, Rhenish Prussia, November 25, 1697, Tersteegen was only six years old when his father died. It had been the plan of his parents that he should become a Reformed minister, but the death of the father made it impossible for the mother to carry out this purpose. At the age of sixteen he was apprenticed to a merchant, and four years later entered business on his own account.

Although he was only twenty years old at this time, he began to experience seasons of deep spiritual despondency. This lasted for nearly five years, during which time he changed his occupation to that of silk weaving, since he desired more time for prayer and meditation. It was not until the year 1724, while on a journey to a neighboring town, that light seemed to dawn on his troubled soul, and he was filled with the assurance that God's grace in Christ Jesus was sufficient to atone for all sin. In the joy and peace which he had found, he immediately wrote the beautiful hymn, "How gracious, kind and good, my great High Priest, art Thou."

From this time until the close of his life, Tersteegen began to devote his energies more and more to religious work and literary activities. An independent religious movement known as "Stillen im Lande" had begun about this time, and he soon became known as a leader among these people.

Tersteegen had already ceased to associate with his friends in the Reformed Church, and had gone over to religious mysticism. In one of his strange spiritual moods he wrote what he called "a covenant between himself and God" and signed it with his own blood.

Finally he gave up business pursuits entirely, and his home became the refuge of multitudes of sick and spiritually troubled people. It came to be known as the "Pilgrim's Hut," from the fact that many found a temporary retreat there, as well as spiritual help and guidance. Tersteegen also traveled extensively in his own district, and made frequent visits to Holland to hold meetings there.

Tersteegen never married, and for this reason he was accused of teaching celibacy. Several sects, including the Moravians, sought to induce him to become one of their number, but he steadfastly refused to identify himself with any organized church body. He died at Mülheim, April 30, 1769.

Tersteegen's hymns, as well as his other writings, reflect his spirit of mysticism. His soul was imbued with the sense of the nearness of God, and, through a life of spiritual communion and a renunciation of the world, he developed a simplicity of faith and a child-like trust that found beautiful expression in his hymns.

Two of these, "Thou hidden love of God whose height" and "Lo, God is here, let us adore," made a deep impression on John Wesley, who translated the former during his visit to Georgia in 1736. Wesley became familiar with Tersteegen's hymns through contact with Moravian pilgrims who were crossing the Atlantic on the same ship on which he sailed. "Lo, God is here, let us adore" has several English versions, including "God is in His temple" and "God Himself is present."

Another of Tersteegen's hymns, "God calling yet! shall I not hear?" is one of the most stirring calls to repentance in all the realm of Christian hymnody. It was rendered into English by Mrs. Sarah Borthwick Findlater in the series of translations known as "Hymns from the Land of Luther."

Other noted hymns by Tersteegen include "Jesus, whom Thy Church doth own," "O Love divine, all else transcending," and "Triumph, ye heavens," the latter a Christmas lyric of exultant strain.

Tersteegen's conception of the high place which hymnody should occupy in Christian worship is revealed in his writings. He says: "The pious, reverential singing of hymns has something angelic about it and is accompanied by divine blessing. It quiets and subdues the troubled emotions; it drives away cares and anxieties; it strengthens, refreshes and encourages the soul; it draws the mind unconsciously from external things, lifts up the soul to joyful adoration, and thus prepares us to worship in spirit and in truth. We should sing with the spirit of reverence, with sincerity, simplicity and hearty desire.... When you sing, O soul, remember that you are as truly communing with the holy and omnipresent God as when you are praying. Consider that you are standing in spirit before the throne of God with countless thousands of angels and spirits of the just and that you are blending your weak praises with the music of heaven. Serve the Lord with fear, and rejoice with trembling."

Following a Heavenly Leader

Jesus, still lead on,
Till our rest be won,
And although the way be cheerless,
We will follow, calm and fearless.
Guide us by Thy hand
To our Fatherland!
If the way be drear,
If the foe be near,
Let not faithless fear o'ertake us,
Let not faith and hope forsake us;
For through many a foe
To our home we go!
When we seek relief
From a long-felt grief,
When temptations come alluring,
Make us patient and enduring,
Show us that bright shore
Where we weep no more!
Jesus, still lead on,
Till our rest be won;
Heavenly Leader, still direct us,

Still support, console, protect us,
Till we safely stand
In our Fatherland!
Nicolaus Ludwig, Count Zinzendorf, 1721

ZINZENDORF AND MORAVIAN HYMNODY

The church of the Moravian Brethren is famous for two things: its missionary zeal and its love for church music. It owes both of these distinguishing characteristics to its great founder and patron leader, Nicolaus Ludwig, Count von Zinzendorf. Not only was this very unusual man a gifted writer of hymns, but he was also an ardent exponent of foreign missions.

Zinzendorf was only ten years old when his soul was fired with a passionate desire to do something to help win the world for Christ. He was a pupil at the famous Pietist school of Francke at Halle, Germany, at the time, and through his endeavors a mission society known as "The Order of the Grain of Mustard Seed," was organized among the lads of his own age.

A few years later he chanced to see a copy of Sternberg's masterpiece, "Ecce Homo," depicting Christ wearing His crown of thorns before Pilate and the Jewish mob. Beneath the famous picture were inscribed the words:

This have I done for thee;
What hast thou done for Me?
From that moment Zinzendorf took as his life motto: "I have but one passion, and that is He and only He." On his wedding day, in 1722, he and his young bride decided to renounce their rank and to dedicate their lives to the task of winning souls for Christ.

The Lord took them at their word. In that same year a number of Protestant refugees from Moravia, who had been compelled to leave their homes because of Roman Catholic persecution, arrived in Saxony and found refuge on Zinzendorf's large estate. They were a remnant of the Bohemian Brethren, a heroic religious communion which dated back to the days of the noble martyr, John Huss. Though relentlessly hunted and persecuted for more than three centuries, this early evangelical body had continued to maintain its existence in the form of secret religious circles known as "the hidden seed."

Under the protection of Count Zinzendorf, the little band of Moravian refugees established a religious center which they called "Herrnhut." Zinzendorf, who was a Lutheran, induced them to adopt the Augsburg Confession as a statement of their doctrine, but they continued to exist as an independent church body. People from all over Europe, hearing that religious freedom was enjoyed on the Zinzendorf estates, flocked to Herrnhut in large numbers to escape persecution, and it soon became a flourishing colony.

In 1737 Zinzendorf accepted ordination as a bishop of the Brethren, and thus became the real leader of the organization. He immediately began to impart his own missionary zeal to the Moravian movement. Two of the earliest missionaries, David Nitschmann and Leonard Dober, were sent to the island of St. Thomas, in the West Indies, to preach the gospel to the negro slaves. The blacks were so embittered because of the cruel treatment received at the hands of their taskmasters that they refused to listen to the missionaries, and very little progress could be made. At last, in order to gain their confidence, Dober sold himself as a slave and shared their hardships with them. He soon died, however, as a result of this deed. The story of his heroic sacrifice so moved the heart of Prime Minister Wilberforce of England that he forthwith determined to begin the movement which eventually led to the emancipation of all slaves in the British empire.

Missionary zeal continued to flourish among the Moravians, and the little colony of Herrnhut became known as one of the most famous missionary centers of Christendom. Every one of its members felt that he possessed no permanent habitation in this world, and was prepared every day to be sent to any part of the globe.

Though still a small organization today, the Moravian Church has never lost its missionary spirit. It is claimed that for every fifty-eight members of the Church at home, there is one missionary in foreign lands. When Carey went to India, the Moravians already had 165 missionaries in the pagan world.

Zinzendorf was a great lover of music. Even as a boy, he wrote hymns. The first was written at the age of twelve, and he was still producing hymns in 1760, the year of his death. Altogether, he is credited with the authorship of more than 2,000 lyrics. His most famous is "Jesus, still lead on," which is also known as "Jesus, lead the way." John Wesley was a great admirer of Zinzendorf's hymns and has given us the beautiful English translation of "Jesus, thy blood and righteousness." James Montgomery, the noted English hymnist, was a member of the Moravian communion.

A Glorious Hymn of Adoration

Beautiful Saviour!
King of Creation!
Son of God and Son of Man!
Truly I'd love Thee,
Truly I'd serve Thee,
Light of my soul, my Joy, my Crown.
Fair are the meadows,
Fair are the woodlands,
Robed in flowers of blooming spring;
Jesus is fairer,
Jesus is purer;
He makes our sorrowing spirit sing.
Fair is the sunshine,
Fair is the moonlight,
Bright the sparkling stars on high;
Jesus shines brighter,
Jesus shines purer
Than all the angels in the sky.

Beautiful Saviour!
Lord of the nations!
Son of God and Son of Man!
Glory and honor,
Praise, adoration,
Now and for evermore be Thine!
Münster Gesangbuch, 1677.

TWO FAMOUS HYMNS AND SOME LEGENDS

Every hymn has a story. Ofttimes, however, the origin is obscure, and it is difficult to trace its birth out of the misty past. Again there are so many legends that have gathered around the great lyrics of the ages, many of them generally accepted, that it becomes a painful process to get rid of these excrescences. Two beautiful German hymns, "Schönster Herr Jesu" and "Stille Nacht! Heilige Nacht!" may serve to illustrate these difficulties.

In innumerable hymn-books the former hymn, sometimes translated "Beautiful Saviour" and sometimes "Fairest Lord Jesus," is designated as "The Crusaders' Hymn." The hymn was first introduced to American worshipers by Richard Storrs Willis, who included it in his "Church Chorals and Choir Studies," published in 1850. It was accompanied with this explanation: "This hymn, to which the harmony has been added, was lately (1850) discovered in Westphalia. According to the traditionary text by which it is accompanied, it was wont to be sung by the German knights on their way to Jerusalem. The only hymn of the same century which in point of style resembles this is one quoted by Burney from the Chatelaine de Coucy, set about the year 1190, very far inferior, however, to this."

In a London hymn-book, "Heart Melodies" by Morgan and Chase, the same error is repeated. There it is referred to as "Crusader's Hymn of the Twelfth Century. This air and hymn used to be sung by the German pilgrims on their way to Jerusalem."

"For these statements," writes James Mearns, "there does not seem to be the shadow of foundation, for the air referred to has not been traced earlier than 1842, nor the words than 1677."

The hymn appeared anonymously in the "Münster Gesangbuch" of 1677, where it was published as the first of "Three beautiful selected new hymns." In a book of Silesian folk songs, published in Leipzig in 1842, the text is found in altered form and the beautiful melody to which it is now sung is given for the first time. Both text and melody, it is explained in this book, were taken down from oral recitation in the district of Glaz, in lower Silesia. From these facts we are compelled to draw the conclusion that this glorious hymn of adoration to the Saviour probably dates back to the seventeenth century, while the melody is undoubtedly a Silesian folk song of much later origin.

The English translation, "Beautiful Saviour," has come to us from the pen of Joseph A. Seiss, the noted Lutheran preacher of Philadelphia.

"Silent night, holy night" also is a hymn around which numerous legends have clustered. The most unfortunate of these deals with its origin. According to this story, the hymn was written on a Christmas Eve by a "Mr. Mohr," whose wife that very day had gone to celebrate Christmas in heaven. In an adjoining room the grief-stricken husband and father could see his little motherless children sleeping. Outside the house of mourning the stillness of the night was broken suddenly by the singing of Christmas carolers. They were singing the very songs his wife and children used to sing. Now, he thought, she is blending her voice with the angels. Then came the inspiration for the hymn, and in a few moments he had penned the now famous "Stille Nacht."

This is a very touching story, but its fatal defect lies in the fact that "Mr. Mohr" was a Roman Catholic priest.

The true story of the origin of the hymn has much less of the emotional appeal. The author, Joseph Mohr, was born at Salzburg, Austria, December 11, 1792. He was ordained as a priest at the age of twenty-three, becoming assistant at Laufen, near his native city. It was here, three years later, that the beautiful Christmas carol was written.

It seems that a shipowner at Oberndorf named Maier and his wife had invited the young priest to be their guest at a pre-Christmas party. As a special surprise for the priest, Maier had invited some wandering minstrels to stage a crude representation of the Christmas story as recounted in the Bible. The thoughtful hospitality of the Maier couple and the touching simplicity of the festival play so stirred the heart of Mohr that, instead of going straightway home, he climbed the so-called "Totenberg," (mountain of the dead) overlooking Oberndorf, and stood in silent meditation.

The silence of the night, the starry splendor of the winter sky, the murmur of the Salzach river thrilled his soul. Quickly he descended to his parish house, and late that night wrote the words of "Stille Nacht." The next day he hurried to his friend and co-worker, Franz Gruber, organist and school teacher, and asked him to write music for his lines. The latter eagerly embraced the opportunity, and thus was given to the world one of the most exquisite of Christmas carols.

A Classical Harvest Hymn

We plow the fields and scatter
The good seed on the land,
But it is fed and watered
By God's almighty hand;
He sends the snow in winter,
The warmth to swell the grain,
The breezes and the sunshine,
And soft, refreshing rain.
He only is the Maker
Of all things near and far;
He paints the wayside flower,
He lights the evening star;
The winds and waves obey Him,

By Him the birds are fed;
Much more to us, His children,
He gives our daily bread.
We thank Thee, then, O Father,
For all things bright and good,
The seedtime and the harvest,
Our life, our health, our food;
No gifts have we to offer
For all Thy love imparts,
But that which Thou desirest,
Our humble, thankful hearts.
Matthias Claudius, 1782.

HYMNODY IN THE AGE OF RATIONALISM

In religion, as in other things, the pendulum often swings from one extreme to the other. Scarcely had the Pietistic movement run its course before the rationalistic tendencies which had thrown religious thought into confusion in France and England began to make their appearance in Germany. Rationalism was an attempt to subject all revealed religion to the test and judgment of the human reason. That which seemed to contradict reason was rejected as superstitious and untrue.

Strangely enough, the University of Halle, which had been the citadel of Pietism, became the stronghold of Rationalism in Germany. Christian Wolff and Johann Semler, noted philosophers of Halle, were leaders in the movement. It was not their purpose to establish a new religion of reason, but to "purge" Christianity of the things that seemed unreasonable. But the results of the movement were devastating. The miracles of the Bible that could not be explained by natural causes were rejected as "fables." Christ was robbed of His glory as a divine Saviour and was regarded only as a teacher of morals. Religion became merely the knowledge of God and the pursuit of virtue. What remained of Christianity was a mere shadow: a hypothesis concerning God and immortality, and a teaching of external morality, the attainment of which was largely a matter of man's own efforts.

Rationalism cast its blight over the hymnody of all Europe, but particularly in Germany. It was the golden age of German literature, but such geniuses as Goethe, Schiller, Lessing and Wieland were not filled with the Christian zeal of earlier poets, and they wrote no hymns. Most of the hymns that were produced were so tinged with the spirit of the "new theology" that they contained no elements of vitality to give them permanent value.

The Rationalists were not satisfied with criticizing the Bible; they also sought to "purge" the hymn-books. The old hymns of Luther, Heermann, Selnecker, and Gerhardt were so completely altered that a noted German hymnologist, Albert Knapp, was moved to observe ironically: "The old hymns were subjected to a kind of transmigration of soul by which their spirits, after having lost their own personality, entered into other bodies."

Only a few writers, such as Friedrich Gottlieb Klopstock, Balthasar Münter, Christian Gellert and Matthias Claudius, wrote hymns of any abiding worth.

Klopstock, the German Milton, whose epic, "Messiah," thrilled Germany as had no other poetic work in centuries, essayed to write a few hymns, but he soared too high. His hymns lacked simplicity of style and were too emotional and subjective to be used for public worship. Only two English translations are familiar—"Blessed are the heirs of heaven," a funeral hymn, and "Grant us, Lord, due preparation," a communion hymn.

Klopstock spent nearly twenty years of his life at the Danish court, having been invited there by King Fredrik V through the influence of Count von Bernstorff, who had become greatly interested in the epic, "Messiah." The Danish monarch gave the poet an annual pension in order to assist him in completing his famous poem without being oppressed by financial worries. In 1770 Klopstock returned to Hamburg, where he died in 1803.

Gellert, who was born in Hainichen, Saxony, July 4, 1715, intended to become a Lutheran pastor. After completing his theological course at the University of Leipzig, however, he found it difficult to deliver sermons without the use of a manuscript, and therefore decided to take up teaching. In 1745 he became a member of the faculty of the University of Leipzig, where he remained until his death in 1769. Among his pupils were many famous men of Germany, including Goethe and Lessing.

Gellert's hymns, although influenced by the age in which he lived, are singular for their genuine, evangelical utterance. It is said that he never attempted to write a hymn except when he was in the proper frame of mind, and only after a season of prayer. His Easter hymn, "Jesus lives! thy terrors now," has gained great popularity, both in England and in America. In the former country it has been sung at the funerals of some of England's greatest churchmen. His communion hymn also breathes a spirit of true faith in Christ:

> Crushed by my sin, O Lord, to Thee
> I come in my affliction:
> O full of pity, look on me,
> Impart Thy benediction.
> My sins are great, where shall I flee?
> The blood of Jesus speaks for me;
> For all my sins He carried.

Matthias Claudius, the author of the splendid hymn, "We plow the fields and scatter," like Gellert, had intended to prepare himself for the Lutheran ministry. While attending the University of Jena, however, the Rationalistic teachings with which he came in contact caused him to lose interest in religion, and he decided to take up journalism instead. In 1777 he became editor of a newspaper at Darmstadt, at which place he became acquainted with Goethe and a group of freethinking philosophers.

Stricken by a serious illness, Claudius began to realize something of the spiritual emptiness of the life he had been living, and in his hour of need he turned again to his childhood faith. When he had recovered, he gave up his position and removed to Wandsbeck, where he edited the "Wandsbecker Bote" in a true Christian spirit.

In the life-story of Claudius we may discern something of the reaction that was already taking place in many quarters against the deadening influence of Rationalism. Men were hungering for the old evangel of salvation, and there were evidences everywhere of the dawn of a happier day. Although Claudius' poems were not essentially Church hymns, they were lyrics that seemed to strike anew some of the strings of Gerhardt's harp. This is seen especially in his surpassingly beautiful ode to evening, "The silent moon is risen," written in the same spirit and meter as Gerhardt's famous evening hymn. The first stanza has been translated:

The silent moon is risen,
The golden star-fires glisten
In heaven serene and bright;
The forest sleeps in shadow,
And slowly off the meadow
A mist is curling, silver-white.

Another stanza, reflecting something of Claudius' own spiritual groping and, at the same time, confessing the futility of all human efforts to attain moral perfection, reads:

We, poor, frail mortals, groping,
Half fearing and half hoping,
In darkness seek our way;
Our airy cobwebs spinning
With erring and with sinning,
Far from the mark we sadly stray.

In the lyrics of Claudius we may observe a transition from the spiritually impoverished hymn production of the rationalistic period to a new type of hymnody, giving expression to the old rugged faith in a more elegant form. Men's souls could no longer be satisfied with the dry husks of philosophical speculation and were turning again to the Bread of God which cometh down from heaven and giveth life unto the world.

Balthasar Münter was another faithful witness to the truth in this unhappy age of widespread skepticism and unbelief. Born at Lübeck in 1735, he became Lutheran court pastor at Gotha and afterwards of the German Church of St. Peter in Copenhagen. He was the writer of about 100 hymns, many of which were set to tunes composed for them by the greatest musicians of the day. Among the best known hymns of Münter are "Lord, Thou Source of all perfection," "Full of reverence, at Thy Word," "Behold the man! how heavy lay," and "Woe unto him who says, There is no God."

A Picture of a Christian Home

O happy home, where Thou art loved the dearest,
Thou loving Friend and Saviour of our race,
And where among the guests there never cometh
One who can hold such high and honored place!
O happy home, where two, in heart united,
In holy faith and blessed hope are one,

Whom death a little while alone divideth,
And cannot end the union here begun!
O happy home, whose little ones are given
Early to Thee in humble faith and prayer,
To Thee, their Friend, who from the heights of heaven
Guides them, and guards with more than mother's care.
O happy home, where each one serves Thee lowly,
Whatever his appointed work may be,
Till every common task seems great and holy,
When it is done, O Lord, as unto Thee!
O happy home, where Thou art not forgotten
When joy is overflowing, full and free,
O happy home, where every wounded spirit
Is brought, Physician, Comforter, to Thee.
And when at last all earthly toil is ended,
All meet Thee in the blessed home above,
From whence Thou camest, where Thou hast ascended—
Thine everlasting home of peace and love.
Carl Johann Philipp Spitta, 1833.

HYMNS OF THE SPIRITUAL RENAISSANCE

In the early part of the nineteenth century a great spiritual revival swept over Germany and other parts of evangelical Europe. In some respects it resembled the earlier Pietistic movement in Germany and the Wesleyan revival in England, except that it was more conservative than either. In Germany the old orthodox conservatives and the more radical Pietists joined forces to fight Rationalism, and the union was of benefit to both groups.

There were many influences that contributed to the overthrow of Rationalism. Chief among these was the widespread suffering and distress in Germany, both physical and spiritual, following the Napoleonic wars. Jacobs has well said: "When earthly props fall and temporal foundations crumble, men turn, almost perforce, to God." The downfall of Napoleon and the great empire he had founded was an object lesson to the world of the transitory character of all things material.

The great thinker, Immanuel Kant, also helped to undermine the walls of Rationalism by pointing out the limitatations of the human reason. He was followed by the famous theologian, Friedrich Schleiermacher, who taught that the seat of religion is not to be found in either the reason or will, but in feeling—"the feeling of absolute dependence upon God." The way was thus paved for the zealous efforts of Claus Harms, who in 1817, the 300th anniversary of the Reformation, published a new set of ninety-five theses and called upon his countrymen to return again to the pure evangelical teachings of Luther.

Spring-time always brings song-birds and flowers. It was spring-time in the religious life of Germany, and the sweet notes of evangelical hymnody again were heard throughout the land.

Carl Johann Philipp Spitta was the greatest German hymn-writer of the nineteenth century. He was born August 1, 1801, in Hannover. His father, who was a descendant of a Huguenot family that fled from France during the Catholic persecutions, died when Carl was only four years old. His mother was a Christian Jewess, and it is a beautiful tribute to her fostering care that the finest hymn ever written on the Christian home came from the pen of her son. No doubt it was the memory of his childhood home that led Spitta to write:

> O happy home, whose little ones are given
> Early to Thee in humble faith and prayer,
> To Thee, their Friend, who from the heights of heaven
> Guides them, and guards with more than mother's care.

Spitta began to write verse at the age of eight. It was his mother's ambition that he should study for the ministry, but, because of his frail health, it was decided that he should become a watchmaker, and a younger brother was sent to school instead. The latter died, however, and now Carl was given his opportunity. He completed his theological studies in 1824, taught school for four years in Lüne, and in 1828 he was ordained to the Lutheran ministry.

During his university days, Spitta had become a bosom friend of Heinrich Heine, the famous poet and prose writer. When the latter visited Spitta at Lüne, however, and scoffed at holy things in the presence of Spitta's pupils, the friendship came to an abrupt end. It was about this time that Spitta passed through a deep spiritual experience, the result of which was the composition of some of his finest hymns. Writing to a friend in 1826, he says, "In the manner in which I formerly sang, I sing no more. To the Lord I dedicate my life, my love, and likewise my song. He gave to me song and melody. I give it back to Him."

Spitta's hymns aroused unparalleled enthusiasm. His "Psalter und Harfe," first published in 1833, appeared in a second and larger edition the following year. Thereafter a new edition appeared every year, and by 1889 no less than fifty-five editions had been published. A second collection of hymns was printed in 1843, and by 1887 it had passed through forty-two editions. The popularity of Spitta's hymns also spread to other lands, and a large number are found in English and American hymn-books.

Spitta's child-like faith and his fervent love to the Saviour may be seen reflected in such a hymn as:

> I know no life divided,
> O Lord of life, from Thee:
> In Thee is life provided
> For all mankind and me;
> I know no death, O Jesus,
> Because I live in Thee;
> Thy death it is that frees us
> From death eternally.

Other well-known hymns from this consecrated writer are "O come, Eternal Spirit," "By the holy hills surrounded," "I place myself in Jesus' hands," "Thou, whose coming seers and sages," "We are the Lord's: His all-sufficient merit," "How blessed from the bonds of sin," "We praise and bless Thee, gracious Lord," "Brethren, called by one vocation," "Withhold not, Lord, the help I crave," "O blessed Sun, whose splendor," and "Say, my soul, what preparation." The beloved German psalmist passed away suddenly while seated at his desk, September 28, 1859.

Most noted among the contemporaries of Spitta was Albert Knapp, who, although his hymns never met with the popular favor that attended Spitta's efforts, nevertheless excelled the latter as a poet. Knapp was born at Tübingen, July 25, 1798, and was educated for the Lutheran ministry in the University at that place. His most important post after ordination was at St. Leonard's church in Stuttgart, where he served from 1845 until his death in 1864.

Knapp was not only a hymnist but also a hymnologist. Perhaps the greatest service he rendered his Church was the editing of a collection of more than 3,000 of the great hymns of Germany. This monumental work, known as "Evangelischer Lieder-Schatz," is the most comprehensive hymn collection ever published in German, and is a veritable gold-mine of the classics of Protestant hymnody. Knapp has been severely criticized, however, for the liberties he took in revising the hymns of some of the older writers. The best known of his own works is a baptismal hymn, "Father, who hast created all." A hymn for church dedication begins with the line, "O God, whom we as Father know."

Carl Bernhard Garve, a Moravian pastor, also contributed a number of compositions to the hymns of this period, the best known of which is the beautiful tribute to the Holy Scripture:

> Thy Word, O Lord, like gentle dews,
> Falls soft on hearts that pine;
> Lord, to Thy garden ne'er refuse
> This heavenly balm of Thine.
>
> Watered by Thee, let every tree
> Forth-blossom to Thy praise,
> By grace of Thine bear fruit divine
> Through all the coming days.

Garve served congregations in Amsterdam, Ebersdorf, Berlin, and Neusalz. He spent the last years of his life in Herrnhut, where he died in 1841. Garve was the most important among the later Moravian hymn-writers. Many of his hymns have been adopted by other communions, particularly the Lutheran Church.

To Friedrich Adolf Krummacher, a Reformed pastor, we owe the highly prized hymn:

> Thou art the Way, the Truth, the Life from heaven,
> This blest assurance Thou to us hast given;
> O wilt Thou teach us, Lord, to win Thy pleasure
> In fullest measure?

Krummacher was a teacher of theology in the Reformed University of Duisburg. After the battle of Jena in 1806 Duisburg was taken from Prussia by Napoleon and the salaries of the professors were cut off. Krummacher continued to lecture, however, until his class consisted of one student! He afterwards served as pastor in a number of cities, finally accepting appointment to St. Ansgarius church in Bremen. He died in Bremen in 1845.

Of the more modern hymn-writers of Germany the best known is Karl von Gerok, chief court preacher at Stuttgart, where he died as recently as 1890. An eloquent preacher and able writer, he attained fame principally through the publication in 1857 of a collection of poems known as "Palmblätter." This work received a marvelous circulation in Germany, and by 1916 no less than 130 editions had been printed. Although most of Gerok's compositions are poems rather than hymns, a few have found their way into hymn-books. A devotional hymn by von Gerok reads:

> Holy, holy, holy, blessed Lord,
> All the choirs of heaven now adore Thee;
> O that I might join that great white host,
> Casting down their golden crowns before Thee.
> Look on me, a creature of the dust,
> Pity me, though I have naught of merit;
> Let me bring to Thee for Jesus' sake
> Humble praises of a contrite spirit.
> Bend Thine ear, dear Lord, and hear my prayer;
> Cleanse me in Thy blood for sinners given;
> Deck me in the robe of spotless white
> Thou hast promised to Thy bride in heaven.

PART III
Scandinavian Hymnody

A Hymn in Luther's Style

> Our Father, merciful and good,
> Who dost to Thee invite us,
> O cleanse us in our Saviour's blood,
> And to Thyself unite us!
> Send unto us Thy Holy Word,
> And let it guide us ever;
> Then in this world of darkness, Lord,
> Shall naught from Thee us sever:
> Grant us, O Lord, this favor!
> O God and man, Christ Jesus blest!
> Our sorrows Thou didst carry.
> Our wants and cares Thou knowest best,
> For Thou with us didst tarry.
> O Jesus Christ, our Brother dear,
> To us and every nation
> Thy Spirit send, let Him draw near
> With truth and consolation,

That we may see salvation.
Come, Holy Ghost, Thy grace impart,
Tear Satan's snares asunder.
The Word of God keep in our heart,
That we its truth may ponder.
Then, sanctified, for evermore,
In Christ alone confiding,
We'll sing His praise and Him adore,
His precious Word us guiding
To heavenly joys abiding.
Olavus Petri, 1530.

THE SWEDISH REFORMERS AND THEIR HYMNS

The Reformation fires kindled by Luther and his contemporaries in Wittenberg spread with amazing rapidity to all parts of Europe. In the year that Luther nailed his famous theses on the chapel door at Wittenberg, two brothers—Olavus and Laurentius Petri—arrived from Sweden to study at the university made famous by Luther and Melanchthon. They were sons of a village blacksmith at Örebro, Sweden.

In 1519 they returned to their native land, full of reforming zeal. Olavus was the more fiery of the two brothers, and he lost no time entering into the political and spiritual storm that was threatening to break over their country. In the Stockholm massacre the following year Olavus almost lost his life when he cried out in protest at the cruel beheading of his friend, the bishop of Strengnäs. Only the intervention of a Wittenberg acquaintance, who asserted that Olavus was a German citizen, saved the young man from a similar fate. The massacre had been instigated by Roman intrigue.

Olavus preached boldly against the sale of indulgences and other abuses of the papal church, and, when the Swedish revolution placed Gustavus Vasa on the throne in 1523, the young reformer found a powerful ally in the new monarch. Despite protests of the ecclesiastical authorities, the king ordered a pulpit placed in the cathedral church of Stockholm and gave Olavus permission to preach to the populace in the native tongue.

The following year the two brothers were summoned to appear before the papal authorities at Upsala, but, when neither threats nor bribes could induce them to desist from their high-minded purpose, they were placed under the ban. This, however, made them only the more determined to carry out their Reformation plans.

Laurentius Andreae, archdeacon of Strengnäs, also had been converted to the principles of the Reformation and powerfully espoused the cause championed by the Petri brothers. In 1523 he was appointed by Gustavus Vasa as chancellor to the king, and it was largely through his influence that the Lutheran teachings were approved by the Diet af Vesterås in 1527. The younger of the Petri brothers, Laurentius, was named Archbishop of Upsala, Primate of Sweden, in 1531.

The Swedish reformers were apt pupils of Luther and quickly made use of the same spiritual weapons in their own country that he had found so effective in Germany. It is significant that the Word of God and a hymn-book in the vernacular were given to the Swedish people in the same year. It was in 1526 that Laurentius Andreae published his translation of the New Testament in Swedish, and simultaneously Olavus Petri issued a little hymn-book entitled, "Swedish Hymns or Songs."

This marked the beginning of evangelical hymnody in Sweden. The little book contained only ten hymns, five of which are believed to have been original productions of Olavus Petri himself, and the other five translations from Luther's first hymn-book of 1524. Although no copy of the first Swedish hymn-book is now known to exist, it is believed that Petri's beautiful hymn, "Our Father, merciful and good," appeared in this historic collection. It occurs in a second edition, called "A Few Godly Songs Derived from Holy Writ," published by the Swedish reformer in 1530. A few fragmentary pages of this hymn-book were discovered in 1871.

How far Olavus Petri had imbibed the spirit of Luther is reflected not only by the fiery zeal with which he proclaimed the doctrines of the Reformation in Sweden, but also in the character of his hymns. "Our Father, merciful and good" is so strongly suggestive of Luther's style that it was regarded for a long time as a translation of one of Luther's hymns. It is now known that there is no such hymn of German origin.

Most of Petri's hymns, however, are translations of German or Latin originals. One of these is the beautiful Advent hymn:

Now hail we our Redeemer,
Eternal Son of God,
Born in the flesh to save us,
And cleanse us in His blood.
The Morning Star ascendeth,
Light to the world He lendeth,
Our Guide in grief and gloom.

Although this hymn was translated by Petri from the German, it is believed that it dates back to a Latin hymn by Ambrose in the fourth century. Another of Latin origin is the glad Easter hymn:

Blest Easter day, what joy is thine!
We praise, dear Lord, Thy Name divine,
For Thou hast triumphed o'er the tomb;
No more we need to dread its gloom.

Petri, like Luther, never ceased praising God for restoring His Word to the Church through the Reformation. This may be seen in one of his more polemic hymns, which is regarded as original. A translation by Ernst W. Olson reads:

Thy sacred Word, O Lord, of old
Was veiled about and darkened,
And in its stead were legends told,
To which the people harkened;
Thy Word, for which the people yearned,

The worldlings kept in hiding,
And into human fables turned
Thy truth, the all-abiding.
Now thanks and praise be to our Lord,
Who boundless grace bestoweth,
And daily through the sacred Word
His precious gifts forthshoweth.
His Word is come to light again,
A trusty lamp to guide us;
No strange and divers teachings then
Bewilder and divide us.

The last hymn-book published by Olavus Petri appeared in 1536. It contained some thirty new hymns, most of them translations from German sources. In addition to his labors in the realm of hymnody, Petri must also be credited with the authorship of the Swedish Church-Book, which appeared in 1529. He was the creator of the liturgy of the Church of Sweden.

His hymnological endeavors were continued by his brother Laurentius, who, as archbishop, brought out in 1567, and later in 1572, the most important of all the earlier hymn-books of the Swedish Church. Laurentius is sometimes given the title, "Father of Swedish hymnody," but the honor more rightly belongs to his older brother, Olavus.

The latter years of Olavus were darkened through an unfortunate misunderstanding with the Swedish king. As a consequence of the reformer's sturdy opposition to Gustavus Vasa's plan to make himself the head of the Church, he fell into royal disfavor. When a plot against the king's life was discovered in 1540, Olavus was convicted of having guilty knowledge of it, and was condemned to die. Through the intervention of the populace of Stockholm, he was pardoned, but the king never forgave him. He was permitted to resume his work in 1543, and continued to preach the gospel with great zeal until his death in 1552.

A Model Hymn of Invocation

O Lord, give heed unto our plea,
O Spirit, grant Thy graces,
That we who put our trust in Thee
May rightly sing Thy praises.
Thy Word, O Christ, unto us give,
That grace and power we may receive
To follow Thee, our Master.
Touch Thou the shepherd's lips, O Lord,
That in this blessed hour
He may proclaim Thy sacred Word
With unction and with power;
What Thou wouldst have Thy servant say,
Put Thou into His heart, we pray,
With grace and strength to say it.
Let heart and ear be opened wide

Unto Thy Word and pleading;
Our minds, O Holy Spirit, guide
By Thine own light and leading.
The law of Christ we would fulfil,
And walk according to His will,
His Word our rule of living.
Jesper Swedberg (1653-1735).

A HYMN-BOOK THAT FAILED

When the Swedish colonists along the Delaware gathered in their temples to worship God in the latter part of the 17th century, they sang songs from a hymn-book the use of which had been prohibited in Sweden. It was the much-mooted hymn-book of Jesper Swedberg. Originally published by the author in 1694 and intended for the Church of Sweden, it immediately came under suspicion on the ground that it contained unorthodox teachings and was promptly confiscated. This, however, did not hinder the authorities from sending the book in large quantities to America, and it was used on this side of the Atlantic for many years.

Swedberg, who was born near Falun, Sweden, in the year 1653, was the first important hymnist of his native land. From the days of the Reformation no noteworthy advance had been made in Swedish hymnody until Swedberg began to tune his lyre. The official "Psalm-book" had been revised on several occasions, but the Upsala edition of 1645 contained only 182 hymns, far too few to meet the needs of church worship and private devotion.

It was in 1691 that Swedberg received the royal commission to prepare a new hymn-book. He was fortunate in having the aid of such gifted poets as Haqvin Spegel, Petrus Lagerlöf, Israel Kolmodin and Jacob Boethius in the execution of his task.

The new book, containing 482 Swedish hymns and a few in Latin, made its appearance in 1694. A large edition was printed, the financial cost of which was borne largely by Swedberg himself. It met with immediate opposition, particularly from Bishop Carl Carlsson, who charged that the hymn-book contained "innumerable heresies of a theological, anthropological, Christological, soteriological and eschatological nature."

It was enough. King Karl XI immediately appointed a new commission to revise Swedberg's work, with the result that 75 hymns were omitted and six new hymns added. It was printed in 1696 and remained in use as the "Psalm-book" of the Church of Sweden for more than a century, until it was succeeded in 1819 by Wallin's masterpiece.

The unsold copies of the first edition, about 20,000 in number, were confiscated and stored away. From time to time quantities of these books were sent to the Swedish colonists in America, for whose "preservation in the true faith," as the hymnologist Söderberg ironically remarks, "the Swedish authorities seemed less concerned."

Swedberg felt the slight keenly and often made significant references in his diary regarding those who had been instrumental in rejecting his work. One of these notations tells how the Cathedral of Upsala was destroyed by fire in 1702, and how the body of Archbishop O. Svebilius, although encased in a copper and stone sarcophagus, was reduced to ashes. "But my hymn-books," he adds, "which were only of paper, unbound and unprotected, were not even scorched by the flames."

The final form in which his hymn-book was published nevertheless still retained so many of his own hymns, and the entire book was so impregnated with his own spirit, that it has always been known as "Swedberg's Psalm-book." A noted critic has called it "the most precious heritage he left to his native land." It was Swedberg who wrote the sublime stanza that has become the doxology of the Church of Sweden:

> Bless us, Father, and protect us,
> Be our souls' sure hiding-place;
> Let Thy wisdom still direct us,
> Light our darkness with Thy grace!
> Let Thy countenance on us shine,
> Fill us all with peace divine.
> Praise the Father, Son, and Spirit,
> Praise Him all that life inherit!

Swedberg was elevated to the bishopric of Skara in 1702. He died in 1735, universally mourned by the Swedish people.

Haqvin Spegel, who collaborated with Swedberg in the preparation of his hymn-book, was the more gifted poet of the two. It was he who, by his hymns, fixed the language forms that subsequently became the model for Swedish hymnody. Although Spegel never stooped to sickly sentimentality, his hymns are so filled with the spirit of personal faith and fervent devotion that they rise to unusual lyric heights. A sweet pastoral fragrance breathes through the hymn, "We Christians should ever consider," as the following stanza testifies:

> The lilies, nor toiling nor spinning,
> Their clothing how gorgeous and fair!
> What tints in their tiny orbs woven,
> What wondrous devices are there!
> All Solomon's stores could not render
> One festival robe of such splendor
> As modest field lilies do wear.

His communion hymn, "The death of Jesus Christ, our Lord," is a classic example of how Spegel could set forth in song the objective truths of the Christian faith.

> The death of Jesus Christ, our Lord,
> We celebrate with one accord;
> It is our comfort in distress,
> Our heart's sweet joy and happiness.
> He blotted out with His own blood
> The judgment that against us stood;
> He full atonement for us made,
> And all our debt He fully paid.
> That this is so and ever true

He gives an earnest ever new,
In this His Holy Supper, here
We taste His love, so sweet, so near.
For His true body, as He said,
And His own blood, for sinners shed,
In this communion we receive:
His sacred Word we do believe.
O sinner, come with true intent
To turn to God and to repent,
To live for Christ, to die to sin,
And thus a holy life begin.

Spegel was given the highest ecclesiastical honor bestowed by his country when he was created archbishop in 1711. He died three years later.

Among the other hymn-writers who contributed hymns to Swedberg's noted book was Jacob Arrhenius, professor of history in the University of Upsala. This man, who devoted a great deal of his time to the financial affairs of the University, was also a richly-endowed spiritual poet. The intimate tenderness with which he sang the Saviour's praise had never before been attained in Swedish hymnody. It was he who wrote:

Jesus is my Friend most precious,
Never friend did love as He;
Can I leave this Friend so gracious,
Spurn His wondrous love for me?
No! nor friend nor foe shall sever
Me from Him who loves me so;
His shall be my will forever,
There above, and here below.

Wallin's Sublime Morning Hymn

Again Thy glorious sun doth rise,
I praise Thee, O my Lord;
With courage, strength, and hope renewed,
I touch the joyful chord.
On good and evil, Lord, Thy sun
Is rising as on me;
Let me in patience and in love
Seek thus to be like Thee.
May I in virtue and in faith,
And with Thy gifts content,
Rejoice beneath Thy covering wings,
Each day in mercy sent.
Safe with Thy counsel in my work,
Thee, Lord, I'll keep in view,
And feel that still Thy bounteous grace
Is every morning new.
Johan Olof Wallin, 1816.

DAVID'S HARP IN THE NORTHLAND

When Longfellow translated Tegnér's Swedish poem, "Children of the Lord's Supper," he introduced Johan Olof Wallin to the English-speaking world in the following lines:

> And with one voice
> Chimed in the congregation, and sang an anthem immortal
> Of the sublime Wallin, of David's harp in the Northland.

Wallin is Scandinavia's greatest hymnist and perhaps the foremost in the entire Christian Church during the Nineteenth century. The Swedish "Psalm-book" of 1819, which for more than a century has been the hymn-book of the Swedish people in the homeland and in other parts of the world, is in large measure the work of this one man. Of the 500 hymns in this volume, 128 are original hymns from his pen, 178 are revisions by Wallin, twenty-three are his translations, and thirteen are semi-originals based on the hymns of other authors. In brief, no less than 342 of the hymns of the "Psalm-book" reflect the genius of this remarkable writer.

Early in life Wallin began to reveal poetic talent. Born at Stora Tuna, Dalarne province, in 1779, he overcame the handicaps of poverty and poor health and at the age of twenty-four he had gained the degree of Doctor of Philosophy at the University of Upsala. In 1805, and again in 1809, he won the chief prize for poetry at the University.

In 1806 he was ordained to the Lutheran ministry. Very soon he began to attract attention by his able preaching. In 1812 he was transferred to Stockholm, and in 1816 he became dean of Vesterås. In 1824 he was elevated to the bishopric, and thirteen years later became Primate of the Church of Sweden when he was made Archbishop of Upsala. He died in 1839.

As early as 1807 Wallin had begun to publish collections of old and new hymns. He possessed the rare ability of translating sacred poetry of other lands in such a way that often the translation excelled the original in virility and beauty.

In 1811 a commission was appointed by the Swedish parliament to prepare a new hymn-book to succeed that of Jesper Swedberg, which had been in use for more than a century. Wallin was made a member of this body. Within three years the commission presented its labors in the form of a first draft. However, it did not meet with universal favor, nor was Wallin himself satisfied with the result. By this time Wallin's genius had been revealed so clearly that the commission was moved to charge him with the entire task of completing the "Psalm-book." He gladly undertook the work and on November 28, 1816, he was able to report that he had finished his labors. A few minor changes were subsequently made, but on January 29, 1819, the new hymn-book was officially authorized by King Karl XIV. It has remained in use until the present day.

Unfortunately, Wallin's hymns have not become generally known outside of his own native land. It is only in recent years that a number have been translated into English. One of these is his famous Christmas hymn, which for more than a century has been sung in every sanctuary in Sweden as a greeting to the dawn of Christmas day. The first stanza reflects something of the glory of the Christmas evangel itself:

> All hail to thee, O blessed morn!
> To tidings long by prophets borne
> Hast thou fulfilment given.
> O sacred and immortal day,
> When unto earth, in glorious ray,
> Descends the grace of heaven!
> Singing,
> Ringing
> Sounds are blending,
> Praises sending
> Unto heaven
> For the Saviour to us given.

Although Wallin reverenced the old traditional hymns of the Church in spite of their many defects in form and language, he was unrelenting in his demand that every new hymn adopted by the Church should be tested by the severest classical standards. "A new hymn," he declared, "aside from the spiritual considerations which should never be compromised in any way, should be so correct, simple and lyrical in form, and so free from inversions and other imperfections in style, that after the lapse of a hundred years a father may be able to say to his son, 'Read the Psalm-book, my boy, and you will learn your mother tongue!'"

The profound influence which Wallin's hymns have exerted over the Swedish language and literature for more than a century is an eloquent testimony, not only to his poetic genius, but also to the faithfulness with which he adhered to the high standards he cherished.

The charge has sometimes been made that a number of Wallin's hymns are tinged by the spirit of rationalism. It is true that in his earlier years the great Swedish hymnist was strongly influenced by the so-called "New Theology," which had swept over all Europe at that time. His poems and hymns from this period bear unmistakable marks of these rationalizing tendencies. Even some of the hymns in the first part of the "Psalm-book," dealing with the person and attributes of God, are not entirely free from suspicion.

However, as Wallin became more and more absorbed in his great task, his own spiritual life seems to have been deepened and a new and richer note began to ring forth from his hymns. In 1816 this change was made manifest in an address Wallin delivered before the Swedish Bible Society, in which he declared war on rationalism and the "New Theology," and took his stand squarely upon the faith and confessions of the Lutheran Church. He said:

"So far had we traveled in what our age termed 'enlightenment' and another age shall call 'darkness,' that the very Word of God ... was regarded as a sort of contribution to the ancient history which had already served its purpose and was needed no more."

The atonement of Christ now became the central theme in his hymn-book, the pure evangelical tone of which may be heard in one of his own hymns:

There is a truth so dear to me,
I'll hold it fast eternally,
It is my soul's chief treasure:
That Jesus for the world hath died,
He for my sins was crucified—
O love beyond all measure!
O blessed tidings of God's grace,
That He who gave the thief a place
To paradise will take me
And God's own child will make me!

Kind Shepherd, Son of God, to Thee
Mine eyes, my heart, so yearningly,
And helpless hands are lifted.
From Thee I strayed; ah, leave me not,
But cleanse my soul from each dark blot,
For I am sore afflicted.
A wandering sheep, but now restored,
Ah, bear me to Thy fold, dear Lord,
And let me leave Thee never,
O Thou who lovest ever!

Again we find him giving expression to faith's certainty in a stanza that has become very dear to the Swedish people:

Blessed, blessed he who knoweth
That his faith on Thee is founded,
Whom the Father's love bestoweth
Of eternal grace unbounded,
Jesus Christ, to every nation
A Redeemer freely given,
In whose Name is our salvation,
And none else in earth or heaven.

The poetic utterance and exalted language of Wallin's hymns made him the hymnist par excellence for festival days, as witness the quotation above from his Christmas hymn and the following stanza from his Ascension hymn:

To realms of glory I behold
My risen Lord returning;
While I, a stranger on the earth,
For heaven am ever yearning.
Far from my heavenly Father's home,
'Mid toil and sorrow here I roam.

His metrical version of the Te Deum Laudamus is also an impressive example of the poetic genius of this master psalmist:

Jehovah, Thee we glorify,
Ruler upon Thy throne on high!
O let Thy Word
Through all the earth be heard.
Holy, holy, holy art Thou, O Lord!
Thou carest gently for Thy flock;
Thy Church, firm-founded on the Rock,
No powers dismay
Until Thy dreadful day.
Holy, holy, holy art Thou, O Lord!
All nations, in her fold comprised,
Shall bow their knees unto the Christ,
All tongues shall raise
Their orisons and praise:
Holy, holy, holy art Thou, O Lord!
Around Thy throne the countless throng
At last in triumph swell the song,
When Cherubim
Shall answer Seraphim:
Holy, holy, holy art Thou, O Lord!

Although a hymn usually loses much of its original expression in translation, something of the rare beauty in Wallin's poetry is still apparent in the following:

Where is the Friend for whom I'm ever yearning?
My longing grows when day to night is turning;
And though I find Him not as day recedeth,
My heart still pleadeth.
His hand I see in every force and power,
Where waves the harvest and where blooms the flower;
In every breath I draw, my spirit burneth:
His love discerneth.

When summer winds blow gently, then I hear Him;
Where sing the birds, where rush the streams, I'm near Him;
But nearer still when in my heart He blesses
Me with caresses.
O where such beauty is itself revealing
In all that lives, through all creation stealing,
What must the Source be whence it comes, the Giver?
Beauty forever!

Other noble hymns by the Swedish archbishop recently translated into English include "Behold, the joyful day is nigh," "Guardian of pure hearts," "I know in Whom I trust," "Great joy and consolation," "He lives! O fainting heart, anew," "Mute are the pleading lips of Him," "Thine agony, O Lord, is o'er," "A voice, a heavenly voice I hear," "Heavenly Light, benignly beaming," "Father of lights, eternal Lord," "In my quiet contemplation," "Jerusalem, lift up thy voice," "Jesus, Lord and precious Saviour," "O blessed is the man who stays," "O let the children come to Me," "Strike up, O harp and psaltery," "Watch, my soul and pray," and "Again Thy glorious sun doth rise."

Wallin's "Psalm-book" has aroused the greatest admiration wherever it has become known. The hymnologists of Germany, including Mohnike, Knapp, Weiss and Wackernagel, have given it undivided praise. Mohnike declared, "This is undoubtedly the most excellent hymn-book in the entire Evangelical Church, and, if translated, it would become the hymn-book for all Christian people." Knapp concurs by saying, "The Scriptural content of this book is clothed in the most beautiful classical language; there is nothing in Evangelical Germany to equal it."

A Vision of Christ's Triumph

Thy scepter, Jesus, shall extend
As far as day prevaileth.
Thy glorious kingdom, without end,
Shall stand when all else faileth,
Thy blessed Name shall be confessed,
And round Thy cross, forever blest,
Shall kings and people gather.
The child when born to Thee we take,
To Thee in death we hasten;
In joy we often Thee forsake,
But not when sorrows chasten.
Where truth and virtue are oppressed,
Where sorrow dwells, pain and unrest,
Thy help alone availeth.
Come, Jesus, then, in weal and woe,
In life and death be near us;
Thy grace upon our hearts bestow,
And let Thy Spirit cheer us,
For every conflict strength afford,
And gather us in peace, O Lord,
When all the world Thou judgest.
Frans Michael Franzén, 1816

THE GOLDEN AGE OF SWEDISH HYMNODY

Archbishop Wallin was not alone in the preparation of that masterpiece of Northern hymnody known as the "Swedish Psalm-book of 1819." Although the lion's share of the task fell to the lot of the gifted psalmist, he was aided by a number of the greatest spiritual poets in Scandinavian history. It was the golden age in Swedish hymnody, when such men as Franzén, Hedborn, Geijer, Åström, Afzelius and Nyström were singing "the glories of the Lamb."

Foremost in this unusual group was the beloved Frans Michael Franzén, a lyric poet of singular talent. Born at Uleaborg, Finland, in 1772, he held a number of positions at the University of Åbo, and later removed to Sweden, where he became pastor of St. Clara church, in Stockholm, and eventually Bishop of Hernösand. He died in 1847.

Franzén early became associated with Wallin and exerted a strong influence over the latter. Though not as prolific a writer as Wallin, the hymns of Franzén are rich in content and finished in form. Because of their artless simplicity it has been said that "the cultured man will appreciate them and the unlettered man can understand them." Among the most popular are two evening hymns—"The day departs, yet Thou art near" and "When vesper bells are calling." The latter is a hymn of solemn beauty:

When vesper bells are calling
The hour of rest and prayer,
When evening shades are falling,
And I must hence repair,

I seek my chamber narrow,
Nor my brief day deplore,
For I shall see the morrow,
When night shall be no more.
O take me in Thy keeping,
Dear Father, good and just,
Let not my soul be sleeping
In sin, and pride, and lust.
If in my life Thou guide me
According to Thy will,
I may in death confide me
Into Thy keeping still.

The voice of gracious invitation heard in Franzén's communion hymn, "Thine own, O loving Saviour," has called millions of hungering souls to the Lord's Supper. His hymn for the first communion of catechumens, "Come, O Jesus, and prepare me," is also regarded as the most appealing of its kind in Swedish hymnody. The stirring note in his hymn of repentance, "Awake, the watchman crieth," reveals Franzén as a poet of power and virility as well as a writer of the more meditative kind. The same solemn appeal, although expressed in less severe language, is also heard in his other call to repentance:

Ajar the temple gates are swinging,
Lo! still the grace of God is free.
Perhaps when next the bells are ringing
The grave shall open unto thee,
And thou art laid beneath the sod,
No more to see this house of God.

Franzén was recently accorded a unique honor in America when his soul-gripping Advent hymn, "Prepare the way, O Zion," was made the opening hymn in the Hymnal of the Augustana Synod. This hymn-book contains more translations of Swedish hymns than any other volume published in America.

When we add to the hymns already mentioned such beautiful compositions as "Thy scepter, Jesus, shall extend," "Look to Jesus Christ thy Saviour," and "The little while I linger here," it will readily be understood why Franzén ranks so high among the foremost hymnists of the North.

To Samuel Johan Hedborn, another of Wallin's contemporaries, posterity will ever be grateful for "Holy Majesty, before Thee," a magnificent hymn of praise that for loftiness of poetic sentiment and pure spiritual exaltation has probably never been excelled. The first stanza suggests something of the heavenly beauty of this noble hymn:

Holy Majesty, before Thee
We bow to worship and adore Thee;
With grateful hearts to Thee we sing.
Earth and heaven tell the story
Of Thine eternal might and glory,
And all Thy works their incense bring.
Lo, hosts of Cherubim
And countless Seraphim
Sing, Hosanna,
Holy is God, almighty God,
All-merciful and all-wise God!

Hedborn, who was the son of a poverty-stricken Swedish soldier, was born in Heda, Sweden, in the year 1783. He began his career as a school teacher, served for a while as court preacher, and finally became pastor at Askeryd, where he died in 1849. He was a gifted writer, and his lyric poetry and folk-songs struck a responsive chord in Swedish hearts. In 1812 he published a collection of hymns, and in the following year a second volume appeared. It is claimed that the Christo-centric note in Hedborn's hymns profoundly influenced Wallin and helped to establish the latter in the orthodox Lutheran teaching.

In addition to the sublime Te Deum mentioned above, two other hymns of Hedborn have been given English dress. One of these is the beautiful Epiphany hymn, "Now Israel's hope in triumph ends"; the other is the communion hymn, "With holy joy my heart doth beat."

Erik Gustav Geijer, professor of history in Upsala University, was another of the poetic geniuses of this golden age in Swedish hymnody. He was born at Ransäter, Värmland, Sweden, in the same year that witnessed Hedborn's birth—1783. Like Hedborn, he also published a little collection of hymns in 1812 which immediately focused attention upon him as a poet of unusual ability. Although his hymns do not rise to the artistic heights attained by his other poems, it is believed that Geijer purposely avoided high-sounding phrases as unworthy of the dignity and spirit of hymnody.

His passion hymn, "Thy Cross, O Jesus, Thou didst bear," is a gripping portrayal of the conquering power of the Saviour's sacrificial love. There is likewise a glorious note of victory heard in his Easter hymn:

In triumph our Redeemer
Is now to life returned.
All praise to Him who, dying,
Hath our salvation earned!
No more death's fetter galls us,
The grave no more appalls us,
For Jesus lives again.

In glory Thou appearest,
And earth is filled with light;
With resurrection radiance
The very tomb is bright;

There's joy in heavenly places
When o'er all earthly races
The dawn of mercy breaks.

In the preparation of the "Psalm-book," there was no one on whom Archbishop Wallin leaned so heavily for help and counsel as Johan Åström, parish priest in Simtuna and Altuna. This man, who was born in 1767, was a lyric poet of unusual ability, and Wallin valued his judgment very highly, even to the extent of seeking his criticism of his own hymns. Eighteen of the hymns in the "Psalm-book" are from Åström's pen. Many of them, however, are unfortunately tinged by the spirit of rationalism, from which influence Åström had not quite been able to free himself. Instead of emphasizing trust in the Saviour's merits as the true way to eternal life, there is a strong suggestion in Åström's hymns that the heavenly goal is achieved by walking in the Saviour's footsteps. Witness, for example:

Lord, disperse the mists of error,
In Thy light let me see light;
Give Thou me that faith and visior
Whereby I may walk aright,
In my Saviour's path discerning,
Through this vale of doubt and strife,
Footsteps to eternal life.

We are immeasurably indebted to Åström, however, for the present form of the glorious All Saints' hymn, "In heaven above, in heaven above." This hymn, in which we almost may discern something of the celestial radiance and beauty of the heavenly country, is ranked as one of the finest hymns in the Swedish "Psalm-book." It is more than three centuries old, dating back in its original form to 1620. It was written by L. Laurentii Laurinus, parish pastor in Häradshammar, at the time of his wife's death, and was appended to the funeral sermon preached by a brother pastor. Åström recognized the rare beauty of the hymn and through his poetic genius it was clothed in immortal language. William Maccall, a Scotchman, has in turn rendered it into English in such a faithful manner that much of its original beauty is preserved.

In heaven above, in heaven above,
Where God our Father dwells:
How boundless there the blessedness!
No tongue its greatness tells:
There face to face, and full and free,
Ever and evermore we see—
We see the Lord of hosts!
In heaven above, in heaven above,
What glory deep and bright!
The splendor of the noon-day sun
Grows pale before its light:
The mighty Sun that ne'er goes down,

Around whose gleam clouds never frown,
Is God the Lord of hosts.
In heaven above, in heaven above,
No tears of pain are shed:
There nothing e'er shall fade or die;
Life's fullness round is spread,
And like an ocean, joy o'erflows,
And with immortal mercy glows
Our God the Lord of hosts.
In heaven above, in heaven above,
God hath a joy prepared
Which mortal ear hath never heard,
Nor mortal vision shared,
Which never entered mortal breast,
By mortal lips was ne'er expressed,
O God the Lord of hosts!

Arvid Afzelius, court chaplain and pastor at Enköping, was another member of this remarkable group of Swedish hymnists that contributed to the "Psalm-book" of Wallin. Afzelius, who was an authority on folk songs, has given us the inspiring hymn of praise beginning:

Unto the Lord of all creation
Thy voice, my soul, in anthems raise.
Let every heart a fit oblation
Bring unto Him with songs of praise.
O contemplate in humbleness
The power and riches of His grace.

Johan Hjertén, an obscure country pastor at Hellstad, was the author of six hymns in the "Psalm-book," among them the devotional hymn, "Jesus, in my walk and living." It is said that the artless simplicity of his hymns provided an excellent pattern for the other writers of his day, many of whom were fond of the grandiloquent phrases so characteristic of the rationalist hymnody.

The last name of this group we would mention is that of a layman, Per Olof Nyström. This man, who was a high naval officer, wrote many excellent hymns, among them a devotional lyric that for more than a hundred years has been cherished almost as a national prayer by the pious folk of Sweden. Its first stanza reads:

O Fount of truth and mercy,
Thy promise cannot fail;
What Thou hast said must ever
In heaven and earth prevail;
"Call upon Me in trouble,
And I will help afford."
Yea, to my latest moment,
I'll call upon Thee, Lord.

A Longing for Home

Jerusalem, Jerusalem,
Thou city ever blest,
Within thy portals first I find
My safety, peace, and rest.
Here dangers always threaten me,
My days in strife are spent,
And labor, sorrow, worry, grief,
I find at best their strength.
No wonder, then, that I do long,
O blessed home, for thee,
Where I shall find a resting-place,
From sin and sorrow free;
Where tears and weeping are no more,
Nor death, nor pain, nor night,
For former things are passed away,
And darkness turned to light.
Now all for me has lost its charm
Which by the world is praised,
Since on the cross, through faith, I saw
My Saviour Jesus raised;
My goal is fixed, one thing I ask,
Whate'er the cost may be,
Jerusalem, Jerusalem,
Soon to arrive in thee.
Carolina Vilhelmina (Sandell) Berg (1832-1903).

THE FANNY CROSBY OF SWEDEN AND THE PIETISTS

As will be noted in a subsequent chapter, the Nineteenth century witnessed the phenomenon of gifted Christian women assuming a place of primary importance among the foremost hymn-writers of the Church. Just as England had its Charlotte Elliott and Frances Havergal, and America had its Fanny Crosby, so Sweden had its Lina Sandell.

The rise of women hymn-writers came simultaneously with the great spiritual revival which swept over America and evangelical Europe in successive tidal waves from 1800 to 1875. In Sweden the religious renaissance received its first impulse, no doubt, from Lutheran Germany. However, the Wesleyan movement in England and America also began to make its influence felt in wider circles, and the coming to Stockholm of such a man as George Scott, an English Methodist, gave added impetus to the evangelical movement which was already under way. Carl Olof Rosenius, Sweden's greatest lay preacher and the most prominent leader in the Pietistic movement in that country, was one of Scott's disciples, although he remained faithful to the Lutheran doctrine and a member of the Established Church to the close of his life.

It was in the midst of the Rosenius movement that Lina Sandell became known to her countrymen as a great song-writer. She was born October 3, 1832, at Fröderyd, her father being the parish pastor at that place. She was a frail child who preferred to spend her hours in her father's study rather than join her comrades in play. When she was twenty-six years old, she accompanied him on a journey to Gothenburg, but they never reached their destination. At Hästholmen the vessel on which they sailed gave a sudden lurch and the father fell overboard, drowning before the eyes of his devoted daughter.

This tragedy proved a turning point in Lina Sandell's life. In the midst of her grief she sought comfort in writing hymns. Her songs seemed to pour forth in a steady stream from the depths of a broken heart. Fourteen of her hymns were published anonymously the same year (1858) in a Christian periodical, Budbäraren. Although she lived to write 650 hymns in all, these fourteen from the pen of the grief-stricken 26-year-old girl have retained a stronger hold on the hearts of her countrymen than most of her later productions. Among these "first-fruits" born in sorrow are such hymns as: "Saviour, O hide not Thy loving face from me," "Others He hath succored," and

> Children of the heavenly Father
> Safely in His bosom gather;
> Nestling bird nor star in heaven
> Such a refuge e'er was given.

The remarkable popularity which Lina Sandell's hymns attained within a comparatively short time was due to a large extent to the music written for them by Oskar Ahnfelt, a "spiritual troubadour" of his day. Ahnfelt not only possessed the gift of composing pleasing melodies that caught the fancy of the Swedish people, but he traveled from place to place throughout the Scandinavian countries and sang them to the accompaniment of a guitar. Miss Sandell once said: "Ahnfelt has sung my songs into the hearts of the people."

The inspiration for her songs came to Miss Sandell at sundry times and places. Sometimes in the midst of the noise and confusion of the city's streets, she would hear the words of a new song. Sometimes she would awake in the still hours of the night with the verses of a hymn ringing in her ears. By her bedside she always kept a slate on which she might instantly record these heaven-born thoughts.

In 1867 Miss Sandell was married to a Stockholm merchant, C. O. Berg, but she continued to sign her hymns with the initials, "L. S." by which she was familiarly known throughout Sweden. She died on July 27, 1903.

Not only Ahnfelt, but also Jenny Lind helped to make Lina Sandell's hymns known. The "Swedish nightingale" was herself a Pietist and found great delight in listening to the preaching of Rosenius and the singing of Ahnfelt. At these conventicles the marvelous singer who had gained the homage of two continents sat with common workingmen on crude benches and joined with her sweet voice in singing the Pietist hymns. Ahnfelt, in visiting the home of the great singer, spoke of his ambition to publish these hymns. When Jenny Lind learned that financial difficulties stood in the way, she quickly provided the necessary funds, and so the first edition of "Ahnfelt's Songs," which in reality were mostly the hymns of Lina Sandell and Rosenius, was made possible.

Rosenius and Ahnfelt encountered much persecution in their evangelical efforts. King Karl XV was petitioned to forbid Ahnfelt's preaching and singing. The monarch refused until he had had an opportunity to hear the "spiritual troubadour." Ahnfelt was commanded to appear at the royal palace. Being considerably perturbed in mind as to what he should sing to the king, he besought Lina Sandell to write a hymn for the occasion. She was equal to the task and within a few days the song was ready. With his guitar under his arm and the hymn in his pocket, Ahnfelt repaired to the palace and sang:

> Who is it that knocketh upon your heart's door
> In peaceful eve?
> Who is it that brings to the wounded and sore
> The balm that can heal and relieve?
> Your heart is still restless, it findeth no peace
> In earth's pleasures;
> Your soul is still yearning, it seeketh release
> To rise to the heavenly treasures.

The king listened with tears in his eyes. When Ahnfelt had finished, the monarch gripped him by the hand and exclaimed: "You may sing as much as you like in both of my kingdoms!"

Mention has already been made of the hymns of Rosenius. These, like the songs of Lina Sandell, were likewise a powerful factor in the spread of the evangelical movement in Sweden.

Rosenius was the son of a parish pastor in Norrland, Sweden. From the time of his birth, February 3, 1816, he was dedicated by his pious parents to the holy ministry. After having pursued studies for a short time at Upsala University, however, he became disgusted with the low moral and spiritual standards existing among the students, and for a while his own faith was severely shaken. During these spiritual difficulties he came in contact with George Scott, the Methodist evangelist in Stockholm, and eventually he began to hold meetings as a "lay preacher."

In 1842 Scott and Rosenius began the publication of Pietisten, a religious monthly that was destined to play a most important part in the spiritual revival in Sweden. When Scott was constrained the same year to leave Sweden because of violent opposition to his movement, Rosenius became his successor, not only as editor of Pietisten, but also as the outstanding leader among those who were trying to bring about the dawn of a new spiritual day.

Rosenius centered his activity in the Swedish capital, preaching and writing. He also traveled extensively throughout the country, and so the movement spread. Numerous lay preachers, known as "läsare," sprang up everywhere, holding private meetings in homes and in so-called "mission houses" that were built nearby the parish churches.

Agitation for separation from the Established Church found no sympathy with Rosenius, who stood firmly on the Lutheran doctrine and regularly took communion at the hands of its ordained ministers.

"How long do you intend to remain within the Church?" he once was asked.

"As long as Jesus is there," was the answer of Rosenius.

"But how long do you think He will be there?"

"As long as men are there born anew, for that is not the work of the devil."

In 1856 Rosenius, together with many earnest-minded ecclesiasts and leaders in the Established Church, organized the National Evangelical Foundation, which originally was intended to promote home and inner mission activities. It subsequently embraced the cause of foreign missions also and became one of the greatest spiritual influences emanating from Scandinavia. Rosenius died in 1868, at the age of fifty-two.

His hymns, like those of Lina Sandell, became known largely through the musical genius of Ahnfelt. Everywhere "Ahnfelt's Songs" were on the lips of the so-called "believers." Emigrants from Sweden to America brought them with them to the New World, where they were a source of solace and strength in the midst of spiritual and material difficulties. Perhaps no song verse was heard more often in their humble gatherings than the concluding stanza of Rosenius' hymn, "With God and His mercy, His Spirit, and Word":

O Shepherd, abide with us, care for us still,
And feed us and lead us and teach us Thy will;
And when in Thy heavenly fold we shall be,
Our thanks and our praises,
Our thanks and our praises we'll render to Thee.

Then there is that other hymn by Rosenius, so dear to thousands of pious souls, "I have a Friend, so patient, kind, forbearing," as well as that other one which Miss Anna Hoppe has so beautifully rendered into English:

O precious thought! some day the mist shall vanish;
Some day the web of gloom shall be unspun.
A day shall break whose beams the night shall banish,
For Christ, the Lamb, shall shine, the glorious Sun!

Although the songs of Lina Sandell and Rosenius do not attain to the poetic excellence and spiritual power of the noble hymns of Wallin's "Psalm-book," it is a significant fact that seven of Lina Sandell's and three of Rosenius' songs were included in an appendix adopted in 1920. This appendix is the first authorized change in Archbishop Wallin's masterpiece in 102 years. The 500 hymns of the "Psalm-book" still remain unchanged, however, as they came from his hand in 1819. Although a number of commissions have endeavored since 1865 to make revisions of Wallin's work, their proposals have been consistently rejected. The addition of 173 hymns in the form of an appendix was a compromise adopted by the Church of Sweden in 1920. It was sanctioned by the king and authorized for tentative use in the churches beginning Nov. 27, 1921, thus being given precedence over a revision made by a commission and sanctioned by the church but indefinitely deferred.

In the 1921 appendix hymn-writers of the Reformed Church are represented for the first time in the Swedish "Psalm-book." Among the Reformed hymns found there may be mentioned Joachim Neander's "Lobe den Herren," Sarah Flower Adams' "Nearer, my

God, to Thee," Henry Francis Lyte's "Abide with me, fast falls the eventide," John Marriot's "Thou, Whose almighty Word," and Lydia Baxter's "There is a gate that stands ajar." Classical Lutheran hymns, such as Gerhardt's "O sacred Head, now wounded" and Luther's "Lord, keep us steadfast in Thy Word," have also been added, while other Lutheran writers, such as the great Danish hymnists, Brorson and Grundtvig, and the Norwegian psalmist, Landstad, are given recognition. Then there is the beautiful Christmas hymn, "Silent night, holy night," by the Catholic priest, Joseph Mohr.

The more important of recent Swedish hymnists are Johan Alfred Eklund, bishop of Karlstad, who is represented by thirty-six hymns in the appendix; Svante Alin, pastor at Sventorp, eleven of whose hymns are included; the late Edvard Evers, pastor in Norrköping and a writer of some note, who contributed twelve hymns, and Erik Söderberg, writer and publicist, who is the author of seven.

Eleven hymns by two of Finland's great poets, Johan Ludvig Runeberg and Zachris Topelius, are also found in the appendix.

Kingo's Sunrise Hymn

The sun arises now
In light and glory,
And gilds the rugged brow
Of mountains hoary;
Be glad, my soul, and lift
Thy voice in singing
To God from earth below,
Thy heart with joy aglow
And praises ringing.
Like countless grains of sand,
Beyond all measure,
And wide as sea and land
Is heaven's treasure
Of grace which God anew
Each day bestoweth,
And which, like pouring rain,
Into my soul again
Each morning floweth.
Keep Thou my soul today
From sin and blindness;
Surround me on my way
With loving-kindness,
And fill my heart, O God,
With joy from heaven;
I then shall ask no more
Than what Thou hast of yore
In wisdom given.
Thou knowest best my needs,
My sighs Thou heedest;

Thy hand Thy children feeds,
Thine own Thou leadest;
What should I more desire,
With Thee deciding
The course that I must take
Than follow in the wake
Where Thou art guiding?
Thomas Kingo (1634-1703).

KINGO, THE POET OF EASTER-TIDE

Denmark's first great hymnist, Thomas Kingo, hailed from the land of Robert Burns. His grandfather, who also bore the name of Thomas, emigrated from Scotland to Denmark near the end of the 17th century to become a tapestry weaver for Christian IV.

The boy who was destined to become one of Denmark's most famous spiritual bards was born in Slangerup, December 15, 1634. At the age of six years he entered the Latin school of his native city, and ten years later became a student of the school in Frederiksborg. The principal of this institution, Albert Bartholin, discovered unusual gifts in the lad and took him into his own home. After completing theological studies at the university, he returned in 1668 to his native city of Slangerup as Lutheran parish pastor.

About this time he began to attract attention as a writer of secular poetry. It was not until 1673, however, that his first collection of hymns appeared under the title, "Spiritual Songs, First Part." The profound impression created by this production is evidenced by the fact that in 1677 he was elevated from an obscure parish to the bishopric of the diocese of Fyen.

Kingo had dedicated his "Spiritual Songs" to Christian V, and thus had attracted the attention of the Danish monarch. In his "address" to the king, Kingo deplored the fact that the Danish people in their worship had depended so largely upon hymns of foreign origin.

"The soul of the Danes," he added significantly, "is not so bound and impoverished but that it can soar as high toward heaven as that of other peoples, even if it be not upborne by strange and foreign wings."

The Second Part of his "Spiritual Songs" appeared in 1681, this collection being dedicated to the Danish queen. Many of Kingo's hymns were written to be sung to popular folk melodies. In justification of this practice the poet wrote:

"If a pleasing melody set to a song of Sodom delights your ear, how much more, if you are a true child of God, should not that same melody delight your soul when sung to a song of Zion!"

In his dedicatory address to Queen Charlotte, the poet of Scotch forebears gave expression to his great love for the Danish language, praised her for her heroic efforts to master the language before coming to Denmark as its queen, and ironically flayed certain foreign courtiers who for "thirty years had eaten the bread of the Fatherland in the service of the king without making an effort to learn thirty Danish words."

By this time the Danish people had come to a full realization that a poet of the first magnitude had risen in their midst. In June, 1679, Kingo was created a member of the nobility, and in 1682 he received the honorary degree of doctor of theology. The following year came the royal appointment to prepare a hymn-book for the Church of Denmark. The king's decree specifically stated that Kingo should include a number of his own hymns, but he was directed to make few changes in the old, traditional hymns, and "under no circumstances to alter the meaning of Luther's hymns."

The first part of Kingo's new book appeared in 1689. It met with a storm of disapproval that was not altogether unmerited. Of the 267 hymns in this book, 136 were by Kingo himself. Members of the Danish court who had been objects of Kingo's merciless satire now found an opportunity to secure revenge. Kingo's book, which had been published at his own expense, was rejected, and Soren Jonassen, dean of Roskilde, was appointed to take over the task. His work, which was completed in 1693, did not contain a single one of Kingo's hymns! It too was promptly disapproved. A commission was then appointed by the king to supervise the work, and again Kingo came into favor. The new hymn-book, which was officially approved in 1699, was based largely on Kingo's work, and contained 85 of his original hymns.

Although Kingo lived to see his life-work crowned with success, he never recovered from the indignity and humiliation he had suffered. His death occurred on October 14, 1703. The day before his death, he exclaimed: "Tomorrow, Lord, we shall hear glorious music."

Kingo has been called "the poet of Easter-tide." A biographer declares that Kingo was "in love with the sun," and that he regarded light as the "true element." This is reflected in his morning hymns, which are among the finest songs of praise ever written. It may also be seen in his Easter hymns, one of which begins with the words, "Like the golden sun ascending." However, Kingo could also dwell on the theme of Christ's passion with gripping pathos:

> Such a night was ne'er before,
> Even heaven has shut its door;
> Jesus, Thou our Sun and Light,
> Now must bear the shame of night.

And in this:

> See how, in that hour of darkness,
> Battling with the evil power,
> Agonies untold assail Him,
> On His soul the arrows shower;
> And the gardens flowers are wet
> With the drops of bloody sweat

From His anguished frame distilling—
Our redemption thus fulfilling.

When the commission appointed by the Danish king was revising his hymn-book, Kingo pleaded that his Lenten hymns might be retained. Among the most soul-stirring of these in the famous hymn, "Over Kedron Jesus treadeth." In its original form it contained fourteen stanzas. Although objective in character, Kingo's hymns never fail to make a strong personal appeal. Witness, for example, the following from his Good Friday hymn:

On my heart imprint Thine image,
Blessed Jesus, King of grace,
That life's riches, cares, and pleasures
Never may Thyself efface;
This the superscription be:
Jesus, crucified for me,
Is my life, my hope's foundation,
And my glory and salvation.

Other hymns of Kingo that have been translated into English include "Praise to Thee and adoration," "Dearest Jesus, draw Thou near me," "He that believes and is baptized," "O dearest Lord, receive from me," "I come, invited by Thy Word," "Softly now the day is ending," and "The sun arises now."

Grundtvig, a later Danish hymn-writer, pays Kingo this tribute: "He effected a combination of sublimity and simplicity, a union of splendor and fervent devotion, a powerful and musical play of words and imagery that reminds one of Shakespeare."

The Great White Host

Behold a host, arrayed in white,
Like thousand snow-clad mountains bright,
With palms they stand—who are this band
Before the throne of light?
Lo, these are they, of glorious fame,
Who from the great affliction came,
And in the flood of Jesus' blood
Are cleansed from guilt and blame;
Now gathered in the holy place
Their voices they in worship raise,
Their anthems swell where God doth dwell
'Mid angels' songs of praise.
Despised and scorned, they sojourned here,
But now, how glorious they appear!
These martyrs stand a priestly band,
God's throne forever near.
So oft, in troubled days gone by,
In anguish they would weep and sigh;
At home above, the God of love
The tears of all shall dry.
They now enjoy their Sabbath rest,

The paschal banquet of the blest;
The Lamb, their Lord, at festal board
Himself is host and guest.
Then hail, ye mighty legions, yea,
All hail! now safe and blest for aye;
And praise the Lord, who with His Word
Sustained you on the way.
Ye did the joys of earth disdain,
Ye toiled and sowed in tears and pain;
Farewell, now bring your sheaves, and sing
Salvation's glad refrain.
Swing high your palms, lift up your song,
Yea, make it myriad voices strong:
Eternally shall praise to Thee,
God, and the Lamb, belong!
Hans Adolph Brorson, 1763.

BRORSON, THE POET OF CHRISTMAS

No Scandinavian hymn has attained such popularity in recent years as "Behold a host." This sublime "glory song" was first given to the world after its writer, Hans Adolph Brorson, had gone to join the "host, arrayed in white" that sings "before the throne of light."

It was published by his son in a collection entitled "Hans Adolph Brorson's Swan-Song," which appeared in 1765, a year after the famous Danish hymn-writer had gone to his final rest. The collection contained seventy hymns, all written in the last year of the poet's life.

Brorson was a product of the Pietistic movement emanating from Halle, in Germany. Born June 20, 1694, at Randrup, Denmark, he early came under the influence of the great spiritual awakening which was then sweeping through the Lutheran Church.

Brorson's father was a Lutheran pastor, and all of his three sons, including the hymn-writer, entered the service of the Church. Brorson's first pastorate was in his native city of Randrup, a place he dearly loved and to which he often returned in later life when he found himself oppressed by manifold cares.

It was during his ministry in Randrup that Brorson began to write his first hymns. He speaks of the eight years spent at this place as the happiest in his life. In 1729 he was called to become Danish preacher at Tonder, where he labored side by side with Johan Herman Schrader, who was also a hymnist of some note. Because of the mixed Danish and German population of Tonder, a curious situation existed in the church worship. Although Brorson preached in Danish, the congregation sang in German! To remedy this, Brorson, in 1732, wrote a number of his famous Christmas hymns, among them 'Den yndigste Rose er funden,' one of the most exquisite gems in sacred poetry. A free rendering of four of its eleven stanzas by August W. Kjellstrand follows:

The sweetest, the fairest of roses
I've found. Among thorns it reposes:
'Tis Jesus, my soul's dearest Treasure,
Of sinners a Friend above measure.
E'er since the sad day when frail mortals
Were thrust from fair Eden's bright portals,
The world has been dark, full of terror,
And man dead in sin, lost in error.
Then mindful of promises given,
God sent from the gardens of heaven
A Rose, 'mid the thorns brightly blowing,
And freely its fragrance bestowing.
Wherever this Rose Tree is grounded,
The kingdom of God there is founded;
And where its sweet fragrance is wafted,
There peace in the heart is engrafted.

As Kingo was known among the Danes as "the poet of Easter," so Brorson from this time was hailed as "the poet of Christmas."

In 1747 Brorson was appointed by Christian VI to become bishop of the diocese of Ribe. It is said that the Danish monarch upon meeting Brorson at a certain occasion inquired of him if he was the author of the hymn, "Awake, all things that God has made." When the poet modestly answered in the affirmative, so the story runs, the king promised him the bishopric. When Erik Pontoppidan, later bishop of Bergen, was appointed to revise Kingo's hymnal, which for forty years had served the churches of Denmark and Norway, he found his task a comparatively simple one through the valuable assistance rendered by Brorson. Kingo's hymns were changed only slightly, and the greater part of the new material was from Brorson's pen.

The later years of the poet were darkened by sad experiences. In the year that Brorson was elevated to the bishopric, his beloved wife died while giving birth to their thirteenth child. This and other troubles served to make him melancholy in spirit, but he did not cease to compose poems of rarest beauty. His thoughts, however, turned more and more toward heaven and the blessedness of the life hereafter. A celestial radiance is reflected in the hymns of his "Swan-Song." This is particularly true of "Behold, a host arrayed in white," a lyric that has become a favorite in America as well as in Europe through its association with Edvard Grieg's famous adaptation of a Norwegian folk song.

Brorson's earnest character and pious nature made him deeply concerned about the salvation of souls. Many of his poems and hymns contain solemn warnings touching on the uncertainty of life and the need of seeking salvation. His gripping hymn, "Jeg gaar i Fare, hvor jeg gaar," gave Archbishop Wallin, the great Swedish hymnist, the inspiration for his noble stanzas:

I near the grave, where'er I go,
Where'er my pathway tendeth;
If rough or pleasant here below,
My way at death's gate endeth.

I have no other choice;
Between my griefs and joys
My mortal life is ordered so:
I near the grave, where'er I go.
I go to heaven, where'er I go,
If Jesus' steps I follow;
The crown of life He will bestow,
When earth this frame shall swallow.
If through this tearful vale
I in that course prevail,
And walk with Jesus here below,
I go to heaven, where'er I go.

Other well-known hymns by Brorson are "Thy little ones, dear Lord, are we," "O Father, may Thy Word prevail," "O watch and pray," "Life's day is ended," "My heart, prepare to give account," "By faith we are divinely sure," "Children of God, born again of His Spirit," "O seek the Lord today," "I see Thee standing, Lamb of God," "Stand fast, my soul, stand fast," "Jesus, Name of wondrous grace," and "Who will join the throng to heaven?" Brorson's childlike spirit may be seen reflected in the first of these, a children's Christmas hymn:

Thy little ones, dear Lord, are we,
And come Thy lowly bed to see;
Enlighten every soul and mind,
That we the way to Thee may find.
With songs we hasten Thee to greet,
And kiss the dust before Thy feet;
O blessed hour, O sweetest night,
That gave Thee birth, our soul's delight.

Now welcome! From Thy heavenly home
Thou to our vale of tears art come;
Man hath no offering for Thee, save
The stable, manger, cross, and grave.
Jesus, alas! how can it be
So few bestow a thought on Thee,
Or on the love, so wondrous great,
That drew Thee down to our estate?
O draw us wholly to Thee, Lord,
Do Thou to us Thy grace accord,
True faith and love to us impart,
That we may hold Thee in our heart.

A Prayer to the Holy Spirit

Holy Spirit, come with light,
Break the dark and gloomy night
With Thy day unending;
Help us with a joyful lay
Greet the Lord's triumphant day

Now with might ascending.
Comforter, so wondrous kind,
Noble Guest of heart and mind,
Fix in us Thy dwelling.
Give us peace in storm and strife,
Fill each weary heart and life
With Thy joy excelling.
Make salvation clear to us,
Who, despite our sin and cross,
Are in Thee confiding.
Lest our life be void and vain,
With Thy light and love remain
Aye in us abiding.
Raise or bow us with Thine arm,
Break temptation's evil charm,
Clear our clouded vision.
Fill our hearts with longings new,
Cleanse us with Thy morning dew,
Tears of deep contrition.
Thou who givest life and breath,
Let our hope in sight of death
Blossom bright and vernal;
And above the silent tomb
Let the Easter lilies bloom,
Signs of life eternal.
Nikolai Grundtvig (1783-1872).

GRUNDTVIG, THE POET OF WHITSUNTIDE

Nikolai F. S. Grundtvig was the last and greatest of the celebrated triumvirate of Danish hymn-writers. As Kingo was the bright star of the 17th century and Brorson of the 18th century, so Grundtvig shone with a luster all his own in the 19th century. The "poet of Easter" and the "poet of Christmas" were succeeded by the "poet of Whitsuntide."

The appellation given to Grundtvig was not without reason, for it was he, above all others, who strove mightily in Denmark against the deadening spirit of rationalism which had dried up the streams of spirituality in the Church. No one as he labored with such amazing courage and zeal to bring about the dawn of a new day.

Nor did Grundtvig strive in vain. Before his life-work was ended, fresh Pentecostal breezes began to blow, the dry bones began to stir, and the Church, moved by the Spirit of God, experienced a new spiritual birth.

The spirit of rationalism had worked havoc with the most sacred truths of the Christian religion. As some one has said, "It converted the banner of the Lamb into a blue-striped handkerchief, the Christian religion into a philosophy of happiness, and the temple dome into a parasol."

Under the influence of the "new theology," ministers of the gospel had prostituted the church worship into lectures on science and domestic economy. It is said that one minister in preaching on the theme of the Christ-child and the manger developed it into a lecture on the proper care of stables, and another, moved by the story of the coming of the holy women to the sepulcher on the first Easter morning, delivered a peroration on the advantages of getting up early! God was referred to as "Providence" or "the Deity," Christ as "the founder of Christianity," sin as "error," salvation as "happiness," and the essence of the Christian life as "morality."

Grundtvig's father was one of the few Lutheran pastors in Denmark who had remained faithful to evangelical truth. The future poet, who was born in Udby, September 8, 1783, had the advantage, therefore, of being brought up in a household where the spirit of true Christian piety reigned. It was not long, however, before young Grundtvig, as a student, came under the influence of the "new theology." Although he planned to become a minister, he lost all interest in religion during his final year at school, and finished his academic career "without spirit and without faith."

A number of circumstances, however, began to open his eyes to the spiritual poverty of the people. Morality was at a low ebb, and a spirit of indifference and frivolity banished all serious thoughts from their minds. It was a rude shock to his sensitive and patriotic nature to observe, in 1807, how the population of Copenhagen laughed and danced while the Danish fleet was being destroyed by English warships and the capital city itself was being bombarded by the enemy.

In 1810 he preached his famous probation sermon on the striking theme, "Why has the Word of God departed from His house?" The sermon produced a sensation, and from this time Grundtvig came to be known as a mystic and fanatic. His career as a pastor was checkered, but throughout his life he exerted a powerful influence by his literary activity as well as by his preaching. His poetry and hymns attracted so much attention that it was said that "Kingo's harp has been strung afresh."

Grundtvig's strongest hymns are those that deal with the Church and the sacraments. The divine character of the Church is continually stressed, for Christ not only founded it, but, as the Living Word, He is present in it and in the sacraments unto the end of time. "Built on the Rock, the Church doth stand" is probably his most famous hymn. Grundtvig was more concerned about the thought he was trying to convey than the mode of expression; therefore his hymns are often characterized by strength rather than poetic beauty. They are also so deeply tinged by national spirit and feeling that they lose much of the color and fragrance of their native heath when translated. That Grundtvig could rise to lyrical heights is revealed especially in his festival hymns. There is a charming freshness in the sweet Christmas hymn:

> Chime, happy Christmas bells, once more!
> The heavenly Guest is at the door,
> The blessed words the shepherds thrill,
> The joyous tidings, "Peace, good will."
> O let us go with quiet mind,
> The gentle Babe with shepherds find,

To gaze on Him who gladdens them,
The loveliest flower of Jesse's stem.
Come, Jesus, glorious heavenly Guest,
Keep Thine own Christmas in our breast,
Then David's harp-strings, hushed so long,
Shall swell our jubilee of song.

The Danish hymnologist Brandt has pointed out the distinctive characteristics of his country's three great hymnists by calling attention to their favorite symbols. That of Kingo was the sun, Brorson's the rose, and Grundtvig's the bird. Kingo extols Christ as the risen, victorious Saviour—the Sun that breaks through the dark shades of sin and death. Brorson glorifies Christ as the Friend of the spiritually poor and needy. They learn to know Him in the secret prayer chamber as the Rose that spreads its quiet fragrance. Grundtvig's hymns are primarily hymns of the Spirit. They laud the Holy Spirit, the Giver and Renewer of life, who bears us up on mighty wings toward the mansions of light.

Among Danes and Norwegians there are few hymns more popular than Grundtvig's hymn on the Church. The first stanza reads:

Built on the Rock the Church doth stand,
Even when steeples are falling;
Crumbled have spires in every land,
Bells still are chiming and calling;
Calling the young and old to rest,
But above all the soul distressed,
Longing for rest everlasting.

Other noted hymns by Grundtvig include "Love, the fount of light from heaven," "As the rose shall blossom here," "The Lord to thee appealeth," "Splendid are the heavens high," "A Babe is born in Bethlehem," "From the grave remove dark crosses," "O let Thy Spirit with us tarry," "Fair beyond telling," "This is the day that our Father hath given," "Hast to the plow thou put thy hand," "The peace of God protects our hearts," "O wondrous kingdom here on earth," "With gladness we hail this blessed day," "He who has helped me hitherto," and "Peace to soothe our bitter woes."

Because of his intensive efforts to bring about reforms in the educational methods of his day, Grundtvig became known as "the father of the public high school in Scandinavia."

In 1861, when he celebrated his golden jubilee as pastor, Grundtvig was given the title of bishop. The good old man passed away peacefully on September 2, 1872, at the age of eighty-nine years. He preached his last sermon on the day before his death.

A distinguished contemporary of Grundtvig's who also gained renown as a Danish hymn-writer was Bernhardt Severin Ingemann, author of the famous hymn, "Through the night of doubt and sorrow." Ingemann was born in Falster, Denmark, in 1789, the son of a Lutheran pastor, Soren Ingemann.

The father died when Bernhardt was 11 years old, but the mother made it possible for the gifted lad to receive a liberal education. At the age of 22 years he published his first volume of poems, and three years later his famous epic, "The Black Knights," appeared. A number of dramas followed, and in 1822 he was appointed lector of Danish language and literature at the Academy of Soro. Here he remained for forty years, writing novels, secular poetry and hymns. He was a warm friend of Grundtvig's, who constantly encouraged him in his literary efforts.

Ingemann's "Morning Hymns" appeared in 1822, and in 1825 his "Hymns of Worship" was published. In 1854 he was charged with the task of completing the "Psalm Book for Church and Private Devotion," edited by the ministerial conference at Roskilde.

A Norwegian Miserere

Before Thee, God, who knowest all,
With grief and shame I prostrate fall;
I see my sins against Thee, Lord,
The sins of thought, of deed, and word,
They press me sore, I cry to Thee;
O God, be merciful to me!
O Lord, My God, to Thee I pray:
O cast me not in wrath away,
Let Thy good Spirit ne'er depart,
But let Him draw to Thee my heart,
That truly penitent I be;
O God, be merciful to me!
O Jesus, let Thy precious blood
Be to my soul a cleansing flood;
Turn not, O Lord, Thy guest away,
But grant that justified I may
Go to my house with peace from Thee;
O God, be merciful to me!
Magnus Brorstrup Landstad, 1861.

LANDSTAD, A BARD OF THE FROZEN FJORDS

This is the story of a man whose chance purchase of two books at an auction sale for the sum of four cents was probably the means of inspiring him to become one of the foremost Christian poets of the North.

Magnus Brorstrup Landstad was a poverty-stricken student at the University of Christiania (now Oslo), Norway, when he happened to pass a house in which a sale of books was being conducted. Moved by curiosity, he entered the place just as a package of old books was being offered. We will let him tell the remainder of the story:

"I made a bid of four cents, the deal was made, and I walked home with my package. It contained two volumes in leather binding. One was 'Freuden-Spiegel des ewigen Lebens' by Philipp Nicolai. On the last few pages of this book four of Nicolai's hymns were printed. The other book was Bishop A. Arrebo's 'Hexaemeron, The Glorious and Mighty Works of the Creation Day.' In this manner two splendid hymn collections, one German and the other Danish-Norwegian, unexpectedly came into my possession. I was not acquainted with either of these works before. Nicolai's hymns made a deep impression on me, and I at once attempted to translate them.... My experience with these hymn collections, I believe, gave me the first impetus in the direction of hymn writing. Furthermore, it gave me a deeper insight into the life and spirit of the old church hymns."

Two of the hymns of Nicolai that Landstad attempted to translate were "Wachet auf, ruft uns die Stimme" and "Wie schön leuchtet der Morgenstern," noble classics that have never been excelled. The young student was so successful in his rendering of the former hymn that it subsequently found a place in the Norwegian church hymnary.

Landstad was born October 7, 1802, in Maaso, Finnmarken, Norway, where his father was pastor of the Lutheran church. This parish is at the extreme northern point of Norway, and so Landstad himself wrote, "I was baptized in the northernmost church in the world." Later the family moved to Oksnes, another parish among the frozen fjords of the Norse seacoast.

"The waves of the icy Arctic," he writes poetically, "sang my cradle lullaby; but the bosom of a loving mother warmed my body and soul."

The stern character of the relentless North, with its solitude, its frozen wastes, its stormy waters and its long months of winter darkness, no doubt left a profound and lasting impression upon the lad whose early years were spent in such environments. The Napoleonic wars were also raging, and it was a time of much sorrow and suffering among the common people. When the boy was nine years old the family removed to Vinje. Although they continued to suffer many hardships, the natural surroundings at this place were more congenial, and in summer the landscape was transformed into a magic beauty that must have warmed the heart and fired the childish imagination of the future hymnist.

Magnus was the third in a family of ten children. Although sorely pressed by poverty, the father recognized unusual talent in the boy, and at the age of twenty years he was sent to the university in Christiania. During his first year at the institution two of his brothers died. Young Landstad was greatly cast down in spirit, but out of the bitterness of this early bereavement came two memorial poems that are believed to represent his first attempt at verse-writing.

In 1827 he completed his theological studies at the university and the following year he was appointed resident vicar of the Lutheran church at Gausdal. During his pastorate at this place he wrote his first hymn. In 1834 he became pastor at Kviteseid, where he continued the writing of hymns and other poems. Five years later he became his father's successor as pastor of the parish at Seljord. It was here, in 1841, that he published his first work, a book of daily devotions that has been highly prized among his countrymen.

For centuries Norway and Denmark had been closely connected politically and culturally. The Lutheran Church was, moreover, the state church of both countries. As a consequence of this relationship Norway had always looked to Denmark for its hymn literature, and no hymnist of any note had ever risen in the northern country.

Now, however, it began to dawn on the Norwegians that a native singer dwelt in their own midst. The political ties with Denmark having been broken as a result of the Napoleonic wars, the spirit of nationalism began to assert itself and the demand for a new hymn-book for the Church of Norway constantly grew stronger. In 1848 the Norwegian ecclesiastical authorities requested Landstad to undertake the task, but not until four years later could he be prevailed upon to assume the arduous duties involved in so great an endeavor.

In 1861 the first draft of his "Kirke-Salmebog" was published. It did not meet with universal approval. In defense of his work, Landstad wrote: "We must, above all, demand that our hymns possess the elements of poetic diction and true song. We must consider the historical and churchly elements, and the orthodox objectivity which shows respect for church tradition and which appreciates the purity, clearness, and force of confession. But the sickly subjectivity, which 'rests' in the varying moods of pious feelings and godly longings, and yet does not possess any of the boldness and power of true faith such as we find in Luther's and Kingo's hymns—this type of church hymn must be excluded. Finally, we must also emphasize the aesthetic feature. Art must be made to serve the Church, to glorify the name of God, and to edify the congregation of worshipers. But it must always be remembered that art itself is to be the servant and not the master."

Nevertheless, Landstad continued for several years to revise his own work, and in 1869 the hymn-book was finally published and authorized for use in the Church of Norway. Within a year it had been introduced into 648 of the 923 parishes of the country.

In 1876 Landstad retired from active service after the Norwegian parliament had unanimously voted him an annual pension of 4,000 crowns in appreciation of the great service he had rendered his country. He died in Christiania, October 9, 1880.

Among the hymns of Landstad that have been translated into English are, "I know of a sleep in Jesus' Name," "I come to Thee, O blessed Lord," "There many shall come from the East and the West," "When sinners see their lost condition," and "Before Thee, God, who knowest all."

Although Landstad's hymns do not attain to lofty poetic heights, they are marked by a spirit of unusual intimacy, deep earnestness, and a warmth of feeling that make a strong appeal to the worshiper.

PART IV
ENGLISH HYMNODY

Ken's Immortal Evening Hymn

Glory to Thee, my God, this night,
For all the blessings of the light:
Keep me, O keep me, King of kings,
Beneath Thine own almighty wings.
Forgive me, Lord, for Thy dear Son,

The ill that I this day have done:
That, with the world, myself, and Thee,
I, ere I sleep, at peace may be.
Teach me to live, that I may dread
The grave as little as my bed;
To die, that this vile body may
Rise glorious at the judgment day.
O then shall I in endless day,
When sleep and death have passed away,
With all Thy saints and angels sing
In endless praise to Thee, my King.
Thomas Ken, 1695.

THE DAWN OF HYMNODY IN ENGLAND

Owing to the strong prejudice in the Reformed Church to hymns of "human composure," the development of hymnody in England, as well as other countries where Calvin's teachings were accepted, was slow. Crude paraphrases of the Psalms, based on the Genevan Psalter, appeared from the hands of various versifiers and were used generally in the churches of England and Scotland. It was not until 1637, more than a century after Luther had published his first hymn-books, that England's first hymn-writer was born. He was Bishop Thomas Ken.

This first sweet singer in the early dawn of English hymnody holds the distinction of having written the most famous doxology of the Christian Church. It is the so-called "long meter" doxology:

Praise God, from whom all blessings flow;
Praise Him, all creatures here below;
Praise Him above, ye heavenly host;
Praise Father, Son, and Holy Ghost.

His sublime evening hymn, "Glory to Thee, my God, this night," is ranked as one of the four masterpieces of English praise. His beautiful morning hymn, "Awake, my soul, and with the sun," is scarcely less deserving of high distinction. As originally written, both hymns closed with the famous doxology given above.

Bishop Ken looms as a heroic figure during turbulent times in English history. Left an orphan in early childhood, he was brought up by his brother-in-law, the famous fisherman, Izaak Walton. Ken's name has been found cut in one of the stone pillars at Winchester, where he went to school as a boy.

When, in 1679, the wife of William of Orange, the niece of the English monarch, asked Charles II, king of England, to send an English chaplain to the royal court at The Hague, Ken was selected for the position. However, he was so outspoken in denouncing the corrupt lives of those in authority in the Dutch capitol that he was compelled to leave the following year. Charles thereupon appointed him one of his own chaplains.

Ken continued to reveal the same spirit of boldness, however, rebuking the sins of the dissolute English monarch. On one occasion, when Charles asked the courageous pastor to give up his own dwelling temporarily in order that Nell Gwynne, a notorious character, might be housed, Ken answered promptly: "Not for the King's kingdom."

Instead of punishing the bold and faithful minister, Charles so admired his courage that he appointed him bishop of Bath and Wells.

Charles always referred to Ken as "the good little man" and, when it was chapel time, he would usually say: "I must go in and hear Ken tell me of my faults."

When Charles died, and the papist James II came to the throne, Ken, together with six other bishops, was imprisoned in the Tower of London. Although he was acquitted, he was later removed from his bishopric by William III.

The last years of his life were spent in a quiet retreat, and he died in 1711 at the age of seventy-four years. He had requested that "six of the poorest men in the parish" should carry him to his grave, and this was done. It was also at his request that he was buried under the east window of the chancel of Frome church, the service being held at sunrise. As his body was lowered into its last resting-place, and the first light of dawn came through the chancel window, his friends sang his immortal morning hymn:

Awake, my soul, and with the sun
Thy daily stage of duty run.
Shake off dull sloth, and joyful rise
To pay thy morning sacrifice.
Wake and lift up thyself, my heart,
And with the angels bear thy part,
Who all night long unwearied sing
High praise to the eternal King.
All praise to Thee, who safe hast kept,
And hast refreshed me while I slept:
Grant, Lord, when I from death shall wake,
I may of endless life partake.

It is said that after Bishop Ken had written this hymn, he sang it to his own accompaniment on the lute every morning as a part of his private devotion. Although he wrote many other hymns, only this one and his evening hymn have survived. The two hymns were published in a devotional book prepared for the students of Winchester College. In this work Bishop Ken urged the students to sing the hymns devoutly in their rooms every morning and evening.

The historian Macaulay paid Ken a beautiful tribute when he said that he came as near to the ideal of Christian perfection "as human weakness permits."

It was during the life-time of Bishop Ken that Joseph Addison, the famous essayist, was publishing the "Spectator." Addison was not only the leading literary light of his time, but a devout Christian as well. From time to time he appended a poem to the charming essays which appeared in the "Spectator," and it is from this source that we have received five hymns of rare beauty. They are the so-called "Creation" hymn, "The spacious firmament on high," which Haydn included in his celebrated oratorio; the Traveler's hymn, beginning with the line, "How are Thy servants blest, O Lord"; and three other hymns, almost equally well-known: "The Lord my pasture shall prepare," "When rising from the bed of death," and "When all Thy mercies, O my God." The latter contains one of the most striking expressions in all the realm of hymnody:

Through all eternity to Thee
A joyful song I'll raise:
But oh, eternity's too short
To utter all Thy praise!

In the essay introducing this hymn, Addison writes: "If gratitude is due from man to man, how much more from man to his Maker. The Supreme Being does not only confer upon us those bounties which proceed immediately from His hand, but even those benefits which are conveyed to us by others. Any blessing which we enjoy, by what means soever derived, is the gift of Him who is the great Author of Good and the Father of Mercies."

The Traveler's hymn, "How are Thy servants blessed, O Lord," was written after Addison's return from a perilous voyage on the Mediterranean.

In addition to his literary pursuits, Addison also occupied several important positions of state with the English government. He died on June 17, 1719, at the age of forty-seven. When he was breathing his last, he called for the Earl of Warwick and exclaimed: "See in what peace a Christian can die!"

The hymns of Addison and Bishop Ken may be regarded as the heralds of a new day in the worship of the Reformed Church. While Addison was still writing his essays and verses for the "Spectator," Isaac Watts, peer of all English hymnists, was already tuning his lyre of many strings. Psalmody was beginning to yield to hymnody.

The Pearl of English Hymnody

When I survey the wondrous cross
On which the Prince of glory died,
My richest gain I count but loss,
And pour contempt on all my pride.
Forbid it, Lord, that I should boast,
Save in the death of Christ, my God;
All the vain things that charm me most,
I sacrifice them to His blood.
See, from His head, His hands, His feet,
Sorrow and love flow mingled down!
Did e'er such love and sorrow meet,
Or thorns compose so rich a crown!
Were the whole realm of nature mine,
That were a tribute far too small;
Love so amazing, so divine,
Demands my soul, my life, my all.

Isaac Watts, 1707.

ISAAC WATTS, FATHER OF ENGLISH HYMNODY

By universal consent the title, "Father of English Hymnody," is bestowed upon Isaac Watts. English hymns had been written before the time of Watts, notably the beautiful classics of Ken and Addison; but it remained for the genius of Watts to break the iron rule of psalmody in the Reformed Church which had continued uninterrupted since the days of Calvin.

Watts was born in Southampton, England, July 17, 1674. His father was a "dissenter," and twice was imprisoned for his religious views. This was during the time when Isaac was still a baby, and the mother often carried the future poet in her arms when she went to visit her husband in prison.

When Isaac grew up, a wealthy man offered to give him a university education if he would consent to become a minister in the Established Church. This he refused to do, but prepared instead for the Independent ministry.

Early in life young Watts had revealed signs of poetic genius. As a boy of seven years he had amused his parents with his rhymes. As he grew older he became impatient with the wretched paraphrases of the Psalms then in use in the Reformed churches. These views were shared generally by those who possessed a discriminating taste in poetry. "Scandalous doggerel" was the term applied by Samuel Wesley, father of the famous Wesley brothers, to the versified Psalms of Sternhold and Hopkins, who had published the most popular psalm-book of the day.

When young Watts ventured to voice his displeasure over the psalm-singing in his father's church in Southampton, one of the church officers retorted: "Give us something better, young man." Although he was only eighteen years old at the time, he accepted the challenge and wrote his first hymn, which was sung at the following Sunday evening services. The first stanza seems prophetic of his future career:

Behold the glories of the Lamb
Amidst His Father's throne;
Prepare new honors for His Name,
And songs before unknown.

The hymn met with such favorable reception that the youthful poet was encouraged to write others, and within the next two years he produced nearly all of the 210 hymns that constituted his famous collection, "Hymns and Spiritual Songs," published in 1707. This was the first real hymn-book in the English language.

Twelve years later he published his "Psalms of David," a metrical version of the Psalter, but, as he himself stated, rendered "in the language of the New Testament, and applied to the Christian state and worship." Indeed, the Psalms were given such a distinctively Christian flavor that their Old Testament origin is often overlooked. Witness, for example, the opening lines of his rendition of the Seventy-second Psalm:

Jesus shall reign where'er the sun
Does his successive journeys run.

In addition to being a preacher and a poet, Watts was an ardent student of theology and philosophy, and wrote several notable books. Always frail in health from childhood, his intense studies finally resulted in completely shattering his constitution, and he was compelled to give up his parish.

During this period of physical distress, the stricken poet was invited to become a guest for a week in the home of Sir Thomas Abney, an intimate friend and admirer. The friendship continued to grow, and inasmuch as Watts did not improve in health, he was urged to remain. He finally so endeared himself to the Abney family that they refused to let him go, and he who had come to spend a week remained for the rest of his life—thirty-six years!

The great hymnist died on November 25, 1748, and was buried at Bunhill Fields, London, near the graves of John Bunyan and Daniel Defoe. A monument to his memory was placed in Westminster Abbey, the highest honor that can be bestowed upon an Englishman.

To Isaac Watts we are indebted for some of our most sublime hymns. "When I survey the wondrous cross" has been named by Matthew Arnold as the finest hymn in the English language, and most critics concur in the judgment. Certainly it is one of the most beautiful. John Julian, the noted hymnologist, declares that it must be classified with the four hymns that stand at the head of all English hymns.

Other hymns of Watts continue to hold their grip on the Christian Church after the passing of two centuries. No Christmas service seems complete without singing his beautiful paraphrase of the ninety-eighth Psalm, "Joy to the world, the Lord is come!" Another hymn, "O God, our help in ages past," based on the ninetieth Psalm, is indispensable at New Year's time. Then there is the majestic hymn of worship, "Before Jehovah's awful throne," as well as the appealing Lenten hymn, "Alas, and did my Saviour bleed?" And who has not been stirred by the challenge in "Am I a soldier of the cross?" Other hymns by Watts include such favorites as "There is a land of pure delight," "Come, Holy Spirit, Heavenly Dove," "O that the Lord would guide my ways," "My dear Redeemer and my Lord," "How beauteous are their feet," "Come, sound His praise abroad," "My soul, repeat His praise," "O bless the Lord, my soul," "Lord of the worlds above," "Lord, we confess our numerous faults," "In vain we seek for peace with God," "Not all the blood of beasts," "So let our lips and lives express," "The Lord my Shepherd is," and "When I can read my title clear."

Although Watts never married, he deeply loved little children, and he is the author of some of the most famous nursery rhymes in the English language. The profound genius that produced "O God, our help in ages in past" also understood how to appeal to the childish mind by means of such happy little jingles as, "How doth the little busy bee" and "Let dogs delight to bark and bite," as well as by the exquisite cradle-song:

Hush, my dear, lie still and slumber;
Holy angels guard thy bed;

Heavenly blessings without number
Gently falling on thy head.
Sleep, my babe, thy food and raiment,
House and home, thy friends provide;
All without thy care or payment,
All thy wants are well supplied.

How much better thou'rt attended
Than the Son of God could be,
When from heaven He descended,
And became a child like thee.
Soft and easy is thy cradle,
Coarse and hard thy Saviour lay,
When His birthplace was a stable,
And His softest bed the hay.

Seeking the Heavenly Prize

Awake, my soul, stretch every nerve,
And press with vigor on;
A heavenly race demands thy zeal,
And an immortal crown.
A cloud of witnesses around
Hold thee in full survey:
Forget the steps already trod,
And onward urge thy way.
'Tis God's all-animating voice
That calls thee from on high;
'Tis His own hand presents the prize
To thine aspiring eye:
That prize with peerless glories bright
Which shall new luster boast,
When victors' wreaths and monarchs' gems
Shall blend in common dust.
Blest Saviour, introduced by Thee,
Have I my race begun;
And, crowned with victory, at Thy feet
I'll lay my honors down.
Philip Doddridge (1702-1751).

DODDRIDGE: PREACHER, TEACHER AND HYMNIST

Philip Doddridge was one of England's gifted evangelical preachers. Like the Wesley brothers, he came from a large family. While there were nineteen children in the Wesley family, Philip Doddridge was the last of twenty children.

The religious background of the Doddridge family was significant. Although his father was an oil merchant in London, his grandfather had been one of the Independent ministers under the Commonwealth who were ejected in 1662. Both of his parents were pious people, and Philip, who was born June 26, 1702, was brought up in a religious atmosphere.

He was such a delicate child that his life was despaired of almost from birth. His parents died while he was yet quite young, but kind friends cared for the orphan boy and sent him to school.

Because he revealed such unusual gifts as a student, the Duchess of Bedford offered to give him a university training on condition that he would become a minister of the Church of England. This, however, Philip declined to do, and he entered a nonconformist seminary instead.

At the age of twenty-one years he was ordained as pastor of the Independent congregation at Kibworth, England. Six years later he began his real life work at Northampton, where he served as the head of a theological training school and preached in the local congregation.

To this school came young men from all parts of the British Isles and even from the continent. Most of them prepared to become ministers in the Independent Church. Doddridge himself was practically the whole faculty. Among his subjects were Hebrew, Greek, Algebra, Philosophy, Trigonometry, Logic, and theological branches.

As a hymn-writer Doddridge ranks among the foremost in England. He was a friend and admirer of Isaac Watts, whose hymns at this time had set all England singing. In some respects his lyrics resemble those of Watts. Although they do not possess the strength and majesty found in the latter's hymns, they have more personal warmth and tenderness. Witness, for instance, the children's hymn:

> See Israel's gentle Shepherd stand
> With all-engaging charms;
> Hark! how He calls the tender lambs,
> And folds them in His arms.

Note also the spiritual joy that is reflected in the hymn so often used at confirmation:

> O happy day, that stays my choice
> On Thee, my Saviour and my God!
> Well may this glowing heart rejoice,
> And tell its raptures all abroad.

Something of Doddridge's own confiding trust in God is expressed in the beautiful lines:

> Shine on our souls, eternal God!
> With rays of beauty shine;
> O let Thy favor crown our days,
> And all their round be Thine.

Did we not raise our hands to Thee,
Our hands might toil in vain;
Small joy success itself could give,
If Thou Thy love restrain.

Other noted hymns by Doddridge include such gems as "Hark, the glad sound, the Saviour comes," "Great God, we sing that mighty hand," "O Fount of good, to own Thy love," and "Father of all, Thy care we bless."

Doddridge wrote about four hundred hymns. Most of them were composed for use in his own congregation in connection with his sermons. None of them was published during his life-time, but manuscript copies were widely circulated among the Independent congregations in England. The fact that about one-third of his hymns are still in common use on both sides of the Atlantic bears witness of their unusual merit.

Though Doddridge struggled under the burden of feeble health, his life was filled with arduous duties. When he was only forty-eight years old it became apparent that he had fallen a victim to tubercular infection. He was advised to leave England for Lisbon, Portugal. Lacking funds for the voyage, friends in all parts of England came to his aid. The journey was undertaken, but on October 26, 1751, he died at Lisbon.

A Hymn of the Ages

Jesus, Lover of my soul,
Let me to Thy bosom fly,
While the nearer waters roll,
While the tempest still is high!
Hide me, O my Saviour, hide,
Till the storm of life is past;
Safe into the haven guide:
O receive my soul at last!
Other refuge have I none;
Hangs my helpless soul on Thee;
Leave, ah, leave me not alone,
Still support and comfort me!
All my trust in Thee is stayed,
All my help from Thee I bring:
Cover my defenseless head
With the shadow of Thy wing.
Thou, O Christ, art all I want;
More than all in Thee I find.
Raise the fallen, cheer the faint,
Heal the sick, and lead the blind.
Just and holy is Thy name,
I am all unrighteousness;
False and full of sin I am,
Thou art full of truth and grace.
Plenteous grace with Thee is found,
Grace to cover all my sin;

Let the healing streams abound,
Make and keep me pure within.
Thou of life the Fountain art,
Freely let me take of Thee:
Spring Thou up within my heart,
Rise to all eternity.
Charles Wesley, 1740.

WESLEY, THE SWEET BARD OF METHODISM

Every great religious movement has witnessed an outburst of song. This was particularly true of the Lutheran Reformation in Germany and other lands and of the Methodist revival in England. John and Charles Wesley, like Martin Luther, understood something of the value of sacred song in impressing religious truths upon the hearts and minds of men. While John Wesley was undoubtedly a preacher of marvelous spiritual power, the real secret of the success of the Wesleyan movement more likely must be sought in the sublime hymns written by his brother Charles.

With Isaac Watts, Charles Wesley holds the foremost place in the realm of English hymnody. No less than 6,500 hymns are said to have been written by this "sweet bard of Methodism." Naturally they are not all of the highest order, but it is surprising how many of them rise to real poetic excellence. Of the 770 hymns in the Wesleyan Hymn Book, 623 are from the pen of Charles Wesley!

Wesley did not write hymns merely as a duty, nor yet as a pastime. His soul seemed filled with music and poetry, and when his genius became touched by the divine spark of Christ's Spirit, it burst into full flame. It has been said of Franz Schubert that "he had to write music." The same was true of Charles Wesley. When his soul was full of song, he had to give expression to it by writing his immortal hymns. The inspiration came to him under all sorts of conditions. Some of his hymns were written on horseback, others in a stage-coach or on the deck of a vessel. Even as he was lying on his deathbed, at the age of eighty years, he dictated his last hymn to his faithful and devoted wife. It begins with the words, "In age and feebleness extreme."

Charles Wesley was the next to the youngest of nineteen children born to Rev. Samuel Wesley and his remarkable wife Susannah. The father, who was a clergyman in the Church of England, possessed more than ordinary literary gifts. He is the author of at least one hymn that has survived the passing of time, "Behold, the Saviour of mankind." The mother presided over the rectory at Epworth, where both of the distinguished sons were born, and also looked after the education of the younger children of the large family. Concerning this very unusual mother and the spiritual influence she exerted over her children, volumes have been written.

Poverty and other tribulations descended upon the Epworth rectory like the afflictions of Job. The crowning disaster came in 1709, when the Wesley home was completely destroyed by fire. John, who was only six years old at the time, was left behind in the confusion and when the entire house was aflame he was seen to appear at a second-story window. The agonized father fell upon his knees and implored God to save his child. Immediately a neighbor mounted the shoulders of another man and managed to seize the boy just as the roof fell in. Thus was spared the child who was destined to become the leader of one of the greatest spiritual movements in the Christian Church.

While John and Charles were students at Oxford University, they became dissatisfied with the spiritual conditions existing among the students. Soon they formed an organization devoted to spiritual exercises. Because of their strict rules and precise methods, they were nicknamed "the Methodists," a name that afterwards became attached to their reform movement.

The hymns of Charles Wesley are so numerous that only a few of the more outstanding can be mentioned here. "Hark! the herald angels sing," "Love divine, all love excelling" and "Jesus, Lover of my soul" form a triumvirate of hymns never surpassed by a single author. Add to these such hymns as "A charge to keep I have," "Arise, my soul, arise," "Christ, whose glory fills the sky," "Come, Thou long-expected Jesus," "Soldiers of Christ, arise," "Hail the day that sees Him rise," and "Suffering Son of Man, be near me," and it will readily be understood why the name of Charles Wesley is graven in such large letters in the hymnody of the Christian Church.

"Jesus, Lover of my soul" is generally recognized as the finest hymn of Wesley. This is all the more remarkable since it was one of the earliest written by him. It was first published in 1740 in a collection of 139 hymns known as "Hymns and Sacred Poems, by John and Charles Wesley." This was at the beginning of the Wesleyan movement, which soon began to spread like fire all over England.

There are several stories extant as to the origin of the hymn. The most trustworthy of these tells how the author was deeply perplexed by spiritual difficulties one day, when he noticed through his open study window a little song bird pursued by a hungry hawk. Presently the bird fluttered exhausted through the window and straight into the arms of Wesley, where it found a safe refuge. Pondering on this unusual incident, the thought came to Wesley that, in like manner, the soul of man must flee to Christ in doubts and fears. Then he took up his pen and wrote:

Jesus, Lover of my soul,
Let me to Thy bosom fly.

The reference to the "tempest" and the "storm of life" may have been prompted by the memory of an earlier experience, when he and his brother John were on their way to the colony of Georgia on a missionary journey. It was in the year 1735 the brothers formed a friendship with a band of Moravians who were sailing on the same ship for America. During the crossing a terrible tempest was encountered and for a while it was feared the ship would sink. While all of the other passengers were filled with terror, the Wesleys were impressed by the calmness and courage of the Moravians, who sang hymns in the midst of the raging storm.

Seeking for a reason for their spiritual fortitude, the brothers found that the Moravians seemed to possess a positive certainty of salvation through faith in Jesus Christ. The Wesleys also made the sad discovery that they themselves did not really possess this assurance, but had been trying to work out their salvation by methods of their own. John Wesley later made the confession that he and his brother had gone to Georgia to convert the people there, whereas they themselves had need to be converted!

Upon their return to London the brothers fell in with other Moravians, and through them they became familiar with Luther's teachings. Charles came to a saving faith in Christ during a severe illness, and a week later his brother had a similar spiritual experience. It was on May 24, 1738, that John Wesley attended a meeting in Aldersgate Street, where some one was reading Luther's preface to the Epistle to the Romans. Then for the first time light dawned on his soul, and he found peace with God through Christ.

Soon afterwards John Wesley left for Halle, Germany, the seat of the Pietist movement, in order to become more familiar with the teachings of Luther and the evangelical methods of the Pietists. At Halle he also became deeply imbued with missionary zeal. Upon his return to England he launched, with John Whitefield, the greatest spiritual movement his country had ever known. Revivals flamed everywhere. No buildings were large enough to house the crowds that gathered to hear the evangelists, and, because the English clergy were hostile to the movement, most of the meetings were held in the open air.

Charles at first aided in preaching, but eventually devoted his time mainly to hymns. It is estimated that John Wesley held no less than forty thousand preaching services, and traveled nearly a quarter of a million miles. It was he who said, "The world is my parish." John wrote some original hymns, but his translations of German hymns are more important. We are indebted to him for the English versions of Paul Gerhardt's "Commit thou all thy griefs," Tersteegen's "Thou hidden love of God whose height," Freylinghausen's "O Jesus, Source of calm repose," Zinzendorf's "Jesus, Thy blood and righteousness," and Scheffler's "Thee will I love, My Strength, my Tower."

Charles Wesley died March 29, 1788, after fifty years of service to the Church. The day before he was taken ill, he preached in City Road chapel, London. The hymn before the sermon was Watts' "I'll praise my Maker, while I've breath." The following evening, although very sick, he amazed his friends by singing the entire hymn with a strong voice. On the night of his death he tried several times to repeat the hymn, but could only say, "I'll praise—I'll praise—," and with the praise of his Maker on his lips, he went home to God. John Wesley survived his brother three years, entering his eternal rest on March 2, 1791. The text of his last sermon was, "Seek ye the Lord while He may be found."

Whether Charles Wesley or Isaac Watts should be accorded first place among English hymnists has been a subject of much dispute. The fact is that each occupies a unique position, and the one complements the other. While Watts dwells on the awful majesty and glory of God in sublime phrases, Wesley touches the very hem of Christ's garment in loving adoration and praise. Dr. Breed compares the two in the following striking manner:

"Watts is more reverential; Wesley more loving. Watts is stronger; Wesley sweeter. Watts appeals profoundly to the intellect; Wesley takes hold of the heart. Watts will continue to sing for the Pauls and Peters of the Church; Wesley for the Thomases and the Johns. Where both are so great it would be idle to attempt to settle their priority. Let us only be grateful that God in His gracious providence has given both to the Church to voice the praises of various classes."

Henry Ward Beecher uttered one of the most beautiful of all tributes to "Jesus, Lover of my soul" when he said: "I would rather have written that hymn of Wesley's than to have the fame of all the kings that ever sat on the earth. It is more glorious. It has more power in it. I would rather be the author of that hymn than to hold the wealth of the richest man in New York. He will die. He is dead, and does not know it.... But that hymn will go singing until the last trump brings forth the angel band; and then, I think, it will mount up on some lip to the very presence of God."

George Duffield, author of "Stand up, stand up for Jesus," called Wesley's lyric "the hymn of the ages."

No one will ever know how much help and consolation it has brought to souls in affliction. Allan Sutherland tells of the following pathetic incident:

"On an intensely warm day, as I stood on the corner of a sun-baked street in Philadelphia, waiting for a car to take me to the cool retreats of Fairmount Park, I heard a low, quavering voice singing, with inexpressible sweetness, 'Jesus, Lover of my soul.' Looking up to an open window whence the sound came, I saw on the sill a half-withered plant—a pathetic oasis of green in a desert of brick and mortar—and resting tenderly and caressingly upon it was an emaciated hand. I could not see the person to whom the voice and hand belonged, but that was unnecessary—the story was all too clearly revealed: I knew that within that close, uncomfortable room a human soul was struggling with the great problem of life and death, and was slowly but surely reaching its solution; I knew that in spite of her lowly surroundings her life was going out serenely and triumphantly. I shall never forget the grave, pathetic pleading in the frail young voice as these words were borne to me on the oppressive air:

> Other refuge have I none;
> Hangs my helpless soul on Thee;
> Leave, ah, leave me not alone,
> Still support and comfort me!"

Another Hymn of the Ages

> Rock of Ages, cleft for me,
> Let me hide myself in Thee:
> Let the water and the blood
> From Thy riven side which flowed
> Be of sin the perfect cure,
> Save me, Lord, and make me pure.
> Not the labors of my hands
> Can fulfil Thy Law's demands;
> Could my zeal no respite know,
> Could my tears forever flow,
> All for sin could not atone;
> Thou must save, and Thou alone.

Nothing in my hand I bring,
Simply to Thy cross I cling;
Naked, come to Thee for dress;
Helpless, look to Thee for grace;
Foul, I to the Fountain fly:
Wash me, Saviour, or I die!
When I draw this fleeting breath,
When my eyelids close in death,
When I soar to worlds unknown,
See Thee on Thy judgment throne,
Rock of Ages, cleft for me,
Let me hide myself in Thee.
August Toplady, 1776.

A GREAT HYMN THAT GREW OUT OF A QUARREL

Although Isaac Watts' beautiful hymn, "When I survey the wondrous cross," is regarded by most critics as the finest hymn in the English language, Toplady's "Rock of Ages" holds the distinction of being the most popular. Perhaps no hymn ever written has so gripped the hearts of Christians of all communions as this noble hymn.

A British magazine once invited its readers to submit a list of the hundred English hymns that stood highest in their esteem. A total of 3,500 persons responded, and "Rock of Ages" was named first by 3,215.

We have tried the same experiment with a group of Bible students, and "Rock of Ages" easily headed the list.

Augustus Montague Toplady, the writer of this hymn, was born on November 4, 1740, at Farnham, England. His father, a major in the English army, was killed the following year at the siege of Carthagena. The widowed mother later removed to Ireland, where her son was educated at Trinity College, Dublin. It was during this period of his life that Augustus, then sixteen years of age, chanced to attend an evangelistic service held in a barn. The preacher was an unlettered layman, but his message so gripped the heart of the lad that he determined then and there to give his heart to God. Of this experience Toplady afterward wrote:

"Strange that I who had so long sat under the means of grace in England should be brought right unto God in an obscure part of Ireland, amidst a handful of people met together in a barn, and by the ministry of one who could hardly spell his own name. Surely it was the Lord's doing and is marvelous."

Toplady was ordained at the age of twenty-two as a minister of the Church of England. He was frail of body, and after some years he was stricken with consumption. It was while fighting the ravages of this disease that he wrote his famous hymn, two years before his death.

The hymn first appeared in the March issue of the Gospel Magazine, of which Toplady was editor, in the year 1776. It was appended to a curious article in which the author attempted to show by mathematical computation how dreadful is the sum total of sins committed by a man during a lifetime, and how impossible it is for a sinner to redeem himself from this debt of guilt. But Christ, who is the sinner's refuge, has paid the entire debt. It was this glorious thought that inspired him to sing:

Rock of Ages, cleft for me,
Let me hide myself in Thee.

For some years John Wesley, the great founder of Methodism, and Toplady had been engaged in a theological dispute. Toplady was a confirmed Calvinist and was intolerant of Wesley's Arminian views. Both men were intemperate in their language and hurled unseemly and sometimes bitter invectives at each other. Wesley characterized Toplady as a "chimney-sweep" and "a lively coxcomb." Toplady retorted by calling Wesley "Pope John" and declaring that his forehead was "petrified" and "impervious to a blush." There are reasons for believing that the article in the Gospel Magazine by Toplady to which we have alluded was for the purpose of refuting Wesley's teachings, and that "Rock of Ages" was written at the conclusion of the article as an effective way of clinching the argument.

In our day, when we find "Rock of Ages" on one page of our hymnals and Charles Wesley's "Jesus, Lover of my soul," on the next, it is hard to understand the uncharitable spirit that existed between these servants of Christ. Perhaps, had they really understood each other, they were more in accord than they suspected.

Nevertheless, God is able to use the most imperfect of human instruments for His praise, and surely "Rock of Ages" has been the means of bringing multitudes to God through Christ. Its strength lies undoubtedly in the clear and simple manner in which it sets forth the glorious truth that we are saved by grace alone, through the merits of Christ. Even a child can understand the meaning of the words,

Nothing in my hand I bring,
Simply to Thy cross I cling.

Or these,

Not the labors of my hands
Can fulfil Thy Law's demands;
Could my zeal no respite know,
Could my tears forever flow,
All for sin could not atone;
Thou must save, and Thou alone.

In this comforting and triumphant faith Toplady himself passed into glory in his thirty-eighth year. A few hours before his death he exclaimed: "My heart beats every day stronger and stronger for glory. Sickness is no affliction, pain no curse, death itself no dissolution." His last words were: "My prayers are all converted into praises."

During his illness some friends had expressed the hope that he might soon be restored. Toplady shook his head.

"No mortal man can live," he said, "after the glories which God has manifested to my soul."

At another time he told how he "enjoyed a heaven already in his soul," and that his spiritual experiences were so exalted that he could ask for nothing except a continuation of them.

Before his death Toplady had requested that he be buried beneath the gallery over against the pulpit of Totenham Court Chapel. Strangely enough, this building was intimately associated with the early history of Methodism. It was built by Whitefield, and here also Wesley preached Whitefield's funeral sermon. Perhaps it was Toplady's way of expressing the hope that all the bitterness and rancor attending his controversy with Wesley might be buried with him.

"Rock of Ages" has been translated into almost every known language, and to all peoples it seems to bring the same wondrous appeal. An old Chinese woman was trying to do something of "merit" in the eyes of her heathen gods by digging a well twenty-five feet deep and fifteen in diameter. She was converted to Christianity, and when she was eighty years old, she held out the crippled hands with which she had labored all her life and sang: "Nothing in my hands I bring."

A missionary to India once sought the aid of a Hindu to translate the hymn into one of the numerous dialects of India. The result was not so happy. The opening words were:

Very old stone, split for my benefit,
Let me get under one of your fragments.

This is a fair example of the difference between poetry and prose. The translator was faithful to the idea, but how common-place and unfortunate are his expressions when compared with the language of the original!

The Coronation Hymn

All hail the power of Jesus' Name!
Let angels prostrate fall;
Bring forth the royal diadem,
And crown Him Lord of all.
Ye seed of Israel's chosen race,
Ye ransomed from the fall,
Hail Him, who saves you by His grace,
And crown Him Lord of all.
Hail Him, ye heirs of David's line,
Whom David Lord did call;
The Lord incarnate, Man divine,
And crown Him Lord of all.
Sinners, whose love can ne'er forget
The wormwood and the gall;

Go, spread your trophies at His feet,
And crown Him Lord of all.
Let every kindred, every tribe,
On this terrestrial ball
To Him all majesty ascribe,
And crown Him Lord of all.
O that with yonder sacred throng
We at His feet may fall!
We'll join the everlasting song,
And crown Him Lord of all.
Edward Perronet, 1779.

THE BIRD OF A SINGLE SONG

Some men gain fame through a long life of work and achievement; others through a single notable deed. The latter is true in a very remarkable sense of Edward Perronet, author of the Church's great coronation hymn, "All hail the power of Jesus' Name."

"Perronet, bird of a single song, but O how sweet!" is the charming tribute of Bishop Fess in referring to this inspired hymn and its author.

Although Perronet was a man of more than ordinary ability, his name probably would have been lost to posterity had he not written the coronation hymn. An associate of the Wesleys for many years, Perronet also wrote three volumes of sacred poems, some of unusual merit. All of them, however, have been practically forgotten except his one immortal hymn. So long as there are Christians on earth, it will continue to be sung, and after that—in heaven!

Perronet came from a distinguished line of French Protestants who had found refuge in England during times of religious persecution in their homeland. His father, Rev. Vincent Perronet, was vicar of Shoreham. Both father and son, though ardent supporters of the Established Church, became intensely interested in the great evangelical revival under Whitefield and the Wesleys. At one time young Perronet traveled with John Wesley. Much opposition had been stirred up against the Wesleyan movement, and in some places the preachers were threatened by mobs. Concerning these experiences, Wesley makes the following notation in his diary:

"From Rockdale we went to Bolton, and soon found that the Rockdale lions were lambs in comparison with those of Bolton. Edward Perronet was thrown down and rolled in mud and mire. Stones were hurled and windows broken."

On another occasion it is recorded that Wesley wanted to hear Perronet preach. The author of our hymn, however, seems to have been somewhat reluctant about preaching in the presence of the great reformer. Wesley, nevertheless, without consulting Perronet, announced in church that the young man would occupy the pulpit on the following morning. Perronet said nothing, but on the morrow he mounted the pulpit and explained that he had not consented to preach. "However," he added, "I shall deliver the best sermon that has ever been preached on earth," whereupon he read the Sermon on the Mount from beginning to end, adding not a word of comment!

"All hail the power of Jesus' Name" has been translated into almost every language where Christianity is known, and wherever it is sung it seems to grip human hearts. One of the most remarkable stories of the power of this hymn is related by Rev. E. P. Scott, a missionary to India. Having learned of a distant savage tribe in the interior to whom the gospel had not yet been preached, this missionary, despite the warnings of his friends, packed his baggage and, taking his violin, set out on his perilous venture. After traveling several days, he suddenly came upon a large party of the savages who surrounded him and pointed their spears at him.

Believing death to be near, the missionary nevertheless took out his violin and with a prayer to God began to sing "All hail the power of Jesus' Name!" He closed his eyes as he sang, expecting every moment to be pierced through with the threatening spears. When he reached the stanza, "Let every kindred, every tribe," he opened his eyes. What was his surprise to see every spear lowered, and many of the savages moved to tears!

He remained for two years and a half, preaching the story of redemption and leading many of the natives to Jesus. When he was about to return to America on furlough, they pleaded, "O missionary, come back to us again!" He did so, and finally passed away in the midst of these people who had learned to love the man who had brought them the gospel of Christ.

It is interesting to know that, while the people of both England and America prize this hymn very highly, they sing it to different melodies. The tune used in America is called "Coronation" and was composed by a carpenter of Charlestown, Mass., by the name of Oliver Holden. This man was very fond of music and spent his spare time in playing a little organ on which he composed his tunes. The organ may still be seen in Boston.

Thus an English minister and an American carpenter have united in giving the world an immortal hymn.

Perronet died January 2, 1792. His last words were:

"Glory to God in the height of His divinity!
Glory to God in the depth of His humanity!
Glory to God in His all-sufficiency!
Into His hands I commend my spirit."

Two other hymn-writers who, like Perronet, were associated with the Wesleyan movement may be mentioned in this connection. They were John Cennick and William Williams. Like Perronet, too, each was the author of one great hymn, and through that hymn their names have been preserved to posterity.

Cennick, who was of Bohemian ancestry, first met John Wesley in 1739. Of that meeting Wesley has the following notation in his diary: "On Friday, March 1739, I came to Reading, where I found a young man who had in some measure known the powers of the world to come. I spent the evening with him and a few of his serious friends, and it pleased God much to strengthen and comfort them."

For a while Cennick assisted Wesley as a lay preacher, but in 1741 he forsook the Methodist movement on account of Wesley's "free grace" doctrines and organized a society of his own along Calvinistic lines. Later he joined himself to John Whitefield as an evangelist, but finally he went over to the Moravians, in which communion he labored abundantly until his death in 1755 at the early age of thirty-seven years.

To Cennick we are indebted for the majestic hymn on the theme of Christ's second coming, "Lo! He comes, with clouds descending." James King, in his "Anglican Hymnology," gives this hymn third place among the hymns of the Anglican Church, it being excelled in his estimation only by Bishop Ken's "All praise to Thee, my God, this night" and Wesley's "Hark! the herald angels sing." Cennick has also bequeathed to the Church the lovely hymn, "Children of the heavenly King." Though he wrote and published many more hymns, they are mostly of an inferior order.

Williams, a Welshman by birth, has also left a hymn that has gone singing down through the centuries. It is the rugged and stirring hymn that sets forth in such striking imagery the experiences of the Israelites in the wilderness, "Guide me, O Thou great Jehovah."

Williams, who earned the title of the "Watts of Wales," wrote the hymn originally in Welsh. Of him it has been said that "He did for Wales what Wesley and Watts did for England, or what Luther did for Germany." His first hymn-book, "Hallelujah," was published in 1744, when he was only twenty-seven years old.

The Welsh hymnist originally intended to enter the medical profession, but, after passing through a spiritual crisis, he was ordained as a deacon in the Church of England. Because of his free methods of evangelism, he was denied full ordination, and later identified himself with the Wesleyan revival. Like Cennick and Perronet, however, he soon forsook the Wesleys, and now we find him a Calvinistic Methodist, having adopted Wales as his parish. He was a powerful preacher and an unusual singer, and for forty-five years he carried on a blessed work until, on January 11, 1791, he passed through "the swelling current" and was landed "safe on Canaan's side."

In Praise of the Word of God

Father of Mercies, in Thy Word
What endless glory shines!
Forever be Thy Name adored
For these celestial lines.
Here the Redeemer's welcome voice
Spreads heavenly peace around;
And life and everlasting joys
Attend the blissful sound.
O may these heavenly pages be
My ever dear delight;

And still new beauties may I see,
And still increasing light.
Divine Instructor, gracious Lord,
Be Thou forever near;
Teach me to love Thy sacred Word,
And view my Saviour there.
Anne Steele, 1760.

ENGLAND'S FIRST WOMAN HYMNIST

While Isaac Watts was working on his immortal version of "Psalms of David," a baby girl was born to a Baptist minister at Broughton, fifteen miles away. The baby was Anne Steele, destined to become England's first woman hymn-writer. This was in 1716.

Her father, who was a merchant as well as a minister, served the church at Broughton for sixty years, the greater part without pay. The mother died when Anne was only a babe of three years. From childhood the future hymnist was delicate in health, and in 1735 she suffered a hip injury which made her practically an invalid for life.

The hardest blow, however, came in 1737, when her lover, Robert Elscourt, was drowned on the day before he and Anne were to have been married. The grief-stricken young woman with heroic faith nevertheless rose above her afflictions and found solace in sacred song. It is believed that her first hymn, a poem of beautiful resignation, was written at this time:

Father, whate'er of earthly bliss
Thy sovereign will denies,
Accepted at Thy throne, let this
My humble prayer arise:
Give me a calm and thankful heart,
From every murmur free;
The blessings of Thy grace impart,
And make me live to Thee.

Let the sweet hope that Thou art mine
My life and death attend,
Thy presence through my journey shine,
And crown my journey's end.

That the Lord heard her prayer may be attested by the fact that she became the greatest hymn-writer the Baptist Church has produced. Throughout her life she remained unmarried, living with her father and writing noble hymns. In 1760 her first poems appeared in print under the pen name of "Theodosia." Her father at this time makes the following notation in his diary: "This day Nanny sent part of her composition to London to be printed. I entreat a gracious God, who enabled and stirred her up to such a work, to direct it and bless it for the good of many. I pray God to make it useful, and keep her humble." The book proved immensely popular, and the author devoted the profits from its sale to charity.

Miss Steele is the author of 144 hymns and 34 paraphrases of the Psalms. That many of them breathe a spirit of melancholy sadness is not to be wondered at, when we consider the circumstances under which they were written. Although they do not rise to great poetic heights, their language is so artless and simple they seem to sing their way into the heart of the worshiper. When Trinity Episcopal Church of Boston, in 1808, printed its own hymn-book of 151 hymns, fifty-nine of them, or more than one-third, were selected from Miss Steele's compositions. The fact that so many of them are still found in the hymnals of today is another testimony of their worth.

Among the more famous hymns from her pen are: "Father of Mercies, in Thy Word," "How helpless guilty nature lies," "Dear Refuge of my weary soul," "O Thou whose tender mercy hears," "Thou only Sovereign of my heart," and "Thou lovely source of true delight."

England's pioneer woman hymnist fell asleep in November, 1788, her last words being, "I know that my Redeemer liveth." Her epitaph reads:

Silent the lyre, and dumb the tuneful tongue,
That sung on earth her great Redeemer's praise;
But now in heaven she joins the angelic song,
In more harmonious, more exalted lays.

The decades during which Miss Steele lived and wrought were remarkable for the number of hymn-writers of her own communion who flourished in England. In addition to Miss Steele, the Baptist Church produced such hymnists as Samuel Medley, Samuel Stennett and John Fawcett. Benjamin Beddome also was a prolific writer of this period, but his hymns are not of a high order.

Medley lived a dissipated life in the navy until he was severely wounded in battle in 1759. The reading of a sermon led to his conversion, and he later became pastor of a Baptist congregation in Liverpool. His most famous hymns are "O could I speak the matchless worth" and "Awake, my soul, to joyful lays." Stennett in 1757 succeeded his father as pastor of a Baptist church in London, where he gained fame as a preacher. His best hymns are "Majestic sweetness sits enthroned" and "'Tis finished, so the Saviour cried." Fawcett was minister of an humble Baptist congregation in Wainsgate when, in 1772, he received a call to a large London church. He preached his farewell sermon and had loaded his household goods on wagons, when the tears of his parishioners constrained him to remain. A few days later he wrote the tender lyric, "Blest be the tie that binds." Among his other hymns are "How precious is the Book divine" and "Lord, dismiss us with Thy blessing."

The Name above All Names

How sweet the Name of Jesus sounds
In a believer's ear!
It soothes his sorrows, heals his wounds,
And drives away his fear.
It makes the wounded spirit whole,
And calms the troubled breast;

'Tis Manna to the hungry soul,
And to the weary Rest.
Dear Name! the Rock on which I build,
My Shield and Hiding-place;
My never-failing Treasury, filled
With boundless stores of grace.
By Thee my prayers acceptance gain,
Although with sin defiled:
Satan accuses me in vain,
And I am owned a child.
Weak is the effort of my heart,
And cold my warmest thought;
But when I see Thee as Thou art,
I'll praise Thee as I ought.
Till then I would Thy love proclaim
With every fleeting breath;
And may the music of Thy Name
Refresh my soul in death.
John Newton, 1779.

A SLAVE-TRADER WHO WROTE CHRISTIAN LYRICS

In one of England's famous old churches there is a tablet marking the last resting-place of one of its rectors, and on the tablet this epitaph:

"John Newton, clerk, once an Infidel and Libertine, a servant of slavers in Africa, was, by the rich Mercy of our Lord and Saviour Jesus Christ, preserved, restored, pardoned, and appointed to preach the Faith he had long labored to destroy."

This inscription, written by Newton himself before his death, tells the strange story of the life of the man who wrote "How sweet the Name of Jesus sounds," and scores of other beautiful hymns.

Newton was born in London, July 24, 1725. His father was a sea captain. His mother, a deeply pious woman, though frail in health, found her greatest joy in teaching her boy Scripture passages and hymns. When he was only four years old he was able to read the Catechism.

The faithful mother often expressed the hope to her son that he might become a minister. However, when the lad was only seven years of age, the mother died, and he was left to shift largely for himself. On his 11th birthday he joined his father at sea, and made five voyages to the Mediterranean. Through the influence of evil companions and the reading of infidel literature, he began to live a godless and abandoned life.

Being pressed into the navy when a war seemed imminent, young Newton deserted. He was captured, however, and flogged at the mast, after which he was degraded.

At this point his life teems with reckless adventures and strange escapes. Falling into the hands of an unscrupulous slave-dealer in Africa, he himself was reduced practically to the abject condition of a slave. In his misery he gave himself up to nameless sins. The memory of his mother, however, and the religious truths which she had implanted in his soul as a child gave his conscience no peace.

The reading of "The Imitation of Christ," by Thomas à Kempis, also exerted a profound influence over him, and a terrifying experience in a storm at sea, together with his deliverance from a malignant fever in Africa, served to bring the prodigal as a penitent to the throne of mercy.

After six years as the captain of a slaveship, during which time Newton passed through many severe struggles in trying to find peace with God through the observance of a strict moral life, he met on his last voyage a pious captain who helped to bring him to a truer and deeper faith in Christ.

For nine years at Liverpool he was closely associated with Whitefield and the Wesleys, studying the Scriptures in Hebrew and Greek, and occasionally preaching at religious gatherings of the dissenters. In 1764 he was ordained as curate of Olney, where he formed the famous friendship with the poet William Cowper that gave to the world so many beautiful hymns.

It was at Newton's suggestion that the two undertook to write a hymn-book. The famous collection known as "The Olney Hymns," was the result of this endeavor. Of the 349 hymns in this book, Cowper is credited with sixty-six, while Newton wrote the remainder. "How sweet the Name of Jesus sounds" appeared for the first time in this collection. It is a hymn of surpassing tenderness, and ranks among the finest in the English language.

Other notable hymns, by Newton are: "Come, my soul, thy suit prepare," "Approach, my soul, the mercy-seat," "While with ceaseless course the sun," "One there is above all others," "For a season called to part," "Safely through another week," "On what has now been sown," "May the grace of Christ our Saviour," "Though troubles assail us, and dangers affright," "Day of judgment, day of wonders," and "Glorious things of thee are spoken."

Newton's life came to a close in London in 1807, after he had served for twenty-eight years as rector of St. Mary Woolnoth. Among his converts were numbered Claudius Buchanan, missionary to the East Indies, and Thomas Scott, the Bible commentator. In 1805, when his eyesight began to fail and he could no longer read his text, his friends advised him to cease preaching. His answer was: "What! shall the old African blasphemer stop while he can speak?"

When he was nearly eighty years old it was necessary for a helper to stand in the pulpit to help him read his manuscript sermons. One Sunday Newton had twice read the words, "Jesus Christ is precious." "You have already said that twice," whispered his helper; "go on." "John," said Newton, turning to his assistant in the pulpit, "I said that twice, and I am going to say it again." Then the rafters rang as the old preacher shouted,

"Jesus Christ is precious!" Newton's whole life may be said to be summed up in the words of one of his appealing hymns:

> Amazing grace! how sweet the sound
> That saved a wretch like me!
> I once was lost, but now am found—
> Was blind, but now I see.

A Hymn on God's Providence

> God moves in a mysterious way,
> His wonders to perform:
> He plants His footsteps in the sea,
> And rides upon the storm.
> Deep in unfathomable mines
> Of never-failing skill,
> He treasures up His bright designs,
> And works His sovereign will.
> Ye fearful saints, fresh courage take:
> The clouds ye so much dread
> Are big with mercy, and shall break
> In blessings on your head.
> Judge not the Lord by feeble sense,
> But trust Him for His grace;
> Behind a frowning Providence
> He hides a smiling face.
> His purposes will ripen fast,
> Unfolding every hour.
> The bud may have a bitter taste,
> But sweet will be the flower.
> Blind unbelief is sure to err,
> And scan His works in vain.
> God is His own interpreter,
> And He will make it plain.
> William Cowper, 1774.

AN AFFLICTED POET WHO GLORIFIED GOD

Paul once wrote to the Corinthians: "God chose the weak things of the world, that he might put to shame the things that are strong."

In a very special sense this truth was exemplified in the life of the poet William Cowper. If God ever made use of a frail instrument through which to glorify Himself, He did it in this man. Feeble in health from childhood, with a sensitive, high-strung mind that ever was on the point of breaking, he still worked and wrought in such a way that his sad and feverish life certainly was not lived in vain.

Cowper was born at Great Berkhamstead, England, in 1731. His father was an English clergyman. His mother died when the child was only six years old. Even as a youth, he was distressed by frequent mental attacks. He once wrote pathetically: "The meshes of that fine network, the brain, are composed of such mere spinner's threads in me that when a long thought finds its way into them it buzzes, and twangs, and bustles about at such a rate as seems to threaten the whole contexture."

In the previous sketch we related how the famous friendship between the poet and John Newton led to the joint publication of "The Olney Hymns." Newton's idea in suggesting this project was not merely "to perpetuate the remembrance of an intimate and endeared friendship," as he states in the preface of the noted collection, but also to occupy Cowper's mind, which already had given signs of approaching madness.

In 1773, two years after the two friends had begun "The Olney Hymns," Cowper passed through a mental crisis that almost ended in tragedy. Obsessed with the idea that it was the divine will that he should offer up his life by drowning himself in the Ouse river, the afflicted poet ordered a post chaise, and instructed the driver to proceed to a certain spot near Olney, where he planned to leap into the river. When he reached the place, Cowper was diverted from his purpose when he found a man seated at the exact place where he had intended to end his life. Returning home, he is said to have thrown himself on his knife, but the blade broke. His next attempt was to hang himself, but the rope parted.

After his recovery from this dreadful experience, he was so impressed by the realization of God's overruling providence that he was led to write the hymn, "God moves in a mysterious way." It is regarded by many critics as the finest hymn ever written on the theme of God's providence. James T. Fields declares that to be the author of such a hymn is an achievement that "angels themselves might envy."

That God had a purpose in sparing the life of the sorely tried man is made clear when we learn that Cowper lived for twenty-seven years after passing through this crisis. Although he continued to experience some distressing periods, it was during these years that he wrote some of his most beautiful hymns. Among these are "O for a closer walk with God," "Sometimes a light surprises," "Jesus, where'er Thy people meet," "In holy contemplation," and "There is a fountain filled with blood."

The latter hymn has often been criticized because of its strong figurative language. The expression, "a fountain filled with blood," has proved so offensive to modern taste that many hymn-books have omitted this touching hymn. Dr. Ray Palmer, writer of "My faith looks up to Thee," opposed these views vigorously. He once wrote:

"Such criticism seems to us superficial. It takes the words as if they were intended to be a literal prosaic statement. It forgets that what they express is not only poetry, but the poetry of intense and impassioned feeling, which naturally embodies itself in the boldest metaphors. The inner sense of the soul, when its deepest affections are moved, infallibly takes these metaphors in their true significance, while a cold critic of the letter misses that significance entirely. He merely demonstrates his own lack of the spiritual sympathies of which, for fervent Christian hearts, the hymn referred to is an admirable expression."

Certainly it is a hymn that has spread blessings in its path, and countless are the stories of how it has broken down the resistance of hardened human hearts. One of these tells how a Belfast minister once visited a mill where two hundred girls were employed, many of them from his own congregation. One girl, when she saw her pastor entering, began to sing "There is a fountain filled with blood." Other girls took up the lines, and soon the glorious song was ringing above the noise of all the looms. The manager, who was an unbeliever, was so moved that he seized his hat and ran from the building. Later he confessed to the minister, "I never was so hard put to it in all my life. It nearly broke me down."

Cowper also wrote a number of secular poems that achieved great fame. "The Task," has been called "one of the wisest books ever written, and one of the most charming." Another poem, "John Gilpin," is a very happy and mirthful narrative.

Although Cowper's mother died in his early childhood, he never forgot her. When he was fifty-six years old, a cousin sent him a miniature of his mother. In acknowledging the gift, he wrote: "I had rather possess my mother's picture than the richest jewel in the British crown; for I loved her with an affection that her death, fifty years since, has not in the least abated."

Cowper died in 1800. Three years before his death, he lost his lifelong comforter and friend, Mrs. Morley Unwin, who had cared for him with the solicitude of a mother. The sorrow was almost too great for his feeble nature, and he again sank into deepest gloom. At times he thought God had forsaken him. Only at intervals was he able to resume his literary work. His last poem was "The Castaway," written March 20, 1799. Through all his spiritual and mental depression, however, he was ever submissive to the will of God. But the time of release for this chastened child of God was at hand.

Bishop Moule tells the story of his departure thus: "About half an hour before his death, his face, which had been wearing a sad and hopeless expression, suddenly lighted up with a look of wonder and inexpressible delight. It was as if he saw his Saviour, and as if he realized the blessed fact, 'I am not shut out of Heaven after all!' This look of holy surprise and of joyful adoration remained until he had passed away, and even as he lay in his coffin the expression was still there. One who saw him after death wrote that 'with the composure and calmness of the face, there mingled also a holy surprise.'"

Mrs. Browning, in her poem entitled "Cowper's Grave," concludes with these lines:

"O poets, from a maniac's tongue was poured the deathless singing!
O Christians, at your cross of hope a hopeless hand was clinging!
O men, this man in brotherhood your weary paths beguiling,
Groaned inly while he taught you peace, and died while you were smiling."
It is a noble tribute to the deathless work of an afflicted man, and reminds us that Cowper is still singing his wondrous theme of "redeeming love," although his

"poor lisping, stammering tongue
Lies silent in the grave."

A Hymn of Gracious Invitation

Come ye disconsolate, where'er ye languish;
Come to the mercy-seat, fervently kneel:
Here bring your wounded hearts, here tell your anguish;
Earth has no sorrow that Heaven cannot heal.
Joy of the desolate, light of the straying,
Hope of the penitent, fadeless and pure!
Here speaks the Comforter, tenderly saying,
"Earth has no sorrow that Heaven cannot cure."
Here see the Bread of Life; see waters flowing
Forth from the throne of God, pure from above,
Come to the feast of love; come, ever knowing
Earth has no sorrow but Heaven can remove.
Thomas Moore (1179-1852).

AN IRISH POET AND HIS HYMNS

There are probably few Protestants who, when they have sung "Come, ye disconsolate, where'er ye languish," have been conscious of the fact that it was written by a Roman Catholic. There is indeed no place where the "communion of saints" becomes so apparent as in the hymn-books of Christendom. The authors of our great hymns have come from practically every Christian communion, proving that in every church group there are souls who are living in the grace that is in Christ Jesus.

Thomas Moore, the author of the hymn mentioned above, is probably better known for his ballads and other poems than for his hymns. Lovers of English lyric poetry will always remember him as the writer of "The last rose of summer," "Believe me, if all those endearing young charms," "The harp that once through Tara's halls," "Oft in the stilly night," and a number of other ballads that have lived through the years and have made the name of Thomas Moore famous.

Moore, who was born in Dublin, Ireland, May 28, 1779, was a man of curious make-up. True to his Celtic nature, he possessed a fiery temper that often brought him into embarrassing situations.

Jeffrey, the famous critic, once aroused Moore's ire by saying unkind things about his poetry. Moore resented this and promptly challenged Jeffrey to a duel. The authorities interfered before any blood was shed. It was then discovered that one of the pistols contained no bullet, whereupon the two men became fast friends.

Moore was one of the few men who ever made a financial success of the business of writing poetry. For "Lalla Rookh" he received $15,000 before a single copy had been sold.

Moore's hymns, thirty-two in number, first appeared in his volume of "Sacred Songs," published in 1816. Most of these hymns were written to popular airs of various nations. They have attained greater popularity in America than in Great Britain. One of the most famous of his hymns is "Sound the loud timbrel o'er Egypt's dark sea."

Like most men of poetic bent, Moore was a poor financier and business man. At one time he accepted a government position in the revenue service at Bermuda. He did not enjoy his tasks, and so he placed his duties in the hands of a deputy, while he went on a tour of America. The deputy, however, absconded with the proceeds of a ship's cargo, whereupon Moore found himself liable for the loss of $30,000.

"Come, ye disconsolate" was so changed by Thomas Hastings, the great American hymnist, that it almost became a new hymn. The second line of the first stanza, as Moore originally wrote it, was:

Come, at the shrine of God fervently kneel.
The second line of the second stanza was also changed by Dr. Hastings, the original version by Moore being:

Hope, when all others die, fadeless and pure.
The third line of the second stanza was greatly improved by the American critic. Moore's line read:

Here speaks the Comforter, in God's name saying.
But the greatest change was made in the third stanza. This was practically rewritten by Dr. Hastings. Moore's third stanza departs very radically and abruptly from true hymn style. It originally read:

Come, ask the infidel what boon he brings us,
What charm for aching hearts he can reveal,
Sweet is that heavenly promise Hope sings us—
Earth has no sorrow that God cannot heal.
The last three years of Moore's life were very unhappy. A nervous affliction rendered him practically helpless. His death occurred on February 26, 1852, at the age of seventy-three years.

A Beautiful Lyric on Prayer

Prayer is the soul's sincere desire,
Uttered or unexpressed;
The motion of a hidden fire
That trembles in the breast.
Prayer is the simplest form of speech
That infant lips can try;
Prayer the sublimest strains that reach
The majesty on high.
Prayer is the contrite sinner's voice,
Returning from his ways;
While angels in their songs rejoice
And cry, "Behold, he prays!"
Prayer is the Christian's vital breath,

The Christian's native air;
His watchword at the gates of death;
He enters heaven with prayer.
O Thou, by whom we come to God,
The Life, the Truth, the Way,
The paths of prayer Thyself hast trod:
Lord, teach us how to pray!
James Montgomery, 1818

THE HYMN LEGACY OF AN ENGLISH EDITOR

Shortly before James Montgomery died, a friend asked him, "Which of your poems will live?" He answered, "None, sir; nothing, except perhaps a few of my hymns."

Montgomery was right. Although he wrote a number of pretentious poems, they have been forgotten. But his hymns live on. A perusal of almost any evangelical hymnbook will probably reveal more hymns by this gifted and consecrated man than by any other author, excepting only Isaac Watts and Charles Wesley.

What a rich legacy was bequeathed to the Christian Church by the man who wrote "Hail to the Lord's Anointed," "Prayer is the soul's sincere desire," "Angels, from the realms of glory," "In the hour of trial," "Who are these in bright array?" "According to Thy gracious Word," "Come to Calvary's holy mountain," "Forever with the Lord," "The Lord is my shepherd, no want shall I know," "Jerusalem, my happy home," and "Go to dark Gethsemane!" Montgomery wrote about four hundred hymns in all, and nearly one-fourth of these are still in common use.

Montgomery began writing hymns as a little boy. He was born at Irvine, Ayrshire, Scotland, November 4, 1771. His father was a Moravian minister, and it had been determined that the son James should also be trained for the same calling. Accordingly he was sent to the Moravian seminary at Fulneck, Yorkshire, England. The parents, however, were sent to the West Indies as missionaries, and their death there made it necessary for James to discontinue his schooling.

For a while he worked as a clerk in a store, but this was entirely distasteful to one who possessed the literary gifts of Montgomery. At the age of nineteen we find him in London with a few of his poems in manuscript form, trying to find a publisher who would print them. In this he was unsuccessful, and two years later we follow him to Sheffield, where he became associated with Robert Gales, editor of the Sheffield Register.

Gales was a radical, and, because he displeased the authorities by some of his articles, he found it convenient in 1794 to leave England for America. Montgomery, then only twenty-three years old, took over the publication of the paper and changed its name to the Sheffield Iris. Montgomery, however, proved as indiscreet as Gales had been, and during the first two years of his editorship he was twice imprisoned by the government, the first time for publishing a poem in commemoration of "The Fall of Bastille," and the second time for his account of a riot at Sheffield.

In 1797 he published a volume of poems called "Prison Amusements," so named from the fact that some of them had been written during his imprisonment. In later years the British government granted him a pension of $1,000 per year in recognition of his achievements and perhaps by way of making amends for the indignity offered him by his two imprisonments.

In Montgomery's hymns we may hear for the first time the missionary note in English hymnody, reflecting the newly-awakened zeal for the evangelization of the world which had gripped the English people. The Baptist Missionary Society had been organized in 1792; Carey had gone to India as its great apostle; and in 1799 the English Church Missionary Society had been formed.

In the fervor aroused for foreign missions in England we may discern a continuation of the impulses which went forth from the Pietistic movement at Halle, Germany, nearly a century earlier, when Bartholomew Ziegenbalg and Henry Plütschau were sent from that cradle of the modern missionary movement as the first missionaries to India. We may also see something of the influences emanating from the great Moravian missionary center at Herrnhut. John Wesley visited both these places before he began his great revival in England, and became deeply imbued with zeal for missions.

Moravian contact with England had resulted in the formation of many Moravian societies, and it was one of these that had sent Montgomery's parents as missionaries to the West Indies. It was not without reason, therefore, that Montgomery became the first English hymnist to sound the missionary trumpet. He could never forget that his parents had given their lives in bringing the gospel to the wretched blacks of the West Indies. His father's grave was at Barbadoes and his mother was sleeping on the island of Tobago. And for the same reason, Montgomery was a bitter opponent of slavery.

The first missionary note is heard in Montgomery's great Advent hymn, "Hail to the Lord's Anointed," written in 1821. One of the stanzas not usually found in hymn-books reads:

Kings shall fall down before Him,
And gold and incense bring;
All nations shall adore Him,
His praise all people sing;

For He shall have dominion
O'er river, sea, and shore,
Far as the eagle's pinion
Or dove's light wing can soar.

Two other missionary hymns are "Lift up your heads, ye gates of brass" and "Hark! the song of jubilee." The latter sweeps along in triumphant measures:

He shall reign from pole to pole,
With illimitable sway;
He shall reign, when like a scroll
Yonder heavens have passed away;
Then the end: beneath His rod

Man's last enemy shall fall:
Hallelujah! Christ in God,
God in Christ, is all in all!

Although "Jerusalem, my happy home!" ranks highest among the hymns of Montgomery, judged by the standard of popular favor, his hymn on prayer and "Forever with the Lord" have aroused the most enthusiasm on the part of literary critics. Julian says of the latter that "it is full of lyric fire and deep feeling," and Dr. Theodore Cuyler declares that it contains four lines that are as fine as anything in hymnody. This beautiful verse reads:

Here, in the body pent,
Absent from Thee I roam,
Yet nightly pitch my moving tent
A day's march nearer home.

Montgomery's last words were words of prayer. After his usual evening devotion on April 30, 1854, he went to sleep, a sleep from which he never woke on earth. And so was fulfilled in his own experience the beautiful thought contained in his glorious hymn on prayer:

Prayer is the Christian's vital breath,
The Christian's native air,
His watchword at the gates of death—
He enters heaven with prayer.

A Sublime Hymn of Adoration

Holy, Holy, Holy, Lord God Almighty!
Early in the morning our song shall rise to Thee:
Holy, Holy, Holy! merciful and mighty;
God in three Persons, blessed Trinity!
Holy, Holy, Holy! all the saints adore Thee,
Casting down their golden crowns upon the glassy sea;
Cherubim and Seraphim falling down before Thee,
Which wert, and art, and evermore shalt be.
Holy, Holy, Holy! though the darkness hide Thee,
Though the eyes of sinful man Thy glory may not see,
Only Thou art holy: there is none beside Thee,
Perfect in power, in love, in purity.
Holy, Holy, Holy, Lord God Almighty!
All Thy works shall praise Thy Name, in earth, and sky, and sea:
Holy, Holy, Holy! merciful and mighty;
God in three Persons, blessed Trinity!
Reginald Heber, 1826.

HEBER, MISSIONARY BISHOP AND HYMNIST

In the glorious hymns of Reginald Heber, missionary bishop to India, we find not only the noblest expression of the missionary fervor which in his day was stirring the

Church, but also the purest poetry in English hymnody. Christians of all ages will gratefully remember the name of the man who wrote the most stirring of all missionary hymns, "From Greenland's icy mountains," as well as that sublime hymn of adoration, "Holy, holy, holy, Lord God Almighty!"

The latter was regarded by Alfred Tennyson as the world's greatest hymn.

Born April 21, 1783, at Malpas, Cheshire, England, Heber was educated at Oxford, where he formed the friendship of Sir Walter Scott. His gift for writing poetry revealed itself in this period of his life, when he won a prize for a remarkable poem on Palestine. It is said that Heber, who was only seventeen years old at the time, read the poem to Scott at the breakfast table, and that the latter suggested one of the most striking lines.

Following the award of the prize, for which young Heber had been earnestly striving, his parents found him on his knees in grateful prayer.

For sixteen years Heber served in the obscure parish of Hodnet as a minister of the Church of England. It was during this period that all of his hymns were written. He was also engaged in other literary activities that brought him some fame. All this while, however, he nourished a secret longing to go to India. It is said that he would work out imaginary journeys on the map, while he hoped that some day he might become bishop of Calcutta.

His missionary fervor at this time is also reflected in the famous hymn, "From Greenland's icy mountains," written in 1819. The allusions to "India's coral strand" and "Ceylon's isle" are an indication of the longings that were running through his mind.

His earnest prayer was answered in 1822, when at the age of forty years he was called to the episcopate as bishop of Calcutta. After three years of arduous work in India, the life of the gifted bishop was cut short. During this period he ordained the first native pastor of the Episcopal Church—Christian David.

A man of rare refinement and noble Christian personality, Heber was greatly beloved by all who knew him. "One of the best of English gentlemen," was the tribute accorded him by Thackeray. It was not until after his death, however, that he leaped into fame through his hymns.

The story of how "From Greenland's icy mountains" was written reveals something of the poetic genius of Heber. It seems that he was visiting with his father-in-law, Dr. Shipley, vicar and dean of Wrexham, on the Saturday before Whitsunday, 1819. The dean, who was planning to preach a missionary sermon the following morning, asked young Heber to write a missionary hymn that could be sung at the service. The latter immediately withdrew from the circle of friends to another part of the room. After a while the dean asked, "What have you written?" Heber replied by reading the first three stanzas of the hymn. The dean expressed satisfaction, but the poet replied, "No, no, the sense is not complete." And so he added the fourth verse—"Waft, waft, ye winds, His story"—and the greatest missionary hymn of the ages had been born.

The story of the tune to which the hymn is sung is equally interesting. A Christian woman in Savannah, Georgia, had come into possession of a copy of Heber's words. The meter was unusual, and she was unable to find music to fit the words. Learning of a young bank clerk who was said to be gifted as a composer, she sent the poem to him. Within a half hour it was returned to her with the beautiful tune, "Missionary Hymn," to which it is now universally sung. The young bank clerk was none other than Lowell Mason, who afterwards achieved fame as one of America's greatest hymn-tune composers. The marvel is that both words and music were written almost in a moment—by real inspiration, it would seem.

Bishop Heber's hymns are characterized chiefly by their lyrical quality. They are unusually rich in imagery. This may be seen particularly in his beautiful Epiphany hymn, "Brightest and best of the sons of the morning." In some respects the hymns of Heber resemble the later lyrics of Henry Francis Lyte, writer of "Abide with me, fast falls the eventide." They ring, however, with a much more joyous note than the hymns of Lyte, in which are always heard strains of sadness.

We have already referred to Tennyson's estimate of Heber's hymn to the Holy Trinity. It should be observed that this great hymn is one of pure adoration. There is nothing of the element of confession, petition or thanksgiving in it, but only worship. Its exalted language is Scriptural throughout, indeed it is the Word of the Most High. It is doubtful if there is a nobler hymn of its kind in all the realm of hymnody. The tune to which it is always sung, "Nicaea," was written by the great English composer, Rev. John B. Dykes, and is comparable to the hymn itself in majesty.

Other fine hymns by Heber include "The Son of God goes forth to war," "God that madest earth and heaven," "O Thou, whose infant feet were found," "When through the torn sail," "Bread of the world in mercy broken," and "By cool Siloam's shady rill."

Altogether Heber wrote fifty-seven hymns, all of which were published in a single collection after his death. It is said that every one of them is still in use, a rare tribute to the genius of this consecrated writer.

Heber's life was closely paralleled in many respects by another great hymn-writer who lived in the same period. His name was Sir Robert Grant. He was born two years later than the gifted missionary bishop and, like Heber, died in India. Although he did not enter the service of the Church but engaged in secular pursuits, he was a deeply spiritual man and his hymns bear testimony of an earnest, confiding faith in Christ. Between his hymns and those of Heber there is a striking similarity. The language is chaste and exalted. The rhythm is faultless. The lines are chiseled as perfectly as a cameo. The imagery is almost startling in its grandeur. Take, for example, a stanza from his magnificent hymn, "O worship the King":

O tell of His might, and sing of His grace,
Whose robe is the light, whose canopy space;
His chariots of wrath the deep thunder-clouds form,
And dark is His path on the wings of the storm.

There is something beautifully tender in that other hymn of Grant's in which he reveals childlike trust in Christ:

When gathering clouds around I view,
And days are dark, and friends are few,
On Him I lean, who, not in vain,
Experienced every human pain;
He sees my wants, allays my fears,
And counts and treasures up my tears.

Nor would we forget his other famous hymn, "Saviour, when in dust to Thee," based on the Litany. When we learn that the man who wrote these hymns was never engaged in religious pursuits, but that his whole life was crowded with arduous tasks and great responsibilities in filling high government positions, we have reason to marvel.

Sir Robert Grant was born in the county of Inverness, Scotland, in 1785. His father was a member of Parliament and a director of the East India Company. The son also was trained for political life, and, after graduating from Cambridge University in 1806, he began the practice of law. In 1826 he was elected to Parliament, five years later became privy counselor, and in 1834 he was named governor of Bombay. He died at Dapoorie, in western India, in 1838.

While a member of Parliament, Sir Robert introduced a bill to remove the restrictions imposed upon the Jews. The historian Macaulay made his maiden speech in Parliament in support of this measure.

Brief mention should also be made here of another of Bishop Heber's contemporaries who gained undying fame by a great hymn. He was John Marriott, a minister of the Church of England, whose missionary hymn, "Thou, whose almighty word," is ranked among the finest in the English language. Marriott was born in 1780, three years before Heber's birth, and he died in 1825, a year before the death of the famous missionary bishop.

A Hymn That Wins Souls

Just as I am, without one plea
But that Thy blood was shed for me,
And that Thou bidd'st me come to Thee,
O Lamb of God, I come, I come!
Just as I am, and waiting not
To rid my soul of one dark blot,
To Thee whose blood can cleanse each spot,
O Lamb of God, I come, I come!
Just as I am, though tossed about
With many a conflict, many a doubt,
Fightings and fears, within, without,
O Lamb of God, I come, I come!
Just as I am, poor, wretched, blind;
Sight, riches, healing of the mind,
Yea, all I need, in Thee I find,

O Lamb of God, I come, I come!
Just as I am, Thou wilt receive,
Wilt welcome, pardon, cleanse, relieve,
Because Thy promise I believe,
O Lamb of God, I come, I come!
Just as I am; Thy love unknown
Hath broken every barrier down;
Now to be Thine, yea, Thine alone,
O Lamb of God, I come, I come!
Charlotte Elliott, 1836.

AN INVALID WHO BLESSED THE WORLD

"Just as I am" will doubtlessly be sung to the end of time, and as often as Christians sing it they will praise God and bless the memory of the woman who wrote it—Charlotte Elliott.

This hymn will have a greater value, too, when we know something of the pain and effort that it cost the writer to produce it. Miss Elliott was one of those afflicted souls who scarcely know what surcease from suffering is. Though she lived to be eighty-two years old, she was never well, and often endured seasons of great physical distress. She could well understand the sacrifice made by one who

Strikes the strings
With fingers that ache and bleed.
Of her own afflictions she once wrote: "He knows, and He alone, what it is, day after day, hour after hour, to fight against bodily feelings of almost overpowering weakness, languor and exhaustion, to resolve not to yield to slothfulness, depression and instability, such as the body causes me to long to indulge, but to rise every morning determined to take for my motto: 'If a man will come after Me, let him deny himself, take up his cross daily, and follow Me.'"

But God seemed to have had a purpose in placing a heavy cross upon her. Her very afflictions made her think of other sufferers like herself and made her the better fitted for the work that He had prepared for her—the ministry of comfort and consolation. How beautifully she resigned herself to the will of God may be seen in her words: "God sees, God guides, God guards me. His grace surrounds me, and His voice continually bids me to be happy and holy in His service, just where I am."

"Just as I am" was written in 1836, and appeared for the first time in the second edition of "The Invalid's Hymn Book," which was published that year and to which Miss Elliott had contributed 115 pieces.

The great American evangelist, Dwight L. Moody, once said that this hymn had probably touched more hearts and brought more souls to Christ than any other ever written. Miss Elliott's own brother, who was a minister in the Church of England, himself wrote:

"In the course of a long ministry, I hope to have been permitted to see some fruit of my labors; but I feel far more has been done by a single hymn of my sister's."

It is said that after the death of Miss Elliott, more than a thousand letters were found among her papers, in which the writers expressed their gratitude to her for the help the hymn had brought them.

The secret power of this marvelous hymn must be found in its true evangelical spirit. It sets forth in very simple but gripping words the all-important truth that we are not saved through any merit or worthiness in ourselves, but by the sovereign grace of God through faith in Jesus Christ. It also pictures the utter helplessness and wretchedness of the human soul, and its inability to rise above its own sins; but very lovingly it invites the soul to come to Him "whose blood can cleanse each spot."

The hymn was born out of the author's personal spiritual experiences. Though a daughter of the Church, brought up in a pious home, it seems that Miss Elliott had never found true peace with God. Like so many other seeking souls in all ages, she felt that men must do something themselves to win salvation, instead of coming to Christ as helpless sinners and finding complete redemption in Him.

When Dr. Caesar Malan, the noted Swiss preacher of Geneva, came to visit the Elliott home in Brighton, England, in 1822, he soon discovered the cause of her spiritual perplexity, and became a real evangelical guide and counsellor. "You have nothing of merit to bring to God," he told her. "You must come just as you are, a sinner, to the Lamb of God that taketh away the sin of the world."

Throughout the remainder of her life, Miss Elliott celebrated every year the day on which her friend had led her to Christ, for she considered it to be her spiritual birthday. Although it was fourteen years later that she wrote her immortal hymn, it is apparent that she never forgot the words of Dr. Malan, for they form the very core and essence of it. The inspiration for the hymn came one day when the frail invalid had been left alone at the home of her brother. She was lying on a couch and pondering on the words spoken by Dr. Malan many years before, when suddenly the whole glorious truth of salvation as the free gift of God flashed upon her soul. Then came the heavenly gift. Rising from her couch, she wrote:

Just as I am, without one plea,
But that Thy blood was shed for me,
And that Thou bidd'st me come to Thee,
O Lamb of God, I come, I come!

Miss Elliott was the author of some 150 hymns. Perhaps her finest, aside from her great masterpiece, is "My God, my Father, while I stray." By common consent, Miss Elliott is given first place among English women hymn-writers.

The Sun That Ne'er Goes Down

Sun of my soul, Thou Saviour dear,
It is not night if Thou be near;

O may no earthborn cloud arise
To hide Thee from Thy servant's eyes.
When the soft dews of kindly sleep
My wearied eyelids gently steep,
Be my last thought, how sweet to rest
Forever on my Saviour's breast.
Abide with me from morn till eve,
For without Thee I cannot live;
Abide with me when night is nigh,
For without Thee I dare not die.
If some poor wandering child of Thine
Have spurned today the voice divine,
Now, Lord, the gracious work begin;
Let him no more lie down in sin.
Watch by the sick; enrich the poor
With blessings from Thy boundless store;
Be every mourner's sleep tonight,
Like infant's slumber, pure and light.
Come near and bless us when we wake,
Ere through the world our way we take;
Till in the ocean of Thy love
We lose ourselves in heaven above.
John Keble, 1827.

HOW HYMNS HELPED BUILD A CHURCH

Many of the classic hymns of the Christian Church have been derived from devotional poems that were never intended as hymns by their writers. This is true of the beautiful morning hymn, "New every morning is the love," and the equally beautiful evening hymn, "Sun of my soul, Thou Saviour dear." Both of these gems in the treasury of hymnody have been taken from one of the most famous devotional books ever written—John Keble's "The Christian Year."

Keble was born at Fairford, England, April 25, 1792, the son of a country vicar. The only elementary training he received was at the hands of his gifted father, but at the age of fifteen years he was ready to enter Oxford University. Here he distinguished himself as a brilliant scholar, and at the age of twenty-three he was ordained as a clergyman of the Church of England. He remained as a tutor at Oxford for a number of years, but when his mother died he returned to Fairford to assist his father. Although he received a number of tempting offers at this time, he preferred to labor in this obscure parish, where he might be of help and comfort to his father and his two sisters.

It was not until 1835, when his father died and the home was broken up, that Keble accepted the vicarage of Hursley, another humble and scattered parish, with a population of 1,500 people. He married in the same year, and here he and his devoted wife labored until 1866, when they passed away within six weeks of each other.

It was in 1827, when Keble was only twenty-seven, that he yielded to the strong entreaties of his father and many of his friends and consented to publish the volume of poems known as "The Christian Year." The verses follow the church calendar, and it was the author's desire that the book should be a devotional companion to the Book of Common Prayer. For this reason it has been called "The Prayer Book in Poetry."

Keble was so modest concerning his work that he refused to permit the volume to bear his name, and so it was given to the world anonymously. The work was a marvelous success. From 1827 to 1867, a year after the author's death, the book had passed through one hundred and nine editions. Keble used a large part of the proceeds derived from the sales of his book in helping to rebuild the church at Hursley. He also was instrumental in having churches built at Otterbourne and Ampfield, hamlets that belonged to his parish.

Religious leaders, as well as literary critics, have been unanimous in rendering tribute to this remarkable volume. Dr. Arnold, the great schoolmaster of Rugby, speaking of Keble's poems, says: "Nothing equal to them exists in our language. The knowledge of Scripture, the purity of heart, and the richness of poetry, I never saw equaled." "It is a book," says Canon Barry, "which leads the soul up to God, not through one, but through all of the various faculties which He has implanted in it." And Dr. Pusey adds: "It taught, because his own soul was moved so deeply; the stream burst forth, because the heart that poured it out was full; it was fresh, deep, tender, loving, because he himself was such; he was true, and thought aloud, and conscience everywhere responded to the voice of conscience."

The publication of "The Christian Year" brought Keble such fame that, in 1831, he was elected professor of poetry at Oxford. He did not remove thither, but in 1833 he preached at Oxford his famous sermon on "National Apostasy" which is credited with having started the so-called "Oxford Movement."

This movement had its inception in the earnest desire on the part of many prominent leaders of the Church of England, including John Newman, to bring about a spiritual awakening in the Church. They looked askance at the evangelistic methods of the Wesleyan leaders and turned to the other extreme of high church ritualism. All England was profoundly stirred by a series of "Tracts for the Times," written by Newman and his friends, among them Keble. A disastrous result of the movement was the desertion of Newman and a large number of others to the Church of Rome; but Keble shrank from this final step and remained a high church Episcopalian.

Although a great part of his later life was occupied with religious controversy, we would like to remember Keble as a consecrated Christian poet and an humble parish pastor. For more than thirty years he labored faithfully among his people, visiting from house to house. If it was impossible for a candidate to attend confirmation instruction during the day, Keble would go to his house at night, armed with cloak and lantern. He gave each candidate a Bible, in which he had marked the passages that were to be learned. These Bibles were highly prized, and some of them are to be found in Hursley to this day. It was noticed that, whenever the Vicar prepared to read and explain a passage of Scripture, he would first bow his head and close his eyes while he asked for the guidance of the Holy Spirit.

Keble's famous morning hymn, "New every morning is the love," is taken from a poem of sixteen verses. The first line reads, "O timely happy, timely wise." It contains the two oft quoted stanzas that ought to be treasured in the heart of every Christian:

The trivial round, the common task,
Will furnish all we ought to ask,
Room to deny ourselves; a road
To bring us daily nearer God.
Only, O Lord, in Thy dear love
Fit us for perfect rest above;
And help us this, and every day,
To live more nearly as we pray.

The evening hymn is also taken from a longer poem, in which the author first describes in graphic words the setting of the sun:

'Tis gone! that bright and orbéd blaze,
Fast fading from our wistful gaze;
Yon mantling cloud has hid from sight
The last faint pulse of quivering light.
In darkness and in weariness
The traveler on his way must press,
No gleam to watch on tree or tower,
Whiling away the lonesome hour.

Then comes the beautiful and reassuring thought:

Sun of my soul! Thou Saviour dear,
It is not night if Thou be near!
O may no earthborn cloud arise
To hide Thee from Thy servant's eyes.

The peculiar tenderness in Keble's poetry is beautifully illustrated in the second stanza:

When the soft dews of kindly sleep
My wearied eyelids gently steep,
Be my last thought, how sweet to rest
Forever on my Saviour's breast.

Other familiar hymns by Keble are "The Voice that breathed o'er Eden," "Blest are the pure in heart," and "When God of old came down from heaven."

The Hymn of a Perplexed Soul

Lead, kindly light, amid th' encircling gloom,
Lead Thou me on!
The night is dark, and I am far from home;
Lead Thou me on!

Keep Thou my feet; I do not ask to see
The distant scene; one step enough for me.
I was not ever thus, nor prayed that Thou
Shouldst lead me on;
I loved to choose and see my path; but now
Lead Thou me on!
I loved the garish day, and, spite of fears,
Pride ruled my will. Remember not past years!
So long Thy power hath blest me, sure it still
Will lead me on
O'er moor and fen, o'er crag and torrent, till
The night is gone,
And with the morn those angel faces smile,
Which I have loved long since, and lost awhile.
John Henry Newman, 1833.

A FAMOUS HYMN BY A PROSELYTE OF ROME

When the children of Israel were about to resume the march from Mount Sinai and Moses had received the command to lead the people into the unknown wilderness, we are told in Exodus that Moses hesitated.

"See," said the great leader, "Thou sayest unto me, 'Bring up this people': and Thou hast not let me know whom Thou wilt send with me." And God answered, "My presence shall go with thee, and I will give thee rest."

It was this sublime thought of the guiding presence of God that gave to John Henry Newman the inspiration for "Lead, kindly Light."

There was much of tragedy in the strange life of Newman. He was born in London, the son of a banker, February 21, 1801. It is said that he was extremely superstitious as a boy, and that he would cross himself, after the custom of Roman Catholics, whenever he entered a dark place. He also came to the conclusion that it was the will of God that he should never marry.

He graduated from Trinity College, Oxford, at the age of nineteen, and four years later was ordained as a minister of the Church of England. He soon began to be attracted by Roman Catholic teachings and to associate with leaders of that communion. In 1833 he was in poor health, and determined to go to Italy. This was the year of the famous "Oxford Movement," which was destined to carry so many high Anglicans into the Roman communion. While in Rome he came still further under the influence of the Romanists, who lost no opportunity to take advantage of his perplexed state of mind. Leaving Rome, he went down to Sicily, where he was stricken with fever and was near death. After his recovery, his one thought was to return to his native shores. He writes:

"I was aching to get home; yet for want of a vessel was kept at Palermo for three weeks. At last I got an orange-boat bound for Marseilles. We were becalmed a whole week on the Mediterranean Sea. Then it was (June 16, 1833) that I wrote the lines: 'Lead, kindly Light.'"

The hymn, therefore, may be said to be the work of a man who found himself in deep mental, physical, and spiritual distress. Newman was greatly dissatisfied with conditions within his own Church. In his perplexity he scarcely knew where to turn, but he had no intention at this time, as he himself states, to forsake the Church of England for the Roman Catholic communion. This step was not taken by him until twelve years later.

"Lead, kindly Light" was published for the first time in "The British Magazine," in the month of March, 1834. It bore the title, "Faith—Heavenly Leadings." Two years later he printed it with the title, "Light in the Darkness," and the motto, "Unto the godly there ariseth up light in the darkness." At a later date he published it under the title, "The Pillar of the Cloud."

Newman ascribed its popularity as a hymn to the appealing tune written for it in 1865 by Dr. John B. Dykes. As to its poetic qualities there has been the widest divergence of opinion. While one critic has called it "one of the outstanding lyrics of the nineteenth century," William T. Stead observes, caustically, that "It is somewhat hard for the staunch Protestant to wax enthusiastic over the invocation of a 'Kindly Light' which led the author straight into the arms of the Scarlet Woman of the Seven Hills."

The hymn has often been attacked on the ground that it is not definitely Christian in character. In this respect it is similar to Mrs. Adams' famous hymn, "Nearer, my God, to Thee." When the Parliament of Religions convened in Chicago a few years ago, Newman's hymn was the only one sung by representatives of all creeds from every part of the world. Bishop Bickersteth of England, feeling the need of the Christian note in the hymn, added the following stanza:

Meantime along the narrow rugged path
Thyself hast trod,
Lead, Saviour, lead me home in childlike faith,
Home to my God
To rest for ever after earthly strife
In the calm light of everlasting life.

This was done, said Bishop Bickersteth, "from a deep conviction that the heart of the belated pilgrim can only find rest in the Light of Light." The additional stanza, however, has not come into general use.

Many interpretations have been given to the closing lines,

And with the morn those angel faces smile,
Which I have loved long since, and lost awhile.

Some have believed that Newman by "angel faces" had in mind loved ones lost through death. Yet others are convinced that the author had reference to the actual visions of angels which are said to have come to him in youth, and the loss of which greatly grieved him in later life. Newman himself, in a letter written January 18, 1879, refused to throw further light on the lines, pleading that he had forgotten the meaning that he had in mind when the hymn was written forty-six years before.

Rome honored its distinguished proselyte by making him a cardinal. It is said, however, that Newman was never again a happy man after having surrendered the faith of his fathers. He died at Birmingham, England, August 11, 1890, at the age of eighty-nine years.

A disciple of Newman's, Frederick William Faber, may be mentioned in this connection, for the lives of the two men were strangely intertwined. Faber, who was the son of an English clergyman, was born at Yorkshire, June 28, 1814. He was graduated from Oxford in 1836, and became a minister of the English Church at Elton in 1843.

While at Oxford he came under the influence of the "Oxford Movement" and formed a deep attachment for Newman. It was inevitable, therefore, that he too should be carried into the Roman Church, which communion he joined in 1846. For some years he labored with Newman in the Catholic church of St. Philip Neri in London. He died in 1863 at the age of forty-nine years.

Faber wrote a large number of hymns, many of them before his desertion to the Church of Rome. Others, written after his defection, containing eulogies of Mary and petitions addressed to the saints, have been changed in order to make them suitable for Protestant hymn-books. His inordinate use of the word "sweet", and his familiar manner of addressing Christ as "sweet Saviour" has called down harsh criticism on his hymns as sentimental and effeminate. However, such hymns as "There's a wideness in God's mercy," "Hark, hark, my soul! angelic songs are swelling," "O Saviour, bless us ere we go," "O Paradise, O Paradise," and "Faith of our fathers, living still" have probably found a permanent place in the hymn-books of the Church Universal, and will be loved and cherished both for their devotional spirit and their poetic beauty.

Faber wrote "Faith of our fathers" after his defection to the Church of Rome. In its original form the author expressed the hope that England would be brought back to the papal fold. The opening lines, as Faber wrote them, were:

Faith of our fathers! Mary's prayers
Shall win our country back to thee.

A Hymn Written in the Shadows

Abide with me! fast falls the eventide;
The darkness deepens; Lord, with me abide!
When other helpers fail, and comforts flee,
Help of the helpless, O abide with me!
Swift to its close ebbs out life's little day;
Earth's joys grow dim, its glories pass away;
Change and decay in all around I see;
O Thou who changest not, abide with me!
I need Thy presence every passing hour:

What but Thy grace can foil the tempter's power?
Who like Thyself my guide and stay can be?
Through cloud and sunshine, O abide with me!
I fear no foe, with Thee at hand to bless:
Ills have no weight, and tears no bitterness.
Where is death's sting? where, grave, thy victory?
I triumph still, if Thou abide with me!
Hold Thou Thy cross before my closing eyes,
Shine through the gloom, and point me to the skies;
Heaven's morning breaks, and earth's vain shadows flee;
In life, in death, O Lord, abide with me!
Henry Francis Lyte, 1847.

HENRY FRANCIS LYTE AND HIS SWAN SONG

Many a man who has labored in obscure places, practically unnoticed and unpraised by his own generation, has achieved a fame after his death that grows in magnitude with the passing years.

When Henry Francis Lyte died in 1847, he was little known beyond his humble seashore parish at Lower Brixham, England; but today, wherever his beautiful hymns are sung throughout the Christian world, he is gratefully remembered as the man who wrote "Abide with me."

In response to a questionnaire sent to American readers recently by "The Etude," a musical magazine, 7,500 out of nearly 32,000 persons who replied named "Abide with me" as their favorite hymn. It easily took first rank, displacing such older favorites as "Rock of Ages" and "Jesus, Lover of my soul."

How often we have sung this hymn at the close of an evening service, and a settled peace has come into our hearts as we have realized the nearness of Him who said, "And lo! I am with you always." Yet, this is not in reality an evening hymn. Its theme is the evening of life, and it was written when Lyte felt the shadows of death gathering about his own head. We catch his meaning in the second stanza:

Swift to its close ebbs out life's little day;
Earth's joys grow dim, its glories pass away.

Lyte was always frail in health. He was born in Scotland, June 1, 1793, and was early left an orphan. Nevertheless, despite the handicap of poverty, he struggled through college, and on three occasions won prizes with poems.

His first ambition was to become a physician, but during his college days he determined to enter the ministry. The death of a young friend, a brother clergyman, brought about a profound change in the spiritual life of Lyte. Called to the bedside of his friend to give him consolation, he discovered to his sorrow that both he and the dying man were blind guides who were still groping for light. Through a prayerful search of the Scriptures, however, they both came to a firm faith in Christ. Lyte wrote of his friend:

"He died happy under the belief that though he had deeply erred, there was One whose death and sufferings would atone for his delinquencies, and that he was forgiven and accepted for His sake."

Concerning the change that came into his own life, he added: "I was greatly affected by the whole matter, and brought to look at life and its issue with a different eye than before; and I began to study my Bible and preach in another manner than I had previously done."

For nearly twenty-five years after this incident Lyte labored among humble fisherfolk and sailors of the parish at Lower Brixham, and his deep spiritual zeal and fervor led him to overtax his physical powers. From time to time he was obliged to spend the winters in more friendly climes.

In the autumn of 1847 he wrote to a friend that the swallows were flying southward, and he observed, "They are inviting me to accompany them; and yet alas; while I am talking of flying, I am just able to crawl."

The Sunday for his farewell service came. His family and friends admonished him not to preach a sermon, but the conscientious minister insisted. "It is better," he said, "to wear out than to rust out."

He did preach, and the hearts of his hearers were full that day, for they seemed to realize that it would probably be the last time they would hear him. The faithful pastor, too, seemed to have a premonition that it would be his last sermon. The service closed with the Lord's Supper, administered by Lyte to his sorrowing flock.

"Though necessarily much exhausted by the exertion and excitement of this effort," his daughter afterward wrote, "yet his friends had no reason to believe that it had been hurtful to him."

This was September 4, 1847. That afternoon he walked out along the shore to watch the sun as it was setting in a glory of crimson and gold. It was a peaceful, beautiful Sabbath evening. Returning to his home, he shut himself up in his study for the brief space of an hour, and when he came out, he handed a near relative the manuscript containing the famous hymn, "Abide with me." He also had composed a tune of his own for the words, but this never came into general use.

During the following week Lyte left his beloved England for Italy. However, he got no farther than Nice, in France, where he was obliged to discontinue his journey. Here he passed away November 20 of the same year. His last words were, "Joy! Peace!" and then he fell asleep.

A little cross marks his grave in the English cemetery at Nice, for he was buried there. Every year hundreds of pilgrims visit his grave and tell touching stories of how Lyte's hymn brought them to faith in Christ Jesus.

It was Lyte's life-long wish that he might leave behind him such a hymn as this. In an earlier poem he had voiced the longing that he might write

Some simple strain, some spirit-moving lay,
Some sparklet of the soul that still might live
When I was passed to clay....
O Thou! whose touch can lend
Life to the dead, Thy quick'ning grace supply,
And grant me, swanlike, my last breath to spend
In song that may not die!

Lyte's prayer was fulfilled. As long as men shall worship the crucified and risen Lord, so long will they continue to sing the sad and beautiful words of Lyte's swan song.

In Lyte we have a hymn-writer of the first rank. Indeed, he is comparable to any of England's greatest hymnists, not excepting Watts or Wesley. His hymns are real lyrics, Scriptural in language, rich in imagery, and exalted in poetic conception. "In no other author," says an eminent authority, "is poetry and religion more exquisitely united."

Aside from the sublime hymn we have mentioned, Lyte has given to the Church such noble lyrics as "Jesus, I my cross have taken," "Pleasant are Thy courts above," "Praise, my soul, the King of heaven," "God of mercy, God of grace," "My spirit on Thy care," "As pants the hart for cooling streams," and "O that the Lord's salvation." The latter hymn is one of the few ever written that voice a prayer for the salvation of Israel.

The poetic rapture to which Lyte's poetry sometimes rises is most beautifully reflected in his hymn of adoration:

Praise, my soul, the King of heaven;
To His feet thy tribute bring;
Ransomed, healed, restored, forgiven,
Who like thee His praise should sing?
Alleluia! Alleluia!
Praise the everlasting King!
Praise Him for His grace and favor
To our fathers in distress;
Praise Him, still the same as ever,
Slow to chide, and swift to bless:
Alleluia! Alleluia!
Glorious in His faithfulness!

A Woman's Gift to the Church

Nearer, my God, to Thee!
Nearer to Thee!
E'en though it be a cross
That raiseth me,
Still all my song shall be,
Nearer, my God, to Thee,
Nearer to Thee!
Though, like the wanderer,

The sun gone down,
Darkness be over me,
My rest a stone,
Yet in my dreams I'd be
Nearer, my God, to Thee,
Nearer to Thee!
There let my way appear
Steps unto heaven;
All that Thou sendest me
In mercy given;
Angels to beckon me
Nearer, my God, to Thee,
Nearer to Thee!
Then with my waking thoughts,
Bright with Thy praise,
Out of my stony griefs
Bethel I'll raise,
So by my woes to be
Nearer, my God, to Thee,
Nearer to Thee!
Or if on joyful wing,
Cleaving the sky,
Sun, moon, and stars forgot,
Upwards I fly;
Still all my song shall be,
Nearer, my God to Thee,
Nearer to Thee!
Sarah Adams, 1840.

SARAH ADAMS AND THE RISE OF WOMEN HYMN-WRITERS

Nineteenth century hymnody was characterized by an extraordinary number of women hymn-writers. It is significant that this development came, as we have noted in a previous chapter, with the great spiritual revivals which aroused evangelical Europe and America from 1800 to 1875. It was also coincident with the general movement resulting in the enlargement of women's influence and activity in all spheres of human endeavor. In the realm of hymnody women have become the chief exponents of church song.

Dr. Breed has pointed out that the large increase of women hymnists, as well as the preponderance of hymn translations, is indicative of a period of decadence in sacred song. While this is probably true of the latter half of the nineteenth century, which saw the rise of the so-called "Gospel song," we must cheerfully recognize the fact that such women as Charlotte Elliott, Sarah Adams, Cecil Alexander and Frances Havergal in England and Mary Lathbury, Anna Warner, Catherine Esling, Harriet Beecher Stowe, Phoebe Gary, Elizabeth Prentiss and Fanny Crosby in America have contributed some of the most precious gems to the treasure-store of Christian hymns. Indeed, the hymnody of the Church would have been immeasurably poorer had these consecrated women failed to make use of their heaven-born talent.

And, although we must deplore the apparent fact that "original utterance in sacred song is departing from the Church," we must be forever grateful to such gifted women as Catherine Winkworth and the Borthwick sisters, who, through their excellent translations, gave to the English-speaking world some of the choicest pearls of German hymnody.

Charlotte Elliott was the forerunner of the long line of women hymnists. Then came Sarah Flower Adams, the writer of "Nearer, my God, to Thee," one of the greatest sacred lyrics ever given to the world, and probably the finest ever written by a woman.

Sarah Flower was born at Harlow, England, February 22, 1805, the daughter of Benjamin Flower, editor of the Cambridge "Intelligencer." The mother died when Sarah was only five years old. A sister, Eliza, was a gifted musician, while Sarah early showed talent along literary lines. In later years Eliza wrote music for the hymns of her sister.

Sarah was fond of the stage. She believed that it could be made to teach great moral truths as well as the pulpit. Her dreams of becoming an actress, however, failed to materialize because of poor health. In 1834 she became the wife of John Bridges Adams, a civil engineer, after which she made her home in London. Her health was seriously impaired through caring for her sister, who died a consumptive in 1846, and she survived her less than two years.

Her great hymn was written in 1840. It was published the following year in a volume of hymns and anthems edited by her pastor, Rev. William Johnson Fox. This man was a Unitarian, and for this reason Mrs. Adams has also been classified with that sect. It is said, however, that she became a Baptist near the close of her life. Other hymns written by her indicate that she had arrived at a living faith in Christ. Perhaps the many trials she suffered proved in the end to be the means of bringing her to the Saviour. And thus was fulfilled in her own life the beautiful lines:

E'en though it be a cross
That raiseth me.

"Nearer, my God, to Thee" has probably aroused more discussion than any other hymn. Because it is based entirely on the story of Jacob at Bethel and omits reference to Christ, it has been called more Unitarian than Christian. Many efforts have been made, but without much success, to write a substitute hymn with a definite Christian note. In 1864 Bishop How of London wrote a hymn, the first stanza of which reads:

Nearer, O God, to Thee!
Hear Thou our prayer;
E'en though a heavy cross
Fainting we bear.
Still all our prayer shall be
Nearer, O God, to Thee,
Nearer to Thee!

Prof. Henry Eyster Jacobs of Philadelphia, in 1887, also wrote a version:

Nearer, my God, to Thee,
Nearer to Thee!

Through Word and Sacrament
Thou com'st to me.
Thy grace is ever near,
Thy Spirit ever here
Drawing to Thee.

The hymn was a favorite with William McKinley, the martyred president. When he was dying, his attending physician heard him murmur, "'Nearer, my God, to Thee, E'en though it be a cross,' has been my constant prayer."

That Sweet Story of Old

I think, when I read that sweet story of old,
When Jesus was here among men,
How He called little children as lambs to His fold,
I should like to have been with them then.
I wish that His hand had been placed on my head,
That His arm had been thrown around me,
And that I might have seen His kind look when He said,
"Let the little ones come unto Me."
Yet still to His footstool in prayer I may go,
And ask for a share in His love;
And if only I earnestly seek Him below,
I shall see Him and hear Him above.
In that beautiful place He has gone to prepare
For all who are washed and forgiven,
Full many dear children are gathering there,
"For of such is the kingdom of heaven"
But thousands and thousands who wander and fall
Never heard of that heavenly home:
I should like them to know there is room for them all,
And that Jesus has bid them to come.
And O how I long for that glorious time,
The sweetest and brightest and best,
When the dear little children of every clime
Shall crowd to His arms and be blest!
Jemima Luke, 1841.

A HYMN WRITTEN IN A STAGE-COACH

Some one has said, "Let me write the songs of a nation, and I care not who may write its laws."

It is a wise saying; for who can estimate the influence of the songs we sing, especially the songs of children? There is no better way to teach Christian truths to children than to have them sing those truths into their hearts and souls.

When Jemima Luke sat in an English stage-coach in 1841 composing the lines of a little poem that had been ringing in her mind, she could scarcely have known she was writing a hymn that would gladden the hearts of thousands of children in many years to come. But that is how she wrote "I think when I read that sweet story of old," and that is the happy fate that was in store for her labor of love.

Her maiden name was Jemima Thompson. Her father was a missionary enthusiast, and she herself was filled with zeal for mission enterprises. Even as a child, at the age of thirteen, she was an anonymous contributor to "The Juvenile Magazine." When she was twenty-eight years old she visited a school where the children had been singing a fine old melody as a marching song.

"What a lovely children's hymn it would make," she thought, "if only there were suitable religious words for it."

She hunted through many books for the words she desired, but could find none that satisfied her. Some time later, as she was riding in a stage coach with nothing to occupy her, she thought of the tune again. Taking an old envelope from her pocket, she recorded on the back of it the words that have come to be loved on both sides of the Atlantic, and some day probably will be sung by the children of all the world.

When she returned home, she taught the words and the melody to her Sunday school class. Her father, who was superintendent of the school, chanced to hear them one day.

"Where did that hymn come from?" he asked.

"Jemima made it!" was the proud answer of the youngsters.

Without telling his daughter about it, the father sent a copy of the words to the "Sunday School Teachers' Magazine," and in a few weeks it appeared for the first time in print. Since that time it has continued to find a place year after year in almost every juvenile hymnal published in the English language.

The last stanza of the hymn, which begins with the words, "But thousands and thousands who wander and fall," was added subsequently by the author, who desired to make it suitable for missionary gatherings. Her interest in foreign missions continued unabated throughout her life. At one time she was accepted as a missionary to the women of India, but poor health prevented her from carrying out her purpose. However, she edited "The Missionary Repository," the first missionary magazine for children, and numbered among her contributors such famous missionaries as David Livingstone, Robert Moffatt and James Montgomery.

In 1843 she married a minister, Rev. Samuel Luke. After his death in 1868 she devoted much of her time to promoting the erection of parsonages in parishes that were too poor to provide them for their pastors.

When an international convention of the Christian Endeavor society was held in Baltimore in 1904, Mrs. Luke sent the following message to the young people:

"Dear children, you will be men and women soon, and it is for you and the children of England to carry the message of a Saviour's love to every nation of this sin-stricken world. It is a blessed message to carry, and it is a happy work to do. The Lord make you ever faithful to Him, and unspeakably happy in His service! I came to Him at ten years of age, and at ninety-one can testify to His care and faithfulness."

She died in 1906 at the age of ninety-three years. Although she wrote a great deal of inspiring Christian literature, it is only her beautiful "Sweet Story of Old" that has come down to us.

Redemption's Story in a Hymn

There is a green hill far away,
Without a city wall,
Where the dear Lord was crucified,
Who died to save us all.
We may not know, we cannot tell,
What pains He had to bear;
But we believe it was for us
He hung and suffered there.
He died that we might be forgiven,
He died to make us good,
That we might go at last to heaven,
Saved by His precious blood.
There was no other good enough
To pay the price of sin;
He only could unlock the gate
Of heaven, and let us in.
O dearly, dearly has He loved,
And we must love Him too,
And trust in His redeeming blood,
And try His works to do.
Cecil Frances Alexander, 1848.

AN ARCHBISHOP'S WIFE WHO WROTE HYMNS

Shortly before the death in 1911 of Archbishop William Alexander, primate of the Anglican Church in Ireland, he remarked that he would be remembered as the husband of the woman who wrote "The roseate hues of early dawn" and "There is a green hill far away."

The humble prelate was right. Although he occupied an exalted position in the Church less than two decades ago, few people today recall his name. But who has not heard the name of Cecil Frances Humphreys Alexander, who, in spite of multitudinous duties as wife and mother, found time to be a parish worker among the poor and to write hymns that shall never die?

When Cecil Frances was only a little girl, she began to reveal poetic talent. Because her father was an officer in the Royal Marines and rather a stern man, she was not sure that he would be pleased with her efforts and therefore she hid her poems under a carpet! When he finally discovered what his nine-year-old daughter was busying herself with, he set aside a certain hour every Saturday evening, at which time he read aloud to the family the poems she had written.

The family numbered among its friends none other than John Keble, writer of the famous collection of devotional poems known as "The Christian Year," and he, too, gave encouragement to the youthful poet.

In 1848, at the age of twenty-five, she published a volume of hymns for little children that probably has never been excelled by a similar collection. Two years later she became the bride of Rev. William Alexander, afterwards Bishop of Derry and Raphoe, and later Archbishop of Armaugh. He was rector of a country parish in the county of Tyrone at the time, and there was much poverty among his people. Among these needy folk the young minister's wife moved about like a ministering angel. A beautiful tribute to her memory from the pen of her husband reads: "From one poor home to another, from one bed of sickness to another, from one sorrow to another, she went. Christ was ever with her, and in her, and all felt her influence."

But the poetic spark within her was not permitted to languish. Even when children began to bless this unusual household and the cares of the mother increased, her harp was tuned anew and sweeter songs than ever began to well up from her joyous, thankful heart.

Practically all of the four hundred hymns and poems written by Mrs. Alexander were intended for children, and for this reason their language is very simple. At the same time she succeeds in teaching some of the most profound truths of the Christian faith. Witness, for example, the simple language of "There is a green hill far away." A child has no difficulty in comprehending it, and yet this precious hymn sets forth in a most touching way the whole story of the Atonement.

> He died that we might be forgiven,
> He died to make us good,
> That we might go at last to heaven,
> Saved by His precious blood.

Again, the infinite value of the sacrifice which Christ made when He, the Sinless One, died for sinners is expressed in these simple, appealing words:

> There was no other good enough
> To pay the price of sin,
> He only could unlock the gate
> Of heaven, and let us in.

Archbishop Alexander mentioned two hymns by which his wife's name, and incidentally his own, would be remembered. He might have added several others, such as the challenging hymn, "Jesus calls us; o'er the tumult," or the two beautiful children's hymns, "Once in royal David's city" and "All things bright and beautiful." And among her splendid poems he might have mentioned the sublime verses entitled "The Burial of Moses." Her own spirit of confiding trust in God is reflected in the lines:

> O lonely tomb in Moab's land!
> O dark Beth-peor's hill!
> Speak to these curious hearts of ours,
> And teach them to be still;
> God has His mysteries of grace,
> Ways that we cannot tell;
> He hides them deep, like the secret sleep
> Of him He loved so well.

Mrs. Alexander died in 1895 at the age of seventy-two years. She was buried in Londonderry, Ireland. At Archbishop Alexander's funeral sixteen years later "The roseate hues of early dawn" was sung in Londonderry cathedral, and when the body was lowered into the grave the mourners sang, "There is a green hill far away."

During the years when Mrs. Alexander was penning her beautiful lyrics, three other women were giving hymns to the English people in another way. They were Catherine Winkworth and the sisters Jane Borthwick and Sarah Borthwick Findlater, all three of whom had conceived a deep love for the wonderful hymns of Germany and were translating them into their native tongue.

Miss Winkworth, who is the foremost translator of German hymns, was born in London, September 13, 1829. Her "Lyra Germanica," published in 1855, met with such favorable reception that a second series was issued in 1858. Her "Christian Singers of Germany" was published in 1869.

Miss Winkworth possessed a marvelous ability of preserving the spirit of the great German hymns while she clothed them in another language. It was she who gave us in English dress such magnificent hymns as Rinkart's "Now thank we all our God," Luther's "Out of the depths I cry to Thee," Decius' "All glory be to God on high," Neander's "Praise to the Lord, the Almighty, the King of creation," Schmolck's "Open now thy gates of beauty," and Gerhardt's "All my heart this night rejoices." Miss Winkworth, more than any other one person, is responsible for having aroused in England and America an appreciation of the treasure store of German hymnody. She died in 1869.

The two Borthwick sisters, Jane Laurie and Sarah, were born in Edinburgh, Scotland, the former in 1813 and the latter in 1823. They came from an old Scotch family. Sarah married a Rev. Eric Findlater and lived for a time in Perthshire.

The Borthwick sisters collaborated in the preparation of the translations entitled "Hymns from the Land of Luther." These appeared first in 1854 and continued in four series until 1862. Although it is difficult to distinguish the individual work of the sisters, Jane is generally credited with the translation of such noble hymns as Zinzendorf's "Jesus, still lead on," and Schmolck's "My Jesus, as Thou wilt," while Sarah is believed to be the translator of Tersteegen's "God calling yet," Spitta's "O happy home, where Thou art loved the dearest," Schmolck's "My God, I know that I must die," and a large number of other famous German hymns.

Jane Borthwick died in 1897, and her younger sister followed her ten years later.

The Voice of Jesus

I heard the voice of Jesus say:
"Come unto Me and rest;
Lay down, thou weary one, lay down
Thy head upon My breast."
I came to Jesus as I was,
Weary, and worn, and sad;
I found in Him a resting-place,
And He has made me glad.
I heard the voice of Jesus say,
"Behold, I freely give
The living water, thirsty one,
Stoop down, and drink, and live."
I came to Jesus and I drank
Of that life-giving stream;
My thirst was quenched, my soul revived,
And now I live in Him.
I heard the voice of Jesus say,
"I am this dark world's Light;
Look unto Me, thy morn shall rise,
And all thy day be bright."
I looked to Jesus, and I found
In Him my Star, my Sun;
And in that Light of life I'll walk,
Till traveling days are done.
Horatius Bonar, 1846.

BONAR, THE SWEET SINGER OF SCOTLAND

One of Scotland's most earnest soul-winners was also its greatest hymnist. He was Horatius Bonar, a name that will be forever cherished by all who are filled with a fervent love for the Saviour and who find that love so beautifully expressed in the spiritual songs of the noble Scotchman.

Like the hymns of Mrs. Alexander, Dr. Bonar wrote his songs for children; but they are so profound and intensely spiritual in their very simplicity they will always satisfy the most mature Christian mind. No matter how old we become, our hearts will ever be stirred as we sing the tender words:

I long to be like Jesus,
Meek, loving, lowly, mild;

I long to be like Jesus,
The Father's holy Child.
I long to be with Jesus,
Amid the heavenly throng,
To sing with saints His praises,
To learn the angels' song.

The subjective, emotional element is strongly present in the hymns of Bonar. In this respect there is a striking resemblance to the hymns of the great German writer, Benjamin Schmolck. Both use the name "Jesus" freely, and both become daringly intimate, yet the hymns of neither are weak or sentimental.

In Bonar we behold the strange anomaly of a man with a strong physique and powerful intellect combined with the gentle, sympathetic nature of a woman and the simple, confiding faith of a child. The warmth and sincerity of his personal faith in Christ may be seen reflected in all his hymns. "I try to fill my hymns with the love and light of Christ," he once said, and certainly he has drawn many souls to the Saviour by the tenderness of their appeal.

Bonar is ever pointing in his hymns to Christ as an all-sufficient Saviour, dwelling in simple language on the blessings of the Atonement and the willingness of God to accept all who come to Him through Christ. In these days of modernistic teachings when practically all stress is placed on "living the Christ-life" while the meritorious work of Christ on behalf of the sinner is largely ignored and forgotten, it would be salutary for the Church to listen anew to such words as these:

Upon a Life I have not lived,
Upon a Death I did not die,
Another's Life; Another's Death:
I stake my whole eternity.
Not on the tears which I have shed;
Not on the sorrows I have known:
Another's tears; Another's griefs:
On them I rest, on them alone.
Jesus, O Son of God, I build
On what Thy cross has done for me;
There both my death and life I read;
My guilt, my pardon there I see.
Lord, I believe; O deal with me
As one who has Thy Word believed!
I take the gift, Lord, look on me
As one who has Thy gift received.

Bonar was born in Edinburgh, December 19, 1808. His father was a lawyer, but he came from a long line of eminent Scottish ministers. His mother was a gentle, pious woman, and it was largely through her influence that her three sons, John, Horatius and Andrew, entered the ministry of the Church of Scotland. Andrew became a noted Bible commentator.

After completing his course at the University of Edinburgh, Horatius began mission work in Leith, under Rev. James Lewis. In one of the most squalid parts of the city he conducted services and Sunday school in a hall. The children did not seem to enjoy singing the Psalm paraphrases, which were still exclusively used by the Church of Scotland at that late date, and therefore Bonar decided to write songs of his own. Like Luther, he chose happy tunes familiar to the children, and wrote words to fit them. His first two hymns were "I lay my sins on Jesus" and "The morning, the bright and beautiful morning." Still others were "I was a wandering sheep" and "A few more years shall roll." Needless to say, the children sang and enjoyed them.

At this time, also, he wrote his first hymn for adults, "Go, labor on! Spend and be spent!" It was intended to encourage those who were working with him among the poor of his district.

After four years Bonar was ordained as a minister of the Church of Scotland, assuming charge of a new church at Kelso. He was a man of prayer, and his first sermon to his people was an exhortation to prayer. It is said that a young servant in his home was converted by his prayers. Hearing his earnest supplications from his locked study, she thought: "If he needs to pray so much, what will become of me, if I do not pray!"

Many stories are related of his methods of dealing with seeking souls. A young man who was troubled by a grievous sin came to Bonar for help. The latter told him that God was willing to forgive and that the blood of Jesus His Son cleanseth from all sin. The despairing young man seemed unable to believe the gospel message, however, and continually reminded Bonar of the greatness of his transgression. Finally an inspiration came to the pastor. "Tell me," he demanded, "which is of greater weight in the eyes of God—your sin, black as it is, or the blood of Jesus, shed for sinners?" Light dawned on the soul of the troubled young man, and he cried joyfully, "Oh, I am sure the blood of Jesus weighs more heavily than even my sin!" And so he found peace.

Bonar was a man of boundless energy. When he was not preaching, he was writing hymns or tracts or books. One of his tracts, "Believe and Live," was printed in more than a million copies, and the late Queen Victoria of England was much blessed by it. His hymns number about 600, and the fact that at least 100 are in common use today is a testimonial to their worth. Dr. Bonar never used his hymns in his own church worship, but when, on a certain occasion near the close of his life, he broke the rule, two of his elders showed their emphatic disapproval by walking out of church.

Perhaps the finest hymn we have received from his pen, if we except "I lay my sins on Jesus," is "I heard the voice of Jesus say." Other familiar hymns are "Thy works, not mine, O Christ," "Not what my hands have done," "Blessing, and honor, and glory, and power," "All that I was, my sin, my guilt," "Thy way, not mine, O Lord," and "A few more years shall roll."

In 1843 Dr. Bonar married Miss Jane Lundie, and for forty years they shared joy and sorrow. She, too, was a gifted writer, and it is she who has given us the beautiful gem, "Fade, fade, each earthly joy."

Sorrow was one of the means used by the Lord to enrich and mellow the life of Bonar. Five of his children died in early years. It required much of divine grace in such experiences to write lines like these:

Spare not the stroke; do with us as Thou wilt;
Let there be naught unfinished, broken, marred.
Complete Thy purpose, that we may become
Thy perfect image, O our God and Lord.

Bonar himself was sorely afflicted during the last two years of his life. He died in 1889, deeply mourned by all Scotland as well as by Christians throughout the world who had come to know him through his tracts and hymns. At his funeral one of his own hymns was sung. It was written on the theme of his family motto, "Heaven at Last."

What a city! what a glory!
Far beyond the brightest story
Of the ages old and hoary:
Ah, 'tis heaven at last!
Christ Himself the living splendor,
Christ the sunlight mild and tender;
Praises to the Lamb we render:
Ah, 'tis heaven at last!
Now, at length, the veil is rended,
Now the pilgrimage is ended,
And the saints their thrones ascended:
Ah, 'tis heaven at last!
Broken death's dread bands that bound us,
Life and victory around us;
Christ, the King, Himself hath crowned us;
Ah, 'tis heaven at last!

The Dayspring from on High

O very God of very God,
And very Light of Light,
Whose feet this earth's dark valley trod,
That so it might be bright!
Our hopes are weak, our foes are strong,
Thick darkness blinds our eyes;
Cold is the night, and O we long
For Thee, our Sun, to rise!
And even now, though dull and gray,
The east is brightening fast,
And kindling to the perfect day
That never shall be past.
O guide us till our path be done,
And we have reached the shore
Where Thou, our everlasting Sun,
Art shining evermore!
We wait in faith, and turn our face

To where the daylight springs,
Till Thou shalt come our gloom to chase,
With healing on Thy wings.
John Mason Neale, 1846.

TWO FAMOUS TRANSLATORS OF ANCIENT HYMNS

Little more than a century ago—in the year 1818, to be exact—there was born in the great city of London a child who was destined to become an unusual scholar. He was christened John Mason Neale, a name that may be found today throughout the pages of the world's best hymn-books.

When he was only five years old, his father died, and, like so many other men who have achieved fame, he received the greater part of his elementary training from a gifted mother.

At Cambridge University, which he entered at an early age, he became a brilliant student, leading his classes and winning numerous prizes. After his graduation he was ordained as a minister in the Church of England.

His interest in the ancient hymns of the Christian Church led him to spend much time in the morning lands of history, particularly in Greece. To him, more than any one else, we owe some of the most successful translations from the classical languages. By his sojourn in eastern lands, he seems to have been enabled to catch the spirit of the Greek hymns to such a degree that his translations read almost like original poems. For instance, in order to do justice to the famous Easter hymn of John of Damascus, written some time during the eighth century, Neale celebrated Easter in Athens and heard the "glorious old hymn of victory," as he called it, sung by a great throng of worshipers at midnight. The result is his sublime translation:

The day of resurrection!
Earth, tell it out abroad!
The Passover of gladness,
The Passover of God!
From death to Life eternal,
From earth unto the sky,
Our Christ hath brought us over,
With hymns of victory.
Another very famous translation from the Greek by Neale is the hymn:

Art thou weary, art thou languid,
Art thou sore distressed?
"Come to me," saith One, "and, coming,
Be at rest."
This hymn is often regarded as an original by Neale, but the author was St. Stephen the Sabaite, a monk who received his name from the monastery in which he spent his life, that of St. Sabas, near Bethlehem, overlooking the Dead Sea. St. Stephen, who was born

in 725 A.D., had been placed in the monastery at the age of ten years by his uncle. He lived there more than half a century until his death in 794 A.D.

Neale was equally successful in the translation of ancient Latin hymns. Perhaps the most notable is his rendering of Bernard of Cluny's immortal hymn:

Jerusalem, the golden,
With milk and honey blest!
Beneath thy contemplation
Sink heart and voice oppressed:
I know not, O I know not,
What blissful joys are there,
What radiancy of glory,
What light beyond compare!

So facile was Neale in the art of writing either English or Latin verse, that he often astounded his friends. It is said that on one occasion John Keble, author of "The Christian Year," was visiting him. Absenting himself from the room for a few minutes, Neale returned shortly and exclaimed: "I thought, Keble, that all your poems in 'The Christian Year' were original; but one of them, at least, seems to be a translation." Thereupon he handed Keble, to the latter's amazement, a very fine Latin rendering of one of Keble's own poems. He had made the translation during his absence from the room.

But Neale did not confine himself to translations. He also wrote a large number of splendid original hymns. He was fond of writing hymns for holy days and festivals of the church year. The hymn printed in connection with this sketch is for Advent. "Oh Thou, who by a star didst guide," for Epiphany, and "Blessed Saviour, who hast taught me," for confirmation, are among his other original hymns.

Because of his "high church" tendencies, accentuated no doubt by the influence of the "Oxford Movement," Neale incurred the suspicion of some that he leaned toward the Church of Rome. However, there is nothing of Roman error to be found in his hymns. The evangelical note rings pure and clear, and for this reason they will no doubt continue to be loved and sung through centuries yet to come.

Neale died August 6, 1866, at the age of forty-eight years, trusting in the atoning blood of Christ, and with the glorious assurance expressed in his version of St. Stephen's hymn:

If I still hold closely to Him,
What hath He at last?
"Sorrow vanquished, labor ended,
Jordan passed."
If I ask Him to receive me,
Will He say me nay?

"Not till earth and not till heaven
Pass away."

Another Englishman who gained renown by translations of the old classical hymns of the Church was Edward Caswall. He was a contemporary of Neale, and, like the latter, came under the influence of the "Oxford Movement," which cost the Church of England some of its ablest men. While Neale, however, remained faithful to his own communion, Caswall resigned as a minister of the English Church and became a Romanist. He was made a priest in the Congregation of the Oratory, which Cardinal Newman had established in Birmingham, a position he continued to fill until his death in 1878.

Two of the most beautiful hymns in the English language—"Jesus, the very thought of Thee" and "O Jesus, King most wonderful"—were derived by Caswall from the famous Latin poem, De Nomine Jesu, by Bernard of Clairvaux. Of the former hymn Dr. Robinson has said: "One might call this poem the finest in the world and still be within the limits of all extravagance."

Among other fine translations from the Latin by Caswall are "Hark! a thrilling voice is sounding" and "Glory be to Jesus." He also has given us some hymns from the German, including the exquisite morning hymn, "When morning gilds the skies." This is such a free rendering, however, that it may rather be regarded as an original hymn by Caswall. Three of its stanzas read:

> When morning gilds the skies,
> My heart, awaking, cries,
> May Jesus Christ be praised!
> Alike at work and prayer,
> To Jesus I repair;
> May Jesus Christ be praised!
>
> In heaven's eternal bliss
> The loveliest strain is this,
> May Jesus Christ be praised!
> Let air, and sea, and sky
> From depth to height reply,
> May Jesus Christ be praised!
> Be this, while life is mine,
> My canticle divine,
> May Jesus Christ be praised!
> Be this the eternal song
> Through all the ages on,
> May Jesus Christ be praised!

A Great Marching Song

> Onward, Christian soldiers,
> Marching as to war,
> With the cross of Jesus
> Going on before.
> Christ, the royal Master,
> Leads against the foe;
> Forward into battle,
> See, His banners go!
> At the sign of triumph

Satan's armies flee;
On, then, Christian soldiers,
On to victory!
Hell's foundations quiver
At the shout of praise;
Brothers, lift your voices,
Loud your anthems raise.
Crowns and thrones may perish,
Kingdoms rise and wane,
But the church of Jesus
Constant will remain;
Gates of hell can never
'Gainst that church prevail;
We have Christ's own promise,
And that cannot fail.
Onward, then, ye people!
Join our happy throng,
Blend with ours your voices
In the triumph-song;
Glory, laud, and honor
Unto Christ the King,
This through countless ages
Men and angels sing.
Sabine Baring-Gould, 1865.

BARING-GOULD AND HIS NOTED HYMN

When Rev. Sabine Baring-Gould, on Whitsunday, 1865, sat up a greater portion of the night to compose a hymn, he did not realize he was writing words that would be sung through the centuries; but that no doubt will be the result of his zeal. The hymn he wrote was "Onward, Christian soldiers."

The story is an interesting one. At that time Baring-Gould was minister of the Established Church at Lew-Trenchard, England. On Whitmonday the children of his village were to march to an adjoining village for a Sunday school rally.

"If only there was something they could sing as they marched," the pastor thought, "the way would not seem so long." He searched diligently for something suitable but failed to find what he wanted. Finally he decided to write a marching song. It took the greater part of the night to do it, but the next morning the children's pilgrimage was made the lighter and happier by "Onward, Christian soldiers."

Commenting on the hymn some thirty years later, the author said: "It was written in great haste, and I am afraid some of the rhymes are faulty. Certainly, nothing has surprised me more than its popularity."

In this instance, as in many others that might be mentioned, the tune to which it is inseparably wedded, has no doubt contributed much to make it popular. Sir Arthur

Seymour Sullivan, the great English organist who wrote "The Lost Chord," in 1872 composed the stirring music now used for Baring-Gould's hymn.

Objection has sometimes been voiced against the hymn because of its martial spirit. However, it should be noted that this hymn gives not the slightest hint of warfare with carnal weapons. The allusion is to spiritual warfare, and the warrior is the Christian soldier.

We are reminded throughout this hymn of Paul's martial imagery in the sixth chapter of Ephesians, where he tells us that "our wrestling is not against flesh and blood, but against the principalities, against the powers, against the world-rulers of this darkness, against the spiritual hosts of wickedness in the heavenly places," and admonishes us to put on "the whole armor of God." We also recall the same apostle's exhortation to Timothy to "war the good warfare," and to "fight the good fight of faith."

It is salutary to be reminded by such a hymn as this of the heroic character of the Christian life. The follower of Jesus is not to sit with folded hands and sing his way into Paradise. A sickly, sentimental religion has no more place in the Christian Church today than it had in those early days when apostles and martyrs sealed their faith with their life-blood. Baring-Gould's hymn seems almost an exultant answer to Isaac Watts' challenging stanza:

> Must I be carried to the skies
> On flowery beds of ease,
> While others fought to win the prize,
> And sailed through bloody seas?

We sometimes hear it said that the Church of Christ has fallen on evil days, and more than one faithful soul fears for the future. Baring-Gould has reminded us here of Christ's "own promise" that, though kingdoms may rise and fall, His kingdom shall ever remain, for the gates of hell shall not prevail against it.

During a desperate battle between the French and Austrians in the Napoleonic wars, a French officer rushed to his commander and exclaimed, "The battle is lost!" Quietly the general answered, "One battle is lost, but there is time to win another." Inspired by the commander's unconquerable optimism, the French army renewed the struggle and snatched victory out of the jaws of defeat. That has ever been the history of the Church of Christ.

Baring-Gould was one of England's most versatile ministers. In addition to his hymn-writing, he was a novelist of considerable reputation. For many years he regularly produced a novel every year. His "Lives of the Saints" in fifteen volumes, his "Curious Myths of the Middle Ages" and his "Legends of the Old Testament" are all notable works. It is said that he did all his writing in long hand without the aid of a secretary. He once declared that he often did his best work when he felt least inclined to apply himself to his task. He never waited for an "inspiration," but plunged into his work and then stuck to it until it was finished.

The beautiful evening hymn, "Now the day is over," is also from Baring-Gould's pen, and, to show his versatility, he also composed the tune for it. He was also the translator of Bernhardt Severin Ingemann's famous Danish hymn, "Through the night of doubt and sorrow."

Despite his arduous and unceasing labors, Baring-Gould lived to the ripe old age of ninety years. He died in 1924, but his hymn goes marching on.

A Rapturous Hymn of Adoration

O Saviour, precious Saviour,
Whom, yet unseen, we love;
O Name of might and favor,
All other names above:
We worship Thee, we bless Thee,
To Thee alone we sing;
We praise Thee and confess Thee,
Our holy Lord and King.
O Bringer of salvation,
Who wondrously hast wrought,
Thyself the revelation
Of love beyond our thought;
We worship Thee, we bless Thee,
To Thee alone we sing;
We praise Thee and confess Thee,
Our gracious Lord and King.
In Thee all fulness dwelleth,
All grace and power divine;
The glory that excelleth,
O Son of God, is Thine.
We worship Thee, we bless Thee,
To Thee alone we sing;
We praise Thee and confess Thee,
Our glorious Lord and King.
O grant the consummation
Of this our song above,
In endless adoration
And everlasting love;
Then shall we praise and bless Thee
Where perfect praises ring,
And evermore confess Thee,
Our Saviour and our King.
Frances Ridley Havergal, 1870.

FRANCES RIDLEY HAVERGAL, THE CONSECRATION POET

The beauty of a consecrated Christian life has probably never been more perfectly revealed than in the life of Frances Ridley Havergal. To read the story of her life is not only an inspiration, but it discloses at once the secret of her beautiful hymns. She lived her hymns before she wrote them.

This sweetest of all English singers was born at Astley, Worcestershire, December 14, 1836. She was such a bright, happy and vivacious child that her father, who was a minister of the Church of England and himself a hymn-writer of no mean ability, called her "Little Quicksilver." Her father was also a gifted musician, and this quality too was inherited by the daughter, who became a brilliant pianist and passionately fond of singing. However, because she looked upon her talents as gifts from God to be used only in His service, she would sing nothing but sacred songs.

Her sunshiny nature became even more radiant following a deep religious experience at the age of fourteen. Of this she afterwards wrote:

"I committed my soul to the Saviour, and earth and heaven seemed brighter from that moment."

At the age of eighteen she was confirmed. It is evident that she looked upon her confirmation as one of the most blessed experiences of her life, for when she returned home she wrote in her manuscript book of poems:

"THINE FOR EVER"

Oh! Thine for ever, what a blessed thing
To be for ever His who died for me!
My Saviour, all my life Thy praise I'll sing,
Nor cease my song throughout eternity.

She also wrote a hymn on Confirmation, "In full and glad surrender." This hymn her sister declared was "the epitome of her life and the focus of its sunshine."

Four years later, while pursuing studies in Düsseldorf, Germany, Miss Havergal chanced to see Sternberg's celebrated painting, Ecce Homo, with the inscription beneath it:

This have I done for thee;
What hast thou done for me?

This was the same painting that once made such a profound impression on the youthful mind of Count Zinzendorf. Miss Havergal was likewise deeply moved, and immediately she seized a piece of scrap paper and a pencil and wrote the famous hymn:

I gave My life for thee,
My precious blood I shed,
That thou might'st ransomed be,
And quickened from the dead.
I gave My life for thee:
What hast thou given for Me?

She thought the verses so poor after she had read them over that she tossed them into a stove. The piece of paper, however, fell out untouched by the flames. When she showed the words to her father a few months later, he was so touched by them he immediately composed a tune by which they could be sung.

This seems to have been one of the great turning points in the life of the young hymnist. Her hymns from this period reveal her as a fully surrendered soul, her one ambition being to devote all her talents to Christ. She did not consider herself to be a poet of a high order, but so filled was she with the love of Christ that her heart overflowed with rapturous praise. Indeed, her hymns may be said to be the record of her own spiritual experiences. Always she was proclaiming the evangel of full and free salvation through Jesus' merits to all who believe.

She is often referred to as "the consecration poet." This is an allusion to her famous consecration hymn, written in 1874:

Take my life, and let it be
Consecrated, Lord, to Thee.
Take my moments and my days;
Let them flow in ceaseless praise.

The circumstances that led to the writing of this hymn are interesting. Miss Havergal was spending a few days in a home where there were ten persons, some of them unconverted, and the others rather half-hearted Christians who seemed to derive no joy from their religion. A great desire came upon her that she might be instrumental in bringing them all to true faith in Christ. Her prayer was wonderfully answered, and on the last night of her stay her heart was so filled with joy and gratitude she could not sleep. Instead, she spent the night writing the consecration hymn.

Her prayer, "Take my silver and my gold; not a mite would I withhold," was not an idle petition with her. In August, 1878, she wrote to a friend: "The Lord has shown me another little step, and of course I have taken it, with extreme delight. 'Take my silver and my gold,' now means shipping off all my ornaments to the Church Missionary House (including a jewel cabinet that is really fit for a countess), where all will be accepted and disposed of for me. I retain a brooch or two for daily wear, which are memorials of my dear parents, also a locket containing a portrait of my dear niece in heaven, my Evelyn, and her two rings; but these I redeem, so that the whole value goes to the Church Missionary Society. Nearly fifty articles are being packed up. I don't think I ever packed a box with such pleasure."

In addition to her other accomplishments, Miss Havergal was a brilliant linguist, having mastered a number of modern languages. She was also proficient in Greek and Hebrew. Her sister records that she always had her Hebrew Bible and Greek New Testament at hand when she read the Scriptures.

The study of the Bible was one of her chief joys. During summer she began her Bible reading at seven in the morning, and in winter at eight o'clock. When, on cold days, her sister would beg her to sit near the fire, she would answer: "But then, Marie, I can't rule my lines neatly. Just see what a find I've got. If one only searches, there are such extraordinary things in the Bible!" Her Bible was freely underscored and filled with notations. She was able to repeat from memory the four Gospels, the Epistles, Revelation and all the Psalms, and in later years she added Isaiah and the Minor Prophets to the list.

Miss Havergal was only forty-two at the time of her death, on June 3, 1879. When her attending physician told her that her condition was serious, she replied, "If I am really going, it is too good to be true!" At the bottom of her bed she had her favorite text placed where she could see it: "The blood of Jesus Christ His Son cleanseth us from all sin." She also asked that these words be inscribed upon her coffin and on her tombstone. Once she exclaimed: "Splendid! To be so near the gates of heaven!" And again, "So beautiful to go! So beautiful to go!" She died while singing:

Jesus, I will trust Thee,
Trust Thee with my soul;
Guilty, lost, and helpless,
Thou hast made me whole:
There is none in heaven
Or on earth like Thee;
Thou hast died for sinners,
Therefore, Lord, for me!

Some of the more popular hymns by Miss Havergal, aside from those already mentioned, are: "O Saviour, precious Saviour," "I am trusting Thee, Lord Jesus," "Thou art coming, O my Saviour," "Lord, speak to me, that I may speak," and "Singing for Jesus, our Saviour and King." While she was writing the hymns that were destined to make her famous, another remarkable young woman, "Fanny" Crosby, America's blind hymn-writer, was also achieving renown by her hymns and songs. Miss Havergal and Miss Crosby never met, but each was an ardent admirer of the other, and on one occasion the English poet sent a very touching greeting to the American hymn-writer. It read:

Dear blind sister over the sea,
An English heart goes forth to thee.
We are linked by a cable of faith and song,
Flashing bright sympathy swift along:
One in the East and one in the West
Singing for Him whom our souls love best;
"Singing for Jesus," telling His love
All the way to our home above,
Where the severing sea, with its restless tide,
Never shall hinder and never divide.
Sister! What shall our meeting be,
When our hearts shall sing, and our eyes shall see!

The Emblem That Survives

In the cross of Christ I glory,
Towering o'er the wrecks of time;
All the light of sacred story
Gathers round its head sublime.
When the woes of life o'ertake me,
Hopes deceive, and fears annoy,
Never shall the cross forsake me;
Lo! it glows with peace and joy.

When the sun of bliss is beaming
Light and love upon my way,
From the cross the radiance streaming
Adds new luster to the day.
Bane and blessing, pain and pleasure,
By the cross are sanctified;
Peace is there that knows no measure,
Joys that through all time abide.
John Bowring, 1825.

A UNITARIAN WHO GLORIED IN THE CROSS

Among the great hymns of the cross, Sir John Bowring's classic, "In the cross of Christ I glory," occupies a foremost place. This is all the more remarkable when we are reminded that Bowring was known as a Unitarian, a communion which not only denies the deity of Christ, but ignores the true significance of the cross. And yet he has given us a hymn that every evangelical Christian rejoices to sing, for it is a hymn that magnifies the cross and makes it the very center of the Christian religion.

In justice to Bowring it ought to be stated that he himself was "a devoted and evangelical believer," and that his connection with the Unitarian Church was merely accidental and nominal. When he died, in 1872, the opening line of his famous hymn was inscribed in bold letters upon his tombstone:

In the Cross of Christ I Glory

Knowing these things, every true Christian will cherish an inner conviction that the man who wrote so beautiful a tribute to Christ and the cross did not really die but only fell asleep, trusting in the atoning death of a Saviour who is God.

Bowring was a learned man, especially famed as a linguist. He is said to have been able to speak twenty-two languages fluently, and was able to converse in at least one hundred different tongues. He found special delight in translating poems from other languages. His published works contain translations from Bohemian, Slavonic, Russian, Servian, Polish, Slovakian, Illyrian, Teutonic, Esthonian, Dutch, Frisian, Lettish, Finnish, Hungarian, Biscayan, French, Provencal, Gascon, Italian, Spanish, Portuguese, Catalonian and Galician sources.

Sir John was particularly fond of the study of hymns. Even at the age of eighty years he was said to begin the day with some new song of thanksgiving.

In addition to all his other accomplishments, Bowring had a very distinguished career in English politics. He was twice a member of the British parliament. Later he became consul general for the English government at Hong Kong, China. During this period he chanced to sail down the Chinese coast to Macao, where nearly 400 years earlier the Portuguese explorer, Vasco da Gama, had built an imposing cathedral. The structure had been wrecked by a typhoon, but the tower still remained, and surmounting it a great bronze cross, sharply outlined against the sky. Far above the wreckage surrounding it, the cross seemed to Bowring to be a symbol of Christ's Kingdom, glorious and eternal, living through the centuries while other kingdoms have come and gone. So inspired was he by the sight, the words of the hymn seemed to suggest themselves to him at once, and in a short while a famous poem had been written.

The plan of the hymn is interesting. The first stanza declares the cross of Christ to be the central fact in divine revelation and the one theme in which the Christian never ceases to glory. The second stanza pictures the cross as the Christian's refuge and comfort in time of affliction, while the third tells how it also adds luster to the days of joy and sunshine. The final stanza summarizes these two ideas, and the hymn closes by telling of the eternal character of the peace and joy that flow from the cross.

An interesting story is told of this hymn in connection with the Boxer uprising in China. All foreigners in Peking had been besieged by the infuriated Chinese for several weeks. When the allied troops finally reached the city and the terrible strain was ended, the Christian missionaries gathered in the Temple of Heaven, the remarkable pagan shrine where the Emperor of China was accustomed to worship, and, lifting up their voices in thanksgiving, the messengers of the cross sang:

In the cross of Christ I glory,
Towering o'er the wrecks of time;
All the light of sacred story
Gathers round its head sublime.

Sir John Bowring eventually became governor of Hong Kong, and wielded great influence in the Orient. He did much to promote Christian benevolences and other enterprises for the good of the peoples in the Far East. When his health began to fail, his friends warned him to cease some of his activities, but in vain. His answer was, "I must do my work while life remains to me; I may not long be here."

He was often gratified to hear his hymns sung at unexpected times and in unusual places. In 1825 he wrote a poem beginning with the words, "Watchman, tell us of the night." He did not know it was being used as a hymn until ten years later, when he heard it sung by Christian missionaries in Turkey. Among other hymns of Bowring that have come into general use is the beautiful one beginning with the words:

God is Love; His mercy brightens
All the path in which we rove;
Bliss He wakes, and woe He lightens:
God is Wisdom, God is Love.

A Hymn That Opens Hearts

O Jesus, Thou art standing
Outside the fast-closed door,
In lowly patience waiting
To pass the threshold o'er:
Shame on us, Christian brothers,
His Name and sign who bear:

O shame, thrice shame upon us,
To keep Him standing there!
O Jesus, Thou art knocking;
And lo, that hand is scarred,
And thorns Thy brow encircle,
And tears Thy face have marred:
O love that passeth knowledge,
So patiently to wait!
O sin that hath no equal,
So fast to bar the gate!
O Jesus, Thou art pleading
In accents meek and low,
"I died for you, My children,
And will ye treat Me so?"
O Lord, with shame and sorrow
We open now the door;
Dear Saviour, enter, enter,
And leave us nevermore.
William Walsham How, 1867.

A MODEL HYMN BY A MODEL MINISTER

It is a significant fact that many of the greatest hymns of the Church have been written by pastors who have been noted for their zeal in winning souls. Their hymns have been a part of their spiritual stratagem to draw the wayward and erring into the gospel net. Bishop William Walsham How, one of the more recent hymnists of England, is a shining example of true devotion in a Christian shepherd.

Bishop How once gave a striking description of the characteristics which he believed should be found in an ideal minister of the gospel. "Such a minister," he said, "should be a man pure, holy, and spotless in his life; a man of much prayer; in character meek, lowly, and infinitely compassionate; of tenderest love to all; full of sympathy for every pain and sorrow, and devoting his days and nights to lightening the burdens of humanity; utterly patient of insult and enmity; utterly fearless in speaking the truth and rebuking sin; ever ready to answer every call, to go wherever bidden, in order to do good; wholly without thought of self; making himself the servant of all; patient, gentle, and untiring in dealing with the souls he would save; bearing with ignorance, wilfulness, slowness, cowardice, in those of whom he expects most; sacrificing all, even life itself, if need be, to save some."

Those who knew How best said it was almost a perfect description of his own life and character.

When Queen Victoria, in 1879, made him Bishop of Bedford, with East London as his diocese, he was tireless in his efforts to alleviate conditions in that poverty-stricken district. When he first began his work in the slums, people would point to him and say, "There goes a bishop." But as they came to know him better, they said, "There goes the bishop." And finally, when they learned to love him, they exclaimed, "There goes our bishop."

Bishop How's most celebrated hymn is "O Jesus, Thou art standing." It is based on the impressive words of the Saviour in the Book of Revelation, "Behold, I stand at the door, and knock: If any man hear my voice, and open the door, I will come in to him, and will sup with him, and he with me."

Though the language of the hymn is commonplace, there are striking expressions here, as in How's other hymns, that arrest the attention of the worshiper. In the first stanza we are reminded that there are many nominal Christians bearing "His Name and sign" who yet are keeping the waiting, patient Saviour outside a "fast-closed door." In the succeeding verse we are told that it is sin that bars the gate. Then there is the concluding stanza with its gripping appeal, picturing the surrender of the human heart to the pleading Christ.

The imagery in the hymn was, no doubt, suggested by Holman Hunt's celebrated painting, "The Light of the World." This was executed by Hunt in 1855, while the hymn by How was written twelve years later. Those who are familiar with the Hunt masterpiece will remember how it pictures the Saviour standing patiently and knocking earnestly at a fast-closed door. The high weeds, the tangled growth of vines, as well as the unpicked fruit lying on the ground before the door, suggest that it has not been opened for a long time. A bat is hovering in the vines overhead.

Ruskin tells us that the white robe worn by the heavenly Stranger shows us that He is a Prophet, the jeweled robe and breastplate indicate a Priest, and the crown of gold a King. The crown of thorns is now bearing leaves "for the healing of the nations." In His scarred hand He carries a lighted lantern, signifying "the Light of the world."

When Holman Hunt's picture was first exhibited, it excited considerable comment. Some one, however, ventured the criticism that there was a fault in the painting inasmuch as Hunt had forgotten to indicate a latch on the door.

"There is no mistake," said the great artist. "I did not put a latch on the outside of the door because it can only be opened from within. The Lord Jesus Christ Himself cannot enter an unwilling heart; it must be opened to Him. He must be invited to enter."

Bishop How's hymn pictures in language what Holman Hunt put into his celebrated canvass.

"O Jesus, Thou art standing" is not the only famous hymn written by Bishop How. His lovely New Year's hymn, "Jesus, Name of wondrous love," and his All Saints' hymn, "For all the saints who from their labors rest," have won a place forever in English hymnody. "O Word of God Incarnate," "We give Thee but Thine own" and "Summer suns are glowing" also have found their way into a large number of the standard hymn-books.

The talented bishop died in the year 1897, mourned not only by those who had learned to love him because of his noble Christian character, but also by those who had come to know him through his beautiful hymns. With the passing of only three decades since his death, there is increasing evidence that Bishop How will be numbered among the great hymn-writers of the Christian Church.

A Blind Man's Hymn of Faith

O Love that wilt not let me go,
I rest my weary soul in Thee:
I give Thee back the life I owe,
That in Thine ocean depths its flow
May richer, fuller be.
O Light that followest all my way,
I yield my flickering torch to Thee:
My heart restores its borrowed ray,
That in Thy sunshine's blaze its day
May brighter, fairer be.
O Joy that seekest me through pain,
I cannot close my heart to Thee:
I trace the rainbow through the rain,
And feel the promise is not vain
That morn shall tearless be.
O Cross that liftest up my head,
I dare not ask to fly from Thee:
I lay in dust life's glory dead,
And from the ground there blossoms red
Life that shall endless be.
George Matheson, 1882.

MATHESON AND HIS SONG IN THE NIGHT

The most recent of English hymn-writers to gain recognition in the standard hymn-books of the Church is George Matheson. The fame of this man will probably rest on a single hymn, "O Love that wilt not let me go," written on a summer evening in 1882.

A deeper appreciation and understanding will be felt for this hymn when we know that it is truly a "song in the night," for Matheson was blind when he wrote it.

Born in Glasgow, Scotland, March 27, 1842, Matheson enjoyed partial vision as a boy. However, after he entered Glasgow University at the age of fifteen, his sight began to fail and he became totally blind. Nevertheless, in spite of this handicap, he was a brilliant scholar and graduated with honor in 1861. Having decided to enter the ministry, he remained four additional years for theological studies.

It was while he was parish minister at Innellan, a seaport summer resort in Scotland, that the famous hymn was written. He tells the story in his own words:

"It was written in the manse of my former parish (Innellan) one summer evening in 1882. It was composed with extreme rapidity; it seemed to me that its construction occupied only a few minutes, and I felt myself rather in the position of one who was being dictated to than an original artist. I was suffering from extreme mental distress, and the hymn was the fruit of pain."

Many conjectures have been made regarding the cause of the "mental distress" from which the author was suffering. Because of the opening line, "O Love that wilt not let me go," it has been suggested that Matheson had been bitterly disappointed in his hopes of marrying a young woman to whom he had become deeply attached. It is said that her refusal to marry him was due to his blindness.

Although this story cannot be vouched for, there are many significant hints in the hymn to his sad affliction, such as the "flickering torch" and the "borrowed ray" in the second stanza, the beautiful thought of tracing "the rainbow through the rain" in the third stanza, and the "cross" referred to in the final stanza. The hymn is so artistically constructed and is so rich in poetic thought and symbolic meaning, it will well repay careful study.

Despite his handicap, Dr. Matheson was blessed with a fruitful ministry. A devoted sister who had learned Greek, Latin and Hebrew in order to aid him in his theological studies remained his co-worker and helper throughout life. In all of his pastoral calls she was his constant guide.

During the early part of his ministry, he wrote all his sermons in full. He possessed such a remarkable memory that after a sermon had been read to him twice, he was able to repeat it perfectly. After he had followed this practice for twelve years, he suffered a complete collapse of memory one Sunday in the midst of a sermon. Unable to proceed, he calmly announced a hymn and sat down. At the conclusion of the singing he told the congregation what had happened, and then preached a sermon of great appeal from another text.

After a ministry at Innellan lasting for eighteen years, he was called as pastor of St. Bernard's church in Edinburgh. Here he remained for thirteen years, attracting large multitudes by his preaching.

The later years of his life were spent in literary work. He was the author of several volumes in prose, among them a very fine devotional book called "Moments on the Mount." He fell asleep August 28, 1906, to await the break of eternity's dawn, confident in the assurance that

> ... the promise is not vain
> That morn shall tearless be.

PART V
AMERICAN HYMNODY

The First American Hymn

I love Thy Zion, Lord,
The house of Thine abode;
The Church our blest Redeemer saved
With His own precious blood.
I love Thy Church, O God;
Her walls before Thee stand,
Dear as the apple of Thine eye,
And graven on Thy hand.
For her my tears shall fall;
For her my prayers ascend:
To her my cares and toil be given,
Till toils and cares shall end.
Beyond my highest joy
I prize her heavenly ways,
Her sweet communion, solemn vows,
Her hymns of love and praise.
Jesus, Thou Friend divine,
Our Saviour and our King,
Thy hand from every snare and foe
Shall great deliverance bring.
Sure as Thy truth shall last,
To Zion shall be given
The brightest glories earth can yield,
And brighter bliss of heaven.
Timothy Dwight, 1800.

THE BEGINNINGS OF HYMNODY IN AMERICA

The rise of hymnody in America ran parallel with the development of hymn-singing in England. The Puritans who came from Holland in the Mayflower in 1620 were "separatists" from the Church of England, hence they used a psalm-book of their own, published by Henry Ainsworth at Amsterdam in 1612. This was the book that cheered their souls on the perilous crossing of the Atlantic and during the hard and trying years that followed their landing at Plymouth.

Amid the storm they sang,
And the stars heard and the sea;
And the sounding aisles of the dim woods rang
With the anthems of the free.

This was also the book that comforted Priscilla, when John Alden stole in and found that

Open wide on her lap lay the well-worn psalm-book of Ainsworth.

The later Puritans who came directly from England, on the other hand, were not "separatists," hence they brought with them the psalm-book of Sternhold and Hopkins, which was the version of the Psaltery approved at that time by the Established Church.

The wretched paraphrases of the Psalms in both the Ainsworth and the "orthodox" version of Sternhold and Hopkins eventually led to an insistent demand among the New England Puritans for an entirely new psalm-book which should also adhere more closely to the Hebrew original. The result was the famous "Bay Psalmist" of 1640, which was the first book printed in British America.

The Puritan editors of this first attempt at American psalmody cared no more for poetic effect than did their brother versifiers across the waters. This they made quite plain in the concluding words of the Preface to the "Bay Psalmist": "If therefore the verses are not always so smooth and elegant as some may desire or expect; let them consider that God's Altar needs not our pollishings: Ex. 20, for wee have respected rather a plaine translation, than to smooth our verses with the sweetness of any paraphrase, and soe have attended to Conscience rather than Elegance, fidelity rather than poetry, in translating the hebrew words into english language, and David's poetry into english meetre: that soe wee may sing in Sion the Lords songs of praise according to his own will; untill hee take us from hence, and wipe away all our tears, & bid us enter into our masters joye to sing eternall Halleluiahs."

The editors scarcely needed to apprise the worshiper that he should not look for artistic verses, for a glimpse within its pages was sufficient to disillusion any one who expected to find sacred poetry. The metrical form given the 137th Psalm is an example of the Puritan theologians' contempt for polished language:

The rivers on of Babilon
there when wee did sit downe:
yea even then wee mourned, when
wee remembred Sion.
Our Harps wee did hang it amid,
upon the willow tree.

Because there they that us away
led in captivitee,
Required of us a song, & thus
askt mirth: us waste who laid,
sing us among a Sions song,
unto us then they said.
The lords song sing can wee? being
in strangers land. Then let
loose her skill my right hand, if I
Jerusalem forget.
Let cleave my tongue my pallate on,
if minde thee doe not I:
if chiefe joyes o'er I prize not more
Jerusalem my joye.

Nevertheless, strange as it may seem, the "Bay Psalmist" passed through twenty-seven editions, and was even reprinted several times abroad, being used extensively in England and Scotland. Gradually, however, psalmody began to lose its hold on the Reformed churches, both in Europe and America, and hymnody gained the ascendancy. The publication in 1707 of the epoch-making work of Isaac Watts, "Hymns and Spiritual Songs," was the first step in breaking down the prejudice in the Calvinistic churches against "hymns of human composure." In America the Great Awakening under Jonathan Edwards, which began in 1734 and which received added impetus from the visit of John Whitefield in 1740, also brought about a demand for a happier form of congregational singing. Then came the influence of the Wesleyan revival with its glorious outburst of song.

Jonathan Edwards himself, stern Puritan that he was, was finally forced to confess that it was "really needful that we should have some other songs than the Psalms of David." Accordingly hymn singing grew rapidly in favor among the people.

The first attempt to introduce hymns in the authorized psalm-books was made by Joel Barlow, a chaplain in the Revolutionary War. Instructed by the General Association of Congregational Churches of Connecticut to revise Watts' "Psalms of David" in order to purge them of their British flavor, he was likewise authorized to append to the Psalms a collection of hymns. He made a selection of seventy hymns, and the new book was published in 1786.

It was received with delight by the Presbyterians, but the Congregationalists who had sponsored it were thoroughly dissatisfied. As an example of the morbid character of Puritan theology, Edward S. Ninde has called attention to the fact that while Barlow failed to include Wesley's "Jesus, Lover of my soul" or Watts' "When I survey the wondrous cross," he did select such a hymn by Watts as "Hark, from the tombs, a doleful sound," and another beginning with the lines,

My thoughts on awful subjects roll,
Damnation and the dead.

A second attempt to make a complete revision of Watts' "Psalms of David" was decided upon by the Congregational churches, and this time the task was entrusted to Timothy Dwight, president of Yale College. Dwight, who was a grandson of Jonathan Edwards, was born in 1752. He entered Yale at the age of thirteen and graduated with highest honors in 1769. At the outbreak of the Revolutionary War he was commissioned a chaplain and throughout the conflict he wrote songs to enthuse the American troops. In 1795 he was elected president of Yale College, in which position he served his Alma Mater for twenty years.

Dwight exhibited a spirit of bold independence when he added to the revised "Psalms" by Watts a collection of two hundred and sixty-three hymns. Of these hymns, one hundred and sixty-eight were also by Watts, indicating the hold which that great hymnist retained on the English-speaking world. Other hymn-writers represented in Dwight's book included Stennett, Doddridge, Cowper, Newton, Toplady, and Charles Wesley. Only one of the latter's hymns was chosen, however, and Toplady's "Rock of Ages" was not included!

Dwight himself wrote thirty-three paraphrases of the Psalms, but they were so freely rendered that they are properly classified as original hymns. Among these is his splendid version of the 137th Psalm, "I love Thy Zion, Lord," which may be regarded as the earliest hymn of American origin still in common use today. It is usually dated 1800, which is the year when Dwight's work was published.

Dwight, who will always be remembered as the outstanding figure in the beginnings of American hymnody, died in 1817. The story of his life is an inspiring one, illustrating how his heroic qualities conquered despite a "thorn in the flesh." A chronicler records that "during the greater part of forty years he was not able to read fifteen minutes in the twenty-four hours; and often, for days and weeks together, the pain which he endured in that part of the head immediately behind the eyes amounted to anguish."

The Hymn of a Wounded Spirit

I love to steal awhile away
From every cumbering care,
And spend the hour of setting day
In humble, grateful prayer.
I love in solitude to shed
The penitential tear,
And all His promises to plead
Where none but God can hear.
I love to think of mercies past,
And future good implore,
And all my cares and sorrows cast
On Him whom I adore.
I love by faith to take a view
Of brighter scenes in heaven;
The prospect doth my strength renew,
While here by tempests driven.
Thus when life's toilsome day is o'er,
May its departing ray
Be calm as this impressive hour
And lead to endless day.
Phoebe Hinsdale Brown, 1818.

AMERICA'S FIRST WOMAN HYMNIST

Less than twenty years after Timothy Dwight's hymns were published, a very poor and unpretentious American woman began to write lyrics that have been treasured by the Church until this present day, nor will they soon be forgotten. Her name was Phoebe Hinsdale Brown, and the story of her life is the most pathetic in the annals of American hymnody.

"As to my history," she wrote near the end of her life, "it is soon told; a sinner saved by grace and sanctified by trials."

She was born at Canaan, N. Y., May 1, 1783. Both parents died before she was two years old and the greater part of her childhood was spent in the home of an older sister who was married to a keeper of a county jail. The cruelties and privations suffered by the orphaned child during these years were such that her son in later years declared that it broke his heart to read of them in his mother's diary. She was not permitted to attend school, and could neither read nor write. She was eighteen years old before she escaped from this bondage and found opportunity to attend school for three months. This was the extent of her education within school walls.

In 1805, at the age of twenty-two, she married Timothy H. Brown, a house painter. He was a good man, but extremely poor. Moving to Ellington, Mass., they lived in a small, unfinished frame house at the edge of the village. Four little children and a sick sister who occupied the only finished room in the house added to the domestic burdens of Mrs. Brown. In the summer of 1818 a pathetic incident occurred that led to the writing of her most famous hymn.

There being no place in her crowded home where she might find opportunity for a few moments of quiet prayer and meditation, she would steal away at twilight to the edge of a neighboring estate, where there was a magnificent home surrounded by a beautiful garden.

"As there was seldom any one passing that way after dark," she afterwards wrote, "I felt quite retired and alone with God. I often walked quite up to that beautiful garden ... and felt that I could have the privilege of those few moments of uninterrupted communion with God without encroaching upon any one."

But her movements had been watched, and one day the lady of the mansion turned on her in the presence of others and rudely demanded: "Mrs. Brown, why do you come up at evening so near our house, and then go back without coming in? If you want anything, why don't you come in and ask for it?"

Mrs. Brown tells how she went home, crushed in spirit. "After my children were all in bed, except my baby," she continues, "I sat down in the kitchen, with my child in my arms, when the grief of my heart burst forth in a flood of tears. I took pen and paper, and gave vent to my oppressed heart in what I called 'My Apology for my Twilight Rambles, addressed to a Lady.'" The "Apology," which was sent to the woman who had so cruelly wounded her began with the lines:

> Yes, when the toilsome day is gone,
> And night, with banners gray,
> Steals silently the glade along
> In twilight's soft array.

Then continued the beautiful verses of her now famous "Twilight Hymn:"

> I love to steal awhile away
> From little ones and care,
> And spend the hours of setting day

In gratitude and prayer.

Seven years later, when Dr. Nettleton was preparing his volume of "Village Hymns," he was told that Mrs. Brown had written some verses. At his request she brought forth her "Twilight Hymn" and three other lyrics, and they were promptly given a place in the collection. Only a few slight changes were made in the lines of the "Twilight Hymn," including the second line, which was made to read "From every cumbering care," and the fourth line, which was changed to "In humble, grateful prayer." Four stanzas were omitted, otherwise the hymn remains almost exactly in the form of the "Apology."

One of the omitted stanzas reveals a beautiful Christian attitude toward death. Mrs. Brown wrote:

I love to meditate on death!
When shall his message come
With friendly smiles to steal my breath
And take an exile home?

One of the other hymns by Mrs. Brown included in "Village Hymns" is a missionary lyric, "Go, messenger of love, and bear." This was written a year earlier than her "Twilight Hymn." Her little son Samuel was seven years old at the time, and the pious mother's prayer was that he might be used of the Lord in His service. It was the period when the English-speaking world was experiencing a tremendous revival of interest in foreign missions, and in her heart she cherished the fond hope that her own boy might become a messenger of the gospel. Then came the inspiration for the hymn:

Go, messenger of love, and bear
Upon thy gentle wing
The song which seraphs love to hear,
The angels joy to sing.
Go to the heart with sin oppressed,
And dry the sorrowing tear;
Extract the thorn that wounds the breast,
The drooping spirit cheer.
Go, say to Zion, "Jesus reigns"—
By His resistless power
He binds His enemies with chains;
They fall to rise no more.
Tell how the Holy Spirit flies,
As He from heaven descends;
Arrests His proudest enemies,
And changes them to friends.

Her prayer was answered. The son, Samuel R. Brown in 1838 sailed as a missionary to China, and eleven years later, when Japan was opened to foreigners, he was transferred to that field. He was the first American missionary to the Japanese.

Mrs. Brown died at Henry, Illinois, October 10, 1861. She was buried at Monson, Mass., where some thirty years of her life had been spent. Her son, the missionary, has written this beautiful tribute to her memory:

"Her record is on high, and she is with the Lord, whom she loved and served as faithfully as any person I ever knew; nay, more than any other. To her I owe all I am; and if I have done any good in the world, to her, under God, it is due. She seems even now to have me in her hands, holding me up to work for Christ and His cause with a grasp that I can feel. I ought to have been and to be a far better man than I am, having had such a mother."

A Triumphant Missionary Hymn

Hail to the brightness of Zion's glad morning!
Joy to the lands that in darkness have lain!
Hushed be the accents of sorrow and mourning,
Zion in triumph begins her glad reign.
Hail to the brightness of Zion's glad morning,
Long by the prophets of Israel foretold!
Hail to the millions from bondage returning!
Gentiles and Jews the blest vision behold.
Lo, in the desert rich flowers are springing,
Streams ever copious are gliding along;
Loud from the mountain-tops echoes are ringing,
Wastes rise in verdure, and mingle in song.
Hark, from all lands, from the isles of the ocean,
Praise to Jehovah ascending on high;
Fallen the engines of war and commotion,
Shouts of salvation are rending the sky.
Thomas Hastings.

THOMAS HASTINGS, POET AND MUSICIAN

High among the names of those who in the early days of America labored to raise the standard of hymnody must be inscribed the name of Thomas Hastings, Doctor of Music. Poet and musician by nature, Hastings may truly be said to have devoted his entire life to the elevation of sacred song.

The story of his life is typical of the struggles and hardships of many American pioneers who conquered in spite of the most adverse circumstances. Born at Washington, Conn., October 15, 1784, young Hastings removed with his parents to Clinton, N. Y., when he was only twelve years old. The journey was made in ox-sleds through unbroken wilderness in the dead of winter.

The frontier schools of those days offered little opportunity for education, but the eager lad trudged six miles a day to receive the instruction that was given. A passionate fondness for music was first satisfied when he secured a musical primer of four pages costing six pence. The proudest moment in his life came when he was named leader of the village choir.

It was not until he was thirty-two years old that Hastings was able to secure employment as a music teacher, but from that time until his death, in 1872, he devoted all his energies to the work he loved.

Hastings was ever tireless in contending that good music should have a recognized place in religious worship. From 1823 to 1832, during which time he edited the Western Recorder, in Utica, N. Y., he had an excellent opportunity to spread his views on music. In the latter year twelve churches in New York City jointly engaged his services as choir director, and for the remainder of his life Hastings made the great American metropolis his home.

Though seriously handicapped by eye trouble, Hastings produced a prodigious amount of work. It is claimed that he wrote more than one thousand hymn tunes. He also published fifty volumes of church music. Some of the finest tunes in our American hymnals were composed by him. Who has not found inspiration in singing that sweet and haunting melody known as "Ortonville"? And how can we ever be sufficiently grateful for the tune called "Toplady," which has endeared "Rock of Ages" to millions of hearts? Besides these there are at least a score of other beautiful hymn tunes that have been loved by the singing Church for nearly a century, any one of which would have won for the composer an enduring name.

Through the composing of tunes, Hastings was led to write words for hymns. More than six hundred are attributed to him, although many were written anonymously. "Hail to the brightness of Zion's glad morning" is generally regarded as his best hymn. It strikingly reflects the spirit of the missionary age in which Hastings lived.

Another very popular and stirring missionary hymn, written by Hastings in 1831, is a song of two stanzas:

Now be the gospel banner
In every land unfurled;
And be the shout, Hosannah!
Reechoed through the world;

Till every isle and nation,
Till every tribe and tongue,
Receive the great salvation,
And join the happy throng.
Yes, Thou shalt reign forever,
O Jesus, King of kings!
Thy light, Thy love, Thy favor,
Each ransomed captive sings:
The isles for Thee are waiting,
The deserts learn Thy praise,
The hills and valleys, greeting,
The songs responsive raise.

A hymn with the title, "Pilgrimage of Life," though very simple, is singularly beautiful and very tender in its appeal. The first stanza reads:

Gently, Lord, O gently lead us,
Pilgrims in this vale of tears,
Through the trials yet decreed us,
Till our last great change appears.

Hastings did not cease writing and composing hymns until three days before his death. It is said that more of his hymns are found in the standard church hymnals of America than those of any other American writer. Their survival through almost a century is a testimony to their enduring quality.

Key's Hymn of Praise

Lord, with glowing heart I'd praise thee
For the bliss Thy love bestows,
For the pardoning grace that saves me,
And the peace that from it flows.
Help, O God, my weak endeavor;
This dull soul to rapture raise;
Thou must light the flame, or never
Can my love be warmed to praise.
Praise, my soul, the God that sought thee,
Wretched wanderer, far astray;
Found thee lost, and kindly brought thee
From the paths of death away;
Praise, with love's devoutest feeling,
Him who saw thy guilt-born fear,
And, the light of hope revealing,
Bade the blood-stained cross appear.
Lord, this bosom's ardent feeling
Vainly would my lips express;
Low before Thy footstool kneeling,
Deign Thy suppliant's prayer to bless;
Let Thy grace, my soul's chief treasure,
Love's pure flame within me raise;
And, since words can never measure,
Let my life show forth Thy praise.
Francis Scott Key, 1823.

FRANCIS SCOTT KEY, PATRIOT AND HYMNIST

Francis Scott Key is known to every American child as the author of our national anthem, "The star spangled banner"; but his fame as a Christian hymnist has not gone abroad to the same degree. And yet, as the author of "Lord, with glowing heart I'd praise Thee," he ranks among the foremost of American hymn-writers.

Key lived during the stirring days of our country's early history. His father was an officer in the Continental army who fought with distinction during the Revolutionary War. Francis was born at Frederick, Maryland, August 1, 1779. After receiving a legal education he began to practice law in Washington, and served as United States district attorney for three terms, holding that office at the time of his death.

The story of how he came to write "Star spangled banner" scarcely needs to be repeated. It was during the War of 1812 that Key was authorized by President Madison to visit the British fleet near the mouth of the Potomac in order to obtain the release of a friend who had been captured.

The British admiral granted Key's request, but owing to the fact that an attack was about to be made on Fort McHenry, which guarded the harbor of Baltimore, Key and his party were detained all night aboard the truce-boat on which they had come.

It was a night of great anxiety. A fierce bombardment continued during the hours of darkness, and as long as the shore fortifications replied to the cannonading, Key and his friends were certain that all was well. Toward morning, the firing ceased, and they were filled with dark forebodings. The others went below to obtain some sleep, but Key continued to pace the deck until the first streaks of dawn showed that the "flag was still there."

His joy was so unbounded that he seized a piece of paper, and hastily wrote the words of his famous anthem. It was not completed until later in the day, when he reached Baltimore and joined in the victorious joy that filled the city.

While "Star spangled banner" is not a Christian hymn, there are noble sentiments in it that reveal the writer at once as a devout Christian, and this was eminently true of Key.

As a member of the Protestant Episcopal Church he held a lay reader's license, and for many years read the service and visited the sick. He also conducted a Bible class in Sunday school. Although he lived in a slave state, he was finally moved by conscientious scruples to free his slaves. He also did much to alleviate conditions among other unfortunate blacks.

When the Protestant Episcopal Church in 1823 appointed a committee to prepare a new hymn-book for that body, Key was made a lay member of it. Another member of the committee was Dr. William Muhlenberg, who in that same year had published a little hymnal for use in his own congregation. It was in this hymnal, known as "Church Poetry", that Key's beautiful hymn, "Lord, with glowing heart I'd praise Thee," was first published.

In Dr. Muhlenberg's hymn-book the hymn had only three stanzas, and that is the form in which it has since appeared in all other hymnals. In 1900, however, Key's autograph copy of the hymn was discovered, and it was found that the hymn originally had four stanzas. The missing one reads:

Praise thy Saviour God that drew thee
To that cross, new life to give,
Held a blood-sealed pardon to thee,
Bade thee look to Him and live.
Praise the grace whose threats alarmed thee,

Roused thee from thy fatal ease,
Praise the grace whose promise warmed thee,
Praise the grace that whispered peace.

Another excellent hymn, "Before the Lord we bow", was written by Key in 1832 for a Fourth of July celebration.

A bronze statue of Key, placed over his grave at Frederick, Md., shows him with his hand outstretched, as at the moment when he discovered the flag "still there," while his other hand is waving his hat exultantly.

Bryant's Home Mission Hymn

Look from Thy sphere of endless day,
O God of mercy and of might!
In pity look on those who stray
Benighted, in this land of light.
In peopled vale, in lonely glen,
In crowded mart, by stream or sea,
How many of the sons of men
Hear not the message sent from Thee!
Send forth Thy heralds, Lord, to call
The thoughtless young, the hardened old,
A scattered, homeless flock, till all
Be gathered to Thy peaceful fold.
Send them Thy mighty Word to speak,
Till faith shall dawn, and doubt depart,
To awe the bold, to stay the weak,
And bind and heal the broken heart.
Then all these wastes, a dreary scene
That makes us sadden, as we gaze,
Shall grow with living waters green,
And lift to heaven the voice of praise.
William Cullen Bryant, 1840.

AMERICA'S FIRST POET AND HIS HYMNS

William Cullen Bryant, America's first great poet, was also a hymn-writer. Although he did not devote much of his thought and genius to sacred lyrics, he wrote at least two splendid hymns that merit a place in every hymn collection. The one, "Thou, whose unmeasured temple stands," is a church dedication hymn of rare beauty; the other, "Look from Thy sphere of endless day," is unquestionably one of the finest home mission hymns ever written.

Born at Cummington, Mass., November 3, 1794, he was educated at Williams College to be a lawyer. It was his writing of "Thanatopsis" as a boy of seventeen years that gave the first notice to the world that America had produced a great poet.

It is said that when the lines of "Thanatopsis" were submitted to Richard H. Dana, editor of the "North American Review," he was skeptical.

"No one on this side of the Atlantic," he declared, "is capable of writing such verses."

Bryant was brought up in a typical New England Puritan home. Family worship and strict attendance at public worship was the rule in the Bryant household. Every little while the children of the community would also gather in the district schoolhouse, where they would be examined in the Catechism by the parish minister, a venerable man who was loved by old and young alike.

While yet a little child Bryant began to pray that he might receive the gift of writing poetry. No doubt he had been influenced to a large degree in this desire by the fact that his father was a lover of verse and possessed a splendid library of the great English poets. The youthful Bryant was taught to memorize the noble hymns of Isaac Watts, and when he was only five years old he would stand on a chair and recite them to imaginary audiences.

Early in life Bryant came under the influence of the Unitarian doctrines which were then sweeping through New England as a reaction against the stern, harsh teachings of Puritanism. When he was only twenty-six years old he was invited to contribute to a volume of hymns then in course of preparation by the Unitarians. He responded by writing five hymns. Six years later he wrote "Thou, whose unmeasured temple stands" for the dedication of the Second Unitarian Church of New York City. He usually attended the First Congregational Unitarian Church of that city.

About thirty years later, however, when Bryant was sixty-four years old, a profound change occurred in his religious convictions. During a trip abroad his wife became critically ill in Naples. At first her life was despaired of, but when she finally was on the road to recovery Bryant sent for a warm friend of the family, Rev. R. C. Waterston, who was in Naples at the time. The latter tells of his meeting with the aged poet in the following words:

"On the following day, the weather being delightful, we walked in the royal park or garden overlooking the Bay of Naples. Never can I forget the beautiful spirit that breathed through every word he (Bryant) uttered, the reverent love, the confiding trust, the aspiring hope, the rooted faith.... He said that he had never united himself with the Church, which, with his present feeling, he would most gladly do. He then asked if it would be agreeable to me to come to his room on the morrow and administer the communion, adding that, as he had never been baptized, he desired that ordinance at the same time.

"The day following was the Sabbath, and a most heavenly day. In fulfilment of his wishes, in his own quiet room, a company of seven persons celebrated together the Lord's Supper.... Previous to the breaking of bread, William Cullen Bryant was baptized. With snow-white head and flowing beard, he stood like one of the ancient prophets, and perhaps never, since the days of the apostles, has a truer disciple professed allegiance to the divine Master."

Twenty years after this experience, in the last year of the poet's life, he made some contributions to the Methodist Episcopal hymnal. A revision of one of the hymns which he had written in 1820 for the Unitarian hymnal reveals his changed attitude toward the Lord Jesus Christ. For the Unitarian book he had written:

Deem not that they are blest alone
Whose days a peaceful tenor keep;
The God who loves our race has shown
A blessing for the eyes that weep.
For the Methodist hymn-book he changed the third line to read:

The anointed Son of God makes known.

The hymn was sung in its changed form at the poet's funeral, as well as another beautiful hymn entitled "The Star of Bethlehem," written in 1875 for the semi-centennial of the Church of the Messiah in Boston.

An Exquisite Baptismal Hymn

Saviour, who Thy flock art feeding
With the shepherd's kindest care,
All the feeble gently leading,
While the lambs Thy bosom share.
Now, these little ones receiving,
Fold them in Thy gracious arm;
There, we know, Thy word believing,
Only there secure from harm.
Never, from Thy pasture roving,
Let them be the lion's prey;
Let Thy tenderness, so loving,
Keep them through life's dangerous way.
Then, within Thy fold eternal,
Let them find a resting place,
Feed in pastures ever vernal,
Drink the rivers of Thy grace.
William Augustus Muhlenberg, 1826.

THE HYMN-WRITER OF THE MUHLENBERGS

William Augustus Muhlenberg, one of America's early hymn-writers, came from a most distinguished family. His great grandfather, Henry Melchior Muhlenberg, was the "patriarch of the Lutheran Church in America," having come to these shores from Germany in 1742, and being the founder in that year of the first permanent Lutheran organization in the new world.

A son of the patriarch and grandfather of the hymn-writer bore the name of Frederick Augustus Muhlenberg. He, too, was a Lutheran minister, but during the stirring days of the Revolutionary period he entered into the political affairs of the struggling colonies. He was president of the convention which ratified the Constitution of the United States and also served as first speaker of the new House of Representatives. His brother, Rev. Peter Muhlenberg, was also a distinguished patriot. When the Revolution broke out, he was serving a congregation at Woodstock, Va. It was he who stood in the pulpit of his church and, throwing aside his clerical robe, stood revealed in the uniform of a Continental colonel.

"There is a time to preach and a time to pray," he cried, "but these times have passed away. There is a time to fight, and that time has now come!"

Thereupon he called upon the men of his congregation to enlist in his regiment. Before the war ended he had risen to the rank of major general.

William Augustus Muhlenberg, the hymn-writer, was born in Philadelphia in 1796. Since the German language was then being used exclusively in the German Lutheran churches, he and his little sister were allowed to attend Christ Episcopal Church. In this way William Augustus drifted away from the Church of his great forbears, and when he grew up he became a clergyman in the Episcopal communion.

It is evident that Muhlenberg brought something of the spirit of the "singing church" into the church of his adoption, for in 1821 he issued a tract with the title, "A Plea for Christian Hymns." It appears that the Episcopal Church at this time was using a prayer-book that included only fifty-seven hymns, and no one felt the poverty of his Church in this respect more keenly than did Muhlenberg.

Two years later the General Convention of the Episcopal body voted to prepare a hymn-book, and Muhlenberg was made a member of the committee. One of his associates was Francis Scott Key, author of "Star spangled banner."

As a member of the committee Muhlenberg contributed four original hymns to the new collection. They were "I would not live alway," "Like Noah's weary dove," "Shout the glad tidings, triumphantly sing," and "Saviour, who Thy flock art leading." The latter is a baptism hymn and is one of the most exquisite lyrics on that theme ever written. Although Muhlenberg never married, he had a very deep love for children. No service seemed so hallowed to him as the baptism of a little child. It is said that shortly after his ordination, when asked to officiate at such a rite, Muhlenberg flushed and hesitated, and then asked a bishop who was present to baptize the babe. The latter, however, insisted that the young clergyman should carry out the holy ordinance, and from that day there was no duty that afforded Muhlenberg more joy.

Muhlenberg often expressed regret that he had written "I would not live alway." It seems that the poem was called into being in 1824, following a "heart-breaking disappointment in the matter of love." Muhlenberg was a young man at the time, and in his later years he sought to alter it in such a way that it would breathe more of the hopeful spirit of the New Testament. He contended that Paul's words, "For me to live is Christ" were far better than Job's lament, "I would not live alway." However, the hymn as originally written had become so fixed in the consciousness of the Church, that all efforts of the author to revise it were in vain.

Nearly all the hymns of Muhlenberg that have lived were written during his earlier years. His later ministry centered in New York City, where he was head of a boys' school for a number of years, and later rector of the Church of the Holy Communion. He soon became an outstanding leader in the great metropolis. After having founded St. Luke's hospital, the first church institution of its kind in New York City, he spent the last twenty years of his life as its superintendent.

His death occurred when he was past eighty years. It is said that when the end was drawing near, the hospital chaplain came to his bedside to pray for his recovery.

"Let us have an understanding about this," said the dying Muhlenberg. "You are asking God to restore me and I am asking God to take me home. There must not be a contradiction in our prayers, for it is evident that He cannot answer them both."

The Way, the Truth, and the Life

Thou art the Way; to Thee alone
From sin and death we flee,
And he who would the Father seek,
Must seek Him, Lord, by Thee.
Thou art the Truth; Thy Word alone
Sound wisdom can impart;
Thou only canst inform the mind,
And purify the heart.
Thou art the Life; the rending tomb
Proclaims Thy conquering arm;
And those who put their trust in Thee
Nor death nor hell shall harm.
Thou art the Way, the Truth, the Life;
Grant us that Way to know,
That Truth to keep, that Life to win
Whose joys eternal flow.
George Washington Doane, 1824.

THE LYRICS OF BISHOP DOANE

Critics will forever disagree on the subject of the relative merits of great hymns. Bishop George Washington Doane's fine hymn, "Thou art the Way; to Thee alone," has been declared by some to be the foremost of all hymns written by American authors. Dr. Breed, on the other hand, declares that it is "by no means the equal" of other hymns by Doane. Another authority observes that it "rather stiffly and mechanically paraphrases" the passage on which it is founded, while Edward S. Ninde rejects this conclusion by contending that although "metrical expositions of Scriptures are apt to be stilted and spiritless ... this one is a success."

Ninde, however, does not agree that it is "the first of American hymns," reserving this honor, as do most critics, for Ray Palmer's "My faith looks up to Thee."

Bishop Doane was born in Trenton, N. J., May 27, 1799. This was the year in which George Washington died. The future hymn-writer was named after the great patriot. At the age of nineteen he was graduated by Union College with the highest scholastic honors. After teaching for a season, he became pastor of Trinity Episcopal Church, Boston, Mass., the church afterwards made famous by Phillips Brooks.

When only thirty-three years old he was elevated to the bishopric of New Jersey, which position he held until his death in 1859. By this time he had already won fame as a hymn-writer. It was in 1824, at the age of twenty-five, that Doane published a little volume of lyrics entitled "Songs by the Way." One of the hymns in this collection was the beautiful paraphrase, "Thou art the Way; to Thee alone." This hymn alone would have been sufficient to have perpetuated the name of the young poet, but there was another gem in the same collection that will always be treasured by those who love Christian song. It is the exquisite evening hymn:

> Softly now the light of day
> Fades upon my sight away;
> Free from care, from labor free,
> Lord, I would commune with Thee.

Among the many achievements of this versatile bishop was the founding of Saint Mary's Hall, a school for young women, at Burlington, N. J. Doane lies buried in the neighboring churchyard, and it is said that the students on every Wednesday evening at chapel services sing "Softly now the light of day" as a memorial tribute to the founder of the institution.

Both of these hymns were quickly recognized as possessing unusual merit, and almost immediately found their way into Christian hymn-books. Today there is scarcely a hymnal published in the English language that does not contain them.

But Bishop Doane's fame does not rest on these two hymns alone. He was destined to write a third one, equally great but of a very different character from the other two. It is the stirring missionary hymn:

> Fling out the banner! let it float
> Skyward and seaward, high and wide;
> The sun that lights its shining folds,
> The cross, on which the Saviour died.

It was written in 1848 in response to a request from the young women of St. Mary's Hall for a hymn to be used at a flag-raising. The third stanza is one of rare beauty:

> Fling out the banner! heathen lands
> Shall see from far the glorious sight,
> And nations, crowding to be born,
> Baptize their spirits in its light.

The hymn, as may be surmised, is based on the passage from the Psaltery: "Thou hast given a banner to them that fear thee, that it may be displayed because of the truth."

Bishop Doane was a zealous advocate of missions. It was during his childhood that the modern missionary movement had its inception and swept like a tidal wave over the Christian world. "Fling out the banner" is a reflection of the remarkable enthusiasm that filled his own soul and that revealed itself in his aggressive missionary leadership. Indeed, he became known in his own Church as "the missionary bishop of America."

A son, William C. Doane, also became one of the most distinguished bishops of the Episcopal Church. Writing of his father's rare gifts as a hymnist, he declares that his heart was "full of song. It oozed out in his conversation, in his sermons, in everything that he did. Sometimes in a steamboat, often when the back of a letter was his only paper, the sweetest things came."

The Quaker Poet's Prayer

Dear Lord and Father of mankind,
Forgive our feverish ways;
Reclothe us in our rightful mind,
In purer lives Thy service find,
In deeper reverence, praise.
In simple trust like theirs who heard,
Beside the Syrian sea,
The gracious calling of the Lord,
Let us, like them, without a word
Rise up and follow Thee.
O Sabbath rest by Galilee!
O calm of hills above,
Where Jesus knelt to share with Thee
The silence of eternity
Interpreted by love.
Drop Thy still dews of quietness,
Till all our strivings cease;
Take from our souls the strain and stress,
And let our ordered lives confess
The beauty of Thy peace.
Breathe through the heat of our desire
Thy coolness and Thy balm;
Let sense be dumb, let flesh retire,
Speak through the earthquake, wind, and fire,
O still, small voice of calm.
John Greenleaf Whittier, 1872.

THE QUAKER POET AS A HYMN-WRITER

Of all American poets, there is none who is so genuinely loved as John Greenleaf Whittier. A man of the people, a true American, and full of the milk of human kindness, Whittier's poetry reflects so much of his own character that it will never lose its singular charm and beauty.

Whittier's life is a story of struggle. He was born of humble Quaker parents at Haverhill, Mass., December 17, 1807. Instead of receiving the advantages of an education, he knew of nothing but drudgery and hard work throughout his childhood. But the poetic spark was in him even as a child. One day, when a small boy, he sat before the kitchen fire and wrote on his slate:

And must I always swing the flail
And help to fill the milking pail?
I wish to go away to school;
I do not wish to be a fool.

No doubt it was the memory of these childhood experiences that later inspired him to write with such depth of feeling and understanding the lines of "The Barefoot Boy":

Blessings on thee, little man,
Barefoot boy, with cheek of tan!
With thy turned-up pantaloons,
And thy merry whistled tunes;

With thy red lips, redder still
Kissed by strawberries on the hill;
With the sunshine on thy face,
Through thy torn brim's jaunty grace:
From my heart I give thee joy—
I was once a barefoot boy!

Through hard work he managed to save enough to attend Haverhill academy two seasons. Though this was the extent of his scholastic training, he never ceased to be a student.

A wandering Scotchman who chanced to visit the quiet Quaker home and sang such rollicking (!) lyrics as "Bonny Doon," "Highland Mary," and "Auld Lang Syne" kindled the boy's imagination. He immediately borrowed a copy of Burns' poems from the village schoolmaster, and now for the first time he seriously began to think of becoming a poet.

When he was only twenty-five years old he had already begun to attract attention by his poetry. He had also achieved some success in politics and was planning to run for Congress. Soon, however, came the call of the Abolition movement, and Whittier, always true to his Quaker conception of "the inner voice," determined to sacrifice all of his political ambitions to become a champion of the slaves.

It was not long before he was recognized as preëminently the poet of anti-slavery, as Phillips was its orator, Mrs. Stowe its novelist, and Sumner its statesman. The fervor with which he threw himself into the cause may be seen reflected in the stirring lines of his poems written in those days, notably "The Star of Bethlehem." However, since his anti-slavery poems are more vehement than inspiring, and as the events which suggested them were temporary, they will be read with constantly waning interest.

The vigor with which he espoused the Abolition cause stirred up deep resentment among his enemies. At Philadelphia, where he published "The Pennsylvania Free-man," the office of the paper was attacked by a mob and burned. But Whittier was not dismayed. When Daniel Webster in 1850 made his notable defense of the Fugitive Slave law in the United States senate, Whittier wrote "Ichabod" in reply.

At a time when the Abolition movement seemed to be losing, rather than gaining, ground, the poet gave expression to his faith in God in the beautiful poem, "Seed-Time and Harvest." His duty, as he saw it, was to sow the seed; God would take care of the harvest.

Because the Quakers do not sing in their services, Whittier knew little of music. However, he once wrote: "A good hymn is the best use to which poetry can be devoted, but I do not claim that I have succeeded in composing one."

And yet, the poems of Whittier, notably "Our Master" and "The Eternal Goodness," have been the source of some of the finest hymns in the English language. There are at least seventy-five hymns now in use that bear his name. Practically all of them are extracts from longer poems. "Dear Lord and Father of mankind," "I bow my forehead to the dust," and "We need not climb the heavenly steeps" are among the best loved of Whittier's hymns. Probably his most famous poem is "Snowbound."

Whittier died in 1892. His last words were, "Love—love to all the world." A friend bent over the dying man and whispered the words of his poem, "At Last."

Palmer's Famous Hymn

My faith looks up to Thee,
Thou Lamb of Calvary,
Saviour divine;
Now hear me while I pray,
Take all my guilt away,
O let me from this day
Be wholly Thine.
May Thy rich grace impart
Strength to my fainting heart,
My zeal inspire;
As Thou hast died for me,
O may my love for Thee
Pure, warm, and changeless be,
A living fire.
When life's dark maze I tread,
And griefs around me spread,
Be Thou my Guide;

Bid darkness turn to day,
Wipe sorrow's tears away,
Nor let me ever stray
From Thee aside.
When ends life's transient dream,
When death's cold, sullen stream
Shall o'er me roll,
Blest Saviour, then, in love,
Fear and distrust remove;
O bear me safe above,
A ransomed soul.
Ray Palmer, 1830.

AMERICA'S GREATEST HYMN AND ITS AUTHOR

Although a number of America's great poets wrote hymns, it was not given to any one of them to compose America's finest Christian lyric. Bryant wrote "Look from Thy sphere of endless day," Whittier was the author of "Dear Lord and Father of mankind," Holmes composed "O Love Divine, that stooped to share," and Longfellow has given us "I heard the bells of Christmas day;" but, beautiful as these hymns are, none of them can compare with "My faith looks up to Thee." This, "the most precious contribution which American genius has yet made to the hymnology of the Christian Church," came from the pen of a very humble but gifted minister, Ray Palmer.

Palmer, who was born at Little Compton, R. I., November 12, 1808, was a direct descendant of John Alden and his good wife, Priscilla. One of his forebears was William Palmer, who came to Plymouth in 1621.

Through pressure of poverty Ray found it necessary to leave home at the age of thirteen, after having received a grammar education. For two years he clerked in a Boston dry goods store, during which time he passed through some deep spiritual experiences, with the result that he gave his heart to God.

Friends who recognized unusual gifts in the young man urged him to attend school. Eventually he graduated from Phillips Andover Academy and from Yale. For a while he taught in New York and New Haven, but in 1835 he was ordained to the Congregational ministry. He served a congregation in Bath, Maine, for fifteen years, and another at Albany, N. Y., for a like period, after which he became Corresponding Secretary of the American Congregational Union, a position which he held until 1878, when he was compelled to retire because of failing health.

It was while he was teaching in New York City that "My faith looks up to Thee" was written. He was only twenty-two years old at the time, and he had no thought when writing it that he was composing a hymn for general use. He tells in his own account of the hymn how he had been reading a little German poem of two stanzas, picturing a penitent sinner before the cross. Deeply moved by the lines, he translated them into English, and then added the four stanzas that form his own hymn.

The words of the hymn, he tells us, were born out of his own spiritual experience.

"I gave form to what I felt, by writing, with little effort, the stanzas," he said. "I recollect I wrote them with very tender emotion, and ended the last lines with tears."

"A ransomed soul!" Who would not have been moved to deep emotion after having written a poem with such a sublime closing line!

This happened in the year 1832, almost a hundred years ago.

Palmer copied the poem into a little note-book which he constantly carried in his pocket. Frequently he would read it as a part of his private devotion. It never seemed to occur to him that it might some day be used as a hymn.

But God was watching over that little poem. One day as Palmer was walking along the busy streets of Boston, he chanced to meet Lowell Mason, the famous musician and composer of Savannah, Ga. Mason was compiling a hymn-book at the time and asked Palmer, who had established something of a reputation as a poet, if he could give him some words for which he could compose music. Palmer remembered the poem in his note-book, and, while the two men stepped into a nearby store, a copy of the poem was made and given to Mason.

When the two men met again a few days later, Mason exclaimed: "Dr. Palmer, you may live many years and do many good things, but I think you will be best known to posterity as the author of 'My faith looks up to Thee.'"

Mason wrote the beautiful tune known as "Olivet" for the hymn, and perhaps the music contributed as much as the words to endear it to the hearts of millions. Certainly here is an instance where words and music are wedded, and should never be parted asunder.

Palmer wrote many other splendid hymns. Some of his most famous are translations from the Latin. His rendering of the noted hymn of Bernard of Clairvaux, "O Jesus, Joy of loving hearts," is a gem of wondrous beauty. It has become a favorite communion hymn.

In his ministry Palmer laid much emphasis on the Lord's Supper, and many of his hymns were written for communion services. He once said, in a communion address: "When the cares and the business of life have hurried me hither and thither with no little distraction of mind, I love to come back again, and sit down before the cross, and gaze on the blessed Sufferer with silent, tender memories. It is like coming once more into the sunshine after long walking through gloom and mist."

Palmer's whole life was characterized by a warm, almost passionate, devotion to Christ. His faith in the Saviour was so childlike and strong that it enabled him to rise above all external burdens and trials. Something of his personal love to Christ may be seen beautifully reflected in his hymn, "Jesus, these eyes have never seen," which was his own favorite and which many regard as inferior only to "My faith looks up to Thee." It is such an appealing lyric, we feel we must quote it in full.

Jesus, these eyes have never seen
That radiant form of Thine!
The veil of sense hangs dark between
Thy blessed face and mine!
I see Thee not, I hear Thee not,
Yet art Thou oft with me!
And earth hath ne'er so dear a spot
As where I meet with Thee.
Like some bright dream that comes unsought,
When slumbers o'er me roll,
Thine image ever fills my thought,
And charms my ravished soul.
Yet though I have not seen, and still
Must rest in faith alone,
I love Thee, dearest Lord, and will,
Unseen, but not unknown.
When death these mortal eyes shall seal,
And still this throbbing heart,
The rending veil shall Thee reveal,
All glorious as Thou art.

Palmer looked upon his hymns as gifts from heaven, and therefore he refused to accept money for their use. He insisted, however, that those who published his hymns should print them exactly as they were written. He regarded the somewhat common practice of tampering with texts as "immoral."

Palmer died in 1887. On the day before he breathed his last, he was heard repeating feebly the last stanza of his favorite hymn:

When death these mortal eyes shall seal,
And still this throbbing heart,
The rending veil shall Thee reveal,
All glorious as Thou art.

A Hopeful Missionary Lyric

The morning light is breaking;
The darkness disappears;
The sons of earth are waking
To penitential tears;
Each breeze that sweeps the ocean
Brings tidings from afar,
Of nations in commotion,
Prepared for Zion's war.
See heathen nations bending
Before the God we love,
And thousand hearts ascending
In gratitude above;
While sinners, now confessing,

The gospel call obey,
And seek the Saviour's blessing,
A nation in a day.
Blest river of salvation,
Pursue thine onward way;
Flow thou to every nation,
Nor in thy richness stay;
Stay not till all the lowly
Triumphant reach their home:
Stay not till all the holy
Proclaim: "The Lord is come!"
Samuel Francis Smith, 1832.

SAMUEL SMITH, A PATRIOTIC HYMN-WRITER

Nearly a century has now elapsed since our national hymn, "America," was written, and, despite all efforts to displace it by other anthems, it seems to retain its hold on the hearts of the people. Samuel Francis Smith will always be gratefully remembered as the author of this hymn, but we should not lose sight of the fact that the New England pastor who gave his country such an inspiring patriotic song has also given to the Christian Church some of the choicest gems in her hymnody.

Associated with "My country, 'tis of thee" will be the stirring missionary hymn, "The morning light is breaking," the two being regarded as the foremost of Dr. Smith's poetical works. Both were written in the winter of 1832, when he was only twenty-four years old. He was a student at Andover Theological Seminary at the time.

Altogether Dr. Smith contributed nearly 150 hymns to American hymnody, many of them on missionary themes. They were written in an era that witnessed a remarkable revival of interest in foreign missions. The famous "Haystack Meeting" at Williams College, which marked the beginning of the modern missionary movement in America, was held in 1806, just two years before Smith was born. Smith himself, while a theological student at Andover, caught the spirit of the times and felt constrained to become a missionary.

At this time reports came from Adoniram Judson in Burmah that, after years of painful disappointment and failure, the light was breaking, and multitudes were turning to Christ. Smith was fired with hopeful enthusiasm, and it was in this spirit of glad exultation that he sat down to write his immortal missionary hymn:

The morning light is breaking,
The darkness disappears;
The sons of earth are waking
To penitential tears.

Many other missionary hymns came from the gifted writer in succeeding years, and immediately after his graduation from Andover he became editor of a missionary magazine, through which he wielded a great influence. When the "Lone Star" mission in India was in danger of being abandoned because of lack of funds, Smith did much to save it by writing a poem with the title, "Lone Star." Another missionary hymn by him begins with the line, "Onward speed thy conquering flight." However, it does not attain to the poetic heights of "The morning light is breaking," which has been compared to Heber's "From Greenland's icy mountains" in spiritual fervor and literary merit.

Another interesting hymn written by Smith during his student days is called "The Missionary's Farewell." The first stanza reads:

> Yes, my native land, I love thee;
> All thy scenes, I love them well;
> Friends, connections, happy country,
> Can I bid you all farewell?
> Can I leave you,
> Far in heathen lands to dwell?

Although Dr. Smith never carried out his earlier resolve to become a missionary, he visited many foreign fields and had the satisfaction of hearing his own hymns sung in many tongues. Referring to "The morning light is breaking," he once wrote:

"It has been a great favorite at missionary gatherings, and I have myself heard it sung in five or six different languages in Europe and Asia. It is a favorite with the Burmans, Karens and Telugus in Asia, from whose lips I have heard it repeatedly."

A son of the distinguished hymn-writer became a missionary to the Burmans.

Dr. Smith filled many important pulpits in New England during his long and illustrious career. At one time he was a professor in modern languages. He was an unusual linguist, being familiar with fifteen tongues. In 1894, a year before his death, he was still vigorous in mind and body, writing and preaching, although he was eighty-six years old. It was in this year that he was found looking around for a textbook that would enable him to begin the study of Russian. It was in this year, too, that he wrote one of his finest hymns, for a church dedication.

> Founded on Thee, our only Lord,
> On Thee, the everlasting Rock,
> Thy Church shall stand as stands Thy Word,
> Nor fear the storm, nor dread the shock.
> For Thee our waiting spirits yearn,
> For Thee this house of praise we rear;
> To Thee with longing hearts we turn;
> Come, fix Thy glorious presence here.
>
> Come, with Thy Spirit and Thy power,
> The Conqueror, once the Crucified;
> Our God, our Strength, our King, our Tower,
> Here plant Thy throne, and here abide.
> Accept the work our hands have wrought;
> Accept, O God, this earthly shrine;
> Be Thou our Rock, our Life, our Thought,

And we, as living temples, Thine.

The celebrated hymnist happily has left a personal account of how he wrote "America." Lowell Mason, the composer, had given him a collection of German books containing songs for children with the request that Smith should examine them and translate anything of merit.

"One dismal day in February, 1832," he wrote long afterward, "about half an hour before sunset, I was turning over the leaves of one of the music books when my eye rested on the tune which is now known as 'America.' I liked the spirited movement of it, not knowing it at that time to be 'God save the King.' I glanced at the German words and saw that they were patriotic, and instantly felt the impulse to write a patriotic hymn of my own, adapted to the tune. Picking up a scrap of waste paper which lay near me, I wrote at once, probably within half an hour, the hymn 'America' as it is now known everywhere. The whole hymn stands today as it stood on the bit of waste paper, five or six inches long and two and a half wide."

Dr. Smith was a member of the celebrated Harvard class of 1829, to which Oliver Wendell Holmes also belonged. The latter wrote a poem for one of the class reunions, in which he referred to the distinguished hymn-writer in the following lines:

And there's a nice youngster of excellent pith—
Fate tried to conceal him by naming him Smith;
But he shouted a song for the brave and the free—
Just read on his medal, 'My country,' 'of thee.'

On November 19, 1895, the venerable pastor and poet was called suddenly to his eternal home. He died as he was taking a train from Boston to preach in a neighboring town.

A Pearl among Christmas Carols

It came upon the midnight clear,
That glorious song of old,
From angels bending near the earth
To touch their harps of gold;
"Peace on the earth, good will to men,
From heaven's all-gracious King:"
The world in solemn stillness lay
To hear the angels sing.
Still through the cloven skies they come
With peaceful wings unfurled,
And still their heavenly music floats
O'er all the weary world;
Above its sad and lowly plains
They bend on hovering wing,
And ever o'er its Babel sounds
The blessed angels sing.
And ye, beneath life's crushing load,

Whose forms are bending low,
Who toil along the climbing way
With painful steps and slow—
Look now! for glad and golden hours
Come swiftly on the wing:
O rest beside the weary road,
And hear the angels sing!
For lo! the days are hastening on
By prophet-bards foretold,
When with the ever-circling years
Comes round the age of gold;
When peace shall over all the earth
Its ancient splendors fling,
And the whole world send back the song
Which now the angels sing.
Edmund Hamilton Sears, 1834.

TWO FAMOUS CHRISTMAS HYMNS AND THEIR AUTHOR

To be the writer of one great hymn classic on the nativity is an enviable distinction, but to be the author of two immortal Christmas lyrics is fame that has probably come to only one man, and he an American. His name was Edmund Hamilton Sears, and so long as Christians celebrate Christmas, they will sing the two hymns he wrote—"It came upon a midnight clear" and "Calm on the listening ear of night."

Strangely enough, an interval of sixteen years separated the writing of the two hymns. Sears had just graduated from Union College at the age of twenty-four when he wrote "Calm on the listening ear of night." It appeared in the "Boston Observer," and was immediately recognized as a poem of unusual merit. Oliver Wendell Holmes spoke of it as "one of the finest and most beautiful hymns ever written."

Sixteen years elapsed, and then at Christmas time in 1850 the Christian world was delighted to find in the "Christian Register" another lyric, "It came upon the midnight clear," which many believe is superior to the earlier hymn. The language of this hymn is so surpassingly lovely and its movement so rhythmical, it fairly sings itself.

There is, in fact, a close resemblance between the two hymns, and yet they are different. While the earlier hymn is largely descriptive, the later one is characterized by a note of joyous optimism and triumphant faith. In Sears' "Sermons and Songs" he published the one at the beginning, and the other at the close, of a sermon for Christmas Eve on 1 Tim. 2:6.

Each of the two hymns had five stanzas in its original form. The fourth stanza of the older hymn is usually omitted. It reads:

Light on thy hills, Jerusalem!
The Saviour now is born;
More bright on Bethlehem's joyous plains

Breaks the first Christmas morn;
And brighter on Moriah's brow,
Crowned with her temple-spires,
Which first proclaim the new-born light,
Clothed with its orient fires.

The stanza omitted from the second Christmas hymn sounds the only minor note heard in that otherwise hopeful and joyous lyric:

Yet with the woes of sin and strife
The world hath suffered long;
Beneath the angel-strain have rolled
Two thousand years of wrong;
And man, at war with man, hears not
The love song which they bring:
O hush the noise, ye men of strife,
And hear the angels sing!

Sears was a native of New England, having been born in Berkshire County, Massachusetts, in 1810. He completed his theological course at Harvard Divinity School in 1837, whereupon he entered the Unitarian Church, serving as a pastor for nearly forty years.

Surprise has often been expressed that a Unitarian could write such marvelous hymns on the nativity; but Sears was a Unitarian in name rather than in fact. He leaned strongly toward Swedenborgian teachings, and believed implicitly in the deity of Christ.

In addition to his hymns, he wrote a few works in prose. His books on "Regeneration," "Foregleams of Immortality," and "The Fourth Gospel the Heart of Christ" were widely read in his day. These have now been almost entirely forgotten, but his two great hymns go singing through the years. They are found in practically all standard hymn-books, although the final stanza of "It came upon the midnight clear" is often altered. Sears died in 1876.

Mrs. Stowe's Hymn Masterpiece

Still, still with Thee, when purple morning breaketh,
When the bird waketh, and the shadows flee;
Fairer than morning, lovelier than the daylight,
Dawns the sweet consciousness, I am with Thee!
Alone with Thee, amid the mystic shadows,
The solemn hush of nature newly born;
Alone with Thee, in breathless adoration,
In the calm dew and freshness of the morn.
When sinks the soul, subdued by toil, to slumber,
Its closing eye looks up to Thee in prayer;
Sweet the repose beneath Thy wings o'ershading,
But sweeter still to wake and find Thee there.
So shall it be at last, in that bright morning,
When the soul waketh, and life's shadows flee;

O for that hour when fairer than the dawning
Shall rise the glorious thought, I am with Thee!
Harriet Beecher Stowe, 1855

HARRIET BEECHER STOWE AND HER HYMNS

Through the fame that her book, "Uncle Tom's Cabin," brought her, the name of Harriet Beecher Stowe has become almost a household word on both sides of the Atlantic. But not many, perhaps, are familiar with Mrs. Stowe the hymn-writer. And yet she wrote a number of hymns that are worthy of finding a place in the best of collections. Indeed, for sheer poetic beauty there is probably not a single American lyric that can excel "Still, still with Thee, when purple morning breaketh."

It was her brother, Henry Ward Beecher, who introduced Mrs. Stowe as a hymn-writer, when he included three of her hymns in the "Plymouth Collection," which he edited in 1865. One of the three was the hymn mentioned above; the other two were "That mystic word of Thine, O sovereign Lord" and "When winds are raging o'er the upper ocean."

Like the Wesley family in England, the Beecher family became one of the most famous in religious and literary circles in America. Harriet Beecher was born in Litchfield, Conn., June 14, 1812. Her father was the noted Dr. Lyman Beecher, a distinguished clergyman of his day. Her mother, a very devout Christian, died when Harriet was less than four years of age. Her dying prayer was that her six sons might be called into the ministry. That prayer was answered, and the youngest of them, Henry Ward Beecher, who was only a boy when the mother died, became one of America's greatest preachers. We do not know what the dying mother's prayer for her daughter was, but we do know that Harriet Beecher achieved fame such as comes to few women. Even as a child she revealed a spiritual nature of unusual depth. An earnest sermon preached by her father when she was fourteen made such an impression on her youthful heart that she determined to give herself wholly to Christ. She tells of the experience in these words:

"As soon as my father came home and was seated in his study, I went up to him and fell in his arms, saying, 'Father, I have given myself to Jesus, and He has taken me.' I never shall forget the expression of his face as he looked down into my earnest childish eyes; it was so sweet, so gentle, and like sunlight breaking out upon a landscape. 'Is it so?' he said, holding me silently to his heart, as I felt the hot tears fall on my head. 'Then has a new flower blossomed in the kingdom this day.'"

In 1832 the father removed to Cincinnati, Ohio, where he became president of Lane Theological Seminary. Here Harriet married Prof. Calvin E. Stowe, a member of the faculty. Many misfortunes and sorrows came into her life, but always she was sustained by her strong faith in God, and she bore them with unusual Christian fortitude. In 1849 her infant boy was snatched from her by the dreadful cholera scourge. Her husband, broken in health, was in an Eastern sanatorium at the time, and all the cares and anxieties of the household fell upon the shoulders of the brave young wife. A letter written to her husband, dated June 29, 1849, gives a graphic description of the plague as it was then raging in Cincinnati. She wrote:

"This week has been unusually fatal. The disease in the city has been malignant and virulent. Hearse drivers have scarce been allowed to unharness their horses, while furniture carts and common vehicles are often employed for the removal of the dead. The sable trains which pass our windows, the frequent indications of crowding haste, and the absence of reverent decency have, in many cases, been most painful.... On Tuesday, one hundred and sixteen deaths from cholera were reported, and that night the air was of that peculiarly oppressive, deathly kind that seems to lie like lead on the brain and soul. As regards your coming home, I am decidedly opposed to it."

Under date of July 26, she wrote again: "At last it is over and our dear little one is gone from us. He is now among the blessed. My Charley—my beautiful, loving, gladsome baby, so loving, so sweet, so full of life, and hope and strength—now lies shrouded, pale and cold, in the room below.... I write as though there were no sorrow like my sorrow, yet there has been in this city, as in the land of Egypt, scarce a house without its dead. This heart-break, this anguish, has been everywhere, and when it will end God alone knows."

The succeeding years brought other tragedies to the sorely tried family. In 1857 the eldest son, Henry, pride of his mother's heart, was drowned at the close of his freshman year at Dartmouth College. Then came the Civil War with its bloody battles. At Gettysburg a third son, Fred, was wounded in the head by a piece of shrapnel. Although it did not prove fatal, his mental faculties were permanently impaired.

Through all these afflictions the marvelous faith of Mrs. Stowe remained firm and unshaken. Many years afterwards, in looking back upon these bitter experiences, she wrote: "I thank God there is one thing running through all of them from the time I was thirteen years old, and that is the intense unwavering sense of Christ's educating, guiding presence and care."

It was in the midst of these dark tragedies that Mrs. Stowe wrote a hymn entitled "The Secret."

> When winds are raging o'er the upper ocean,
> And billows wild contend with angry roar,
> 'Tis said, far down, beneath the wild commotion,
> That peaceful stillness reigneth evermore.
> Far, far beneath, the noise of tempests dieth,
> And silver waves chime ever peacefully;
> And no rude storm, how fierce soe'er it flieth,
> Disturbs the Sabbath of that deeper sea.
> So to the heart that knows Thy love, O Purest!
> There is a temple sacred evermore,
> And all the babble of life's angry voices
> Dies in hushed stillness at its sacred door.
> Far, far away, the roar of passion dieth,
> And loving thoughts rise calm and peacefully;
> And no rude storm, how fierce soe'er it flieth,
> Disturbs that deeper rest, O Lord, in Thee!
> O Rest of rests! O Peace serene, eternal!

Thou ever livest, and Thou changest never;
And in the secret of Thy presence dwelleth
Fulness of joy, forever and forever.

It was the writing of "Uncle Tom's Cabin" that brought world-wide fame to this unusual mother. The family had moved from Cincinnati to Brunswick, Maine, where Professor Stowe had accepted a position in the faculty of Bowdoin College. There were six children now and the father's income was meager. In order to help meet the family expenses, Mrs. Stowe began to write articles for a magazine known as the "National Era." She labored under difficulties. "If I sit by the open fire in the parlor," she wrote, "my back freezes, if I sit in my bedroom and try to write my head and my feet are cold.... I can earn four hundred dollars a year by writing, but I don't want to feel that I must, and when weary with teaching the children, and tending the baby, and buying provisions, and mending dresses, and darning stockings, I sit down and write a piece for some paper."

The passage of the Fugitive Slave Act aroused the deepest feeling among Abolitionists in the North. While living in Cincinnati her family had aided the so-called "underground railway," by which runaway slaves were helped in their efforts to reach the Canadian boundary. Now Mrs. Stowe's spirit burned within her. "I wish," she writes at this period, "some Martin Luther would arise to set this community right."

It was then she conceived the idea of writing "Uncle Tom's Cabin." In the month of February, 1851, while attending communion service in the college church at Brunswick, the scene of the death of Uncle Tom passed before her mind like the unfolding of a vision. When she returned home she immediately wrote down the mental picture she had seen. Then she gathered her children around her and read what she had written. Two of them broke into violent weeping, the first of many thousands who have wept over "Uncle Tom's Cabin."

The first chapter was not completed until the following April, and on June 5 it began to appear in serial form in the "National Era." She had intended to write a short tale of a few chapters, but as her task progressed the conviction grew on her that she had been intrusted with a holy mission. Afterwards she said: "I could not control the story; it wrote itself." At another time she remarked: "The Lord himself wrote it, and I was but the humblest of instruments in His hand. To Him alone should be given all the praise."

Mrs. Stowe received $300 for her serial story! However, scarcely had the last instalment appeared when a Boston publisher made arrangements to print it in book form. Within one year it had passed through 120 editions, and four months after the book was off the press the author had received $10,000 in royalties. Almost in a day Mrs. Stowe had become one of the most famous women in the world, and the specter of poverty had been banished forever. "Uncle Tom's Cabin" exerted a profound influence not only over the American people, but its fame spread to Europe. The year following its publication Jenny Lind came to America. Asked to contribute to a fund Mrs. Stowe was raising for the purpose of purchasing the freedom of a slave family, the "Swedish Nightingale" gladly responded, also writing a letter to Mrs. Stowe in the following prophetic vein: "I have the feeling about 'Uncle Tom's Cabin' that great changes will take place by and by, from the impression people receive from it, and that the writer of that book can fall asleep today or tomorrow with the bright, sweet consciousness of having been a strong means in the Creator's hand of having accomplished essential good."

Tributes like this came to Mrs. Stowe from the great and lowly in all parts of the world.

Concerning Jenny Lind's singing, Mrs. Stowe wrote to her husband from New York: "Well, we have heard Jenny Lind, and the affair was a bewildering dream of sweetness and beauty. Her face and movements are full of poetry and feeling. She has the artless grace of a little child, the poetic effect of a wood-nymph."

Mrs. Stowe died in 1896 at the ripe age of eighty-four. Not long before her death she wrote to a friend: "I have sometimes had in my sleep strange perceptions of a vivid spiritual life near to and with Christ, and multitudes of holy ones, and the joy of it is like no other joy—it cannot be told in the language of the world.... The inconceivable loveliness of Christ!... I was saying as I awoke:

'Tis joy enough, my All in all,
At Thy dear feet to lie.
Thou wilt not let me lower fall,
And none can higher fly."

Bishop Coxe's Missionary Hymn

Saviour, sprinkle many nations,
Fruitful let Thy sorrows be;
By Thy pains and consolations
Draw the Gentiles unto Thee.
Of Thy cross the wondrous story,
Be it to the nations told;
Let them see Thee in Thy glory,
And Thy mercy manifold.
Far and wide, though all unknowing,
Pants for Thee each mortal breast:
Human tears for Thee are flowing,
Human hearts in Thee would rest.
Thirsting as for dews of even,
As the new-mown grass for rain,
Thee they seek, as God of heaven,
Thee as Man, for sinners slain.
Saviour, lo, the isles are waiting,
Stretched the hand, and strained the sight,
For Thy Spirit, new-creating,
Love's pure flame, and wisdom's light.
Give the word, and of the preacher
Speed the foot, and touch the tongue,
Till on earth by every creature,
Glory to the Lamb be sung.
Arthur Cleveland Coxe, 1851.

A HYMN WRITTEN ON TWO SHORES

"Saviour, sprinkle many nations" has been called the "loveliest of missionary hymns." The praise is scarcely too great. All the elements that make a great hymn are present here. Scriptural in language and devotional in spirit, it is fervent and touching in its appeal and exquisitely beautiful in poetic expression. It was given to the Church by Arthur Cleveland Coxe, an American bishop, in 1851, and since that time it has made its victorious course around the world.

A study of the hymn is interesting. The first stanza at once suggests the words of Jesus, uttered in the last week of His life, when Greek pilgrims in Jerusalem came seeking for Him: "And I, if I be lifted up from the earth, will draw all men unto me." In the second stanza the author no doubt had in mind the immortal words of St. Augustine: "Thou, O Lord, hast made me for Thyself, and my heart can find no rest till it rest in Thee." And in the final stanza we find almost an echo of the thought expressed by Paul in Romans: "How then shall they call on him in whom they have not believed? and how shall they believe in him of whom they have not heard? and how shall they hear without a preacher? And how shall they preach, except they be sent? as it is written, How beautiful are the feet of them that preach the gospel of peace, and bring glad tidings of good things!"

Curiously enough, this beautiful missionary lyric was written on two shores of the Atlantic. It was on Good Friday, in the year 1850, that the first stanza was written by Bishop Coxe at his home in Hartford, Conn. For lack of time, however, or because the needed inspiration did not come to him the unfinished manuscript was laid aside.

The next year he visited England, and one day, while wandering about the campus of Magdalen College, Oxford, the thought flashed through his mind that he had never completed the hymn. Finding a scrap of paper and a pencil, he sat down to write, and in a few moments the touching words of the two concluding stanzas were composed, and the hymn was sent on its way to stir the heart of the world.

Bishop Coxe was not primarily a hymn-writer. His fame rests chiefly on his religious ballads. It was in 1840, when a young student of twenty-two, that he published his first volume, entitled "Christian Ballads." These are mostly moral poems, impressive and challenging in character, but not usually suitable as hymns. One of them, however, bearing the name of "Chelsea," has yielded the famous hymn, "O where are kings and empires now?"

An interesting story is told concerning this hymn. In 1873 the General Conference of the Evangelical Alliance was held in New York City. It was a period when many scientific objections had been raised regarding the value of prayer, and many anxious souls were fearful that the faith of the Church was being shaken to its foundations. President Woolsey of Yale University gave the opening address. After he had referred to the wave of skepticism that had swept over the world, particularly in regard to prayer, he looked out upon the assembly with a quiet, confident smile lighting his features, and then quoted the first stanza of Bishop Coxe's hymn:

O where are kings and empires now,

Of old that went and came?

But, Lord, Thy church is praying yet,
A thousand years the same.

"For a moment," writes an eye-witness, "there was silence. In another moment the full significance of the reference had flashed on every mind, and the response was instantaneous and universal. Shouts, waving of handkerchiefs, clapping of hands, stamping of feet—I never knew anything like it. Round after round continued, until the storm of applause ended in a burst of grateful tears. No one doubted that the Church still believed in prayer and that the tempest had passed without the loss of a sail."

In the same volume of "Christian Ballads" there appears another little poem, most appealing in its simplicity:

In the silent midnight-watches,
List—thy bosom door!
How it knocketh, knocketh, knocketh,
Knocketh, evermore!
Say not 'tis thy pulse is beating:
'Tis thy heart of sin;
'Tis thy Saviour knocks, and crieth,
"Rise, and let Me in!"

For a time Coxe gave promise of becoming the "John Keble of America," but after his election as a bishop in the Episcopal Church, pressing duties interfered with his literary work, and in later years he wrote few poems.

Bishop Coxe was the son of a noted Presbyterian minister, Rev. Samuel H. Cox. He was born in Menham, N. J., in 1818. After his graduation from the University of the City of New York, he decided to leave the Presbyterian Church and to enter the Episcopalian fold. At the same time he added an "e" to the end of his name, much to his father's displeasure! He died in 1896 at the age of seventy-eight years.

The Hymn of a Consecrated Woman

More love to Thee, O Christ,
More love to Thee;
Hear Thou the prayer I make
On bended knee;
This is my earnest plea,
More love, O Christ, to Thee,
More love to Thee.
Once earthly joy I craved,
Sought peace and rest;
Now Thee alone I seek,
Give what is best;
This all my prayer shall be,
More love, O Christ, to Thee,
More love to Thee.

Then shall my latest breath
Whisper Thy praise;
This be the parting cry
My heart shall raise;
This still its prayer shall be,
More love, O Christ, to Thee,
More love to Thee.
Elizabeth Payson Prentiss, 1856.

A HYMN THAT GREW OUT OF SUFFERING

The fruits of a sanctified life are often seen long after the person who lived that life has ceased from earthly strivings. This was true in a very special sense of Elizabeth Payson Prentiss, author of "More love to Thee, O Christ." Although it is fifty years since Mrs. Prentiss went home to glory, her beautiful Christian life still radiates its spirit of trust and hope through her hymns and devotional writings.

As a child she was blessed with an unusual home. Her father, Edward Payson, was one of New England's most famous clergymen, revered and beloved by thousands because of his saintly life. It is said that after his death the name of "Edward Payson" was given in baptism to thousands of children whose parents had been blessed through his consecrated ministry.

The daughter, who was born in 1818, was much like her father. Spiritually minded from childhood, she possessed unusual gifts as a writer. When she was only sixteen years old she contributed verses and prose to "The Youth's Companion." Later she taught school at Portland, Me., her birthplace, and in Ipswich, Mass., and Richmond, Va., at each place being greatly beloved by her pupils.

In 1845 she became the bride of Rev. George L. Prentiss, who later was a professor in Union Theological Seminary, New York City.

Her home life was beautiful. Those who knew her best, described her as "a very bright-eyed little woman, with a keen sense of humor, who cared more to shine in her own happy household than in a wide circle of society."

But all the while she was carrying a heavy burden. Throughout life she was a sufferer, and scarcely knew what it meant to be well. Chronic insomnia added to her afflictions, but as her body languished under physical chastening her spirit rose above pain and tribulation, daily growing more radiant and beautiful. It was out of these trying experiences that she wrote her famous story, "Stepping Heavenward." The purpose of the book, as she herself explained, was "for strengthening and comforting other souls."

It met with instant success, more than 200,000 copies being sold. It also was translated into many foreign languages. Another story, "The Flower of the Family," likewise became very popular.

It was as poet and hymn-writer, however, that Mrs. Prentiss was destined to achieve fame. Her volume, "Religious Poems," numbering one hundred and twenty-three, breathes a spirit of fervent devotion to Christ. "To love Christ more," she said, "is the deepest need, the constant cry of my soul.... Out in the woods, and on my bed, and out driving, when I am happy and busy, and when I am sad and idle, the whisper keeps going up for more love, more love, more love!"

It is easy to understand how such a longing should finally find expression in her most famous hymn, "More love to Thee, O Christ." The hymn in reality was the prayer of her life. It was born in 1856 during a time of great physical suffering and spiritual anxiety. It was written in great haste, and the last stanza was left incompleted. Not until thirteen years later did Mrs. Prentiss show it to her husband. She then added a final line with a pencil and gave it to the printer, intending it only for private distribution. The following year, however, the "Great Revival" swept over America, and the hymn sprang into popularity everywhere.

When in August, 1878, the mortal remains of the sanctified singer were lowered into the grave, a company of intimate friends stood with bared heads and sang "More love to Thee, O Christ." The whole Christian world seemed to join in mourning her death. From far-off China came a message of sympathy to the bereaved husband in the form of a fan on which Christian Chinese had inscribed the famous hymn in native characters.

After her death the following verse was found written on the flyleaf of one of her favorite books:

One hour with Jesus! How its peace outweighs
The ravishment of earthly love and praise;
How dearer far, emptied of self to lie
Low at His feet, and catch, perchance, His eye,
Alike content when He may give or take,
The sweet, the bitter, welcome for His sake.

A Hymn of the Sea

Jesus, Saviour, pilot me
Over life's tempestuous sea;
Unknown waves before me roll,
Hiding rock and treacherous shoal;
Chart and compass came from Thee:
Jesus, Saviour, pilot me.
As a mother stills her child,
Thou canst hush the ocean wild;
Boisterous waves obey Thy will
When Thou say'st to them, "Be still!"
Wondrous Sovereign of the sea,
Jesus, Saviour, pilot me.
When at last I near the shore,
And the fearful breakers roar
'Twixt me and the peaceful rest,

Then, while leaning on Thy breast,
May I hear Thee say to me,
"Fear not, I will pilot thee."
Edward Hopper, 1871.

A FAMOUS HYMN WRITTEN FOR SAILORS

It does not surprise us that the writer of "Jesus, Saviour, pilot me" was the pastor of a sailors' church. Rev. Edward Hopper, who for many years was minister of the Church of Sea and Land in New York harbor, had in mind the daily life of the seamen attending his church when he wrote his famous lyric. A hymn on the theme of the stormy sea, picturing Jesus as the divine Pilot—this, he felt, would appeal to sailors and be a source of constant comfort and encouragement.

Perhaps Hopper got his idea from Charles Wesley. It was a common practice of the great English hymn-writer to compose hymns that were particularly adapted to the audiences he addressed. When he visited the men who worked in the Portland quarries in England, he wrote the hymn containing the lines:

Strike with the hammer of Thy Word,
And break these hearts of stone.

In any event, Hopper's beautiful hymn at once sprang into popular use, not only with sailors, but with Christians everywhere. It appeared for the first time anonymously in "The Sailors' Magazine," but several hymn-books adopted it. It was not until 1880, nine years after it was published, however, that the author's name became known. In that year the anniversary of the Seamen's Friend Society was held in Broadway Tabernacle, New York City, and Hopper was asked to write a hymn for the occasion. He responded by producing "Jesus, Saviour, pilot me," and the secret was out.

Hopper wrote several other hymns, but only this one has lived. Like Edward Perronet, the author of "All hail the power of Jesus' Name," he was "a bird of a single song." We could have wished that the fires of inspired genius had continued to burn with both of these men. Here, however, apply the words: "Happy is the man who can produce one song which the world will keep on singing after its author shall have passed away."

The author of "Jesus, Saviour, pilot me" was a child of the city. He was born in America's great metropolis, New York City, in the year 1818. His father was a merchant. His mother was a descendant of the Huguenots, the persecuted French Protestants. He was educated for the ministry, and, after serving several churches in other places, he returned to New York in 1870 to begin his work among the men who go down to the sea in ships. He remained as pastor of the Church of Sea and Land until his death in 1888, and we scarcely need to add that his ministry was singularly successful.

The beautiful prayer in the third stanza of Hopper's hymn was answered in his own passing. He was sitting in his study-chair, pencil in hand, when the final summons came. On the sheet before him were found some freshly written lines on "Heaven." Thus was fulfilled in his own death the beautiful prayer expressed in the final stanza of his hymn:

When at last I near the shore,
And the fearful breakers roar
'Twixt me and the peaceful rest,
Then, while leaning on Thy breast,
May I hear Thee say to me,
"Fear not, I will pilot thee."

A Rally Hymn of the Church

Stand up, stand up for Jesus,
Ye soldiers of the cross;
Lift high His royal banner,
It must not suffer loss;
From victory unto victory
His army He shall lead,
Till every foe is vanquished,
And Christ is Lord indeed.
Stand up, stand up for Jesus,
The trumpet call obey;
Forth to the mighty conflict
In this His glorious day:
Ye that are men, now serve Him
Against unnumbered foes;
Your courage rise with danger,
And strength to strength oppose.
Stand up, stand up for Jesus,
Stand in His strength alone;
The arm of flesh will fail you,
Ye dare not trust your own;
Put on the gospel armor,
And watching unto prayer,
Where duty calls or danger,
Be never wanting there.
Stand up, stand up for Jesus,
The strife will not be long;
This day the noise of battle,
The next the victor's song:
To him that overcometh,
A crown of life shall be;
He with the King of glory
Shall reign eternally.
George Duffield, 1858

A TRAGEDY THAT INSPIRED A GREAT HYMN

    The Christian Church has many stirring rally hymns, but none that is more effective when sung by a large assembly than George Duffield's "Stand up, stand up for Jesus."

Who has not been moved to the depths of his soul by the inspiring words and resounding music of this unusual hymn?

A tragedy lies in its background. It was in the year 1858, and a great spiritual awakening was gripping the city of Philadelphia. Men referred to this revival afterwards as "the work of God in Philadelphia."

One of the most earnest and zealous leaders in the movement was a young pastor, Dudley A. Tyng, not quite thirty years old. Because of his evangelical convictions and his strong opposition to slavery he had shortly before been compelled to resign as rector of the Church of the Epiphany, and in 1857 he had organized a little congregation that met in a public hall.

In the midst of the revival in 1858 he preached a powerful sermon at a noon-day meeting in Jayne's Hall to a gathering of 5,000 men. His text was Exodus 10:11: "Go now, ye that are men, and serve the Lord." It is said that the effect was overwhelming, no less than a thousand men giving themselves to the Lord.

A few weeks later the young pastor was watching a corn-shelling machine when his arm was caught in the machinery and terribly mangled. Though every effort was made to save his life, he died within a few hours. Shortly before the end came he cried to the friends who were gathered about him, "Sing, sing, can you not sing?" He himself then began the words of "Rock of Ages," with the others trying to join him in the midst of their grief. When his father, the distinguished clergyman, Stephen H. Tyng, bent over him to ask if he had a last message for his friends, the dying soldier of the cross whispered:

"Tell them to stand up for Jesus!"

Rev. George Duffield, also of Philadelphia and a close friend of the greatly lamented Tyng, felt that the words were too impressive to be lost. On the following Sunday he preached a sermon in his own church on Ephesians 6:14, "Stand, therefore, having your loins girt about with truth, and having on the breastplate of righteousness." As he concluded his sermon, he read the words of a poem he had written, "Stand up, stand up for Jesus."

Not only did Duffield preserve the dying words of his devoted friend, but it will be noted that the second stanza also contains the challenge of Tyng's last revival sermon: "Go now, ye that are men, and serve the Lord."

The superintendent of Duffield's Sunday school printed the words of the poem for distribution among his scholars. One of these leaflets found its way to a religious periodical, where it was published. Soon it began to appear in hymn-books, being generally set to a tune composed by George J. Webb a few years earlier. It is said that the first time the author heard it sung outside of his own church was in 1864, when the Christian men in the Army of the James sang it in their camp, just before they were about to enter into a bloody battle.

As originally written, the hymn contained six stanzas. The second and fifth are omitted from most hymn-books. These stanzas read:

> Stand up, stand up for Jesus,
> The solemn watchword hear;
> If while ye sleep He suffers,
> Away with shame and fear;
> Where'er ye meet with evil,
> Within you or without,
> Charge for the God of Battles,
> And put the foe to rout.
> Stand up, stand up for Jesus,
> Each soldier to his post:
> Close up the broken column,
> And shout through all the host:
> Make good the loss so heavy,
> In those that still remain,
> And prove to all around you
> That death itself is gain.

The omission of these lines is really no loss, since they sink far beneath the literary level of the remaining verses. They also carry the military imagery to needless length.

A Hymn of Spiritual Yearning

> We would see Jesus, for the shadows lengthen
> Across this little landscape of our life;
> We would see Jesus, our weak faith to strengthen
> For the last weariness, the final strife.
> We would see Jesus, the great Rock-foundation
> Whereon our feet were set by sovereign grace:
> Nor life nor death, with all their agitation,
> Can thence remove us, if we see His face.
> We would see Jesus: other lights are paling,
> Which for long years we have rejoiced to see;
> The blessings of our pilgrimage are failing:
> We would not mourn them, for we go to Thee.
> We would see Jesus: this is all we're needing;
> Strength, joy, and willingness come with the sight;
> We would see Jesus, dying, risen, pleading;
> Then welcome day, and farewell, mortal night.
> Anna Bartlett Warner, 1851.

ANNA WARNER AND HER BEAUTIFUL HYMNS

In the last week of our Saviour's life, a very beautiful and touching incident occurred in the city of Jerusalem. The Evangelist John tells the story in the following words:

"Now there were certain Greeks among those that went up to worship at the feast: these therefore came to Philip, who was of Bethsaida of Galilee, and asked him, saying, Sir, we would see Jesus. Philip cometh and telleth Andrew: Andrew cometh, and Philip, and they tell Jesus. And Jesus answereth them, saying, The hour is come, that the Son of man should be glorified."

It was the petition of these Gentile pilgrims from the land of the Spartans and Athenians that inspired an American young woman to write one of our beautiful hymns, "We would see Jesus."

Her name was Anna Bartlett Warner, and for almost a century she lived at a beautiful retreat in the Hudson river known as Constitution island, under the very shadows of the great military academy at West Point. She had a sister named Susan who achieved even greater literary fame than she, but it is Anna's name, after all, that will live on and be cherished for her songs. We wonder if any child in America during the last half century has not learned to know and to love the little hymn—

Jesus loves me, this I know,
For the Bible tells me so.

Children throughout the world are singing it now, and missionaries tell us that the simplicity of its message also makes a wonderful appeal to the newly-converted heathen. This hymn is one of the reasons why the name of Anna Warner will never be forgotten.

An exquisite lullaby, also written by Miss Warner, begins with the words, "O little child, lie still and sleep."

Two volumes of sacred song were composed by this gifted young woman. The first bore the title, "Hymns of the Church Militant," and was published in 1858. The second, called "Wayfaring Hymns, Original and Translated," appeared in 1869. "We would see Jesus" was included in the first of these collections. It appears, however, that it was written at least seven years before its publication. An interesting item from her sister Susan's diary, under date of February 8, 1851, tells of the impression the hymn made on her when she first read it. She writes:

"The next day, Sunday, in the afternoon, Anna had been copying off some hymns for Emmelin's book, and left them with me to look over. I had not read two verses of 'We would see Jesus,' when I thought of Anna, and merely casting my eye down, the others so delighted and touched me that I left it for tears and petitions. I wished Anna might prove the author—and after I found she was, I sat by her a little while with my head against her, crying such delicious tears."

Another hymn that has found a place in many hearts bears the title, "The Song of the Tired Servant." It was inspired by a letter received by Miss Warner from a friend who was a pastor, in which he spoke of the weariness he felt after the tasks of an arduous day, but of the joy that his soul experienced in serving the Master. The first stanza reads:

One more day's work for Jesus,

One less of life for me!
But heaven is nearer,
And Christ is dearer
Than yesterday, to me;
His love and light
Fill all my soul tonight.

Although the two Warner sisters lived in a corner apart from the busy world, they made their influence felt in widespread circles. They felt a particular responsibility in reference to the many thousands of young men from all parts of the United States who were being trained at West Point for service in the army, and for many years they conducted a Bible class for the cadets.

Military honors were accorded each of the sisters when they were buried. Anna Warner was ninety-five years old when she died in 1915.

A Famous Christmas Carol

O little town of Bethlehem
How still we see thee lie;
Above thy deep and dreamless sleep
The silent stars go by;
Yet in thy darkness shineth
The everlasting Light;
The hopes and fears of all the years
Are met in thee tonight.
For Christ is born of Mary,
And gathered all above,
While mortals sleep, the angels keep
Their watch of wondering love.
O morning stars, together
Proclaim the holy birth,
And praises sing to God the King,
And peace to men on earth.
How silently, how silently,
The wondrous Gift is given!
So God imparts to human hearts
The blessings of His heaven.
No ear may hear His coming,
But in this world of sin,
Where meek souls will receive Him still,
The dear Christ enters in.
O holy Child of Bethlehem!
Descend to us, we pray;
Cast out our sin, and enter in,
Be born in us today.
We hear the Christmas angels
The great glad tidings tell:
O come to us, abide with us,

Our Lord Immanuel!
Phillips Brooks, 1868.

PHILLIPS BROOKS AND HIS CAROLS

Phillips Brooks was a great man. Not only was he a giant in stature, but he possessed a great mind and a great heart. Also, he was a great preacher—one of America's greatest—and he just missed being a great poet. Indeed, the flashes of poetic genius revealed in the few verses he wrote indicate that he might have become famous as a hymn-writer had he chosen such a career.

His poetic gift had its roots in childhood. Phillips was brought up in a pious New England home. Every Sunday the children of the Brooks household were required to memorize a hymn, and, when the father conducted the evening devotion on the Lord's day, the children recited their hymns. When Phillips was ready to go to college, he could repeat no less than two hundred hymns from memory. In his later ministry this knowledge proved to be of inestimable value, and he frequently made effective use of hymn quotations in his preaching. But, more than that, the childhood training unconsciously had made of him a poet!

"O little town of Bethlehem," his most famous Christmas carol, was written for a Sunday school Christmas festival in 1868, when Brooks was rector of Holy Trinity Episcopal Church in Philadelphia. He was only thirty-two years old at the time. Three years earlier he had visited the Holy Land, and on Christmas eve he had stood on the star-lit hills where the shepherds had watched their flocks. Below the hills he had seen the "little town of Bethlehem," slumbering in the darkness just as it had done in the night when Jesus was born. Later he had attended midnight services in the Church of the Nativity in Bethlehem.

He could never entirely forget the impressions of that sublime night, and, when he was asked in 1868 to write a Christmas hymn for his Sunday school, he put down on paper the song that long had been ringing in his mind.

The beautiful tune "St. Louis," to which the hymn is usually sung, also has an interesting story. It was composed by Lewis H. Redner, who was organist and Sunday school superintendent of Dr. Brooks' church. When Brooks asked Redner to write a suitable tune for the words, the latter waited for the inspiration that never seemed to come. Christmas eve arrived and Redner went to sleep without having written the tune. In the middle of the night, however, he dreamed that he heard angels singing. He awoke with the melody still sounding in his ears. Quickly he seized a piece of paper, and jotted it down, and next morning he filled in the harmony.

Redner always insisted that the hymn tune was "a gift from heaven," and those who have learned to love its exquisite strains are more than willing to believe it!

Phillips Brooks, though he never had a family of his own, possessed a boundless love for children. That, perhaps, is one reason why the Christmas season so fascinated him, and why he wrote so many Christmas carols for children. One of these is famous for its striking refrain, "Everywhere, everywhere, Christmas tonight." "The voice of the Christ-child" is the title of another Christmas carol. He also wrote a number of Easter carols, among them, "God hath sent His angels."

But Phillips Brooks not only made a strong appeal to children; it was not long before the great and learned men of America began to realize that a great preacher and prophet had risen among them. There was need of such a spiritual leader, for Unitarianism had threatened to engulf all New England.

In its beginnings this movement was merely a protest against the stern and forbidding aspects of the Christian religion as it had been exemplified in New England Puritanism. It grew more and more radical, however, until the deity of Christ was denied.

The old-fashioned religion of "Christ and Him crucified" was all but forgotten in the intellectual circles of New England when a young man thirty-four years of age began preaching in Trinity church, Boston. He was preaching Jesus Christ, but he was presenting Him in a new and wonderful light. Crowds began to fill the church. Even sedate old Harvard was stirred.

That was the beginning of the ministry of Phillips Brooks in Boston, a ministry that made him famous throughout the land. It marked the turning point in religious tendencies in New England, and perhaps was the most potent factor in checking the spread of the Unitarian doctrine. Brooks was later elevated to a bishopric in his Church. He died in 1893.

It is said that when a little girl of five years was told by her mother that "Bishop Brooks has gone to heaven," the child exclaimed, "Oh, mamma, how happy the angels will be!"

The Story that Never Grows Old

I love to hear the story
Which angel voices tell,
How once the King of glory
Came down to earth to dwell.
I am both weak and sinful,
But this I surely know,
The Lord came down to save me,
Because He loved me so.
I'm glad my blessed Saviour
Was once a child like me,
To show how pure and holy
His little ones should be;
And if I try to follow
His footsteps here below,
He never will forget me,
Because He loves me so.
To sing His love and mercy

My sweetest songs I'll raise!
And though I cannot see Him,
I know He hears my praise;
For He has kindly promised
That even I may go
To sing among His angels,
Because He loves me so.
Emily Huntington Miller, 1867.

WOMEN WHO WROTE HYMNS FOR CHILDREN

Everybody loves the hymns the children sing. And that, perhaps, is the reason why Emily Huntington Miller's name will not soon be forgotten, for the hymns she wrote were children's hymns indeed—hymns that came from the heart of one who understood the heart of a child.

The daughter of a Methodist clergyman, Emily Huntington was born in Brooklyn, Conn., October 22, 1833. The spiritual and cultural influence of a New England parsonage was not lost on this little child, who early in life began to reveal unusual literary gifts. It was very unusual in those days for young women to attend college, but Emily enrolled at Oberlin College and graduated in the class of 1857.

Ten years later she became one of the editors of "The Little Corporal," a very popular magazine for children. Each month she contributed a poem to this publication. Like all other contributors, she often found it difficult to have her poem ready each month on the required day. One month in 1867 she was handicapped by illness. The final day came, and her poem was not written. In spite of her weakness, she aroused herself to the task. The inspiration seemed to come immediately, and, so she tells us, "in less than fifteen minutes the hymn was written and sent away without any correction."

The hymn referred to was "I love to hear the story." Almost immediately it sprang into popularity. In England it was admitted in 1875 to "Hymns Ancient and Modern," the hymn-book of the Church of England. This was a very unusual honor, since very few hymns of American origin have been included in that famous collection. It is said that no one was more surprised at the popularity achieved by the hymn than the author herself.

Another of her hymns that has won a place in the hearts of the smaller children is the sweet little gem:

Jesus bids us shine
With a clear, pure light
Like a little candle
Burning in the night;
In the world is darkness,
So we must shine,
You in your small corner,
And I in mine.

Another of her hymns for children, though not so well known as the other two mentioned, possesses unusual merit:

> Father, while the shadows fall,
> With the twilight over all,
> Deign to hear my evening prayer,
> Make a little child Thy care.
> Take me in Thy holy keeping
> Till the morning break;
> Guard me thro' the darkness sleeping,
> Bless me when I wake.

Emily Huntington became the wife of Prof. John E. Miller in 1860. After his death she became dean of the Woman's College of Northwestern University, in which position she exerted a blessed influence over large numbers of young women. She died in 1913.

Another American woman who at this time was also writing hymns for children was Mrs. Lydia Baxter. Although born at Petersburg, N. Y., September 2, 1809, it was not until nearly fifty years later that she seems to have begun to exercise her gifts as a song writer. Her "Gems by the Wayside" were published in 1855, after which she became a frequent contributor to hymn collections for Sunday schools and evangelistic services.

Mrs. Baxter may be regarded as one of the forerunners of the Gospel hymn movement of America. Her lyrics fall short of the severer standards required in a true hymn, and for this reason few of her hymns have been admitted to the authorized collections of the principal church communions. However, the woman who wrote "Take the Name of Jesus with you" and "There is a gate that stands ajar" will not soon be forgotten by pious Christians, even though the author receives scant notice at the hands of hymnologists. It is a significant fact that in 1921 the Church of Sweden included a translation of the latter hymn in the appendix to its "Psalm-book," one of the most conservative hymn collections in Christendom. Mrs. Baxter died in New York, June 22, 1874.

A Hymn of Sweet Consolation

> Safe in the arms of Jesus,
> Safe on His gentle breast,
> There by His love o'ershaded,
> Sweetly my soul shall rest.
> Hark! 'tis the voice of angels,
> Borne in a song to me,
> Over the fields of glory,
> Over the jasper sea.
> Safe in the arms of Jesus,
> Safe from corroding care,
> Safe from the world's temptations,
> Sin cannot harm me there.
> Free from the blight of sorrow,
> Free from my doubts and fears;

Only a few more trials,
Only a few more tears!
Jesus, my heart's dear refuge,
Jesus has died for me;
Firm on the Rock of Ages
Ever my trust shall be.
Here let me wait with patience,
Wait till the night is o'er;
Wait till I see the morning
Break on the golden shore.
Frances Jane Crosby, 1869.

FANNY CROSBY, AMERICA'S BLIND POET

Blindness is not always an affliction. If it serves to give the soul a clearer vision of Christ and of His redeeming love, as it did with Fanny Crosby, it may rather be regarded as a blessing.

America's most famous hymn-writer could never remember having seen the light of day, nevertheless her life was one of the most happy and fruitful ever lived. Always she radiated a sweet and cheerful spirit, refusing to be pitied, while her soul poured out the songs that brought joy and salvation to countless multitudes.

Born of humble parents at Southeast, N. Y., March 24, 1823, she was only six weeks old when, through the application of a poultice to her eyes, her sight was forever destroyed. Such a disaster would have cast a perpetual gloom over most lives, but not so with Fanny Crosby. Even at the age of eight years she gave evidence not only of her happy optimism but also of her poetic genius by penning the following cheerful lines:

O what a happy soul am I!
Although I cannot see,
I am resolved that in this world
Contented I will be.
How many blessings I enjoy,
That other people don't;
To weep and sigh because I'm blind,
I cannot, and I won't!

When she was fifteen years old she entered the Institution for the Blind in New York City, where she soon began to develop her remarkable talent for writing verse. At first she wrote only secular songs. One of these, "Rosalie, the Prairie Flower," brought the blind girl nearly $3,000 in royalties.

Strange to state, it was not until she was forty-one years old that her first hymn was written. It was in 1864 that she met the famous composer, W. B. Bradbury, and it was at his request that she made her first attempt at hymn-writing. Her first hymn began:

We are going, we are going,

To a home beyond the skies,
Where the fields are robed in beauty,
And the sunlight never dies.

She now felt that she had found her real mission in life, and she wrote that she was "the happiest creature in all the land." Until her death in 1915, hymns flowed from her inspired pen in a ceaseless stream. For a long time she was under contract to furnish her publishers, Biglow & Main, with three hymns every week. It has been estimated that no less than 8,000 hymns and songs were written by this unusual woman.

Not all of her hymns possess high poetical excellence. In fact, they have been subjected to the most severe criticism. John Julian, the English hymnologist, with his usual candor, declares that "they are, with few exceptions, very weak and poor, their simplicity and earnestness being their redeeming features."

However, whether we consider her hymns of high poetic standard or not, the fact remains that no one has written more hymns that are being sung and loved today than Fanny Crosby. Certainly the hymnody of the Christian Church is infinitely richer for "Pass me not, O gentle Saviour," "Sweet hour of prayer," "Safe in the arms of Jesus," "All the way my Saviour leads me," "Jesus is tenderly calling thee home," "I am thine, O Lord," "Rescue the perishing," "Speed away," "Blessed assurance, Jesus is mine," "Jesus keep me near the Cross," "Some day the silver cord will break," and scores of other inspiring gems that have come to us from this blind genius.

Practically all her hymns are very subjective in character. Although this is doubtless an element of weakness, it probably explains their unusual personal appeal. It was the prayer of Miss Crosby that she might win a million souls for Christ, and there are many who believe that her prayer has been more than realized. A strong Scriptural note is heard in most of her hymns. When she was yet a child, she committed to memory the first four books of the Old Testament, as well as the four Gospels, and this proved a rich treasure store from which she drew in later life.

Fanny Crosby's fault apparently lay in the fact that she was too prolific a writer. Most of her songs were composed in a few minutes. Often the lines came as rapidly as they could be dictated. It was this circumstance that led Dr. S. W. Duffield to observe rather facetiously that "It is more to her credit as a writer that she has occasionally found a pearl than that she has brought to the surface so many oyster shells." However, before his death he evidently had altered his opinion, for he wrote: "I rather think her talent will stand beside that of Watts or Wesley, especially if we take into consideration the number of hymns she has written."

Certainly there are many pearls among the 8,000 songs she wrote, and perhaps none has given more solace to broken hearts than "Safe in the arms of Jesus." Often the themes of her hymns were suggested to her by publishers or musical composers. At other times a musician would play a tune for her and ask her to write words for it. It was in 1868 that William H. Doane, the popular hymn composer, came to her one day and said: "Fanny, I have a tune I would like to have you hear." He played it for her, and she exclaimed, "That says 'Safe in the arms of Jesus!'" She went to her room immediately, and within half an hour the words had been written.

Although Fanny Crosby never permitted the fact of her blindness to make her life gloomy, there are many touching allusions in her hymns to her affliction. "All the way my Saviour leads me" suggests how much a guiding hand means to the blind. The same thought appears in the song, "God will take care of you," especially in the lines,

Tenderly watching, and keeping His own,
He will not leave you to wander alone.

There also are pathetic passages in her hymns that reflect the hope that some day the long night of blindness would be ended—in heaven.

Here let me wait with patience,
Wait till the night is o'er;
Wait till I see the morning
Break on the golden shore.

That is also the constant refrain heard in the exquisite hymn, "Some day the silver cord will break."

And I shall see Him face to face,
And tell the story—Saved by grace.

Nevertheless, she never permitted any one to express sympathy on account of her blindness. Once a Scotch minister remarked to her, "I think it is a great pity that the Master, when He showered so many gifts upon you, did not give you sight."

She answered: "Do you know that, if at birth I had been able to make one petition to my Creator, if would have been that I should be made blind?"

"Why?" asked the surprised clergyman.

"Because, when I get to heaven, the first face that shall ever gladden my sight will be that of my Saviour," was the unexpected reply.

At a summer religious conference in Northfield, Mass., Miss Crosby was sitting on the platform when the evangelist, Dwight L. Moody, asked her for a testimony concerning her Christian experience. At first she hesitated, then quietly rose and said: "There is one hymn I have written which has never been published. I call it my Soul's poem, and sometimes when I am troubled I repeat it to myself, for it brings comfort to my heart." She then recited:

Some day the silver chord will break,
And I no more as now shall sing:
But, the joy when I shall wake
Within the palace of the King!
And I shall see Him face to face,
And tell the story—Saved by grace.

The sight of her uplifted face, with its wistful expression, made a deep impression upon the vast audience, and many were moved to tears.

In 1858 Miss Crosby married Alexander Van Alstyne, a blind musician, wherefore she is often referred to as Mrs. Frances Jane Van Alstyne. She died on February 12, 1915.

The Call of the Gospel Song

Sing them over again to me,
Wonderful words of life,
Let me more of their beauty see,
Wonderful words of life.
Words of life and beauty,
Teach me faith and duty;
Beautiful words,
Wonderful words,
Wonderful words of life.
Christ, the blessed One, gives to all
Wonderful words of life;
Sinner, list to the loving call,
Wonderful words of life.
All so freely given,
Wooing us to heaven,
Beautiful words,
Wonderful words,
Wonderful words of life.
Sweetly echo the gospel call,
Wonderful words of life;
Offer pardon and peace to all,
Wonderful words of life.
Jesus, only Saviour,
Sanctify forever,
Beautiful words,
Wonderful words,
Wonderful words of life.
Philip P. Bliss (1838-1876).

ONE OF AMERICA'S EARLIEST GOSPEL SINGERS

Among hymn-books that have exerted a profound influence over the spiritual lives of Christian people none has probably achieved greater fame or wider circulation than the volume known as Gospel Hymns. It was issued in a series of six editions, but now is usually found combined in a single book.

Philip P. Bliss, the subject of this chapter, was the first editor of Gospel Hymns. Associated with him in the publication of the first two editions was the renowned Ira D. Sankey, who gained world-wide fame through his evangelistic campaigns with Dwight L. Moody.

The story of the life of Bliss reads like romance.

Like many a poor lad endowed with love for the artistic, he was compelled to struggle almost all his life for the opportunity that finally came to him. Born at Rome, Pa., in 1838, he early revealed a passion for music when, as a boy, he made crude instruments on which he tried to produce tones.

The story is told of how Philip, when a ragged and barefoot boy of ten years, heard piano music for the first time. So entranced did he become that he entered the home unbidden, and stood listening at the parlor door. When the young woman at the instrument ceased playing, the child who hungered for music cried:

"O lady, play some more!"

Instead of complying with the request, the startled young woman is said to have invited young Bliss to leave the house forthwith!

Although he received practically no musical education, except from occasional attendance at a singing school, he wrote his first song at the age of twenty-six years. It was called "Lora Vale," and because of its popular reception, Bliss was encouraged to devote all his time to writing songs and giving concerts.

Bliss usually wrote both the words and music of his hymns. His work was done very quickly, the inspiration for the whole song, text and melody, being born in his mind at once.

Any incident of an unusually impressive nature would immediately suggest a theme to his mind. He heard the story of a shipwreck. The doomed vessel was abandoned, and the captain ordered the sailors to exert their utmost strength to "pull for the shore." Immediately he wrote his well-known song with the words as a refrain.

One night he listened to a sermon in which the preacher closed with the words, "He who is almost persuaded is almost saved, but to be almost saved is to be entirely lost." He went home from the service and wrote "Almost persuaded," a hymn that is said to have brought more souls to Christ than anything else Bliss ever composed.

In 1870 he heard Major Whittle, an evangelist, tell the story of how the message, "Hold the fort!" was signalled to the besieged garrison at Allatoona Pass. The words suggested the passage from Revelations 2:25, "That which ye have, hold fast till I come." The result was one of his most famous Gospel songs, the chorus of which runs:

"Hold the fort, for I am coming,"
Jesus signals still,
Wave the answer back to heaven,—
"By Thy grace we will."

Other popular songs by Bliss are "Whosoever heareth, shout, shout the sound," "I am so glad that our Father in heaven," "There's a light in the valley," "Sing them over again to me," "Let the lower lights be burning," "Free from the law, Oh, happy condition," "Down life's dark vale we wander" and "Where hast thou gleaned today?"

These songs, like the greater number of the Gospel Hymns, do not possess high literary merit. The most that can be said for them is that they are imaginative and picturesque. They are usually strong in emotional appeal. The same is true of the tunes composed for them. They are usually very light in character, with a lilt and movement that make them easily singable, but lacking in the rich harmony found in the standard hymns and chorales. No doubt there will always be a certain demand for this type of religious song, and a few of the Gospel Hymns will probably live on, but the present trend in all of the principal Christian denominations is toward a higher standard of hymnody.

A terrible tragedy brought the life of the Gospel singer to a close in his thirty-eighth year. He had visited the old childhood home at Rome, Pa., at Christmas time in 1876, and was returning to Chicago in company with his wife when a railroad bridge near Ashtabula, Ohio, collapsed on the evening of December 29. Their train plunged into a ravine, sixty feet below, where it caught fire, and one hundred passengers perished miserably.

Bliss managed to escape from the wreckage, but crawled back into a window in search for his wife. That was the last seen of him.

The song-writer's first name was originally "Philipp." He disliked the unusual spelling, however, and in later years he used the extra "P" as a middle initial.

Chautauqua Vesper Hymn

Day is dying in the west;
Heaven is touching earth with rest:
Wait and worship while the night
Sets her evening lamps alight
Through all the sky.
Refrain:
Holy, holy, holy, Lord God of Hosts!
Heaven and earth are full of Thee!
Heaven and earth are praising Thee,
O Lord Most High!
Lord of life, beneath the dome
Of the universe, Thy home,
Gather us who seek Thy face
To the fold of Thy embrace,
For Thou art nigh.
While the deepening shadows fall,
Heart of Love, enfold us all;
Through the glory and the grace
Of the stars that veil Thy face,
Our hearts ascend.
When forever from our sight
Pass the stars, the day, the night,
Lord of angels, on our eyes
Let eternal morning rise,

And shadows end.
Mary Artimisia Lathbury, 1880, 1890.

THE LYRIST OF CHAUTAUQUA

Those who have had the privilege of attending a vesper service in the great Chautauqua Institution auditorium on the shores of beautiful Lake Chautauqua, N. Y., have come away with at least one impression that is lasting. It is the singing by the vast assembly of Mary Lathbury's famous vesper hymn, "Day is dying in the west."

This beautiful evening lyric, which was written especially for the Chautauqua vesper hour, has been called by a distinguished critic "one of the finest and most distinctive hymns of modern times," and there are few who will not concur in his judgment.

The "lyrist of Chautauqua" was born in Manchester, N. Y., August 10, 1841. As a child she began to reveal artistic tendencies. She developed a special talent in drawing pictures of children, and her illustrations in magazines and periodicals made her name widely known. She also wrote books and poetry, illustrating them with her own sketches.

Very early in life she felt constrained to dedicate her talent to Christian service. She tells how she seemed to hear a voice saying to her: "Remember, my child, that you have a gift of weaving fancies into verse, and a gift with the pencil of producing visions that come to your heart; consecrate these to Me as thoroughly and as definitely as you do your inmost spirit."

An opportunity to serve her Lord in a very definite way came in 1874, when Dr. John H. Vincent, then secretary of the Methodist Sunday School Union, employed her as his assistant. The Chautauqua movement had just been launched the previous year and the formal opening on the shores of the beautiful lake from which the institution has received its name took place on August 4, 1874. Dr. Vincent became the outstanding leader of the movement, and he began to make use of Miss Lathbury's literary talent almost immediately.

Dr. Jesse Lyman Hurlbut, historian of Chautauqua, writes: "In Dr. Vincent's many-sided nature was a strain of poetry, although I do not know that he ever wrote a verse. Yet he always looked at life and truth through poetic eyes. Who otherwise would have thought of songs for Chautauqua and called upon a poet to write them? Dr. Vincent found in Mary A. Lathbury a poet who could compose fitting verses for the expression of the Chautauqua spirit."

The beautiful evening hymn, "Day is dying in the west," was written in 1880, at Dr. Vincent's request, for the vesper services which are held every evening. It originally consisted of only two stanzas, and it was not until ten years later that Miss Lathbury, at the strong insistence of friends, added the last two stanzas. We are happy that she did so, for the last two lines, with their allusion to the "eternal morning" when "shadows" shall end, bring the hymn to a sublime conclusion.

It was also in 1880 that she wrote another hymn of two stanzas that has shared in the fame that has come to her evening hymn. It was composed for the Chautauqua Literary and Scientific Circle, and Miss Lathbury called it "A Study Song." Its beautiful reference to the Sea of Galilee is made the more interesting when we are reminded that the hymn was written on the shores of lovely Lake Chautauqua. The hymn is particularly adapted for Bible study, and it is said that the great London preacher, G. Campbell Morgan, always announced it before his mid-week discourse. The hymn reads:

>Break Thou the Bread of life,
>Dear Lord, to me,
>As Thou didst break the loaves
>Beside the sea;
>Beyond the sacred page
>I seek Thee, Lord;
>My spirit pants for Thee,
>O living Word!
>Bless Thou the truth, dear Lord,
>To me, to me,
>As Thou didst bless the bread
>By Galilee;
>Then shall all bondage cease,
>All fetters fall;
>And I shall find my peace,
>My All-in-all!

Miss Lathbury was greatly esteemed, not only for her lovely lyrics which have given inspiration to thousands of souls, but also for her gentle, Christian character. There was an indescribable charm about her personality, and she exerted an abiding influence over those who came in contact with her devout and consecrated spirit. She died in New York City in 1913.

In His Footsteps

>O Master, let me walk with Thee
>In lowly paths of service free;
>Tell me Thy secret, help me bear
>The strain of toil, the fret of care.
>Help me the slow of heart to move
>By some clear winning word of love;
>Teach me the wayward feet to stay,
>And guide them in the homeward way.
>Teach me Thy patience; still with Thee
>In closer, dearer company,
>In work that keeps faith sweet and strong,
>In trust that triumphs over wrong.
>In hope that sends a shining ray
>Far down the future's broadening way,
>In peace that only Thou canst give,
>With Thee, O Master, let me live!

Washington Gladden, 1879.

GLADDEN'S HYMN OF CHRISTIAN SERVICE

For more than half a century, until his death in 1918, the name of Washington Gladden was known throughout the length of the country as one of America's most distinguished clergymen. A prolific writer, his books and his magazine contributions were widely read by the American people.

Like most literary productions, however, his books and pamphlets have already been largely forgotten. It is only a little hymn, written on a moment's inspiration, that seems destined to preserve Gladden's name for posterity. That hymn is "O Master, let me walk with Thee."

The author was born in Pottsgrove, Pa., February 11, 1836. After his graduation from Williams College in 1859, he was called as pastor to a Congregational church in Brooklyn. In 1882 he removed to Columbus, O., where he remained as pastor until 1914, a period of thirty-two years.

During these years he exerted a profound influence, not only over the city of Columbus, but in much wider circles. Gladden was deeply interested in social service, believing that it is the duty of the Christian Church to elevate the masses not only spiritually and morally, but in a social and economic sense as well. By sermons, lectures and by his writings, he was ever trying to bring about more cordial relationship between employer and employee.

Gladden was often the center of a storm of criticism on the part of those who charged him with liberalism. His beautiful hymn, written in 1879, seems to be in part an answer to his critics. It originally consisted of three stanzas of eight lines each. The second stanza, which was omitted when the poem was first published as a hymn, indicates how keenly Gladden felt the condemnation of his opponents:

O Master, let me walk with Thee
Before the taunting Pharisee;
Help me to bear the sting of spite,
The hate of men who hide Thy light,
The sore distrust of souls sincere
Who cannot read Thy judgments clear,
The dulness of the multitude,
Who dimly guess that Thou art good.

Dr. Gladden always insisted that he was nothing but a preacher, and he gloried in his high calling. In spite of busy pastorates, however, he always found time to give expression to his literary talent. At one time he was a member of the editorial staff of the New York Independent. Later he was an editor of the "Sunday Afternoon," a weekly magazine. It was in this magazine that "O Master, let me walk with Thee" was first published.

The writer had no idea of composing a hymn when it was written, and no one was more surprised than he at its popularity. He himself agreed that the second stanza quoted above was not suitable for hymn purposes.

Whatever judgment may be passed on Dr. Gladden's liberalistic views, it will be agreed that he looked upon Christianity as an intensely practical thing; and, if he underestimated the value of Christian dogma, it was because he emphasized so strongly the necessity of Christian life and practice.

He was always buoyed up by a hopeful spirit, and he believed implicitly that the Kingdom of Light was gradually overcoming the forces of evil. In one of his last sermons, he said:

"I have never doubted that the Kingdom I have always prayed for is coming; that the gospel I have preached is true. I believe ... that the nation is being saved."

Something of his optimism may be seen reflected in the words of his hymn.

A Hymn of the City

Where cross the crowded ways of life,
Where sound the cries of race and clan,
Above the noise of selfish strife,
We hear Thy voice, O Son of man!
In haunts of wretchedness and need,
On shadowed thresholds dark with fears,
From paths where hide the lures of greed,
We catch the vision of Thy tears.
From tender childhood's helplessness,
From woman's grief, man's burdened toil,
From famished souls, from sorrow's stress,
Thy heart has never known recoil.
The cup of water given for Thee
Still holds the freshness of Thy grace;
Yet long these multitudes to see
The sweet compassion of Thy face.
O Master, from the mountain-side,
Make haste to heal these hearts of pain,
Among these restless throngs abide,
O tread the city's streets again,
Till sons of men shall learn Thy love
And follow where Thy feet have trod;
Till glorious from Thy heaven above
Shall come the city of our God.
Frank Mason North, 1905.

A HYMN WITH A MODERN MESSAGE

Among the more recent hymns that have found their way into the hymn-books of the Christian churches in America, there is none that enjoys such popularity and esteem as Frank Mason North's hymn, "Where cross the crowded ways of life." It is a hymn of the highest order, beautiful in thought and unusually tender in expression. It is typical of the trend in modern hymns to emphasize the Church's mission among the lowly and the fallen.

From beginning to end this hymn is a picture of the modern city with its sins and sorrows and spiritual hunger. We see the city as the meeting place of all races and tongues; we hear the din and noise of selfish striving; we behold the haunts of poverty and sin and wretchedness; we catch a glimpse of the sufferings of helpless childhood, of woman's secret griefs and man's ceaseless toil. And all these multitudes are hungering for Christ!

North has, consciously or unconsciously, made a striking distinction between mere social service work, which aims at the alleviation of human need and suffering, and inner mission work, which seeks to help men spiritually as well as physically. "The cup of water" is never to be despised, but when it is given in Christ's Name it has double value; for it is Christ Himself, after all, that men need, and it is only Christ who can truly satisfy. Social service can never take the place of salvation.

What a beautiful prayer is that contained in the fifth stanza, where the Master is entreated to "tread the city's streets again!" And then, as a fitting climax to this whole remarkable poem, comes the triumphant thought expressed in the final lines of the coming of the New Jerusalem from above—"the city of our God."

North was well qualified to write such a hymn. He himself was a child of the city, having been born in America's greatest metropolis in 1850. His early education, too, was received in New York City and after his graduation from Wesleyan University in 1872 he served several congregations in the city of his birth. In 1892 he was made Corresponding Secretary of the New York City Church Extension and Missionary Society and in 1912 he was elected a Corresponding Secretary of the Methodist Episcopal Board of Foreign Missions. Thus, almost his whole life has been devoted to missionary activities at home and abroad.

It was in 1905, in response to a request from the Methodist hymnal committee, that North wrote his celebrated hymn. He tells the story in the following words:

"My life was for long years, both by personal choice, and official duty, given to the people in all phases of their community life. New York was to me an open book. I spent days and weeks and years in close contact with every phase of the life of the multitudes, and at the morning, noon and evening hours was familiar with the tragedy, as it always seemed to me, of the jostling, moving currents of the life of the people as revealed upon the streets and at great crossings of the avenues; and I have watched them by the hour as they passed, by tens of thousands. This is no more than many another man whose sympathies are with the crowd and with the eager, unsatisfied folk of the world, has done.

"As I recall it, I came to write the hymn itself at the suggestion of Professor C. T. Winchester, who, as a member of the committee on the new hymnal, was struggling with the fact that we have so few modern missionary hymns. He said to me one day, 'Why do you not write us a missionary hymn?' I wrote what was in my thought and feeling.... That it has found its way into so many of the modern hymnals and by translation into so many of the other languages, is significant not as to the quality of the hymn itself but as to the fact that it is an expression of the tremendous movement of the soul of the gospel in our times which demands that the follower of Christ must make the interest of the people his own, and must find the heart of the world's need if he is in any way to represent his Master among men."

Another lovely hymn by North was written in 1884. The first stanza reads:

Jesus, the calm that fills my breast
No other heart than Thine can give;
This peace unstirred, this joy of rest,
None but Thy loved ones can receive.

The spirit of this hymn reminds us very much of the two classic hymns of Bernard of Clairvaux—"O Jesus, joy of loving hearts" and "Jesus, the very thought of Thee." The last line quoted above is evidently inspired by a line from the latter hymn.

A Gripping Hymn by a Girl

O'er Jerusalem Thou weepest
In compassion, dearest Lord!
Love divine, of love the deepest,
O'er Thine erring Israel poured,
Crieth out in bitter moan,
"O loved city, hadst thou known
This thy day of visitation,
Thou wouldst not reject salvation."
By the love Thy tears are telling,
O Thou Lamb for sinners slain,
Make my heart Thy temple dwelling,
Purged from every guilty stain!
O forgive, forgive my sin!
Cleanse me, cleanse me, Lord, within!
I am Thine since Thou hast sought me,
Since Thy precious blood hath bought me.
O Thou Lord of my salvation,
Grant my soul Thy blood-bought peace.
By the tears of lamentation
Bid my faith and love increase.
Grant me grace to love Thy Word,
Grace to keep the message heard,
Grace to own Thee as my Treasure,
Grace to love Thee without measure.
Anna Hoppe, 1919.

A LUTHERAN PSALMIST OF TODAY

It is gratifying to know that the spirit of hymnody is not dead, and that still today consecrated men and women are being inspired to "sing new songs unto Jehovah," In Milwaukee, Wis., lives a young woman who for several years has been attracting widespread attention by her Christian lyrics. Her name is Anna Hoppe, and the hymns she writes suggest strongly something of the style and spirit of the Lutheran hymns of a bygone age.

Born of German parents in Milwaukee in 1889, she began to write verse in early childhood. Most of them were on patriotic themes, such as Washington, Lincoln, The Battle of Gettysburg, and Paul Jones.

"At the age of about eleven," Miss Hoppe tells us, "I wrote a few lines on Angels."

It was at the age of twenty-five years, however, that she began in earnest the writing of spiritual poetry. Many of her poems were published in religious periodicals and aroused much interest. In the hymnal of the Augustana Synod, published in 1925, twenty-three of her hymns were included. Since that time a collection of her hymns under the title, "Songs of the Church Year," has appeared. In 1930 eight of her lyrics were published in the "American Lutheran Hymnal."

As a prolific writer of hymns, Miss Hoppe probably has no equal in the Lutheran Church today. Her unusual talent seems all the more remarkable when it is known that she is practically self-educated. After she had finished the eighth grade in the Milwaukee public schools, she entered a business office. Since that time she has worked continuously, and has received the benefit of only a few months' training at evening schools. At present she is employed in the office of the Westinghouse Company.

Her hymns are composed in the midst of the stress and hurry of modern life.

"Many of my hymns," she writes, "have been written on my way to and from church, and to and from work. I utilize my lunch hours for typing the hymns and keeping up correspondence. I used to do quite a bit of writing on Sunday afternoons, but now we have a Layman's Hour in our church at that time, and I do not like to miss it. I also attend our Fundamentalist Bible lectures, Jewish mission meetings, and the like. Still I find a minute here and there in which to jot down some verse."

Although few of Miss Hoppe's hymns rise to heights of poetic rapture, they are characterized by a warmth of feeling and fervency of spirit that make them true lyrics. They are thoroughly Scriptural in language, although they sometimes become too dogmatic in phraseology. A deep certainty of faith, however, breathes through their lines and saves them from becoming prosaic.

One of her most beautiful hymns is for New Year's. Its opening stanza reads:

Jesus, O precious Name,

By heaven's herald spoken,
Jesus, O holy Name,
Of love divine the token.
Jesus, in Thy dear Name
This new year we begin;
Bless Thou its opening door,
Inscribe Thy Name within.

A hymn for Epiphany reflects something of the same spirit of adoration:

Desire of every nation,
Light of the Gentiles, Thou!
In fervent adoration
Before Thy throne we bow;
Our hearts and tongues adore Thee,
Blest Dayspring from the skies.
Like incense sweet before Thee,
Permit our songs to rise.

The final stanza of her Ascension hymn is full of poetic fire:

Ascend, dear Lord!
Thou Lamb for sinners slain,
Thou blest High Priest, ascend!
O King of kings, in righteousness e'er reign,
Thy kingdom hath no end.
Thy ransomed host on earth rejoices,
While angels lift in song their voices.
Ascend, dear Lord!

Her fidelity to Scriptural language may be seen in the following simple verses:

Have ye heard the invitation,
Sinners ruined by the fall?
Famished souls who seek salvation,
Have ye heard the loving call?
Hark! a herald of the Father
Bids you of His supper taste.
Round the sacred table gather;
All is ready; sinners, haste!
O ye chosen, have ye slighted
This sweet call to you proclaimed?
Lo! the King hath now invited
All the halt, the blind, the maimed:
Come, ye poor from out the highways,
Come, a feast awaits you, come!
Leave the hedges and the byways,
Hasten to the Father's home.

We have heard Thee call, dear Father,
In Thy Word and sacrament;

Round Thy festal board we'll gather
Till our life's last day is spent.
Ours the risen Saviour's merit,
Ours the bounties of Thy love,
Ours Thy peace, till we inherit
Endless life in heaven above.

Miss Hoppe speaks in glowing terms of the spiritual impressions received in childhood from pious parents and a consecrated pastor, the sainted John Bading, who both baptized and confirmed her. Her father died in 1910.

"He was a very pious Lutheran," she writes, "and so is mother. They often spoke of afternoon prayer meetings they attended in Germany."

Some of her hymns not already mentioned are, "By nature deaf to things divine," "Heavenly Sower, Thou hast scattered," "How blest are they who through the power," "Lord Jesus Christ, the children's Friend," "O dear Redeemer, crucified," "O precious Saviour, heal and bless," "O'er Jerusalem Thou weepest," "Precious Child, so sweetly sleeping," "Repent, the Kingdom draweth nigh," "The Sower goeth forth to sow," "Thou camest down from heaven on high," "Thou hast indeed made manifest," "Thou Lord of life and death," "Thou virgin-born incarnate Word," "O Lord, my God, Thy holy law," "Jesus, Thine unbounded love," "He did not die in vain," "I open wide the portals of my heart," "Rise, my soul, to watch and pray," "O joyful message, sent from heaven," "O Thou who once in Galilee," and "Thou goest to Jerusalem." She is the translator of "O precious thought! some day the mist shall vanish," a hymn from the Swedish, as well as some eighty gems from German hymnody. Thirty-two of her German translations appeared in "The Selah Song Book," edited by Adolf T. Hanser in 1922.

Many of Miss Hoppe's hymns have been written on the pericopes of the Church Year. She has consistently refused to have her hymns copyrighted, believing that no hindrance should be put in the way of any one who desires to use them.

Up to 1930 nearly 400 hymns had appeared from Miss Hoppe's pen. Her ambition is to write a thousand original Christian lyrics.

A Song of Victory

Rise, ye children of salvation,
All who cleave to Christ, the Head!
Wake, arise, O mighty nation,
Ere the foe on Zion tread:
He draws nigh, and would defy
All the hosts of God Most High.
Saints and heroes, long before us,
Firmly on this ground have stood;
See their banner waving o'er us,
Conquerors through the Saviour's blood!
Ground we hold whereon of old
Fought the faithful and the bold.

Fighting, we shall be victorious
By the blood of Christ our Lord;
On our foreheads, bright and glorious,
Shines the witness of His Word;
Spear and shield on battlefield,
His great Name; we cannot yield.
When His servants stand before Him,
Each receiving his reward—
When His saints in light adore Him,
Giving glory to the Lord—
"Victory!" our song shall be,
Like the thunder of the sea.
Justus Falckner, 1697.

SURVEY OF AMERICAN LUTHERAN HYMNODY

It is a significant fact that the first Lutheran pastor to be ordained in America was a hymn-writer. He was Justus Falckner, author of the stirring hymn, "Rise, ye children of salvation."

Falckner, who was born on November 22, 1672, in Langenreinsdorf, Saxony, was the son of a Lutheran pastor at that place. He entered the University of Halle in 1693 as a student of theology under Francke, but for conscientious reasons refused to be ordained upon the completion of his studies. Together with his brother Daniel he became associated with the William Penn colony in America and arranged for the sale of 10,000 acres of land to Rev. Andreas Rudman, who was the spiritual leader of the Swedish Lutherans along the Delaware.

Through Rudman's influence Falckner was induced to enter the ministry, and on November 24, 1703, he was ordained in Gloria Dei Lutheran Church at Wicacoa, Philadelphia. The ordination service was carried out by the Swedish Lutheran pastors, Rudman, Erik Björk, and Andreas Sandel. Falckner was the first German Lutheran pastor in America, and he also had the distinction of building the first German Lutheran church in the New World—at Falckner's Swamp, New Hanover, Pa. Later he removed to New York, where for twenty years he labored faithfully among the German, Dutch, and Scandinavian settlers in a parish that extended some two hundred miles from Albany to Long Island.

It seems that Falckner's hymn, "Rise, ye children of salvation," was written while he was a student at Halle. It appeared as early as 1697 in "Geistreiches Gesangbuch," and in 1704 it was given a place in Freylinghausen's hymn-book. There is no evidence that Falckner ever translated it into English.

Since the Lutheran Church in America to a large extent employed the German and Scandinavian languages in its worship, it was content for nearly two hundred years to depend on hymn-books originating in the Old World. Not until the latter half of the nineteenth century were serious efforts made to provide Lutheran hymn-books in the

English language. Writers of original hymns were few in number, but a number of excellent translators appeared.

Through the efforts of these translators, an increasing number of Lutheran hymns from the rich store of German and Scandinavian hymnody are being introduced in the hymn-books of this country. Pioneers in this endeavor about half a century ago were Charles Porterfield Krauth, noted theologian and vice-provost of the University of Pennsylvania; Joseph A. Seiss, of Philadelphia, pastor and author, to whom we are indebted for the translation of "Beautiful Saviour" and "Winter reigns o'er many a region"; and Charles William Schaeffer, Philadelphia theologian, who translated Held's "Come, O come, Thou quickening Spirit" and Rambach's beautiful baptism hymn, "Father, Son, and Holy Spirit." Mrs. Harriet Krauth Spaeth also belongs to this group, her most notable contribution being the translation of the medieval Christian hymn, "Behold, a Branch is growing."

Later translators of German hymns were Matthias Loy, for many years president of Capital University, Columbus, Ohio; August Crull, professor of German at Concordia College, Fort Wayne, Ind., and Conrad H. L. Schuette, professor of theology at Capital University and later president of the Joint Synod of Ohio. Loy was not only a translator but also an author of no mean ability. Among his original hymns that seem destined to live are "Jesus took the babes and blessed them," "I thank Thee, Jesus, for the grief," and "O great High Priest, forget not me." His splendid translations include such hymns as Selnecker's "Let me be Thine forever," Schenck's "Now our worship sweet is o'er" and Hiller's "God in human flesh appearing." From Schuette we have received in English dress Behm's "O holy, blessed Trinity," while Crull's most successful translations are Homburg's "Where wilt Thou go, since night draws near?" and Ludaemilia Elizabeth of Schwartzburg-Rudolstadt's beautiful hymn, "Jesus, Jesus, Jesus only."

Among the living translators of German hymns, H. Brueckner, professor at Hebron College, Hebron, Nebraska, takes first rank. In the American Lutheran Hymnal, published in 1930 by a Lutheran intersynodical committee, he is represented by some seventy translations from the German, three from the French, and four original hymns. Although Brueckner's work is too recent to be properly evaluated, his hymns reveal evidences of genuine lyrical quality and true devotional spirit.

Other successful translators of German hymns are John Caspar Mattes, Lutheran pastor at Scranton, Pa.; Emmanuel Cronenwett, pastor emeritus at Butler, Pa., and Paul E. Kretzmann, of Concordia Seminary, St. Louis, Mo., Lutheran theologian and commentator. To Mattes we are indebted for the English version of Gotter's "Friend of the weary, O refresh us" and Albinus' "Smite us not in anger, Lord." Cronenwett and Kretzmann have written a number of excellent original hymns in addition to their translations. The American Lutheran Hymnal contains nine of these by the former and seventeen from the pen of the latter. Cronenwett's hymns are chiefly didactic, but occasionally he soars to lyrical heights, as in "Of omnipresent grace I sing." Among Kretzmann's best efforts are "Lead on, O Lord" and "Praise and honor to the Father." A note of praise to the Holy Trinity is heard in practically all of Kretzmann's hymns.

The foremost translator of Swedish hymns is Ernst W. Olson, office editor of Augustana Book Concern, Rock Island, Ill. From his gifted pen we have received the English version of such gems as Wallin's "All hail to thee, O blessed morn," "From peaceful slumber waking," "Jerusalem, lift up thy voice," "Mute are the pleading lips of Him," and "Heavenly Light, benignly beaming"; Franzén's "Ajar the temple gates are swinging," "Come, O Jesus, and prepare me," and "When vesper bells are calling"; Söderberg's "In the temple where our fathers," Geijer's "In triumph our Redeemer," Petri's "Now hail we our Redeemer" and "Thy sacred Word, O Lord, of old," and Carl Olof Rosenius' "With God and His mercy, His Spirit and Word." Olson has also written a number of excellent original hymns, including "Mine eyes unto the mountains," "Behold, by sovereign grace alone," and "Glorious yuletide, glad bells proclaim it."

Other translators of Swedish hymns include Claude W. Foss, professor of history at Augustana College, Rock Island, Ill.; Victor O. Peterson, formerly with the same institution, but now deceased; George H. Trabert, Lutheran pastor at Minneapolis, Minn.; Augustus Nelson, Lutheran pastor at Gibbon, Minn.; Olof Olsson, for many years president of Augustana College, and August W. Kjellstrand, who until his death in 1930 was professor of English at the same institution. Among the finest contributions by Foss are translations of Nyström's "O Fount of truth and mercy," Hedborn's "With holy joy my soul doth beat," and Franzén's "Thy scepter, Jesus, shall extend." Nelson has given us beautiful renderings of Franzén's "Prepare the way, O Zion" and "Awake, the watchman crieth," and Wallin's "Jesus, Lord and precious Saviour." Peterson is the translator of Arrhenius' "Jesus is my friend most precious" and Wallin's Advent hymn, "O bride of Christ, rejoice." Olsson, who was one of the earliest translators of Swedish lyrics, has given us Franzén's communion hymn, "Thine own, O loving Saviour," and another on the Lord's Supper by Spegel, "The death of Jesus Christ, our Lord." Kjellstrand's version of Hedborn's sublime hymn of praise, "Holy Majesty, before Thee," is one of the most successful efforts at converting Swedish hymns into the English language. To these translators should also be added the name of Anders O. Bersell, for many years professor of Greek at Augustana College, who gave poetic English form to Lina Sandell's "Jerusalem, Jerusalem" and Rutström's "Come, Saviour dear, with us abide."

A number of translators and writers besides those here named made new contributions to the Hymnal of the Augustana Synod published in 1925.

About twenty-five years ago a group of literary men within the Norwegian Lutheran Synods undertook the task of translating some of the gems of Danish and Norwegian hymnody. Among these were C. Doving, now a city missionary in Chicago; George T. Rygh, also residing at the present time in Chicago; C. K. Solberg, pastor of St. Paul's Lutheran Church, Minneapolis, Minn.; O. T. Sanden, and O. H. Smedby, former Lutheran pastor at Albert Lea, Minn., now deceased. Doving's masterpiece undoubtedly is his translation of Grundtvig's "Built on the Rock, the Church doth stand," although he will also be remembered for his rendering of Holm's "How blessed is the little flock," and Landstad's "Before Thee, God, who knowest all." Rygh's contribution consists of the translation of such hymns as Grundtvig's "Peace to soothe our bitter woes," Kingo's "Our table now with food is spread," Landstad's "Speak, O Lord, Thy servant heareth," Boye's "O Light of God's most wondrous love," and Brun's "Heavenly Spirit, all others transcending." Sanden has translated Brun's "The sun has gone down," while Smedby has left us a fine version of Boye's "Abide with us, the day is waning." While Solberg has translated some hymns, he is known better as a writer of original lyrics. Among these are "Lift up your eyes, ye Christians," "Fellow Christians, let us gather," and "O blessed Light from heaven."

Foremost among recent translators of Danish hymns are J. C. Aaberg, pastor of St. Peter's Danish Lutheran church, Minneapolis, Minn., and P. C. Paulsen, pastor of Golgotha Danish Lutheran church, Chicago, Ill. In the American Lutheran Hymnal there are nineteen translations by Aaberg, while Paulsen is represented by a like number. Through the efforts of these men, both of whom possess no mean poetic ability, many of the finest hymns of Brorson, Kingo, Grundtvig, Ingemann, Vig, and Pawels have been introduced to American Lutherans. Paulsen is the author of three original hymns, "Blest is he who cries to heaven," "Take my heart, O Jesus," and "Let us go to Galilee," while Aaberg has written "There is a blessed power."

One of the most richly endowed hymn-writers in the Lutheran Church today is A. F. Rohr, pastor at Fremont, O. From his pen we have received such hymns as "Eternal God, omnipotent," "Lord of life and light and blessing," "From afar, across the waters," and "Living Fountain, freely flowing." For poetic expression and graceful rhythm his hymns are unsurpassed by any contemporary writer. He also combines such depth of feeling with the lyrical qualities of his hymns, they no doubt possess enduring qualities. Witness the following hymn:

> Living Fountain, freely flowing
> In the sheen of heaven's day,
> Grace and life on us bestowing,
> Wash Thou all our sins away.
> Fountain whence alone the living
> Draw the life they boast as theirs,
> By Thy grace, a gift whose giving
> Life of life forever shares.
> Who Thy mighty depths can measure?
> Who can sound, with earthly line,
> Thy profundity of treasure,
> Thy infinity divine?
> They who quaff Thy wave shall never
> Thirst again; for springing free
> In their hearts, a fount forever
> Thou to them of life shall be.
> May we drink of Thee rejoicing,
> Till on heaven's sinless shore
> We Thy virtues shall be voicing
> With the blest for evermore.

Samuel M. Miller, dean of the Lutheran Bible Institute, Minneapolis, Minn., is the writer of a number of spiritual songs and hymns that have become popular in Bible conference circles. Among his hymns are "In the holy Father's keeping" and "When Jesus comes in glory."

W. H. Lehmann, superintendent of home missions in the American Lutheran Church, has written "Take Thou my life, dear Lord," and "Beneath Thy cross I stand," the latter a passion hymn of rare beauty:

> Beneath Thy cross I stand
> And view Thy marrèd face;
> O Son of man, must Thou thus die
> To save a fallen race?
> Alone Thou bear'st the wrath
> That should on sinners fall,
> While from Thy holy wounds forthflows
> A stream of life for all.
> O Lamb of God so meek,
> Beneath Thy cross I bow:
> Heart-stricken, all my sins confess—
> O hear, forgive me now!
> O Son of God, look down
> In mercy now on me
> And heal my wounds of sin and death,
> That I may live to Thee!

Printed in Great Britain
by Amazon